MONSTROUS POWER

EVA CHASE

SHADOWBLOOD SOULS · BOOK 2

Monstrous Power

Book 2 in the Shadowblood Souls series

First Digital Edition, 2022

Cover design: Sanja Balan (Sanja's Covers)

Ebook ISBN: 978-1-998752-12-6

Paperback ISBN: 978-1-998752-13-3

ONE

Riva

The room smells like death.

That's probably because of the copious number of dead bodies sprawled all across it.

It's like a house party of corpses, three dozen or so limp forms gathered around the kitchen and open concept living and dining room of Ursula Engel's expansive but homey cottage in the woods. Some slump on the floorboards and tiles, others loll across leather and hardwood furniture.

Most of them died because of me.

It's pretty easy to tell which ones I took out—at least, the ones I killed with the shrieking power that's now settled down inside me rather than with my claws. Those corpses are definitely not enjoying this undead party.

While the unearthly scream tore out of me, I saw right inside our enemies. I knew exactly where to twist and what to snap to wring every drop of pain out of them before their bodies shut down completely.

Limbs lie askew at impossible angles. Faces have locked in contortions of anguish.

The meaty, metallic tang of blood laces the air, but also the nauseating odors of urine and shit. A lot of my victims lost control over their bladders and bowels in the grips of my brutal talent.

I close my eyes for a second, but removing the gristly view doesn't stop my stomach from churning. Partly because it's not just the scene that's making me queasy, but also the stares of the four other figures who are still standing with me.

My guys. My fellow shadowbloods, who have the same dark smoke winding through their veins that I do that gives them their own unnerving talents.

The four gorgeous, tormented, vicious men who spent most of the past two weeks punishing me for a betrayal I didn't even commit.

They believed I was a monster. I wasn't back then, back when we were separated four years ago.

But looking at the carnage around us with my shriek still ringing in our ears, it must be difficult for them to see me as anything else right now.

I swallow thickly, willing down my nausea and the protests that want to bubble out.

I didn't want *to do this. It was the only way to save us.*

But those claims aren't totally true. Some part of me *did* want to wreak all this havoc, to savage and maim with wild abandon.

Some part of me reveled in it, drew strength from it. It

took all my self-control to shield the guys from the sadistic hunger inside me.

I want to say it isn't me but some other being inside me, but I know that's not true. There's no alien in my chest that can be carved out and burned away.

The hunger is woven into my body, mind, and soul. It's etched in my DNA.

And the woman who lived in this house wrote that code, even if she didn't realize at the time exactly what abilities would emerge and grow in us.

I glance behind me at the mangled body of our creator at the same time Jacob does. The chiseled planes of his stunning face harden even more with the clenching of his jaw.

"Engel said reinforcements were too far out to get here quickly, but we don't know how true that was," he says, breaking the shocked silence. "Let's grab anything that could be useful and get out of here."

Dominic follows his gaze too, his dark auburn hair falling across his tan forehead to shade his eyes. He sways a little and catches the edge of the blood-streaked kitchen island for balance.

He's just spent the past several minutes healing the worst of the other guys' wounds—with the slim, orange tentacles arcing from the top of his shoulder blades to the backs of his knees. He grabbed most of the life energy he needed from the assailant now lying dead by our feet, but the process must have taken a lot out of him as well.

His voice comes out in a low rasp. "She really hated us."

The accusations our creator threw at us echo from the

back of my mind. *You're monsters of the worst kind. Abominations. A catastrophe I set in motion.*

Of course, the bloodbath we're surrounded by doesn't exactly stand as evidence in our favor. I'm not sure any bystander would accept "She started it!" as a reasonable excuse.

Andreas rakes his hand back through the tight coils of his hair, his mouth twisting into a grimace. "Yeah. Well, I can't say I liked *her* all that much either."

None of us laughs at the darkly wry remark, but the rough attempt at humor stirs us all into motion. We tramp over the shattered chunks of the dining table that formed one side of our makeshift fort and pick our way between the bodies.

The search feels unnervingly familiar. I scanned a similar scene just a couple of weeks ago, appropriating weapons and cash, in the arena where I'd been forced into cage fights.

I don't look at the guys, but every now and then I see one pause with a flick of his gaze from a distorted body to me. Each time, my gut knots tighter.

They're moving slowly through the mess. Zian is still favoring one brawny shoulder, though it looks like Dominic was able to stop the bleeding. His wolfish features have vanished, but his normally peachy-brown skin has lost some of its warmth.

Andreas leans a little to the left and bends his knees when he checks something on the floor rather than tilting his torso. A bloody hole marks his shirt where the bullet caught him minutes ago, the wound sealed now but no doubt still painful.

And Jacob's blond hair is dappled crimson from the shrapnel cut that's closed but still an angry pink on his pale forehead.

Dominic speaks up again, quiet as usual and with a wary note in his voice that pricks at me more than I like. "You're not injured, are you, Riva?"

I shake my head quickly. "I'm fine."

I'm actually better than fine. The influx of our enemies' pain has left me energized and rejuvenated.

As the guys have probably noticed.

I shove my uneasiness aside and grab a rifle from where it's lying next to a hand lumpy with shattered bones.

We each pick up every gun we can find that hasn't been broken by Zian's wolfman strength or Jacob's telekinetic powers. I hold on to those that still have at least a few bullets, tucking one pistol into the back of my sweats and setting the other weapons in a growing common pile near the front door.

There's no way of knowing who we might have to fight next… and I'd rather fight with gunfire if I have the option.

That thought brings me to the huge living room windows that stretch from waist-height to the vaulted ceiling, two stories high. Most of their glass now lies in scattered shards on the floor, crunching beneath my sneakers.

A significant number of our attackers crashed in through these windows. I lean over the ledge into the cool autumn air and peer between the trees for any sign of where they came from—and any colleagues who might be on their way.

I can't see anything suspicious, and the fresh breeze filling my lungs is a welcome relief. My braid slipping over my shoulder, I tip farther out into the forest air just for a second.

Glass crackles just a few feet away, and I jerk to the side instinctively. A burning sensation sears across my waist.

I flinch again, glancing down. A shard still lodged in the frame has sliced into my bare flesh where my hoodie and tank top rode up.

Biting my lip against the pain, I jerk my shirts down over the cut and the puff of smoky stuff that started to waft from it and spin around. The wound throbs against my pressing elbow.

Zian has come up by the windows, his massive body looming more than a foot taller than me even in totally human form. He studies me with his dark brown eyes, probably wondering why I flinched so badly.

Or wondering if I'm going to hurl my power at him in response.

Before he can outright ask anything, I let out a stilted giggle. "Just a little jumpy after… all this. I'm going to check the second floor."

I hustle over to the stairs and dart up them, gritting my teeth against the deepening ache in my side. I am *not* going to beg Dominic for help, not when he's already wiped out.

Not when I now know that every bit of healing talent

he uses, the beastly appendages he's so ashamed of grow even longer.

Engel's bedroom is painfully tidy, not a drawer ajar, not a wrinkle in her duvet. I can't help wondering whether she'd be more pissed off about the fact that I killed her or the mess I've made of her home below.

In the ensuite bathroom, I tear a chunk of thick fabric off a towel and fold it into a pad to stem the bleeding. Then I tie that firmly in place with a strip of one of Engel's sheets.

Such lovely linens she's outfitted her home with. I'm sure the thread count made her proud.

They bind my wound well enough. With my baggy hoodie overtop, you can't tell there's anything unusual underneath.

I stand in front of the bathroom mirror for a moment, digging my hands into my pockets and pressing the hasty bandage against my side. The throbbing makes my jaw tick, but a strange sense of peace settles over me.

This is one small fragment of what I inflicted on all our attackers downstairs. A reminder of what I did—what I don't ever want to have to do again.

If having that reminder helps ensure that I keep my most vicious hungers under control, it's a good thing.

The stairs creak, and I pull myself out of the ensuite into Engel's bedroom where I can make myself useful again.

It isn't Andreas coming upstairs after me, I realize with a faint tingling on my clavicle. I can sense him moving around on the level below through the little dark blotch on my skin—the mark that formed after we merged our bodies in more ways than we recognized at the time.

The mark that also appeared at the top of his sternum, that maybe he now wishes he could scrub off along with any other association with me.

I yank open the bedside and dresser drawers and find an envelope with a wad of hundred dollar bills in one and a jewelry box tucked into another. Well, we need any extra cash we can get from pawning Engel's valuables more than she's inclined to wear them in her current state.

I stuff the envelope into the ebony jewelry box and carry it into the hall just as Jacob makes an eager noise from the room next door. He comes out with a laptop clutched in his hands.

"Who knows how much useful info she's got stashed on this," he says, aiming a sharp but seemingly genuine smile at me.

I don't know how to respond when the vast majority of the smiles Jacob has shot at me in the past couple of weeks were cold and cruel. But I'm saved from needing to when Dominic calls up from the first floor.

"I found Engel's cell phone—and her car keys."

Jacob's smile widens. "All right. We make a swift getaway and then ditch it as soon as possible."

As we hustle back down the stairs, Zian rubs his jaw. "Should we drive back to the car we took most of the way here?"

Andreas shakes his head. "We don't know who might have found it by now. I say we head straight to the nearest active trainline and hitch a few more rides."

"Perfect." Jacob tucks the laptop under his arm. "Let's get moving."

His motion toward the door encompasses me as well as the guys. We all stoop to grab a couple more guns from the pile on our way out.

None of the other men look at me. As we tramp around the log house to the 4x4 parked off to the side, uneasiness prickles over my limbs.

We all need to leave—me getting caught would be a danger to the guys. Are they going to kick me to the curb after that?

Don't I *want* to leave, after everything they put me through?

We are blood, we always said to each other. But they've broken the promise of those words so many times since I found my way back to them.

I only came this far with them to get answers… and while we got plenty of those from Engel, what she told us only spawned new questions. I need to know more, and whatever Engel kept on her devices could be the key.

So I guess I'm sticking with them for now, at least during this brief reprieve while we save our skins. But who knows what horrible thoughts about me are winding through the guys' heads as we clamber into the vehicle.

This could be the very last ride we share.

Two

Riva

The glow of the laptop screen turns Jacob's face an even eerier pale than usual in the darkness of the train car. He glares at it and lets out a string of colorful curses before shoving it away.

Andreas glances over at him from where he's sitting by the wall and raises his eyebrows. "You didn't really think the genius scientist would forget to put password protection on her devices, did you?"

Jacob scowls. "It didn't seem like she got a whole lot of visitors she'd need to worry about prying into her stuff. There was hope."

He leans back against the stack of crates behind him, swaying a little with a bump on the tracks, and folds his muscular arms over his chest. "You'll just have to scrounge up another hacker for us."

Andreas tugs at the length of rope he picked up in the train yard and has been winding into knots to pass the time. "I can do that, as soon as we figure out where we're landing."

The smell of sawdust itches at my nose. I draw my knees up to my chest where I'm sitting across from Andreas and risk a question.

"Do you figure we should stay in Canada for now or head back to the States?"

We decided before we hitched our ride that it was better not to try to cross the border right away, not when we're so close to where the guardians may already realize we've come over. But we haven't picked a final destination yet.

Dominic stirs where he's been slouched near the car door. During our short wait for the train, he drained some of the life from a towering pine tree to heal up the other guys' wounds a little better, but the effort seems to have exhausted him.

His voice comes out steady enough, if typically quiet. "The guardians never sent us on any missions outside of the country. They'd probably expect us to cross back to more familiar territory."

Zian lifts his head from where he's been sorting through our collection of firearms, consolidating ammo where he can. "As far as we know, all of the facilities were in the States, right? The guardians probably know their way around better down there too."

Jacob nods. "I think we should stay up north while we regroup, until we've decided on our next steps."

His cool blue gaze slides to me, as if he wants my approval of the plan. As if my opinion suddenly matters to him after weeks of sneering at any suggestion I made.

He admitted to being an asshole and an idiot, with something like an apology… after he tore into me so brutally I had to run straight at a speeding train to make sure I didn't unleash my shrieking power on him. That was only a couple of days ago.

I don't know what to believe. Especially now that they know just how brutal *I* can be.

I press my elbow against the wound on my side—starting to seal on its own with the heightened ability to recover that all our bodies have, but still sore when I prod it. The pain lances through my torso, grounding me.

As I open my mouth to make a brief comment of agreement, the train car lurches. My arm bumps my side harder than before, and what comes out instead is a strained squeak.

All four of the guys sitting around me stiffen. A whiff of nervous pheromones reaches me.

I snap my mouth shut, my stomach flipping over. But I knew we weren't going to avoid this subject forever.

There's a moment of silence other than the rattle of the train over the tracks. Then Andreas speaks up, with a weird mix of wariness and concern in his tone.

"What happened at Engel's house—you didn't tell us you'd developed new abilities too."

I drop my chin to my knees, staring at the scuffed floor rather than holding his gaze. "It'd only… come out once before. I didn't want to think it would happen again."

I close my eyes and add, "I didn't want to think I'd done it in the first place."

I hadn't wanted my guys to realize I had something so horrifying in me. So much for that.

There's a rustle as Dominic pulls his parka closer around him in the cooling evening air. "It didn't look like you just killed them," he ventures.

My throat constricts, but I don't see any point in lying about it.

They saw everything. We might as well get it all out now so they can be as revolted as they're going to be.

My voice comes out scratchy. "The power latches on to any place it can cause pain. Like it feeds off hurting people as much as possible before they die."

"With that scream." Jacob taps the floor. "Like a banshee."

"A what?" Zian says.

I can hear Jacob's baleful glower without even opening my eyes. "Don't you remember that big fat mythology book we all passed around when we were kids? The one Griffin loved."

His voice goes just a little rough with those last few words, mentioning his twin. My hand rises automatically to grip my cat-and-yarn necklace, the one Griffin gave me.

The only thing any of us has left of him.

I can't grip it too hard, though—can't snap the rotating pieces open and shut like I used to when I was feeling tense. I broke it during that last argument with Jacob, and he was only able to partly fix it on his own.

As I let myself take in the darkened train car again, Dominic tilts his head to the side. "Weren't banshees the ones that screamed to warn that death was coming? I don't think they did the actual killing."

Jacob shrugs. "It's not as if our powers fit into neat little boxes. I don't remember any monsters that grew poison spikes and moved things with their minds." He runs his fingers over one forearm where his deadly spines can emerge.

The guys lapse into another momentary silence. Then Andreas fixes me with his gaze, almost like he's going to peer inside my memories, though no ruddy light comes into his dark grey eyes.

"That night at the farmhouse," he says carefully. "When you ran toward the train… You said you didn't want to hurt us. You were trying to stop the new power from coming out?"

I have the urge to curl up inside myself, to recoil from the question. But he obviously already knows.

I got so close to the verge that night, a little sound burst out of me. I saw him flinch. He's putting the pieces together.

I make myself speak. "I was—after everything—"

The words clog in my throat. *After we had sex. After the shadows in our blood tied us together.*

The act felt so precious in the moments after—until I overheard Andreas admitting that he'd gotten close to me just to dig for information. To figure out how much of a traitor I was.

He's apologized too. He's claimed that he wasn't trying to use me when we melded together like one being. But I don't know how much to believe that either.

I swallow thickly and propel myself onward. "After what we did, my nerves were all keyed up, my emotions whirling—and then with the argument, it was even worse

—I *didn't* want to hurt any of you, not like that, but I could tell I was losing control."

More silence. I hug my knees tighter.

This is the worst. Not just the pain I can wield and revel in, but that some part of me was ready to inflict it on them.

No matter how awful they've been, they didn't deserve that—that all-encompassing, soul-rending torture.

Zian clears his throat. "So you… you would have let that train kill you…"

He doesn't seem to know how to go on.

"I wasn't really thinking," I mumble. "It was the only way I could stop myself for sure."

That's how bad it was. That's how close I got to tormenting the guys who were my only family, who I swore to protect, in the most horrific way imaginable.

I brace myself for accusations or recriminations. So I'm not at all prepared when Zian pushes away from his pile of guns and hunches down by my feet.

"We hurt you so badly," he says raggedly, his face so low to the floor his forehead must brush the gritty surface. "With everything we said, the way we'd been treating you —and you still would rather have *died* than hurt us."

My mouth opens and closes, my voice dried up in shock.

Zian goes on in my silence. "I'm so sorry, Riva. I should have been better. I shouldn't have trusted anything the guardians said. You were always there for us, doing everything for us—I am never going to forget that again."

I stare at the massive man kowtowing his apology to

me for several beats of my heart before I can even process what's happening.

He isn't horrified. My confession has made him *more* regretful?

"Zee," I say softly, and don't know how to go on. My heart is aching as much with the memory of times he snapped at me as with the anguish he's expressing now.

He hasn't so much as lifted his head, as if he's waiting for some kind of judgment. My hand reaches out of its own accord toward the short tufts of his silky black hair.

My fingertips graze the top of his head, and Zian jerks away from my touch. Just an inch, but enough of a rejection that I yank my hand back.

"Sorry," he mutters to the floor. "Sorry. I—"

"It's okay," I say before he can go on. I'd rather not hear him explain why he's so adverse to me touching him.

He regrets a lot of things, clearly, but that doesn't mean he wants to get cozy with me either.

Zian eases up a little, his dark eyes searching mine. They're stormy, but lit with enough hope to send the ache in my chest jabbing even deeper.

I fumble for a fuller answer. "We've been through a lot. All of us. I don't really know where we go from here. But I'm not asking for anything."

At this point, I know better than to ask for anything.

Zee pushes upright, looking as if he's not totally satisfied with that answer but uncertain about what he would want instead.

By the door, Dominic draws himself a little straighter, his expression tightening. "You used the power at Engel's house. Are you sure… Are you sure you can control it *now*?"

He obviously isn't. And that's fair—that's closer to the reaction I was expecting.

I set my chin on my knees again. "No. That's why I want to understand everything Engel told us. How she made us—what she made us out of. I was hoping I could get rid of it, but if I can't, then there's got to be a way to at least rein it in more."

Ursula Engel admitted that she'd created us by combining human DNA with the essence of what she called "monsters." Maybe something on her laptop or phone will help us understand exactly what that means.

"We've all had issues with our talents getting away from us," Andreas says, but his tone is still wary.

When the rest of them lose control, none of them risks putting the rest of us through indescribable torture.

"It was only that one moment," I can't help replying. "There were other times when I could have used it, when it wanted me to let it loose, and I kept it under wraps. I *decided* to use it in Engel's house, because it was either that or we died."

"And it was fucking amazing." Jacob pushes to his feet, his penetrating stare sliding over the other guys. In the faint light with that resolute stance, he looks like a warrior guardian angel, just missing the wings.

He jabs his forefinger toward me. After the past couple of weeks, I can't restrain a wince even though his frown obviously isn't directed my way.

"Riva gave the pricks everything they deserved," he says fiercely. "She threw all the pain they've put us through back at them, right where it belongs. And she didn't give us so much as a papercut in the process. So don't any of you dare act like she's anything but a goddamned superhero."

I blink at him, startled speechless for the second time in minutes. How the hell did the guy who's been going out of his way to bully me at every opportunity suddenly become my biggest supporter?

Is he really, or is his attitude going to turn on a dime with the next shift in the wind?

The corner of Zian's mouth kicks up with a hint of a smile. "It was pretty spectacular watching them all go down."

Andreas tips his head to me. "We'll find answers—for all of us."

Dominic's attention has been drawn away by something beyond the door. He leans toward it before glancing back at us.

"We're coming up on the first junction. We wanted to switch trains here, right?"

"Yes." Jacob snatches up the laptop he cast aside. "The more times we divert course, the harder it'll be for the guardians to track us."

Zian stuffs the guns into the sack we found and peers around us through the walls of the car with his X-ray sight. "I don't see anything strange nearby."

A squeal pierces the air as the train's brakes grip the tracks. Dominic peeks out through the door again and motions to us when the coast is clear.

We hop out into the thickening night and slink along

the side of another, motionless train to get a look at our options for transport.

As Jacob pushes ahead in his typical mode as our self-declared leader, Andreas touches my arm—just a fleeting gesture to draw my attention. He slows purposefully, and I match his pace even as tension winds around my gut.

What does he want?

He ducks his head with a slant of his mouth that looks more embarrassed than anything else and then glances sideways at me. "I realized—we got so caught up in the moment that night—I didn't even think about protection. Do we need to worry that you could be—"

I catch on before he even finishes the question.

"No," I interrupt hastily, my cheeks flaring. "The guardians fitted me with some birth control thing before we started going on missions, and they'd updated it just a few months before we tried to escape. It should still be working."

Even if it wasn't, with the stress and physical strain of my captivity at the cage-fighting arena, I haven't had a period in years.

"And that was the first time I ever… did anything like that," I add awkwardly, not really wanting to put a name on the act out loud. "So no diseases or whatever to worry about." I pause. "At least from me."

It's hard to tell in the dim light from the security lamps up ahead, but I think Andreas's face flushes beneath his coppery brown skin. His gaze drops to the gravel-strewn ground.

"There was only once before for me, and it was—the guardians arranged it, a couple months after they took you away. I think they figured we needed some kind of outlet. I didn't *want* to. But they would have been careful about health and all that."

A rush of cold washes over me. My feet stumble for a second before I recover. "You—they *forced* you? All of you?"

My gaze flicks to the guys ahead of us, but Andreas is already shaking his head. "They tried, but it… didn't go so well. That's why it was only the once, and only me."

His voice has gotten strained, but I have to ask. "What happened?"

Andreas's jaw ticks. He raises his head, but I can't tell which of his friends he's looking at. "That's one story that is definitely not mine to tell. You should just know, while you were dealing with all that crap where they took you… a lot of shit went down for us too."

I'd already realized that, but I'd had no idea the guardians had gone that far.

Jacob motions to us, and Andreas picks up the pace to catch up. I follow him, my stomach churning.

Just how badly did our former captors damage the boys I loved?

And was it too much for them to ever really be those guys again, even if they want to?

Three

Andreas

I grip the handle of the door between our motel room and the adjoining one, and catch Dominic's eyes where he's sitting cross-legged on the bed. He looks a little bizarre, slouched there in his parka that disguises the bulge of his extra appendages.

He doesn't like any of us seeing his tentacles more than we have to. As if hiding them will make them less real.

"All good?" I mouth at him.

He nods, our phone pressed to his ear and his other hand resting on the laptop's keyboard. Then his attention veers back to the computer.

"Okay," he says to the woman on the other end as he taps a few keys.

The hacker I managed to connect with—by searching the right kinds of online forums for the telltale signals I've learned—is theoretically going to walk Dominic through the process of cracking the laptop's password from a distance. We decided Dom was the best choice for that job since he's definitely got the rest of us beat when it comes to staying calm and focused.

I don't want to see what Jacob or Zian would do to the computer after a few frustrating failures.

Me, I'd probably get distracted wondering about the hacker's other exploits and wishing I could peek inside her memories from over the phone.

I slip into the other room and shut the door with a click. When I turn around, I find Jacob perched on the edge of one of the double beds.

He hasn't got anywhere to go, but he's poised like he's about to charge into battle. Typical.

The muffled sound of sloshing water filters through the bathroom door. Jake notices my glance.

"Zee wanted to take a *bath*," he mutters with a combination of derision and bafflement that's almost funny.

My mouth twitches into a smile. "This is the first time he's really had a chance in ages. Might as well."

Even when we commandeered the townhouse on the college campus right after our escape, all its tiny bathrooms had were shower stalls. And I have a hazy recollection from the swimming lessons the guardians insisted on when we were kids: Zian stopping to simply float on the surface of the water in the big glass tank they used.

It might feel pretty incredible having that huge body buoyed up. Taking all the weight off.

Of course, I don't know how much water he can

actually fit in the motel tub around all those muscles of his.

I make a mental note, adding to the long, invisible list I've been keeping in my head: We'll find a place with a proper swimming pool.

Eventually. When the guardians are no longer at our heels.

If that day ever comes.

Jacob jerks his head toward the door to my and Dominic's room. "You're sure this computer guru is going to come through?"

I shrug. "She only gets the rest of the money if she does. I didn't get the impression it'd be that hard for her."

"How long are we going to be waiting while she holds Dom's hand?"

I resist the urge to grimace at him. He doesn't really mean to be insulting, even if he sounds like it.

I know from experience and observation that the vast majority of the bitterness that spills out of Jake is actually directed at himself.

"She said it depends on the exact firmware on the laptop. A simple one could take just a few minutes. A more secure setup, she figured two to three hours. Shouldn't be more than that."

Jacob lets out a huff. "Engel would have had plenty of fucking security."

No doubt. But I'm not sure taking a few hours to unwind is a bad thing—for any of us.

My gaze darts to the door at the other end of the space. The one that leads into Riva's room.

A soft tingle ripples through the spot at the top of my

chest where our interlude in the farmhouse marked me. I can sense her on the other side of the door, still there.

She looked so surprised when Jacob pointed out the room that was hers, without messing with the locks or posting a guard outside. So fucking surprised it kills me.

The ache reverberates through my chest alongside the urge I've been fighting ever since that night at the farmhouse. Every particle in my body wants to go to her, to wrap her up in my arms, to tell her I've got her, I love her, it'll all be okay.

But it isn't okay. She thinks I betrayed her.

Because I *did* betray her… just not quite as badly as she believes.

Riva doesn't want me touching her. She barely wants to talk to me.

And maybe she isn't entirely wrong, because the other image that flashes through my mind when I think of her is from Engel's cottage.

Jaw stretched open impossibly wide. Every plane of her face gone taut. Her eyes hazed white.

And the little quivers that passed through her body with each pulse of her scream—eager, almost *giddy*. Like twisting and snapping those bodies while they cried out in agony was a thrill.

I swallow, ignoring the twinge of nausea that ripples through my stomach at the memory. She called on that power to save us—and however she felt about it in the moment, there was no mistaking the horror and revulsion in her expression when we prodded her about it after.

She didn't ask for her new talent any more than Zian asked for his feral rages or Dominic his growing tentacles.

I have to show her I understand that too.

I turn back to Jacob. "I'm going to take Riva to go pick up supplies at the mall. We need to replace what we lost at the townhouse now that we have a chance."

Jacob springs to his feet, his gaze immediately twice as intense. "I'll come with you."

I hold up my hand, not at all surprised by his declaration. "It's better if you stay here. Dom's occupied, and Zian obviously needs a break. Someone needs to be standing guard, right?"

Jacob's eyes narrow. "The mall is more exposure. If they find you there—"

I raise my eyebrows. "We're in the middle of nowhere, four train hops and a drive from the last place the guardians could locate us. And if they find us anyway, Riva can look after herself."

"But—"

"Jake," I say, and he stops at the firmness of my tone.

I hesitate, because this isn't the kind of thing we've normally talked about. It isn't the kind of thing we've normally been *able* to talk about with the guardians watching over us in the facility and charting every weakness.

But I suspect it'd be good if we were all a little more honest about how we feel.

"I screwed up with her," I say quietly. "In some ways worse than you did. I need to take my chances to make it up to her when I can get them."

Jacob's jaw tightens, but he lowers his eyes at the same time, looking vaguely abashed.

"Fine," he mutters. "Get more phones too. If we're

going to be splitting up sometimes, we need to be able to reach each other."

I nod. "Totally agreed. Thank you."

His gaze flicks back to me, his pale blue eyes now stormy. "Just don't be gone too long."

I grab some of the money from our stash and knock on the door to Riva's room. My gut clenches in apprehension about her response before her voice calls out, clear but hesitant. "You can come in."

She can probably sense that it's me just like I'm aware of her presence beyond the door. I ease it open to see her setting down the TV remote next to her where she's poised in the middle of the bed.

I felt her there and she's been at the forefront of my mind for days, but seeing her directly sends an extra jolt of anguished affection through my heart.

She looks so small and delicate with her hoodie hugged tight around her and her shoulders warily hunched. Her skin shines nearly as pale as the silvery strands of her hair that twine with the darker gray underneath.

She flips her braid over her shoulder and studies me with her bright brown eyes. They gleam with feline alertness even when she's in fully human form.

Riva isn't weak or fragile, not really. I've seen so many times how much strength her tiny frame contains.

But somehow that knowledge makes it worse. She endured so much from us, took the accusations and the venom—both metaphorical and literal—and even when she finally cracked, her first instinct was to sacrifice herself to save us.

It's hard to imagine how we let ourselves question her devotion. I have to find a way to show just how devoted to her *I* can be.

I don't care how vicious her new abilities are or how well she can control them. It doesn't matter if she ends up hurting me by accident.

Anything she could deal out would be worth it just to stand by her side like I should have to begin with.

"I'm going to that mall we passed to pick up some changes of clothes for all of us and a few other things," I say. "Do you want to come along? I figured you might like getting to choose your own outfits this time."

Riva blinks, and that flash of startled emotion flits across her face again. The last time we bought new clothes, Jacob forced her to stay back in the car under guard.

And I let him get away with it.

She unfolds her limbs with her usual careful grace and pushes herself off the bed. "All right. I would like that."

We leave through her outer door, Riva stepping close enough to me that I catch a whiff of her sweetly metallic scent. My fingers itch to stroke over her hair or trail along her jaw, but I curl them into my palms.

She'd only flinch away.

She tucks herself into the passenger seat of the sedan we made off with—clunky but functional enough. I let her sit in silence as I start the engine and turn onto the country highway toward the suburban mall about ten minutes down the road, nestled between a couple of minor towns.

There isn't a whole lot else on the highway other than a diner that looks like it caters mostly to truckers and a building that's not much more than a shack with granite lawn ornaments poised for sale out front. Just after noon on a weekday, the mall's parking lot is pretty desolate too.

That suits our preferences just fine.

Riva tugs her hood up over her distinctive hair before we get out of the car. I run my hand over my tight coils and hope that they and my brown skin won't stand out too much in small-town Manitoba.

The guardians always sent us to decently big cities for our missions. I've gotten more uneasy glances roaming across the more out-of-the-way parts of the continent in the past couple of weeks than in my whole life beforehand.

Before we reach the mall doors, I pass several bills to Riva. "Grab whatever you want, wherever you want."

Another flicker of surprise passes through her eyes. "You want me to go off on my own?"

As we push inside, I offer her a crooked smile. "As much as I'd like to offer my services as bodyguard, I know you can kick a hell of a lot more ass than I can."

We both know that's not what she meant, but she ducks her head in acknowledgment. As she takes in the sprawl of shops ahead of us, just a hint of a smile touches her lips.

I spot a clock mounted near the entrance and point to it. "We'll meet back here in an hour?"

"Sounds good."

Riva sets off at a more energetic pace, making a beeline for a store with sporty tank tops and sweats in the display window. I watch her go for a few seconds before propelling myself in my own direction.

I don't actually like leaving her to her own devices, but

only because I won't immediately know if she's under threat.

There isn't a whole lot I'd be able to do that she couldn't. What I said to her about our relative self-defense skills was accurate, though.

And there's no denying how much the freedom meant to her.

I've tried apologizing for my epic screw-up with my words, and that hasn't been enough, understandably. So I'll just have to prove how much I trust her—how much she matters to me—with how I act as well.

It's not as if I've completely lost track of her anyway. As I move briskly through the men's section of the one department store grabbing the shirts and pants I know the other guys will want that aren't too pricy, as I pick up cheap but sturdy looking backpacks at a luggage shop and four more prepaid phones at an electronics kiosk, I'm constantly aware of Riva's position relative to me in the building.

But I can't sense anything other than where she is—no emotions, no other impressions. If she was in distress, I'd have no idea.

I work through my mental shopping list so quickly that I still have plenty of time left when I reach the end. I pause by a store directory and scan the other options.

What else could I offer Riva as a gift of sorts? A token of my affection?

I riffle through my large collection of captured stories —from other people's memories, from TV shows and movies and books. How do you pamper the woman you love?

I've never had the chance to before. I doubt Riva's ever been pampered enough to have any idea how she'd like it to happen.

Which only makes it more important that *someone* start doing it now.

She's already getting whatever clothes she likes. I can't imagine her wanting any jewelry other than the necklace from Griffin that I've never seen her take off except that one night when everything went to hell.

My gaze settles on a bath and body shop. If even Zian can appreciate a nice soak in the tub, why wouldn't Riva?

It seems like as good a place to start as any.

I pop into the shop, the mingling floral perfumes flooding my nose, and try to pick out something to Riva's tastes. I don't think she wants to smell like a rose garden— but then, what do I know?

In the end, I grab a selection of different options and stuff the bag into one of the backpacks so I can keep it sort of a surprise.

When I make it back to the front entrance with ten minutes to spare, Riva is already waiting there. The jeans she's wearing look the same as before, but they're tucked into a pair of lace-up leather boots totally ready for ass-kicking.

She waggles one foot at me with a slightly larger smile than I saw before. "I figured I should be prepared for more forest hikes. And snow. If we keep ahead of the guardians for much longer, we'll be dealing with winter weather too."

"Very wise," I say casually, like my heart hasn't skipped a beat taking in the rest of her. She's swapped her old navy hoodie for a deep maroon one that brings out the gold tones in her vibrant eyes.

A couple of plastic shopping bags dangle from her arms, so obviously she hasn't held back. Good.

A little of her previous uncertainty returns as we head across the parking lot. "Do you need the cash I didn't use back?"

I shake my head immediately. "We should all have at least a little money on us in case we get separated. Oh, and I got a phone for you. We'll have to program in each other's numbers once we're back at the motel."

She takes the package from me and holds it tightly for a second before slipping it into her bag. "We're really getting our act together this time."

"It should have been like this from the start." I open the trunk and toss my bags inside, then glance back toward the mall. "We should probably do a little grocery shopping too. Non-perishables. The money'll go a lot farther that way than with restaurants."

"Good point." Riva rubs her hands together as if she's already envisioning the meals to come.

The supermarket attached to the mall contrasts starkly with the rest of the space, a chill in the air and the overhead lights twice as harsh. I can't help noticing one of the clerks drifting along behind me while supposedly checking that the shelves are properly organized.

Does he think I'm going to rob the soup and sauces aisle?

I fill the basket I picked up hastily, including a box of cookies and a tray of tarts in recollection of Dominic's sweet tooth. I rejoin Riva in the fruits and vegetables section, where she's contemplating bags of lemons.

"Looking for something to stuff down Jacob's throat?" I ask wryly.

The corner of Riva's mouth quirks upward, and she shakes her head. "I was thinking that I kind of liked that drink I got… with Brooke… at the club. It was kind of citrusy and sour. But I'd rather have it without the alcohol."

Brooke—who lived in the townhouse next to the one we were squatting in on campus. Who died when the guardians ambushed us there.

I wince inwardly at the memory and motion to the lemons. "You should get them, then. Experiment. Why not?"

"Yeah. There's no one to tell us what to do now. Why not."

I wouldn't call her peppy, but by the time we return to the car for a second time, her stance has definitely gotten looser. So when we reach the motel and I'm sorting out her bags from mine, I only feel a little awkward getting out the bath and body stuff.

"I bought something else for you," I say, handing it over. "In case you want to just chill out for a bit while we can. There's regular salts and a bunch of different scented stuff…"

Riva peeks inside with a trace of confusion and lifts out one bottle full of pearly blue liquid. "Bubble bath?"

I grin and spread my hands. "Maybe you want to relive the childhood we never got."

When she gives me a pensive look, I let my hands fall

back to my sides. "You've been through a lot, in general and recently… and a lot of it is because of us. You deserve a chance to relax."

I can't read her expression, but at least she doesn't appear to be pissed off. She glances into the bag again and cocks her head.

"Maybe I will."

She goes in through her door and I knock on Jacob and Zian's, not wanting to disturb Dominic if he's still deep in hacker-consultation mode.

Jake flings the door open as if he thinks I've come to warn him of the impending apocalypse. Zee only pauses briefly where he's pacing the room, his hair still damp from his own earlier bath.

"No emergency." I hold up the bags. "I've got clothes, phones, and food—and packs to stash them in so we can keep everything with us wherever we go."

Naturally, Jacob grabs the bags from me and immediately starts sorting the clothes into their respective backpacks, deciding without asking what belongs to who. But he knows us—it's not like I can say he's wrong.

"Is Dominic still on the call?" I ask Zian.

The big guy nods and resumes his pacing. He's only crossed the floor a few times before he pauses to contemplate the grocery bags. "What did you get to eat?"

I suppress a laugh. "Mostly stuff we don't have to worry about going bad anytime soon, like protein bars and dried fruit. But for tonight I did find some premade subs. Yours is meatball."

Despite his obvious tension, his eyes light up. I pick up that bag and stick the subs in the fridge before he gets any ideas about having that dinner just a couple of hours after the drive-through lunch we gulped down on the way here.

At his frown, I toss him an apple. "You do need a few nutrients other than protein."

He glowers at my teasing tone but takes a bite as he goes back to his pacing.

Jacob carries one fresh change of clothes into the bathroom and takes the world's fastest shower, probably worried we'll somehow descend into catastrophe if he leaves us alone for more than a few minutes. The hiss of the running water tugs my thoughts back to Riva in the other room.

Is she soaking in her bathtub right now? My mind conjures the image of her small but soft curves, the pert nipples I stroked my fingers over, the slim hips that rose to meet me...

Heat floods my body. Now *I* need a shower—a cold one.

Maybe one day she'll trust me enough to invite me into a bath with her.

That idea sets my mind down on another dangerous path. I borrow Jacob's tactic and start pacing to distract myself.

Jake stalks out of the bathroom with a flick of his gaze toward the door to Riva's room. I can tell from the momentary tensing of his expression that he wants to go check on her and is holding himself back.

He looks at me next, and the heat that filled me earlier fades away under his scrutiny.

I'm not totally sure if Zee and Dom realize just how

close Riva and I got the other night, but Jacob has definitely guessed. Knowing that sends a weird pang of guilt through me.

As far as I know, I'm the only one of us who's experienced sex once, let alone twice. Even if the first time wasn't by choice, some part of me enjoyed it by the end.

It's pretty hard for a teenage boy to convince his body not to react to certain kinds of stimulation.

I sure as hell hope the other guys don't envy me that first time. The suffocating agony of fighting against your physical reactions with all your willpower and still losing… I wouldn't wish it on anyone.

They might envy me about Riva, though.

She turned to me out of the four of us because I was the one who was there for her. But the allegiance I offered her was partly under false pretenses.

I'm not sure I really deserved to get to know her that way first. She admitted she had feelings for all of us.

There's nothing I can do about it now, though.

I hold up another apple. "Hungry?"

Jacob is just tossing the gnawed core into the trash bin when Dominic shoves open the adjoining door, the laptop clutched in his hands. We all freeze.

"I'm in," he says breathlessly, his hazel eyes unusually wild. "And I found something—we had no idea—"

Riva nudges open the door opposite, obviously having heard him. She's rebraided her hair, but a few strands stick damply to the sides of her pretty face, and I can't repress a shiver of satisfaction that she used my gift.

"What?" she demands. "What have you got?"

Dominic motions us over and sits on the end of one of

the beds where we can easily gather around him. The open folds of his parka pool around him.

He points to a file open on the screen. A tremor runs through his hand.

"There could be others," he says. "Other shadowbloods like us."

FOUR

Riva

In the first few moments after Dominic's declaration, all of us simply stare—at him, at the laptop screen. My head is spinning too fast for me to concentrate on the words.

"What do you mean?" I blurt out. "We never saw— the guardians never said—"

Dominic waves at the screen with a rustle of his parka. He must be sweltering in the thick coat even with it unzipped, but I've never seen him display his tentacles unless he absolutely has to.

"It's not obvious whether they actually *did* create more hybrids. But I found a file that refers to different processes that Engel used. There's an original one, labeled first gen and dated almost twenty-two years ago."

"Around the time we would have been conceived, however that happened," Andreas fills in, looking ill.

Dominic nods. "And then there are two others, one from about five years after that and then another after two more. Some of it is in shorthand notation I don't understand. But it seems like she's reminding herself of where she left certain things out."

My stomach has balled into a massive knot. "She didn't want to make more people like us. She didn't even want *us* to keep living. She said by the time we were toddlers, she'd already changed her mind."

Jacob frowns, leaning his weight onto his hand where it's resting on the comforter next to me. He isn't paying any attention to me, but I'm abruptly aware of how close he is.

How close they all are.

I scrambled onto the bed at Dominic's beckoning without thinking, just wanting to know what he's found. Now I'm perched on my knees with Jacob just a few inches at my right and Andreas equally close at my left.

And Dom is right in front of me. I could tip my head onto his shoulder if I wanted to.

An unwelcome tingle of warmth races over my skin. Suddenly I wish I never took Andreas's suggestion of a soak in the tub, as brief as I made it.

I figured the regular salts he got might be good for the wound on my side that's still raw. If it gets infected, I'll *have* to ask Dominic for help.

But now my skin is scrubbed clean under my crisply new clothes. The sensation is energizing in ways I'd rather not tap into.

No matter how badly these men hurt me, some part of

my body—maybe even my soul—believes that I belong with them. As close to them as I can get.

Thankfully, it's my mind that gets to make those decisions.

I stay stiffly still where I can still see the screen but avoiding easing any closer to the guys.

Jacob makes a vague gesture at the computer. "She was the one who figured out how to make us, but she said there were other people who had control over the facility —who could boss her around. They wanted to keep us. Maybe they wanted to make more too."

Zian lets out a rough chuckle. "She could have given them instructions that were missing pieces so it wouldn't actually work. Pretended it was a fluke they produced us."

"Or the new process worked, but without the parts she thought made us too dangerous," Dominic says quietly.

I shudder. "There could be a bunch of shadowblood teenagers being put through all the same tests we were."

Or even younger kids. There's no saying the guardians wouldn't have used Engel's processes more than once after she handed them over.

"Is there anything else in there that would tell us for sure?" Jacob demands.

As Dominic starts clicking through more files, I scoot farther back on the bed. Could there have been other people like us, with wisps of smoke in their blood and monstrous powers, at the facility where we grew up?

There were an awful lot of doors on the same levels as our cells. For all we know, the guardians had separate training rooms elsewhere in the building.

And we know we lived in at least three different

facilities over the course of our captivity. It's also possible they kept younger test subjects in a totally different place.

Or maybe Engel screwed her colleagues over and they never managed to create anyone else even sort of like us. She didn't seem bothered that it was just the five of us who showed up, other than wondering about Griffin's absence.

Dominic makes a discontented sound. "There are more documents with that weird system of notation I don't know how to read. I don't see anything definite about other 'shadowbloods,' but she doesn't seem to have any files even on us here. I'll keep digging."

"You got into her phone too?" Andreas asks.

"Yeah, but she must have deleted everything whenever she used it. No call history, no saved contacts, nothing."

I restrain a sigh and push myself right to the edge of the bed. My limbs itch to return to my own room where the guys' presence won't niggle at me, but I want to hear the second Dominic finds something.

It could be there's nothing useful on the laptop at all. That we're even more adrift than when I first broke them out of the facility, when they had the goal of finding Engel to see what she knew.

The TV remote is sitting on the bedside table. Aimlessly, I pick it up and start flicking through the channels.

Zian gets up and comes around to get a better view of the TV, but he sits carefully on the other bed, a few feet away. I know I don't have to worry about *him* getting up in my personal space.

He shoots me a cautious glance, but his voice comes out

with a friendly warmth despite its gruffness. "Do you figure a massacre in that little cabin will make the news? Stuff like that can't happen very often near some tiny town."

I consider the question seriously, lingering on a news report about traffic conditions. "Engel's place was so isolated, it'd have been the guardians who found it. And they'd have covered it up."

"Like it never happened."

"Yeah." I cross my arms, tapping my elbow against the rebandaged wound that's hidden under my hoodie.

I wish I could erase what I did completely out of existence, as thoroughly as Andreas can wipe out memories.

I wish I could erase the ability right out of *me*.

I flip the channels a few more times and pause with a jolt of recognition. The faces on the screen, the slightly hazy lighting, and the dramatic swell of music are all so familiar they send me back more than four years to the TV breaks we got in the middle of training.

A woman with billowy hair and an elegant dress wags a manicured finger at a stern-looking man with slicked-back hair. "Don't you dare," she says, drawing the words out.

He squares his shoulders, glowering down at her dramatically. "You're the last person who should be threatening me, Carolina."

Andreas has lifted his head to see what I'm watching. A soft chuckle escapes him. "That's the crazy soap opera Griffin always wanted to watch."

Jacob's gaze jerks up too. At the flexing of his jaw, I

feel like I have to explain—to make it clear I didn't mean to rub salt in a wound.

Even though my own heart aches with the memory of watching these storylines play out tucked next to his twin on the sofa.

Heat tickles across my cheeks as I make myself speak. "It was actually—I liked it. Griffin just knew, and he knew you guys would tease me about it if I said *I* wanted to watch the show."

From the tick of Jacob's eyelid, I can't tell whether my admission made things better or worse.

Andreas arches his eyebrows, but his tone stays mild. The same careful way he's been speaking to me ever since his last apology.

"I think you're allowed one or two interests that are a little girly, Tink. We would never have forgotten that you could take us down in two seconds flat in a sparring match."

Zian gives a huff. "The rest of you, maybe."

I squirm a little, still embarrassed. "Everything in this show was just so different from the facility. They were always going to fancy places and meeting fancy people. And when they got angry, they'd just stare and snap at each other instead of stabbing or shooting."

Not to mention that watching the characters' melodramatic relationship issues made me feel a little less ridiculous having a crush on all five of my best friends.

Before anyone can talk about the soap I secretly adored any more—before it can provoke any further painful memories—I shut the TV off and turn back toward Dominic. "Anything else on the laptop?"

He's brought one hand to his mouth, resting his knuckle against his lips as he scans the current batch of files. "I mean, there's a lot on here. Some of this is kind of interesting—she's got notes on different types of 'monsters.'"

We all perk up.

"Like, what kinds we were made out of?" Zian asks.

Dominic shakes his head. "Nothing connecting them specifically to us. Just observations and data, abilities and possible weaknesses."

Jacob grimaces. "Either to figure out what she wanted to fuse into us or how we were supposed to go take the things down."

Engel had said that she originally created us in the hopes that we'd be powerful enough to fight the creatures she called monsters. Then she decided we were even more dangerous than the original monsters were.

I draw my legs up to my chest. "We've got to figure out more about what we are and what we can do, somehow. If the full monsters can go around mingling with humans without most people noticing, *they* can obviously control their abilities just fine."

So there ought to be ways that we can too. Ways to make it easier to contain my urge to shriek when I get angry.

Ways to ensure Andreas doesn't fade away after he uses his ability to turn invisible. Ways to tame Zian's wolfish rage.

Maybe even a way to get Dominic's tentacles to shrink back into him instead of growing.

Dominic rubs his chin. "It doesn't seem like anyone at

the facilities would know. Engel made us, and I don't think she ever shared the full process with anyone else."

"We'd have a hell of a time trying to go straight at the guardians on their home territory anyway," Andreas says.

Zian hesitates and then catches my gaze. "What about —the place they sent you to, after we tried to escape?"

I suppress a shudder at the thought of the cage-fighting arena where I was held—the weekly matches against armed men twice my size, the shackles that weighed down my arms in between, and the mix of fear and hatred that emanated off my keepers.

"They didn't know anything," I said. "I'm not sure they had any idea what I was other than, to them, a freak."

Jacob's eyes narrow. "We need to pay them back too. They're going to regret everything they put you—"

"They already regretted it," I break in, and jerk my gaze away. I don't want to watch their expressions while I admit this. "That's the first time my new power came out. I took out the boss and all his people who were around… and the whole audience."

My shoulders come up defensively, but I refuse to outright cringe. The memory of that much larger massacre still makes me queasy, but it got me free. It brought me back to my guys, even if our reunion hasn't exactly gone the way I hoped.

If it wasn't for the carnage I dealt with my scream, I'd still be in those shackles in the room where the boss kept me, all alone.

There's a moment of silence, like the other guys aren't sure what to say. Then Zian grunts. "Good."

Jacob's mouth curves into one of the hard little smiles

that until recently were normally aimed at me. This one is on my behalf. "Yes. They got what they deserved."

I'm not sure the other two guys feel quite the same way, but Andreas at least changes the subject so we don't need to dwell on my past brutality.

"If we can't get more answers about our 'monstrous' talents from the people who put them into us," he says, "what if we asked the things that have their own talents?"

Zian knits his brow. "You want to talk to the *monsters*?"

Andreas holds up his hands. "I'm just saying, they're the only other direct source of information. We don't have to make friends or anything, just find one or two and question them."

As his suggestion sinks in, I find myself nodding. "And we don't know how monstrous those monsters actually are. Engel said they're horrible… but she thought *we* were horrible too."

The guardians are against the things they call monsters, and they want to enslave us. So we share at least one other thing with the creatures: a common enemy.

"We'd still need to be cautious," Dominic points out.

"Of course. Trust no one." Jacob rolls his shoulders as if he's warming up to launch into an interrogation right now. "Any idea from her notes where we'd be best off looking for these creatures?"

Dominic tilts his head to the side, studying the screen. "It sounds like most of the ones that mix with humans regularly like to do it where there are lots of people to blend in with. So a big city seems like it'd be our best bet."

Zian relaxes a little. "That'll mean more people for us

to blend in with too. Should we stick to Canada still? What's the biggest city up here?"

"That would be Toronto. Bigger than most of the cities in the States too." Andreas glances around at us with a slow-stretching grin. "What do you say we head a little farther east to do some monster-hunting?"

FIVE

Riva

"This is part of downtown too?" I ask, peering through the windshield at the buildings we're cruising by. "How much of it is there?"

Andreas laughs from behind the wheel. "I told you it was a big city."

He brakes at a red light and glances over his shoulder toward the guys. They're crammed together in the backseat... because Zian insisted I should get to ride shotgun even though his bulky body needs the space way more than I do.

I'm not totally sure whether he was being considerate or ensuring there was no chance he'd end up squished next to me if Jacob demanded the front seat instead.

"One time I crossed paths with a guy who grew up in Toronto," Andreas says, falling into the slightly lilting cadence he takes on in story-telling mode. "He had a bunch of memories of this place. Worked somewhere downtown. Lots of hustle and bustle."

"I don't suppose he had any memories of monster encounters?" Jacob asks with a hint of impatience.

Andreas lets any implied criticism roll right off his back. "Nah. The most interesting thing I saw was he climbed that whole tower once."

He points toward one of the back windows where a slim building with a bulge partway up, like an olive speared on a toothpick only a whole lot bigger, juts up toward the clouded sky. It's got to be twice as tall as the highest skyscrapers nearby.

"Climbed the outside?" Zian says doubtfully.

Andreas chuckles. "The inside, going up the stairs. Seemed like they went on forever. Then he got to the top and puked."

"And that's your idea of a fun story?" Jacob mutters.

"It didn't seem like he minded so much. He laughed about it after, and then his friends caught up and they had a little celebration in this restaurant up there."

I frown at the pedestrians ambling by on the crowded sidewalks. Just like all the other sidewalks we've passed, none of them stand out as anything other than human.

Curiosity tickles up inside my head. "I wonder if you've ever looked inside a monster's memories. I wonder if you *could*."

Andreas cocks his head. "I don't know. I've never run into anyone whose memories I couldn't see. But hopefully the real monsters aren't blending in so well that I wouldn't notice pretty quick once I peeked inside."

"If they don't remember doing anything monstrous,

then they're probably not all that bad," Dominic remarks in his quietly thoughtful way.

We all sit with that thought for a minute as the car creeps along through the traffic. Then Zian sets his hand on his belly.

"Since we haven't figured out where to go yet anyway… maybe we should grab some dinner?"

Jacob lets out a huff, but Andreas nods. "It'd give me some time to concentrate on the people around and see if I can stumble on any unusual memories that'd point us in the right direction."

"Fine," Jacob says. "But let's pick someplace low key where they don't expect us to be dressed up or anything."

He looks pulled together enough, wearing a combination of collared shirt and slacks that Andreas picked up for him at the mall. Andreas could probably blend in anywhere that's not high-level fine dining in his Henley and khakis.

The rest of us, though… I've got on my new favorite hoodie, the inside velvety soft against my arms, and a new pair of cargo pants with a couple of knives stashed in the pockets and a pistol in the back of the waist, just in case.

Zian's in his preferred athletic casual, sweats and tee under a track jacket, and Dominic—well, he's going to look a little strange keeping that parka on inside no matter where we go.

Every one of the men is still absolutely stunning, though. I jerk my gaze back to the windshield and instruct myself to stop noticing, as if that strategy is going to work this time after it's gone *so* well before.

"I think I see a good option." Andreas pulls the car

into a tight parking spot and motions to a storefront farther down the street.

We all clamber out into the cool autumn air. I suck in a deep breath, both to clear my lungs and to see if I catch any unusual tastes that might lead us to our target —and Dominic twitches where he's stepped out next to me.

I only see it from the corner of my eye, and when I glance at him he looks perfectly calm, but I think that was a flinch. A faint tang of nervous adrenaline reaches my nose before the breeze washes it away.

I probably gulped a bunch of air like that right before I let out my killer shriek.

The thought weighs on me as I tramp alongside the guys to a restaurant with a faded sign proclaiming it the Daffodil Diner. The windows are a tad grimy and the leather seats I can see inside are sporting a few cracks, but it's not crowded and definitely not fancy.

I'll take it.

Jacob pushes inside first with his usual commanding air and scores us a booth in the corner next to the front windows. I'd imagine he wants to keep an eye on everyone passing by outside throughout the meal.

This may be a big city that we're blending into, but that doesn't mean the guardians couldn't track us down here.

Apprehension prickles over my skin. I hardly notice how Jacob has ushered the guys into the seats until he's motioning for me to sit down across from him.

He's arranged so that I get to sit on the end of the bench, where I'm not boxed in. The exact opposite of how he'd have handled this scenario a week ago with his fears that I'd take off on them.

I'm next to Zian, who's left me plenty of space beside his brawn—for both of our benefits, no doubt.

I accept one of the menus the waitress brings us, my gaze darting between it and the window.

If the guardians *did* somehow find us here, we'd see them coming, right? It looks like there's a back entrance over by the washrooms.

And if we really need to make a fast getaway, glass is always breakable.

When I finally convince myself to give the menu my full attention, my mouth starts watering. We haven't eaten anything except grocery store offerings and drive-through fast food in days.

The burgers look tasty, but I've had a ton of those already. And so many of the other options sound good.

Even if this place isn't five-star dining, it'll at least be different from the stuff I've spent most of my life subsiding on.

I lick my lips. Andreas catches the movement with apparent amusement.

"Already know what you want, Tink?"

"I want the whole menu," I mutter. "They have fish and chips *and* lasagna. How am I supposed to decide?"

One corner of his mouth ticks upward. "I was eyeing the lasagna. How about I get that and promise you a piece of it?"

My eyes flick to him. I evaluate his expression, but he looks totally relaxed about the offer—and maybe a little hopeful.

I don't want to feel like I owe him for the kindness. But I also really want both dinners.

I set down my menu. "It's a deal. We'll trade part."

Zian hums to himself. "Ribs or steak? They should have a combo."

Dominic casts his pensive gaze around the restaurant's interior. "At a place like this, I think ribs would be a better bet."

"Not like I'm that picky about my steaks," Zian replies.

I've generally been trying to look at Jacob as little as possible, but it's hard when he's sitting in front of me. When my gaze snags on him next, his eyes are just narrowing, his attention fixed on the window.

My head snaps around with a hitch of my pulse, just as a man on the sidewalk outside fumbles his cup of takeout coffee. The steaming liquid splashes all down his shirt, and he yelps loud enough for me to hear it through the glass.

As the guy hustles away, I glance back at Jacob. A small but satisfied smile has curled his lips.

He catches me watching him and draws himself up a little straighter. "That jerk was eyeing you like he figured he'd have *you* for dinner."

So it wasn't just clumsiness but a little telekinetic push that spilled the coffee.

I glower at Jacob. "Being looked at isn't going to hurt me. And if he tried to do more, I can handle some random dude just fine."

Jacob shrugs. "A more subtle approach is better for us than bringing out claws in public."

He has a point, but I fold my arms over my chest. "Or you could just not pick fights over imaginary insults."

Jacob pins me with the full force of his cool stare. Somehow it doesn't feel all that chilly at the moment, though.

"You can still be angry at me, and that's fine," he says, low and even but with a terse edge that suggests he isn't really all that happy about my feelings. "It's not going to stop me from protecting you."

Says the guy who spent most of the last few weeks torturing me every way he could. It's really not fair that the vehemence behind his words sends a flood of heat licking over my skin.

"We all are," Zian puts in, glancing toward the window as if he thinks there might be some new threat out there for him to take on next.

Before I have to figure out what to say to my self-declared bodyguards, the waitress swoops in to take our orders.

After she leaves, Jacob turns to Dominic, taking the pressure off me. "You kept looking through Engel's notes while we were driving. Did you find anything else that could help us ID the monsters?"

Dominic's mouth twists. "I'm not sure. Even in the parts that aren't using her special shorthand at all, I can tell there are a lot of gaps, things she didn't bother explaining because she already understood."

"There has to be something, or no one would ever realize they're around," Zian says.

"I mean, in the write-ups on different types, she mentioned 'common characteristics.' Things like a werewolf is likely to have pointed ears or fangs or claws. But obviously they don't go walking around like that all the time."

Andreas rubs his jaw. "Maybe they do show some outward signs, though. Otherwise, why mention it?"

Zian frowns. "None of us have anything noticeable." He pauses, with an expression like he's just swallowed his tongue. "I mean…"

"Other than me," Dominic says mildly, though he's looking at his napkin rather than at us.

"It'd be hard for anyone who did have obvious inhuman physical features to blend in," I point out. "So maybe they'd hang out places where it's usually darker, like nightclubs or bars or whatever."

Jacob lets out a short laugh. "Places where everyone's a little weird. Every city's got venues like that."

I try to think of any I saw, but… "It's hard to tell which ones are weirdest from the outside."

"Maybe we need to start popping into some places, then."

Zian's forehead furrows. "I don't know. The more we stick ourselves out there, doesn't it get more likely that *we'll* be noticed?"

I let the guys hash out their concerns a little longer while I peer out the window to where evening is falling. The streetlamps flicker on, casting their glow over the sidewalk.

Dozens more people walk by, but none of them are flashing fangs or swishing tails.

If it was easy to tell who the monsters are, wouldn't *everyone* know about them?

The waitress bustles over with our food fast enough that my stomach has only just started to pinch with hunger. The sight of the golden battered fish and thick but crisp fries raises my spirits.

I definitely made the right choice—both of them. Andreas's lasagna bulges with heaps of meaty tomato sauce and creamy cheese.

I half expect him to balk, but he immediately sets about cutting off a quarter of the slab. He drops it onto his saucer and slides it over to me.

"If you like it enough that you want more, let me know."

I glance down at my main plate and lift one of the three battered filets onto my own saucer to offer up. "It's a trade."

"You really don't have to—"

"It's a trade," I repeat firmly. "I do want to still be able to *walk* after this dinner."

A fleeting smile crosses Andreas's face. "Okay, fair."

I would grapple with the weird sense of friendship that I don't want, except right then Jacob stabs his fork down on my plate. The metal tines clang against the china.

I arch an eyebrow at him as he lifts the fry he speared off my plate. "Defending me from my dinner now?"

He swivels the fork in his fingers to show a black blob pierced by one tine. "A fly landed on it."

For a second, I can't speak. He must have used his power to hold the fly in place for him to have caught it like that.

I think.

Without missing a beat, Jacob pushes out of his seat,

walks to the counter, and sets the utensil down on the formica surface.

"I need a new fork," he says, calm but insistent.

The waitress who's working behind the counter area slides one over to him without bothering to ask why. She probably figures he just dropped his on the floor.

My insides are starting to feel all jumbled up, so I dig into my now fly-free dinner to distract myself. The fish is perfectly tender and the sauce that came with it deliciously tart. When I pop a forkful of the lasagna into my mouth, I have to close my eyes in a silent swoon.

Tomorrow we'll be back to protein bars and grocery store sandwiches. I'd better savor all this while I can.

To no one's surprise, Dominic ordered breakfast for dinner to suit his sweet tooth. He's got a plate heaped with syrup-drenched blueberry pancakes and a couple of pieces of bacon on the side.

After five hasty bites, he's waving his fork at Andreas. "Put maple syrup on the grocery store list for next time. I think I could live on this stuff."

Then he turns to me, with a gentler motion of the utensil and a hint of hesitation. "Do you want some? It's way better than table syrup, and the pancakes are great too."

I open my mouth and close it again.

He hasn't gotten to have food like this any more often than I have. The guardians usually kept our meals very plain so that we'd appreciate any little treats they rewarded us with—and every now and then they'd let us go without as some kind of test.

He's probably *never* eaten fresh pancakes like this—and he's offering a portion to me.

Is he trying to make up for his reaction when we got out of the car?

Before I can answer, Zian's eyes widen. He tears another rib off the row he's been working through and holds it out in offering. "The ribs are really good too, if you want to try."

"Um," I say, starkly aware that they're not offering to share with each other. This generosity is all about me.

An easy way to prove a point? Am I supposed to forgive everything that happened before because of a bite of pancake and a BBQ rib?

My gaze darts to Jacob of its own accord—somehow he's the safe one since he's the only one who hasn't attempted to share. He meets my gaze and glances down at his plate, the same fish and chips I ordered.

"It seems a little redundant, or I'd join the club," he says, as if he thinks I was looking at him as a demand rather than an escape.

"It's okay," I say quickly. "Really. I've got lots of food already."

I should probably thank them, but somehow right now that feels too close to accepting apologies I don't think I'm ready to yet.

I'm saved from getting even more flustered by the return of the waitress. "How're you all doing?" she asks with a warm smile.

It occurs to me then that we have a perfect resource right here.

I push my own mouth into a smile. "Great! We were

wondering though… Are there any good places you'd recommend around here if we wanted to go out for drinks or to, er, party a little after dinner? Somewhere really interesting, like a crowd you wouldn't normally find outside the city. We want to get the full experience."

I don't know if my attempt at explaining sounded odd to her, but either it sounded like a reasonable request or she just wants to make sure she gets a good tip. She taps her pen against her lips.

"Well… if you want something on the quirky side, more of an extreme atmosphere, there's a punk venue just a few blocks east from here. And a little farther than that, there's a bar that I think still does Goth nights. Those are the closest ones I can think of."

"Sounds perfect," I say brightly, whipping out my phone. "What are the names? I don't want to forget."

She dredges them from her memory, and I tap them into my notes app. As she walks away, Andreas lets out a soft whistle.

"Very smooth, Tink."

Jacob is grinning, which if you know him is simultaneously both breathtaking and terrifying. "We know what our next stop is. Finish up, and let's get back on the road."

Six

Jacob

It's possible that none of the people in this club are monsters.

It's also possible that all of them are.

The patrons swarming the place are doing a good job of imitating dangerous beasts, at least. The streaks of ruddy light that cut through the dimness keep catching on spikes that I mistake for spines or horns for an instant before the full picture becomes clear and I see they're only embellishments on a jacket, wrist cuff, or choker.

The smell of leather permeates the large, low-ceilinged room, mingling with the sour notes of various alcoholic spirits. The same material's texture covering so many of the figures gives brief impressions of animalistic hides.

And then there are the tattoos and piercings sinking right into the patrons' actual skin. Rings and gems and more spikes, flashing in the light. Dark imprints crawling across forearms and necks and even faces, sometimes with clear images but sometimes just abstract patterns.

I scan every one of them, my body tensed for the first sign of anything definitely inhuman. But every pair of eyes I glance into and every form I consider appears normal enough once I've studied it.

Those pairs of eyes are studying us in turn. Most with skepticism, mixed with either curiosity or hostility.

We don't really fit in. I didn't realize this place would require a uniform.

Andreas, Zian, and I look way too overtly normal in our varying styles of college-guy clothes, no piercings and no tattoos within view. Dominic just looks odd, wading through the crowd in his parka.

Imagine how this bunch of supposed toughs would react to what he's hiding under that coat.

Riva is the only one who looks like she could belong. She strides along in her combat boots, her hands tucked into the pockets of her dark hoodie, the silver layer of her hair reflecting the lights.

She's always moved with a certain assurance, the knowledge that she can tackle any physical challenge that comes her way. I remember watching her stride through the arena, her eyes flashing with determination to take on whatever crap the guardians were going to throw at us next.

That confidence has hardened in her over the years we were apart. If before she was fire, now she's got plenty of steel in her too.

But also a tender underbelly she protects so well, I

almost convinced myself it wasn't there until the truth of it was smacking me in the face.

I stick close to her—as close as I can walk without provoking a flinch. There aren't a whole lot of women in here in general, and none as pretty as her. Most of the gazes that travel over her body are at least curious if not outright leering.

My hands stay balled at my sides. If we weren't on a reconnaissance mission where we need to not stick out any more than we already do, I'd jab all their fucking eyes out.

It doesn't help that Riva is swaying just a bit with the chaotic rhythm of the music blaring from the overhead speakers. Every motion makes her lithe, athletic grace more obvious.

I want to slide my hands down her sides and tug her tight against me. I want to bury my face in her hair and drink in the scent I never let myself appreciate before.

But she'd probably jab *my* eyes out if I even tried. I wouldn't even blame her.

I jerk my gaze away. My nerves jump with the restless energy winding through my limbs that I have no outlet for.

There's so much emotion churning inside me that I don't know what to do with. Regret and desire and shame and devotion.

I've been so empty of anything other than vengeful rage for so long that the deluge sets me off-balance. Like I'm a ship, and sudden swells of waves keep rocking me in directions I can't always predict.

I fucked up. I fucked up so utterly and completely.

I put the woman next to me—the woman I spent so

much of my life loving—through total agony, both physical and emotional. I did it on purpose.

It's a fucking miracle she even accepts being in the same room with me.

I have no idea how to heal the damage I did, how to make her feel good in any way that could come close to making up for the awfulness I put her through.

All I can do is be right here to protect her from the slightest threat. Make room for her voice when she has something to say.

Bit by bit, I *will* make her believe that I treasure her. That I know she's my equal.

That she never deserved one particle of the shit I threw at her.

And if that's not enough for her to ever do more than tolerate my presence, well, it'll be my own damn fault, won't it?

The thought sends a harsher smack of anguish through my chest. My hands squeeze tighter.

I'll protect her from everyone out there and from *me*.

And from the power inside her she's still afraid of. We need to find one of these monsters and get them to cough up their secrets.

I haven't spotted a single clue around us so far. My jaw clenches with frustration, a looming sense of failure—and a jump of my nerves as my own power sparks.

One of the lights overhead crackles out with a spurt of shattering glass. A few of the patrons shout as the tiny shards drift down on them like vicious snow.

Shit. I didn't mean to do that.

Well, there's no way any of these dorks could connect

the little mishap to me. Still, I grasp at the shifting energy inside me, grappling for a better hold on it.

We veer to the left, making a circuit of the space. The music isn't quite as ear-rattling near the bar.

The crimson lights help disguise Andreas's talent as he flicks his attention from one head to another. I can tell from the brief, starker flares of red over his dark irises that he's delving into the patrons' memories, searching for anything that might identify a target.

Zian is carrying out his own inspection, using his X-ray sight to peer beneath layers of clothing for any monstrous appendages they might be hiding like Dominic does. There's no outward sign of his talent other than the twitches of grimaces that cross his broad face.

All the flesh he glimpses must be human if not particularly enjoyable to look at, because he keeps stalking on without nudging me.

A guy who's about my height, his short hair dyed like green leopard spots, bumps his shoulder against mine—hard. My head jerks toward him.

"What the fuck are *you* idiots doing in here?" he demands over the rumble of bass guitar. "Get lost on the way to a kegger?"

I smile sharply at him, resisting the urge to bare my teeth like I'm as much a wolfman as Zian. "We're right where we wanted to be."

He opens his mouth again—and, oh what a tragedy, his mug of beer on the bar counter next to him suddenly topples over.

As he yelps and the bartender rushes to mop up the mess, the five of us merge deeper into the mass of bodies.

The others have been too focused on other things to notice the minor altercation. But when we get farther down the bar, a guy in a studded leather vest reaches out his hand and snaps his fingers at Riva like she's a dog.

"Why're you hanging out with these dipshits, beautiful?" he hollers. "Come over here and let a real man buy you a drink."

Riva rolls her eyes, but my shoulders have stiffened with a jolt of fury—and jealousy, as if some stupid part of me thinks she'd actually take this imbecile up on his offer.

Three bottles whip off the shelves behind the bar. One of them whacks the jerk in the back of his skull.

Oops.

Somehow I can't summon any grief over that little slip-up.

But as the asshole whirls around to yell at the bewildered bartender, Riva's gaze snaps to me. So do my friends'.

Riva gives a brusque motion for us to move away from the bar. The second the crowd filling the room has closed around us, she spins on me.

"What the hell was that?"

"He was being a prick," I protest, and wince inwardly. I don't want to argue with her.

And I really shouldn't have let my power slip the reins again. What the hell *is* wrong with me?

I already know the answer to that.

She's glowering at me from just a foot away, and there's nothing wrong about *her* at all, only how badly I screwed things up.

"We're supposed to be keeping a low profile," she says, crossing her arms in front of her.

Andreas nods with an apologetic grimace. "We should keep any visible talents to a minimum, right? Don't want to scare off any monsters *or* risk the guardians catching wind somehow."

"Yeah, yeah, I know," I mutter.

How can I admit that I didn't even mean to brain that guy? I'm the one who's kept us all on track.

I can't go flying off the rails now. Not when Riva needs me too.

As much as she needs any of us. Her steps might bounce a bit with the rhythm, showing the fluid grace that compact body is capable of, but I can see the strength in every motion.

I remember how she brought all those soldiers to their knees with her voice alone.

She isn't a monster. She's a fucking marvel.

But we still need to find the actual monsters.

I catch Zian's gaze, and he shakes his head. Andreas is frowning, a crease forming in his brow as he stretches his abilities again and again.

Maybe Engel's fearsome creatures aren't into the punk scene. It's not doing much of anything for me.

I turn toward Dominic, who's looking even more hunched and awkward than usual in his parka. I'm about to suggest to him that we leave and check out some other place, because if he agrees then I'm probably being strategic rather than just giving up, but right then a bellowed voice socks my ears from behind me.

"What the fuck did you just say?"

I pause and glance over, my body going even more tense. Two beefy guys who could almost rival Zian in size are glaring at each other while several others who might be their friends look on with uneasy scowls.

"You heard me," the one guy growls through his thick red beard. "Twilight Zombduds totally sold out with that last album, and they should be dead to all of us."

The other guy jabs his thick finger at the bearded guy's face. "They paid their fucking dues, and that's my uncle's best friend's cousin you're talking about."

I don't really understand what the hell they're so worked up over, but the next thing I know, Beardie is swinging his fist. Suddenly the cluster of figures around them transforms into a seething mass of angry yells and bashing hands.

The atmosphere in the room goes from mildly ominous to war zone in an instant. I shove between Riva and one of the combatants who ricochets her way, taking an elbow to the ribs before I heave him out of range.

If they mark her with so much as a bruise…

My pulse thunders; my nerves sizzle like they've been tapped into an electric current. Two more lights shatter across the ceiling.

Didn't mean to do that either. Fucking hell.

I whip around toward the others, every cell in my body buzzing. I have to get us out of here—both to get Riva and my friends away from the fight, and to make sure *I* don't expose us.

The others are already pushing through the crowd toward the door, but the club patrons are jostling in every direction. Some are shoving toward the fight, either to join it or cheer them on.

My heart starts hammering twice as fast. I slam between them to push my way back to Riva's side.

Bodycheck one asshat to the side here. Punt a slowpoke out of the way there.

Clear a way to the door.

Ignore the bottles flying off the bar shelves and smashing every which way.

Ignore the groaning of the floor that might be some part of me prying at the boards.

Just get out. Just get away. There was nothing in this dump for us anyway.

We stumble out onto the sidewalk with a stream of other people who weren't interested in the fight. Some asshole grabs Riva's arm.

I lunge at him, but she gets there first, slamming her knuckles into his nose. He swears at her and staggers off, and I jar to a stop beside her with a growl.

The sign over the club windows screeches, one end starting to wrench forward.

Riva looks at me. I clamp down on my power with all the will I have in me, every muscle going rigid.

I'm going to defend her. I won't be one of the things that's threatening her—not ever again.

Get your head on straight, Jake.

The storm of emotions I still don't know how to master roils on inside me, but nothing else breaks. I feel as wiped out as if I've sprinted a mile just from tamping it down.

I'm way too out of practice at feeling things.

Andreas nudges us all on down the street. I breathe evenly through my nose, letting the chilly night air wash over me.

In that moment, I wish I was back in the forest. Nothing but trees around us and bare earth beneath my feet.

Then Riva freezes in her tracks a couple of steps ahead of me.

We all halt too. She points toward the other side of the street, farther down.

"That woman there," she murmurs. "The one with the green dress. I think she's what we're looking for."

SEVEN

Riva

I don't know how to explain it, which is too bad because the guys will probably think I'm insane. But the longer my gaze remains on the woman down the street, the surer I am that somehow she's one of the creatures Engel would have called a monster.

A quiver runs through my veins, small but tangible, like the faintest breeze rippling the shadows in my blood. Like I recognize her on a bodily level even if I don't with my eyes.

Then she's vanishing from view, slipping through a doorway on a storefront near the corner.

"I could just… feel it," I say to the guys, who are staring after her from where they're standing around me. "That there's something about her that's like us and not like regular people."

Zian nods slowly, his eyes wide. "After you pointed her out—I think I could sense it too."

He shoots me a hopeful smile, and my mouth returns it automatically. My heart skips a beat at the gleam of affection in his eyes even though the rest of me knows it doesn't mean what I want it to.

What I *used* to want it to.

The other guys still look puzzled. Maybe it makes sense that Zian and I would have the keenest awareness of other beings that are kind of like us, since we're the ones with the most honed physical senses in general.

There's always been something a little more beastly about us than the others, at least in the most literal sense.

The feeling isn't even all that strange. A different sort of shiver passes through me like an icy finger down my spine.

I've had the same sensation of recognition before. I had no idea what it meant at the time, but during my missions, there were at least a couple of people who set off that tiny quiver through my blood.

And that skyscraper in San Francisco—the one I couldn't help stopping and staring at, what must have been almost ten years ago. Was that a place built by monsters, or for them?

The clap of Jacob's hands brings me back to the present. His gaze is fixed on the building the woman slipped into.

"Let's go see what she is and what she can tell us, then."

His gaze flicks to me, but not in challenge or accusation. It's happened often enough in the past few days that I know I'm not imagining that he's looking to me for *approval*.

My certainty doesn't make the act any less confusing. But really, what else are we going to do?

I suck in a breath and nod.

We cross the street and amble toward the building. I usually avoid paying much attention to Jacob at all, shying away from the uncomfortable memories his presence stirs up, but now I study him surreptitiously.

He got a little wilder in the punk venue than I've seen him… ever. Or at least since we were little kids.

He's always prided himself in being coolly incisive, staying in control and on top of every scenario we could encounter. He'd dive into any exercise requiring strategy with a fierce sort of focus, tugging us all along with his swift observations and decisions.

From what I've seen since we reunited, those habits have only amplified.

Except after that one attack from the guardians, when we were at the campus townhouse, that is. While we were driving away, it seemed like he'd gone into a sort of daze, lost in his head somewhere.

He practically destroyed the front passenger seat with his telekinesis before I shook him out of it.

He wasn't in a daze in the bar, though. Tonight he's appeared as alert and focused as ever.

But then, I haven't had much of a chance to really get to know all the nuances of who he or the other guys have become in the past four years. They've kept me at a hostile distance until just recently… and I can feel how much painful history they're still keeping bottled up inside.

We ease to a stop outside the building. The cursive letters on the sign up top declare it *The Royal Lounge*.

Most of the front windows are covered by a purple velvet curtain, only a sliver of the interior visible near the door. There, amber light washes over pale, glossy wood and delicately pebbled leather.

The few patrons I can see are dressed similarly to the woman I spotted: subdued but elegant evening wear.

Andreas's gaze has already slid over the five of us. "I don't think we want to stick out in there like we did in the punk club. Jake and I are probably fine. Zee, I got you the one polo shirt in case we all needed to dress up a bit."

Zian makes a face. "Let's go get it then."

We've been keeping our backpacks full of all our new clothes and other belongings in the trunk of the car. As long as we have them nearby at all times, we can hope that we won't lose everything again.

As Zian digs through his pack, I open up mine. "I got a sweater that'll look better than the hoodie."

My dark jeans might go over better than the cargo pants in a swanky setting, but I'm not going to strip down that much. Angling my body so the side of my waist with the bandage is hidden from the guys, I peel my hoodie off and pull the soft black sweater on over my tank top.

When I turn around, Zian is tugging the collar of the navy polo shirt. His mouth is slanted at an awkward angle, but I have to suppress a swoon.

The color compliments his dark hair and peachy brown skin perfectly. And I've never seen him in anything other than athletic gear before.

Zee cleans up nice.

He glances toward me, and I jerk my gaze away before he can realize the flush creeping across my cheeks has anything to do with him. Instead, I find myself facing Dominic, who's looking even more awkward in his parka.

He ducks his head, the short ponytail he's pulled his smooth auburn hair into sliding across his shoulder. "No one needs to say it. I realize there's no way I won't stick out like a sore thumb."

In a shirt or a coat thinner than the parka like the trench coat he used to wear, the lumps of his tentacles will be obvious on his upper back. He doesn't have any workable options.

A pang resonates through my chest. This isn't the first time we've left him behind.

All the childhood training sessions that required immense strength and endurance, Dominic and Griffin always faltered first. The echo of a flinch rises up from the memory of watching the guardians zap them with their electric prods if we slowed down too much to help them along.

Sometimes they didn't mind us working together, but other times the goal was for all of us to be pushed to our limits… whether we liked it or not.

Jacob hesitates. It's clear he doesn't want to say anything that would make Dominic feel worse about his limitations.

I can't help appreciating his obvious concern, as much as I want to be annoyed by everything about him.

"You can stake out the place from outside," he says after a moment. "Pretend you're waiting for someone to show up. Give us a warning if it looks like trouble's brewing."

We don't have any reason to think we'll face a sudden

onslaught of danger from outside, but it's a reasonable compromise.

Dominic offers Jacob a tight smile. "It's a plan."

Trying to look casual, we walk back to the lounge. Dominic props himself against the wall next to the neighboring building, and the rest of us venture inside.

As we step into the warmly lit space, moody classical music wraps around us, full of swelling violin and a tinkling of piano. It smells a hell of a lot nicer than the punk venue, the alcohol tang still present but mingled with a mix of smoky florals. I suspect there's incense burning somewhere beyond view.

The long, narrow room in front of us holds a bar that's only smallish, a semi-circle with a glossy black counter about halfway through the space. In the front half of the room, several sleek leather sofas and armchairs squat in clusters around low mahogany tables. At the far end, patrons stand clustered around taller, smaller circular tables.

A couple of groups are relaxing with their drinks on the seats near us, but I don't see the woman in the green dress among them. Most of the activity appears to be happening at the back anyway.

We stroll over, Andreas stopping at the bar to order drinks for him and the other guys, I guess to keep up our front of being regular customers. He glances at me, but I shake my head.

I don't have Jacob's poison winding through my body anymore, but just remembering the dizzying effects of the one cocktail I drank while I did makes me queasy. I'd rather not even hold one.

A couple dozen people are gathered around the high tables in the back. Once we've approached, I see it expands to twice the width of the front, as if the lounge intrudes on the neighboring building.

The other patrons are chattering and laughing and sipping from their drinks demurely. Nothing about them looks at all monstrous.

The woman in the green dress isn't among them. Has she left already?

Or maybe there's a second floor or a basement level.

I'm about to suggest that to the guys when the faint quiver that drew my attention to her ripples through my veins again.

My gaze snaps to a slim man who looks to be in his late twenties, standing in the far corner by a table on his own. His fingers curl loosely around the stem of his wine glass.

He's watching the other patrons with a nonchalant expression, but I'm abruptly sure that he's actually sizing them up. As prey?

Zian nudges me with a brief tap of his elbow against my arm. He flicks his eyes toward another man, a little older, with a stout frame and a broad grin as he says something that gets his several companions laughing.

The moment I look at him, another quiver hits me. The sensation is more obvious now that I'm getting used to feeling for it.

Jacob motions for us to head to one of the few tables that's unoccupied, over by the wall where we can talk somewhat discreetly. He's only taken a few steps when one of the elegant women sashays up to him and lays her slender hand on his forearm.

"I haven't seen you here before," she purrs.

I've witnessed the kind of interest these guys get from women before—at the dance club where I had that one drink. It's not really surprising considering how stunningly handsome they are.

And I don't even *want* Jacob, any way at all.

But the second she touches him, a growl catches in my throat and my claws itch to spring from my fingertips.

Last time he got this kind of attention, he didn't seem to mind. Tonight, he pulls his arm smoothly but firmly away and steps to the side.

His pale blue eyes turn icy cold. "Not interested," he says in a voice that could slice through glass.

The woman winces, clearly startled by his forceful rejection, and Andreas steps in. He holds up his hands in a placating gesture, keeping his own tone mild. "Sorry. We're taken."

They are?

The woman's gaze darts to me, and my cheeks flare twice as hot as they did just checking Zian out.

Oh. Er.

I kind of want to shout that I'm not taking *any* of them, let alone all of them, but that would send all hope of keeping a low profile right out the window.

It's better if the guys stay focused on our current mission anyway, right? No matter what excuses they give to explain it.

I march on to the table we were heading for without commenting on the situation. By the time the guys have followed me a few moments later, I've willed my blush to retreat.

"No green dress," Andreas comments in a low voice for just us to hear.

"There are two more. I think," I say. "That guy by himself over in the corner and the chubby one with the big crowd around his table."

Zian nods. "That's what I'm sensing too. Can you look into their memories, Drey?"

Andreas turns the glass he hasn't actually drunk from between his hands, considering his potential targets. "I'm a little concerned that they'll notice if I use my power on them. We don't want to put them on the defensive right away."

"It's not their memories we need anyway," Jacob puts in. "We want to know their basic supernatural tactics. But once we have one of them ready for interrogation, you might as well take a peek then. It could be useful to know what they're up to in general."

I study the two men as subtly as I can manage. "How do we get them 'ready'? We wouldn't want to get aggressive up front when we're not sure what they're capable of."

Zian follows my gaze and frowns. "The loner seems like he'd be easier. We'd want to get him outside where no one else is going to interfere, right?"

Jacob hums thoughtfully and brings his drink to his lips, but I can tell he doesn't actually sip the amber liquid. "Let's do a bit of a test run. Zee, you're the most intimidating out of the four of us. Take a walk around the tables, going past both of them, and we'll see if there are any interesting reactions. Could be the loner is way more dangerous."

If Zian minds being put forward as bait, he doesn't show it. He picks up his own drink and immediately sets off to navigate the room.

He keeps a casual pace and doesn't linger anywhere for too long, but it's impossible for him to be completely unnoticeable. He's got to be the tallest and brawniest guy in the lounge, and gorgeous on top of that.

He brushes past the loner's table without looking at the guy. The slim man's gaze only rests on Zian for a moment before it returns to the other patrons. I don't catch any hint of supernatural talent.

The popular man glances over his shoulder before Zian has even reached him, as if sensing some kind of approaching threat. I think I glimpse a brief yellowish sheen passing over his eyes before he returns his attention to his fan club.

Jacob tenses at the same moment. He saw the reaction too.

As Zian circles back toward us, a woman who's been giggling with a few friends spins away from her table. The wobble of her legs suggests she's had a few too many of those martinis.

But I don't think her stumble is entirely accidental. She falls right into Zian, grabbing the front of his shirt and already aiming a sly smile up at him.

I yank my hands below the level of the table just in time to hide the instinctive spring of my claws before I can will them back into my fingertips. At the same moment, eyelashes fluttering, the woman parts her lips as if to make some coy remark.

But Zian shoves away from her.

His mouth clamps tight as if he's bitten back a yell. His eyes have gone wild and his muscles rigid, as if she attacked him rather than making a pass—albeit a forceful one.

"No," he says with a tremor in his voice that he masters a second later. His arms had come up as if to ward her off and now sink to his sides.

"Are you okay?" he adds gruffly, his stance still tensed.

The woman blinks at him, looking totally bewildered, and then sways back to her friends, who are all giving Zian the stink-eye. He hustles back to us with his head low.

My stomach has knotted. I've seen women fawn over Zian before, but not quite so aggressively.

It isn't just me he doesn't want touching him. The flash of emotion that contorted his face in that first instant—it looked like *panic*.

I'm obviously not the only one who noticed. Andreas has knit his brow.

"Zee," he starts when the other guy reaches us.

Zian shakes his head brusquely. "I'm fine. Who are we going for?"

Jacob waits for a beat as if checking to confirm Zian really is fine and then tilts his head toward the loner. "The guy in the corner didn't show any sign of powers or seem to notice anything unusual about you. I think your first instinct was right—we go for him."

Well, if we're all going to pretend nothing weird just happened, it's easiest to play along.

I raise my eyebrows. "So now we just have to convince the monster-dude to leave the lounge without looking like we're harassing him. So simple."

A small smile crosses Andreas's lips. "Maybe it's time I took a little risk and peeked inside his head, then."

His eyes flare briefly with a ruddy light. Then he motions to us. "I've got something I can use. Come on."

Jacob lets Andreas take the lead this once. We weave our way over to the loner's table as a group.

With all four of us in front of him, the slim man can't really look anywhere else. He cocks his head. "Can I do something for you?"

"We've got a message for you from Frond," Andreas says.

Whatever he saw in the possible-monster's head, it delivers. The man twitches straighter, his nonchalance fading away. "About what?"

Andreas jerks his thumb toward the lounge's back door. "I think it's better if we discussed it with fewer people around, yeah?"

The man nods slowly, casting another wary glance over us before moving from his table. We all tramp out of the lounge and into the wide, shadowy lane out back.

There, the slim man turns to us and crosses his arms over his chest. "All right, let's hear it."

The words have barely left his mouth before he's slammed back into the opposite wall by an invisible force. Jacob strides forward in the wake of his power and adds his hand to the man's throat.

Apparently he's decided there's no point in even

pretending this could be a friendly conversation. To be fair, he might not be wrong about that.

As we all stalk closer, Jacob fixes the monster-man with his icy stare. "We have some questions. It shouldn't take too long if you answer quickly."

The man sputters a choked guffaw. "Who do you think you are?" His eyes narrow, and all at once, his face goes sallow. "What the fuck *are* you?"

"None of your fucking business. Now, we can—"

Jacob isn't even finished saying the first part of his threat when the man simply... vanishes.

One second he's there, shoved up against the wall, and then next, Jacob is lurching forward with his hand smacking into the bricks. He whirls around with an angry grunt.

I spin on my feet, craning my neck to scan the alley, but I can't see the slightest hint of our target.

"What the hell?" Zian says, his muscles flexing.

Andreas wets his lips, his expression tense. "It looks like the real monsters have more tricks up their sleeves than we realized."

Eight

Riva

"You're not welcome in here anymore," the stately woman says from the front entrance of the lounge.

We stall on the threshold, where she cut us off. The back door had locked behind us, so we'd come around thinking maybe we could get something out of the portly man or even find the woman in the green dress after all.

Instead, our way is blocked.

Jacob lifts his chin. "Why not?"

The woman raises her own head at a haughty angle, a little taller even than Zian thanks to her heels and being up a step from the street. "We don't allow anyone to harass our patrons. Leave before I have to take further measures."

Oh, shit.

We retreat down the street, Dominic moving to join us. An uneasy vibe runs between all of us.

Andreas is frowning. "Someone must have looked out back while we were confronting the guy."

"In the split-second we had him before he disintegrated," Jacob mutters, and glances at Andreas. "He didn't just turn invisible—not like you do anyway."

Andreas nods. "I still have some kind of physical presence. It looked like he simply wasn't there anymore."

Zian makes a discontented sound. "How the hell are we supposed to get any answers out of them if they can disappear in a snap?"

Dominic has been watching and listening silently, and must be able to put enough of the pieces together to understand what happened. "Whatever skills one monster has, the others don't necessarily have too," he points out. "We don't share many abilities."

I pull myself straighter with a renewed sense of purpose. "That's right. We just have to find another one."

The slight movement pulls at the lingering wound on my side with a jab of pain. I think I broke the scab again when I leapt to search for the vanished monster-man in the alley.

That's fine. It's a reminder of how dangerous any of these creatures could be, considering I got the sadistic power inside me from their kind.

"Come on," I say to distract myself from the deepening ache. "The more ground we cover, the more likely we'll find someone tonight."

As we head back to the car, Jacob nudges Andreas. "Did you see anything interesting in the monster's memories?"

Andreas grimaces. "I only dipped in briefly, just long

enough to pick up a name that seemed meaningful to him. I was trying to avoid freaking him out. Looks like we did anyway."

The guy did act particularly startled right before he vanished. What was that all about?

"He's probably not used to people who seem human recognizing what he is," I say.

We pile back into the car, me taking the front passenger seat again. I want a good view so I can notice anyone who gives me that weird quivery feeling right away.

Jacob takes the wheel this time, his hands squeezing tight around it. He's pissed off that the woman barred us from the lounge.

"Maybe when we do find another one, we should try a more diplomatic approach first," I suggest, a little tartly.

Jacob lets out a huff, but he doesn't argue. "Let's see *who* we find before we make any decisions."

We cruise along the streets through the thickening night, sticking to the commercial areas with shops and restaurants. It doesn't seem likely monsters would be hanging around in the middle of a residential street.

Do they own houses? Do they hide away in caves in ravines and forests?

We have no idea how these things even live. Engel said they were like the supernatural beasts from stories, but how much of those stories are true?

Plenty of pedestrians are still out on the streets, most of them in pairs or groups. I watch a girl who looks about my age rush up to a cluster of other women and throw her arms around each in turn.

I almost had a girl friend. Brooke, our neighbor on campus, tried to be there for me.

Maybe if we'd stayed there, eventually she and I could have become BFFs or besties or whatever the current word for it is. But because she was trying so hard to be there for me, she got caught in the crossfire when the guardians found us.

I can't make any friends other than the uncertain ones I have right now. It's too risky—for them far more than for me.

The thought sends a jab of loss through me that's sharper than the ache from my injury. I swallow thickly and keep skimming my gaze over the sidewalks outside.

We're passing the thicker shadows of a large, treed park when one of those quivers finally races through my veins again. I jerk forward in my seat, biting back a wince at the jolt of pain that sears through my side at the sudden movement.

"There," I say, pointing toward the far end of the park. "There's someone… Someone's sitting there next to that bench."

The figure is barely more than a lump of layered fabric topped by frizzy hair, but there's no denying the increasingly familiar sensation tingling through my blood. Jacob parks by the curb, and we walk over cautiously.

It's a middle-aged woman, hunched next to the bench with a grimy blanket pulled around her shoulders. Dirt smudges her plump face.

She looks like a homeless person. Is that a disguise she's putting on, or can a monster actually be down and out just like a regular human being can?

Or are my senses going haywire, and she *is* just a regular human being?

Zian prowls ahead of the rest of us, his muscles taut beneath the preppy clothes he's still wearing. He shoots us a look with a swift nod of confirmation.

He can sense it too. I'm not going crazy—well, any crazier than I might already be.

The woman stares up at him with a scowl, even less friendly than the guy we tried before. I aim a warning glance at Jacob and step past Zian to stand in front of her.

"Hey," I say in the warmest voice I can manage, and think that I should have volunteered Andreas for this role rather than me.

Too late now, I've already committed.

I force a smile. "We were hoping we could ask you a few questions. Because… we think you're kind of like us."

The woman's gaze flicks over the five of us. Her scowl deepens.

"I'm not an info booth," she says in a dry rattle of a voice.

I hold up my hands, tuning out the increased ache in my side at the motion. "I understand that. But we've been pretty out of the loop when it comes to… unusual stuff. Things those people wouldn't understand." I wave vaguely toward the pedestrians sauntering by on the other side of the road.

Andreas must be able to tell I'm floundering a bit, because he comes around beside me to join in with his smoother warmth. "We don't want to make any trouble for you. Just to get a little advice on using certain skills that we wouldn't want the average person noticing. You have some experience with that, I'm guessing?"

His smile looks a lot less stiff than I'm sure mine does. His eyes stay their normal dark gray, not attempting to scan her mind.

He doesn't want to freak her out either. We don't know what *she* might be capable of.

The woman studies us again, her tongue flicking over her lips, and a shudder ripples through her pudgy frame. She pushes abruptly to her feet.

"I'm not having anything to do with you."

"Wait!" Jacob snaps, lunging forward.

As the woman rushes backward, away from us, his hand snatches at her arm. An instant later, his fingers close around nothing but air.

The woman is gone, wisped away as abruptly and completely as the man in the alley.

Jacob glares down at his hand and then at the spot where the woman disappeared. "Seems like they can *all* give us the slip just like that. Fucking hell."

Dominic shifts his weight on his feet. "It's getting late, and we don't really know what we're dealing with. Maybe we should head back to the apartment, get some rest, and do some new planning tomorrow morning."

My throbbing waist thinks that's a great idea. All I want is to flop on a bed away from the guys and will my emotions back into order as well as my body.

"Dominic's right," I say.

His glance my way looks a bit startled, but Zian nods too, if with apparent reluctance. "We're not getting anything done like this."

Jacob sighs. "Fine. There's got to be a way to make these pricks stick around and talk."

Andreas cuffs him lightly on the shoulder. "We'll figure it out, Jake. We haven't come this far for nothing."

The Airbnb he was able to arrange for us is located in a dingy neighborhood on the outskirts of the city proper, which is probably why it was available on such short notice. But it's got three bedrooms with four beds between them and a pull-out sofa, so at least there's enough space for all of us.

One benefit to my guys' newfound sense of generosity is that they announced that I should take the main bedroom that comes with its own ensuite bathroom. The moment we've stepped into the boxy three-story house we're renting the top two floors of, I pull the pistol out of my waistband to leave it with the duffel of weapons and make a beeline for the stairs.

Even after sitting still for the drive, my side is still aching. As I reach the staircase, I adjust my backpack on my shoulders, careful not to let too much weight rest on that side.

I mustn't be as subtle about it as I intended, because Dominic speaks up from behind me. "Are you feeling okay, Riva?"

"Yeah," I say quickly. "Just tired and kind of disappointed. I'm going to go take a bath and chill out."

In theory, that should stop any of the guys from insisting on keeping me company. In actuality, Andreas follows me up the stairs to the door to my bedroom.

When I pause with my hand on the doorknob and raise my eyebrows at him, he holds up his phone. "I figured out how to download music onto the prepaids. I could show you if you want to have some tunes going with your bath."

There's something so hopeful in his dark eyes that my stomach twists with my refusal. "That's okay. I think silence might be good right now."

I just want to get away from all of them, to have some space where I don't have to keep my vulnerabilities walled off. Where I'm not constantly having to remind certain parts of me that these guys are as likely to hurt me as help me.

Andreas nods, his face only falling a little. "Maybe later."

"Yeah." I might actually like that, even if I don't feel like telling him so right now.

He pauses, his gaze searching mine, and his voice drops. "You know if there's anything you think of that I could do—that would make you happier or feel safer or *anything*—you only have to tell me, and I'll make it happen. Whatever it takes."

The tightness in my stomach climbs up my chest to squeeze my throat. When he looks at me like that, talks to me like that, I can't totally suppress the memory of the night when everything went so horribly wrong.

Of the part before everything went wrong, when he made me feel like I was someone worthy of being cherished rather than punished. When he told me he loved me in the same voice he used just now.

And then I found out he'd been *pretending* to support me from the start just to see if I'd betray some secret evil agenda.

The boy I knew before, the one who could always find the right wry remark to break a sour mood, the one who'd enrapture us with dramatic retellings of tales he'd read and movies we'd watched—or, once we started our missions, true stories pulled right from the minds of people he'd crossed paths with… He would never have been that callous and calculating with his charm.

I have to keep reminding myself that I don't entirely know who these men actually are anymore.

My teeth set on edge. "I don't know what it would take for me to totally trust you again. I don't know if I ever will. But me telling you to do something and having no idea if you're just going through the motions definitely isn't going to work."

Andreas winces. "Fair. But the offer still stands, whether it helps you trust me or not. I won't try to rush you."

He steps back, and I slip into the bedroom.

The moment the door closes behind me, my breath rushes out of me. I toss my backpack on the bed and peel off my sweater.

Lifting the hem of my tank top, I find that a little blood has seeped through my latest bandage. Thankfully I grabbed some gauze when the guys weren't looking at one of the stores we stopped at for supplies, so I can re-dress it.

After that bath.

The wafts of steam that rise from the running water settle my nerves. I let the sensation carry my mind away from everything but the scratched-up but deep tub.

I hadn't been sure I'd actually enjoy baths, considering anything more than a brief swim is about as much water as

I can generally appreciate. But anytime I've been dunked before, it's been in water with at least a bit of a chill.

Turns out even the cat-girl can find an approximation of a hot tub relaxing, at least in small doses.

I still have some of the bath stuff Andreas bought for me, so I toss the plain kind of salts in as well. Then I sink into the hot water.

It encloses my limbs in warmth and licks around my neck. I slide down until the back of my head is completely submerged. Then I loosen my braid and let my hair flow out around my shoulders.

My hand moves to my cat-and-yarn necklace, nestled against my sternum, making sure it's still holding together. I haven't taken it off since Jacob gave it back to me.

Then my fingers drift lower to trail over the tattoo of the crescent moon on my outer thigh. The moon with the dark droplet dangling from its upper tip—the one all the guys have too.

Shadowbloods, Ursula Engel called us. Because we were made with essence from the things she saw as monsters woven into our DNA, and we can see it in the smoky stuff that wisps from our veins when we bleed.

Maybe it's fitting that the full monsters seem to somehow merge into the shadows when we try to confront them. Would it be easier to restrain them by daylight?

My mind lingers over that idea, contemplating scenarios. The heat of the water lulls me into a mild daze.

But when a thud and a shout carry through the walls from downstairs, I spring to my feet in an instant.

"Back off!" Zian growls, and there's a smash that could be from either my guys or some unknown intruder.

My heart thudding against my ribs, I snatch the towel and wrap it around me as I race through my bedroom. I burst into the hall, charge down the stairs to the living room—and jerk to a halt on the bottom step.

All four of my guys are poised there in defensive stances, staring at the new fifth figure in the room.

A figure that's eight feet tall with horns poking from its purple skin and menace glowing in its ruddy eyes.

NINE

Riva

The purple, horned man—I assume, because he looks more male than female with that square jaw and those bulging pecs—glowers at the five of us. He's standing just a few feet from the apartment's front entrance, but I know none of the guys would have opened the door for him.

He got inside without them needing to.

A shiver runs through my ears as they sharpen into furred points. My hand that's holding the towel closed around my torso clenches tighter. Claws prick through the nubby fabric and spring from my free hand.

Those are the only weapons I have. My knives are in my discarded cargo pants upstairs, and all our guns are piled in the duffel bag near the intruder's feet.

If a blade or a bullet could do anything against a creature like this anyway.

I slide one foot back, bracing in case I need to spring. All my attention remains on the intruder.

His horns, glowing eyes, and purple skin aren't his only inhuman features. All he's wearing is a black strip of fabric like a loincloth around his hips, and a short tail with a devilish tip protrudes from a gap in it.

The tail lashes back and forth like he's a pissed-off cat. And as I watch, his immense form rises several inches off the floor.

He's hovering in mid-air. A ripple of energy washes over me, jangling through my nerves.

I don't need to strain any of my senses to recognize this man as a monster.

"What do you want?" Jacob demands, his voice taut enough that I can tell he's nervous. One of the dining-room chairs floats next to him as if he's readying it to hurl at the intruder.

I'm guessing he was responsible for the smashing sound I heard, via the vase now lying in pieces on the floor a few feet from the purple beast.

The monster bares his teeth in what could maybe be considered a grin if it wasn't full of so many sharp, ominous fangs.

"I came here to ask *you* exactly that question," he says in a guttural rumble of a voice that shakes up my insides even more. "I heard you've been hassling beings who'd rather be left alone."

His gaze slides over us again, and his mouth curves into what is definitely a frown. He adjusts his pose in the air with a twitch of his muscles.

As if he's preparing *himself* in case he needs to go on

the defensive. A strange wobbly sensation travels down the center of me.

Nervous pheromones lace the air, but I think most if not all of those are from my men. Maybe monsters don't give off the same kinds of chemicals humans do.

But I can see that this beastly man is definitely a little afraid… of us. What the hell?

Andreas's eyes have flared with their own reddish glow, but it fades as he focuses back on the present. "We didn't mean to bother anyone. We were just hoping to ask a few simple questions."

The creature lets out a derisive sound. "Your approach hasn't sounded all that peaceful to me. What *are* you? Where did you come from?"

Zian folds his brawny arms over his chest. The wolfish hair that's sprung from his neck and the tops of his shoulders ruffles with a flex of his muscles, but he's managed to keep the full wolfman face under wraps.

"How's that any of your business?" he asks with strained bravado. "We didn't go breaking into anyone's apartment like you just did."

"Unexpected situations call for unexpected measures," the monster retorts. "You want to ask some questions? Answer mine, and maybe I'll have a little advice for you."

There's a sneering note to those last words, but his stance remains wary. What exactly is he afraid that *we* might do?

The guys hesitate, but I don't see any point in drawing out this confrontation longer than we need to. It's not as if we need to worry about this beast reporting what we tell him back to the guardians—and anyway, I wouldn't be sharing anything they don't already know.

I lift my chin a little higher, tucking the ends of my towel under my armpit to free both hands. "We were being held captive by people who made us… kind of like you. We managed to get away from them, but there are a lot of things we don't understand about our powers."

Dominic speaks up in his usual softly even voice. "The people we ran from don't want to tell us anything. Mostly we'd like to get better control over our abilities."

"People," the purple giant says. "You mean humans?"

The five of us exchange a glance. "As far as we know," Andreas says.

The monster's lips curl with what looks like disgust. "And they *made* you? From…" He shakes his head as if he doesn't even want to consider the possibilities.

"We don't really get it either," Jacob says, sounding peeved. "We wouldn't have 'hassled' anyone if we did."

"But you're part human, part shadowkind," the beastly man clarifies. "The two mixed together?"

"Shadowkind?" I repeat, confused.

His gaze veers to me, and he flashes his fangs again. "That's what we call ourselves. Maybe your makers called us 'monsters.' Most humans use that word."

Gosh, I wonder why that would be.

But his words send a quiver of rightness through me at the same time. Shadowkind. Like the shadowy haze that seeps from our wounds.

I swallow thickly. "They called us shadowbloods."

The monster —shadowkind—whatever he is—makes a

sound like a snort. "And what do you bleed? Red liquid or black smoke?"

"Both."

Somehow he manages to look even more upset about that fact than he already was. He draws back toward the door.

"I'm not interested in playing anyone's mentor. I just look out for my city to make sure no one's stirring up trouble."

"We'd stir up a lot less trouble if any of you would actually talk to us," Jacob mutters.

The beastly man glares at him. Then he pauses, a more pensive expression coming over his fearsome face.

"I have heard that there's a powerful shadowkind down south who caters to odd ones. He has a hotel—in the city called Miami. You could go down there."

I can't tell how much he's trying to help us and how much just hoping to get us out of his territory.

From the twist of Dominic's mouth, he's wondering the same thing. "How would we find the right hotel? Who is this guy?"

"I believe his name is Rollick. But I don't promise anything." The purple giant shoots us another glower. "Leave the shadowkind here alone and go ask your questions someplace else."

His gaze falls on the small duffel full of our confiscated guns. His lips draw back in a silent snarl.

"You brought mortal weapons. Is there *silver* in some of those?"

I have no idea why he'd object to silver—or whether

we've got any fancy firearms. But the monster doesn't wait for an answer.

"You'll be a little less trouble without these."

He whips the bag off the ground into his arms. Then he blinks out of existence just like the two monsters we tried to interrogate earlier did, taking our entire stash of guns with him.

"Shit," I mumble.

The room's ceiling fixtures are shining brightly. So much for my hope that light might help us keep the monsters in one place.

When he doesn't reappear, the tension wound through me releases just a little. I pull my claws back into my fingertips and hug myself over the towel.

"Well," Andreas says wryly, "that was a fun little visit. I guess bullets won't do much against things like him anyway."

Then his gaze slides toward me—and jars to a halt. The other guys glance over too, and suddenly a different sort of scent wafts through the air alongside the heat that's sparked in their eyes.

I'm abruptly aware of my wet hair sending a trickle of water down my back… and of the fact that I really am wearing *just* a towel. My body is totally naked underneath.

The towel only falls halfway down my thighs, and the two ends have opened to show a triangle of flesh almost to my hip. Damp patches cling to the sides of my breasts.

I try to tug the fabric over more of me without flashing any extra skin in the meantime. "I didn't know what was going on—I didn't have time to get dressed."

Jacob is staring at me with his normally cool eyes

searing, as if he's on the verge of marching across the room and peeling the towel right off me. I'm torn between the conflicting desires to recoil and to welcome that hunger.

Zian makes a rough noise and jerks his head to the side.

Dominic clears his throat, his tan cheeks gone ruddy, and tears his gaze away to look at the other guys again. "It seems like at least in this city, the monsters communicate with each other. Look out for each other."

Yes, thank God, let's focus on something other than my state of undress.

I nod. "I don't think it'd be a very good idea to try to approach any others around here. I don't know what abilities that guy had, but he felt like he had a *lot*."

"Yeah." Zian frowns at the spot where the purple shadowkind was floating, still keeping his eyes carefully averted from me. "Do you think we should believe what he said about that guy in Miami?"

Jacob seems to shake himself out of a trance. He grimaces. "He just wanted to get rid of us."

"He was pretty specific about it," Andreas puts in, and pauses. "I mean, maybe this Rollick monster—or shadowkind or whatever—is actually a dude who eats humans for breakfast and our new purple friend figured that was an easy way to eliminate us for good, but I'm pretty sure a Rollick with a hotel in Miami actually exists."

"Did you see anything in his memories about that?" I ask.

Andreas shakes his head. "There were some dark, murky moments that I couldn't make much sense of, and some where he just appeared to be watching people around the city. One time when he beat up a smaller, creepy-looking dude for reasons I don't know. Nothing very useful. I didn't have much time."

"That's okay," Jacob says. "We can look up hotels in Miami, see if we can figure out which place someone named Rollick owns before we head all the way down there."

Dominic exhales with apparent relief. "Yeah. Get all the information before we make a decision."

Jacob cuts his gaze back toward me, with another flare of heat that flushes my skin. "And you'd better go finish your bath, Wildcat."

He says it mildly enough. But maybe because of that show of self-control combined with his obvious hunger and his use of my old, fond nickname, an unwelcome ache forms between my thighs.

Yes, I had better.

I whirl toward the stairs. "I'll be out quick to hear what you've dug up."

Then I flee from the longing that tugs at me from each of my men—and the answering pang rising up inside me.

TEN

Riva

There's something inexplicably satisfying about twisting half a lemon around the notched peak of a juicer. Feeling the ridges dig into the pulpy flesh against the pressure of my fingers, watching the glass base fill with pale yellow juice.

It makes me feel like I'm actually accomplishing something, which isn't a sensation I've had much in the past couple of days.

Andreas watches from where he's nursing a mug of coffee at the apartment's small dining table. "Had a craving you couldn't resist?" he asks in a lightly teasing tone.

I make a face at him. "I had to take advantage of the equipment while I have it. No motel is going to have a juicer. And I've been carrying around that bag of lemons since The Middle of Nowhere, Manitoba."

Zian stirs at the other side of the table, where he's been

gulping down breakfast sausages—another benefit of having a proper kitchen for once. "We don't know for sure that we're leaving today, do we?"

His gaze slides to Jacob, who's sitting on the sofa across from the kitchen with Engel's laptop propped open on his knees, now connected to the apartment's Wi-Fi. I turn toward the kettle that's just started to whistle.

We took shifts all night keeping watch in case the big purple dude decided to encourage us to leave town more forcefully. The guys tried to insist that I should sleep straight through until I pointed out that they weren't going to convince me that they trust me now by refusing to let me do my bit to protect us.

But I'm not sure how much Jacob slept at all, even when it wasn't his shift. He stayed up into the wee hours in the same pose he's in now.

When it was my turn on watch, he made a point of going into the bedroom he's sharing with Dominic, but I thought I heard keys clicking when I came back up to get more sleep.

As I pour the hot water into a measuring cup, he sighs. "I haven't been able to find *anything* about a person—or whatever he is—named Rollick in Miami. Or the whole state of Florida either."

"Maybe it's time for some fresh eyes," Andreas suggests mildly. "Dominic got pretty comfortable with that computer—he could—"

"I know what I've already tried," Jacob interrupts with an irritated edge. "And that's just about everything."

He shoves the laptop onto the coffee table and sinks back into the sofa cushions.

I dip a spoon into the bag of white sugar that came with the Airbnb and drop the grains into the hot water before consulting the recipe on my phone. It *says* that I should use two tablespoons, but I'm going for alcohol-level sour here.

I stir the one spoonful in and reach for the lemon juice. I can always add more sweetness later if I want.

"What else do we really need to know?" I say as I add the juice and fill most of the rest of the cup with cold water. "It'd be dangerous continuing to talk to shadowkind around here. The only other place we know for sure we should be able to find some is Miami."

Dominic has just stepped into the kitchen area to pour himself some coffee from the pot Andreas brewed. He glances over at me. "We have no idea how dangerous following that one monster's advice might be."

I shrug. "We don't know how dangerous *anyplace* might be. And… we're pretty dangerous too. I think these 'monsters' can tell. Why do you think they all ran away from us?"

I don't really like bringing up the threat we can pose, especially when I seem to be the biggest threat of all. But we can't just sit here playing house.

Zian makes a thoughtful sound. "Even the big guy yesterday seemed kind of nervous of us."

I pour my mixed liquids into a drinking glass I've already added several ice cubes to. They tinkle against the sides. Picking up the glass, I turn to face the guys.

Jacob studies me as I raise the glass to my lips. I'm not sure what he's looking for, so I focus on the first sip of lemonade washing over my tongue.

Oh, that's fucking good. So tart it wakes up my taste buds like a punch in the face.

Who needs coffee when you've got this? And I'm never drinking a cocktail again.

As I take a larger gulp, restraining a pleased shiver at the shock of sourness, Jacob rubs his mouth. "It is our only lead."

Andreas nods. "And there's a chance the guy was telling the truth. It's not like shadowbloods are crashing his city so often he'd have a system set up for screwing us over."

"I vote that we try Miami," Dominic says quietly. "Being careful, but we would be anyway."

Zian swallows another bite of sausage. "If you all think it's the best idea, then I'm in."

"All right." Jacob grabs the laptop and stands up. "We should get going right away then. The faster we get there, the less time there is for these shadow monsters to make their own plans if they want to screw with us after all. Everyone eat what you need to and pack up anything that isn't packed up, and we head out in an hour."

Andreas throws back the last of his coffee. "I call first dibs on the shower!"

As he and Jacob head upstairs, Zian digs into his ample breakfast with even more haste. Dominic takes a long gulp of his own coffee.

I drain the rest of my lemonade, reveling in every bite of the tang, and set the glass down by the sink. There's a grocery store danish left, cherry and cream cheese, but I'm not sure how much that appeals.

Without thinking, I stretch upward to tug open one of

the higher cabinets—and pain lances from my side from my re-opened wound.

My fingers twitch. My mouth snaps shut against a gasp, my jaw clenching tight.

I slow the movement, relaxing my torso as I ease the cupboard door open. The pain quickly fades to a dull ache.

I'm okay. No big deal.

But nothing in the cupboard makes the sacrifice worthwhile. I scowl at the stacks of dishes for a moment and then grab the danish. "I'm going to get packed up."

Dominic sets down his mug and trails behind me up the stairs. I assume he's going to his own room to pack as well, but as I open my bedroom door, he catches me by the elbow.

The second I stop, my pulse jumping at the unexpected physical contact, he drops his hand. His hazel eyes search mine.

"When did you get hurt?"

My stance goes rigid, and I curse my carelessness downstairs. Of course Dominic would notice the signs of an injury.

"It's fine," I say. "I'm taking care of it. Nothing to worry about."

His mouth tightens. "It's not *fine*. We haven't gotten into a fight since Engel's house—that was days ago. If it's still bothering you—"

"I'll deal with it. It isn't your problem."

A shadow of anguish crosses his face, so blatant I can't miss it. He swallows audibly and then tips his head toward the room behind me.

"Can we talk—just the two of us?"

I could be a brat and point out that it's just the two of us right now, but we both know that the other guys could walk into the hall at any moment. With those sharp ears of his, Zian might even be able to pick up on this conversation from downstairs if he tried.

If Dominic had demanded rather than asking, I'd have said no regardless of that fact. But the agony in his expression has left my gut all twisted up.

I step into the room without speaking and prop myself against the wall a few feet inside, my arms crossing over my chest.

Dominic follows cautiously. He nudges the door shut behind him and stays poised in front of it, his posture awkwardly stiff.

"I'm sorry," he blurts out in a tone much rougher than his usual measured voice. "I can't remember if I've ever said it this clearly before—I should have. I'm sorry I made you feel like healing you was a problem."

I glance at the lumps vaguely visible under the shoulders of the new trench coat Andreas picked up for him—so that when he's only around us, he can cover up with something lighter than the parka. "It is a problem, though, isn't it? Every time you use your power, they grow."

"That doesn't fucking matter. Making sure you're okay matters a hell of a lot more."

He pauses and swipes his hand over his face. "I messed up before. A lot. I know that, and you have no idea how sorry I am for everything. I should never have let Jake do his trick with the poison in the first place—I should have figured out that the guardians lied. *You* never gave us any reason not to trust you."

My response bubbles from my throat with a sourness that's less pleasant than my lemonade. "You still don't trust me."

Dominic goes even more rigid than he was before. "What do you mean?"

I might as well spit it out now.

"You're scared of me because of what I did at Engel's house. I saw how you looked at me—and on the train, you were worried about me controlling that power. I've noticed you flinch like you think I'm suddenly going to scream at you."

Dominic closes his eyes for a second. His jaw works. When he looks at me again, his eyes have darkened so much they make my chest ache.

"That's not because of you either," he says, and taps the side of his head. "I know up here that you'd never hurt me. It was just that seeing you destroying all those people like that… it reminded me of the worst parts of *my* power. It isn't your fault. That's my damage to deal with."

I frown. "What do you mean? You only hurt things when you have to so that you have the energy to heal someone."

His head droops. "No. It seems like my extra limbs added another new dimension to my original powers. The guardians forced me to test it out plenty of times."

There's no mistaking the bitterness in his tone. My body tenses up with instinctive defensiveness.

In so many ways, they hurt my guys. Does it ever fucking end?

"What did they do?" I ask with a vibration of the caustic energy inside me that for once I don't even totally mind.

Dominic's voice drops even lower than before. "I can steal the life out of things even if there's nothing to heal. And it's the most incredible feeling…"

His expression contorts with revulsion—at himself, nothing to do with me.

"I've never done it except when they insisted, when they said they'd hurt one of the other guys if I didn't," he adds. "But once I got started—I don't know if I could have stopped before whatever plant or animal they wanted me to work on that time was dead."

"Dom." I don't know what else to say.

In the back of my head, I can see the quiet, pensive boy who'd always dash in to help if any of us showed the slightest injury. Who used to spend a bunch of the little free time we got poring over the medical books the guardians agreed to bring him.

He always hoped he could get even better at using his talent, help even more. Instead he got saddled with a matching curse.

And the guardians forced him to act out that curse over and over.

The ache has crept right up my throat, clogging it. I want to reach out to him, but part of me still balks.

Dominic lifts his gaze again to meet mine. "I told you before that the things that are broken, they broke before you came back. It's true. I think it's true for all of us. And it's our own fault for letting our damage get tangled up with what we believed about you. I won't get mixed up like that again. You've always been here for me, and *nothing* would make me happier than being here for you too. However you need me. Whatever it does to me."

Sudden tears prick at the back of my eyes. I blink, grappling with the growing surge of emotion inside me.

I believe him. He's standing here in an enclosed room with me just a few feet away, talking about things that he has every reason to think would make me angry, and I can't taste even a hint of fear in the air.

Really, he's always been the one I was the least angry with anyway. Jacob was horrible, and Andreas manipulated me. Zian snapped at me and berated me more than once.

All Dominic really did was not interfere—and fail to totally hide his discomfort. I completely understand his conflicted feelings about using his powers now.

But there is still one hitch.

"*I* don't like the idea of making things worse for you," I say, my voice strained.

A little of the tension gripping Dominic's face fades with the smallest of smiles. "It wouldn't be worse, in the balance of things. I swear to you, I'd rather know I did everything I could to make sure you're not in pain than keep these stupid things a tad shorter."

The lumps of the tentacles twitch under the thin coat.

I wet my lips, still torn. Not least of all because when he looks at me like that, every inch of my body tingles, and definitely not with pain.

But we don't know what we're going to face in Miami. It'll be better if I'm not working around an injury.

And it isn't as if I really need the constant reminder of

how awful my new ability is. My memories have been vivid enough to cover that just fine.

I grasp the hem of my hoodie. "I guess you could take a look at it. There's nothing in the apartment you could draw energy from anyway."

As I lift the bottom of the hoodie and the tank top underneath away from the bandage on my waist, Dominic steps closer. He rests his fingers gently at the edge of the bandage, waking up my skin even more.

"Go ahead," I say, struggling to keep my voice steady.

He peels back the adhesive ever so gently and considers the mostly-scabbed-over cut. His mouth slants downward. "When did this happen?"

"Engel's house. After the fight. I had an unfortunate encounter with a shard of glass in the window frame."

"It's barely healed. You've been prodding it so it won't totally seal up on its own?"

I grimace. "I... I wanted the pain to remind me of the kinds of pain I'm trying *not* to inflict unless I absolutely have to."

Dominic looks up at me with so much compassion in his eyes that I forget how to breathe. He's less than a foot away now, and the familiar urge tugs at me to bring him even closer.

"I can heal it by myself," he says. "It'll only take a little out of me—the same amount of hurt spread out over my whole body. Easy to recover from."

"Dom..."

He ignores my conflicted protest. "Please, let me?"

It's the "please" that does me in. I incline my head, not trusting myself to speak.

Dominic rests his palm over the wound, just barely grazing the scab. It only takes a moment before the warmth of his healing energy flows into my waist.

The severed flesh knits together. The scab smooths over. The lingering ache melts away.

And more warmth washes through the whole rest of my body.

It's less than a minute, and then Dominic lowers his hand. He doesn't look any worse for wear.

He looks as pensively handsome as usual, his face just inches from mine.

He doesn't draw back. He lifts his other hand to touch my cheek, and our gazes lock together.

"Thank you," he says softly, as if I've done *him* a favor.

My pulse skitters. I want to lean into his touch—but the longing brings a jolt of panic.

The last time I let one of the guys get this close to me, my heart ended up torn in two.

Before I can clamp down on my nerves, my body is jerking away, taking a few steps back.

Dominic stays where he was, his fingers curling toward his palm. His face has shadowed again.

But this is for the best, isn't it?

I shouldn't be letting myself get distracted from the larger mission. I shouldn't be indulging in my teenage fantasies of some kind of epic romance anyway.

"Thank you," I say, because I definitely owe him that much. "We should get packed up before Jacob starts cracking the whip."

Dominic manages another little smile, although it's tighter than before. "Right. I'll see you downstairs."

After he's left, I don't actually have much to do. I wash up in the bathroom, not bothering with a shower after my soak in the tub last night, and stuff a few lingering odds and ends into my backpack.

When I tramp down to the lower floor, I find the guys gathered in the living room already, packs slung over their shoulders. I guess we're heading out a little early.

Jacob motions us toward the front door wordlessly. As we follow him, Zian's head snaps to the side as if he's tracking a sudden sound. He halts in his tracks.

"Wait," he mutters, and moves to the window.

He scans the street outside, holding perfectly still, his eyes narrowing. His broad shoulders tense.

He glances back at us, wide-eyed. "There are guardians out there, staked out around the building. They've found us."

ELEVEN

Riva

"Are you sure?" Jacob asks as he edges toward the window. As if Zian would make up an invasion of guardians.

Zian is staring at the street outside again. He nods.

"There's this clinking sound their stupid armor makes... It's not very loud so I almost didn't hear it, but I'd know that noise anywhere."

His muscles twitch with restrained power.

My own body has gone rigid with alarm. "How many are there?"

"I've only seen two." He tips his head toward the window. "There's one around the corner of a building across the street, and another ducked next to a car."

Dominic frowns. "I doubt they'd only send a squad of two to try to take us down. There are probably others too far out of view for even your X-ray vision to catch them."

Zian lets out a faint growl. "Yeah."

"At least you caught on so you could warn us," Andreas says in a typical attempt at optimism, though he looks as unnerved as the rest of us. He grips the strap of his backpack against his shoulder and jerks his chin toward the door. "We've got to get to the car."

Jacob lets out his breath in a huff. "Yeah. No good waiting here for them to finish ambushing us. If that fucker yesterday hadn't taken our guns…"

Zian draws back from the window. "We managed without shooting anyone before. Out in public, and in daylight too, they'll have to be careful how they attack us, right?"

A shiver runs down my back. "We have no idea how far they might be willing to go. But I hope so."

"Be ready," Jacob says. "They might simply try to tranq us like before, or they might have decided it's better to just take us out, no matter what Engel said. I'll use my powers to keep them as far away as possible."

Zian glances at me. "Riva and I can smash anyone who gets close."

"I'll muddle anyone I can see with projected memories," Andreas says. "It's worked before. We're not trapped this time. We can make it."

"As long as it's just them." My throat constricts. "Do you think the shadowkind monster last night tipped them off somehow? What if more of *them* are out there too?"

We all pause for a moment in uneasy consideration. Then Jacob shakes his head.

"The guardians won't negotiate with us, and they *know* us. I can't see them collaborating with the things they wanted us to kill."

"That doesn't mean it wasn't the shadowkind who gave us away somehow," Dominic says quietly. "Maybe we didn't get out of the city fast enough to make him happy."

Zian grimaces. "It doesn't matter. Let's just get going now, and then we'll all be happy."

He has a point. I roll my shoulders to loosen them and move with the others toward the door.

The house we're staying in has an outer staircase built against the side of the building to allow outside access to the second floor. Our car is parked by the garage around back.

So close and yet so far.

Jacob goes first, easing the door open and peeking outside. I'm immediately grateful for the solid concrete wall that runs along the landing and the stairs to waist height, even though it looked dreary to me when we first showed up.

"No sign of them yet," Jacob mutters. "Stay low, but move fast. Maybe we can get out of here before they're even fully in position."

He launches himself toward the stairs, his knees bent and shoulders hunched to keep him mostly below the level of the wall. It's more a scuttle than a run.

Zian motions for the rest of us to go ahead of him. He's planning on bringing up the rear, which isn't a bad strategy.

Once we get to the bottom of the stairs, we may need someone big and strong to cover the rest of us in our sprint to the car.

I slink forward behind Jacob, extending my claws from my fingertips. The tension of our escape brings the caustic vibration into my chest, but I suppress it with gritted teeth.

I can't let out a shriek like that without knowing where my targets are. I'm not sure I could even hone the power enough to make sure it only captured our enemies and not random bystanders as well.

The busy activity of the city makes it an ideal spot for us to hide away … but also difficult to avoid collateral damage.

Jacob has almost reached the middle landing when his feet appear to slip from under him. He stumbles and sprawls forward on his hands and knees.

"What the—?" He scrambles up, his head jerking around as if he's looking to see what he tripped over.

Before I can say anything, it hits me too: an invisible surface smacking against my ankles. I teeter and snatch at the railing for balance.

Not a surface, I register through the sudden thudding of my heart. An invisible *force*, like Jacob's telekinetic talent—

Footsteps thunder across the pavement below us. Jacob snarls and slashes out his hand.

The rest of us barrel down to catch up with him, to help him.

Something clatters on the ground; projectiles rattle against the side of the stairwell. A dart whizzes past my ear.

They're still not trying to kill us. But what the hell was that energy that tripped us?

I catch the flashes of sunlight glancing off helmets below—a fuckload more than just two of them. The guardians sway this way and that as Jacob shoves them back.

He dashes farther down the stairs with the rest of us at his heels. Andreas's eyes flash red, and a couple of shouts ring out with a familiar tremor of confusion.

Then a spurt of flame roars into being partway down the stairs.

We jerk to a halt, gaping. A glint of movement catches in the corner of my eye just in time for me to yank Dominic down.

Another dart streaks by, inches from his head.

Then dark vines ripple out of nowhere over the top of the wall. Swallowing a yelp, I aim a punch at one that looks ready to snatch at us.

My hand flies straight through it, my knuckles banging against the concrete.

I stare, and something clicks in my head. "It's an illusion. How—"

As my head spins, there's only one explanation I can think of. I bob up just for a second, my gaze searching.

Most of our talents require seeing our target, if not being directly within reach. Whoever's responsible is probably nearby.

There. By a bus shelter beyond the end of the driveway, a girl who doesn't look like she could be more than sixteen is poised with a guardian on either side of her.

When our eyes lock, her mouth drops open. Then I'm ducking low again to avoid a barrage of darts.

"There's a guy on the other side of the street," Zian mutters to me as he crouches at the back of our pack. "A *kid*, but he's doing something."

I swallow thickly, a difficult task now that my mouth has gone totally dry. "They really did make other shadowbloods."

There are kids out there, teens just like we once were, and somehow or other the guardians are forcing them to attack us.

What kinds of torture have *they* been through across their lifetimes?

Jacob swings his arm, and a few more bodies thump on the ground beyond the stairs. But he can't focus enough to do a ton of damage when he's dealing with a whole army of them at once.

The flames lick up toward the sky, but they haven't expanded beyond their patch. Andreas jabs his forefinger toward them.

"Just charge right through them and keep going until we get to the car," he says. "Same plan as before."

Jacob pushes the attackers back, Andreas confuses them, and Zian and I rip apart anyone who gets through them. And Dominic is here to patch up whatever wounds our attackers deal out along the way.

We all nod and dash forward.

The guardians have been keeping their voices down, but more mutters and footsteps carry from beyond the staircase. We hurtle onward.

I veer to the side so the fire only flicks across my limbs with a brief searing before I'm past it. Then we're out in the open.

Jacob swings around, darts flicking this way and that with the movements of his arms and head. They clatter against the side of the building or plummet to the ground rather than hitting us.

A few of the incoming guardians stumble, their hands flying out as if to grapple with something only they can see, but more are rushing toward us.

Zian barrels straight into one who's wielding a taser. He roars, his distorted wolfish muzzle protruding from his face, and wrenches his thick claws straight down the man's torso.

I duck under the swipe of a baton and plunge my own narrower claws into my attacker's gut. As I yank sideways to ensure this one won't come at us again, blood and bits of flesh splatter me.

I leap and tumble, slashing a throat here and kicking out hard enough to break a thigh bone there. I'm only vaguely aware of Zian fighting alongside me and the other three guys racing to the car.

The engine roars. The sedan zooms toward us and screeches to the side, the trunk ramming into another guardian who'd just lunged forward.

The back door whips open. Dominic beckons us from inside.

I punch the nearest attacker with a crunch of shattering jaw and fling myself into the seat.

Zian springs after me and fumbles to haul the door shut in his wake. Andreas is already slamming on the gas pedal.

As the car lurches around and races onto the road ahead, I crash into Zian's lap with the turn. He grasps my arm to help right me, and his posture goes abruptly taut.

"Riva!" he cries out, half protest, half groan.

When my head snaps up, his expression is frozen in an expression of horror, his face caught halfway between its fully human and wolfman forms. His wrinkled jowls draw back from uneven fangs; the whites of his eyes gleam with apparent panic.

A howl bursts from his lips, one so agonized that my heart nearly stops. At the same time, it raises the hairs on the back of my neck.

Any guardians out there trying to follow us won't miss that sound.

"Zee!" I hiss, trying to push myself away in case our closeness is the problem. But he keeps clutching my arm, his gaze raking down over me.

His whole massive frame shudders. "No, Riva, no, no."

All at once he jerks back from me, his shoulder slamming against the car door hard enough to dent it. "Dom, you have to help her—you have to—I didn't mean—"

The warbled words make no sense until I follow his gaze, looking down at myself. I'm drenched in blood and gore—does he think some of it is *mine*?

You'd think he'd be able to tell from my face that I'm not in the middle of death spasms, but he's gripped by some response beyond logic.

Dominic has reached over from my other side to clasp Zian's shoulder.

"Hey," he says in a gentle but nervous tone. "Zee, we got away from the guardians. Riva isn't hurt. Everything's all right."

But Zian's attention is fixed completely on me. His

breath is coming in hoarse pants. He shakes his head frantically.

I've only seen him close to this panicked once—almost ten years ago, when the guardians took us out to some lake for swimming practice. I plunged in right to the silty bottom and glided around seeing how long I could hold my breath, and when I surfaced Zee was crashing through the water shouting my name.

But that time, he calmed down pretty quickly as soon as he saw my apologetic smile. I don't know what's wrenching so badly at him now.

With a stutter of my pulse at the memory of his reactions to my touch before, I move my free hand to curl my fingers around his, squeezing tight when he tries to jerk it away.

I'm not letting him this time. I don't understand his reactions, but my instincts propel me onward.

He needs to know I'm okay.

I hold his gaze and manage a smile. "I'm good, Zee. Nothing's wrong. Just the blood of our enemies—like it's meant to be, huh?"

I stroke my thumb over his palm. He blinks at me, his head twitching.

His posture starts to relax. I carefully pull at the wet fabric of my open hoodie and the tank top beneath so he can see there are no tears.

"I'm totally fine. Not hurt at all. Only the ones who deserved it are."

A long, shaky breath rushes out of Zian. His wolfish features fully contract, leaving him as the gorgeous man he normally is, if slightly sickly looking at the moment.

His fingers twist against mine—and squeeze back, just for a second.

He doesn't always hate my touch.

"You're all right?" he croaks, scanning my face.

"Absolutely, one hundred percent all right," I assure him. "Other than being annoyed that those assholes ruined my new favorite hoodie."

He lets out a startled guffaw and then pulls his hand from mine. This time I let him go.

His head droops. "I'm sorry. I just—I got so worried—"

"It's okay," Dominic says before I can figure out how to answer. "It could have happened to any of us."

Zian shoots him a look as if he's thinking that it really couldn't, but he sags deeper into his seat rather than arguing. I ease away from him onto the middle seat and tug off my backpack.

At least those made it with us through the fray.

"I *am* going to need to get changed soon," I announce to the car at large.

Zian isn't coated with gore. Benefits of being bigger than most of your opponents so they aren't bleeding all over you as they die.

The thought of the battle we just fled surges back into my mind, and my stomach lurches.

"Did you see them?" I add. "The teenagers who were there?"

Dominic knits his brow. "Teenagers?" He mustn't have heard Zian's comment.

"Around the building. I saw one with the guardians, watching from farther away, and Zian did too."

As Zian dips his head in acknowledgment, Andreas lets out a rough sound. "I did see a high-school age kid watching from a window on one of the other buildings with a weird expression. I thought he was just watching the fight as a startled bystander…"

"Something tripped me and Jacob," I say. "And there was the fire that started out of the blue, and the vines that were only an illusion. Things like what we can do."

Dominic sucks in a sharp breath. "That's right. You said something about shadowbloods—I was so focused on getting out of there."

"We all were," Jacob says. "And it doesn't matter anyway. We're heading to Miami now."

I scowl. "Of course it matters. We can't just— If they have other kids they're torturing like they did to us, we have to help them."

"Why? If you're right, then those kids just helped attack us."

"They might not have had a choice," Zian says, his voice still ragged. "Or they might have thought that we were the real problem. We know what kinds of tactics the guardians use."

If they could turn the guys I grew up with against me, it would be pretty easy to convince a bunch of strangers who have no idea who we are that we were a greater enemy.

"We don't have to figure it out yet," Andreas says. "It's not like we're in a position to stage a prison break right now anyway."

He pauses. "But I agree with Riva. When we *do* have

the chance… we can't let them keep doing to other people what they did to us."

I manage a tight smile in gratitude, and then another unnerving thought hits me. "What if that's how they found us? What if the other shadowbloods can use their talents to track us down?"

An uneasy silence settles over the car. Jacob's voice breaks it, even grimmer than before.

"Then we'll just have to keep on moving so they never have the chance to catch up."

TWELVE

Riva

I t turns out that I didn't really need my new favorite hoodie anyway, because Miami in September is freaking hot.

We cruise along the main strip with the air conditioning blasting, but I can still feel the heat radiating through the windows of our new car alongside the bright late-afternoon sunlight. Jacob and Andreas nabbed this one not far outside Toronto, since it seems likely the guardians who survived the battle will have taken note of our previous vehicle.

The station wagon is clunky and a bit of an eyesore, but the back seat is more spacious than our most recent rides. I stretch out my legs where I'm perched next to the lefthand window.

Just this once, I managed to convince the guys that Zian should get a chance at riding shotgun. Both he and I need to be scanning the streets for possible monsters. Or shadowkind. Or whatever we're going to call them.

The sun isn't the only thing radiating through the windows. Thumping bass seems to reverberate out of buildings on every street and through the windows of open car windows on the road around us.

I kind of like it. It's like the city is one big dance party.

Which is a good thing, because we're doing a lot of cruising without any success so far.

There are a lot of hotels in Miami, and none of them come with signs announcing "Get your monsters here!" So we figure our best shot of finding the one we want is hitting up the local potential clientele.

Hopefully at least one of them will be a little more open to answering questions when that question is a simple, "Do you know where we can find a guy named Rollick?" But in the four hours since we crossed the city limits, Zian has spotted one woman who gave us the monster vibe, and she took off on us before we could even get the whole question out.

"We could go down to the beach," Zian suggests with an unmistakably hopeful note in his voice.

Jacob kicks the back of his seat. "We're not here to sunbathe. If the guardians have some way of getting the younger shadowbloods to track us, we can't stick around here any longer than we absolutely have to."

Zian lowers his head, abashed. "I know. But maybe monsters like the beach too."

He pauses. "It's supposed to be that in the ocean you can float no matter how heavy you are—because of all the salt. I never had the chance to try that."

Andreas lifts his right hand from the steering wheel to tap Zian's arm with his knuckles. "We'll get you some beach time in there somewhere."

At the obvious fondness in his voice and the fact that he wanted to reassure Zian at all, a twinge runs through my gut. That's Andreas for you, always keeping his friends' spirits up.

When he talks like that with Zian, he totally means it, no hidden agenda. Not like all those words of encouragement and reassurance he offered me in the first couple of weeks.

"After we've made some progress," Jacob grumbles.

I jerk my mind back to the present and frown at the high rises we're passing by. "We might have better luck after it gets darker. We only found the two monsters in Toronto when it was getting on into the evening."

"Shadowkind sticking to the shadows," Dominic murmurs from beside me. He's been looking even more pensive than usual since we left Toronto.

He's going to be uncomfortable even in his thinner trench coat anyplace without air conditioning. When we stopped to approach that one woman, he stayed in the car.

Maybe the creatures that call themselves shadowkind can teach him something to help with that problem too. Even if he can't get rid of the tentacles, it's possible there are other techniques for hiding or distracting attention from them that we simply haven't discovered.

We leave behind the commercial strip for a row of ritzy-looking condo buildings, stark white against the deepening blue of the sky. As Andreas flicks on the turn signal to head back downtown, my gaze slides over the front courtyards—and stalls on two kids playing on a tiled walkway.

There shouldn't be anything remarkable about them. It's a boy and a girl, both of them I'd estimate around seven years old.

At least, that's how old they *appear* to be. Because when my attention halts on them at the first niggling awareness, the now familiar tingle of recognition shivers through me.

It hits me twice, as I study each of them.

"Wait!" I call out.

Andreas takes the turn he already committed to but pulls over to the curb just a few car-lengths down the intersecting street. "What's up? Did you see something?"

He twists in his seat to meet my eyes as the other guys watch me too.

I motion over my shoulder toward the condo buildings. "I know it's going to sound ridiculous, but there were a couple of kids back there, hanging out in front of a building. They both gave off that shadowkind feeling."

Zian's forehead furrows. "Kids?"

Andreas cocks his head. "They might not actually be young. It could be some kind of illusion or other supernatural effect they're putting on."

Jacob tilts forward to get a full look at my face. "It was definitely them you got the vibe from?" he asks, with no sign of dismissiveness, only concern.

I nod. "I did a double-take after I got the first impression. It didn't make sense to me either."

"Let's see what the kiddies have to say for themselves, then." He glances at Zian. "Maybe you'd better hang back with Dominic, Zee. We don't want to look like we're ganging up on a couple of children."

Zian grunts but stays put while Jacob, Andreas, and I climb out of the car. At the corner, I tip my head toward the two kids who are giggling as they poke at something on the ground with sticks.

They still look exactly like real, human kids. But I can't ignore the jittering awareness that something isn't quite right about them.

Something a lot like what isn't quite right about me.

We walk over with a casual air that Andreas doesn't even need to remind Jacob to maintain. The kids don't glance our way until we veer off the sidewalk into the courtyard.

They pause, eyeing us, and the fat beetle they were prodding trundles away.

Andreas slings his hands in the pockets of his slacks and aims a warm smile at the two of them. "We're a little lost and were hoping you might be able to help. Any idea where we could find a man by the name of Rollick?"

"He owns a hotel around here, we heard," I put in.

The boy's face pales. He flings himself away from us so fast I don't have time to react, and then he's vanished by the hedge.

The girl scrambles up too, but there's a flicker of curiosity in her expression that stops her from outright fleeing.

"Please," I say, taking another step toward her. "We won't bother you any more than this."

Her gaze darts over me, and she hugs herself. "Beach

Bliss," she spits out, and takes off in the same direction her partner went.

Jacob prowls after them with a huff of frustration, but Andreas already has his phone out. His thumb whips over the keypad, and a wider grin curves his lips.

"Beach Bliss Hotel and Nightclub," he says, raising his head. "It's just a twenty-minute drive from here."

On the outside, the Beach Bliss Hotel fits perfectly with the other hotels along the prominent beachfront strip where it's located. All white-washed walls and sleek modern styling, it stands a little taller than its nearest neighbors, though hardly a skyscraper at ten stories.

Its street-facing front glows with scarlet neon in the dwindling daylight. I can't help thinking that color choice seems a little ominous compared to the pinks and blues on either side.

Even from across the street, my ears catch the pulsing of rhythmic music from the nightclub section that fills one half of the first two floors. More vivid lights flash through the otherwise dark windows.

It might be early in the evening, but the party appears to be in full swing already.

In the short while we've been watching, we haven't seen anyone go in except for a few obvious travelers dragging wheeled suitcases. Either the club-goers are all hotel guests who've already checked in, or there's an outer entrance beyond our view, maybe on the beach side.

"So…" Zian says with a doubtful expression. "We just walk right into the place?"

Jacob draws his already rigid frame up a little straighter. "Walk in, look for anyone monster-y, ask them how we'd speak to Rollick. Simple enough."

He glances at Dominic, who's still in the car, eyeing the hotel through one of the open car windows.

"I'm coming too," Dominic says. "I shouldn't be too noticeable in the club lighting."

He gets out, the sleeves of his trench coat rolled past his elbows to allow him more relief from the heat. The air is just starting to cool as the sun sinks out of view.

We set off across the street and skirt the side of the hotel, picking up our pace when we spot a trickle of patrons heading into the building from a patio around back. Just in that first glimpse, the quiver of supernatural awareness wriggles through me.

I don't have time to figure out which of the figures triggered the sensation before they've stepped out of view. Thankfully, it looks like the club dress code is awfully loose—there's a woman going in with just a sarong over her bikini and sandaled feet, and a couple of men in khaki shorts and tees.

My tank top and cargos should blend in just fine.

It doesn't appear that security is particularly tight. No one is vetting people right at the door, although I do spot a couple of big dudes in professional-looking uniforms standing off to the sides just past the doors.

Because it's early, the dance floor is only about half full, and most of those people are simply talking in clusters and maybe bobbing a little with the rhythm rather than outright dancing. I have to suppress the spring that wants to come into my step at the emphatic melody winding around me.

We're not here to dance. We have a mission—one that's all our own.

My gaze skims over the drifting groups, and my feet stall beneath me. Zian jerks to a halt too.

Inside… this place doesn't look normal at all. The quivers hitting me are melding together into an electric shock.

At least a third of the people I glance at set off that reaction in me. It might be closer to half.

The whole club is packed with monsters.

Welp, we're definitely in the right place.

The other guys pause and look at Zian and me, taking in our reaction. I motion them all over to a quieter corner beyond the end of the marble-topped bar.

"There are tons of them," Zian says in a low mutter before I can speak. His muscles flex beneath the thin fabric of his tee. "I don't like this."

My fingers curl instinctively around my pendant, itching to pop and click the cat around the yarn like I used to. "Yeah. If we piss anyone off… we could be in big trouble."

Jacob inhales sharply and studies the room again, his mouth tightening. "We have to try."

"Why don't we ask someone on staff?" Dominic suggests. "The security guys or the bartenders? Even if they're not shadowkind, they've got to have some idea how to reach out to their boss."

Andreas snaps his fingers. "That's the ticket. Come on."

He strolls over to the not-yet-crowded bar and leans his elbows on the counter. The nearest of the two bartenders—a tall, slim guy with a cleft chin—comes right over, sending another quiver through me.

I don't know if all the staff are shadowkind, but that dude definitely is.

"Hey," Andreas says in his usual easygoing way. "We'll get a round of Sangrias—and we were hoping to have a word with the guy who owns this place. I think his name is Rollick?"

The bartender's eyes narrow. He looks us up and down, and I catch a tick in his expression that looks like surprise.

"He doesn't normally chat with random visitors," he says, calmly enough.

"Well, if there's a way to make an appointment or something, we'd appreciate any tips you can give us." Andreas offers a warm smile. "We were pointed this way by someone who thought he could give us a hand."

"And who was this someone, so I can pass on a name?"

"He didn't give us one," I pipe up, speaking just loud enough for the bartender to hear us but not any nearby fully human patrons. "It was a big purple dude with lots of horns who enjoyed floating, hanging out in the Toronto area, if that rings any bells."

The bartender's jaw works. I can't tell whether he looks more unnerved or irritated.

"Give me a minute, and then I'll get to those drinks."

As he walks off, Jacob grimaces. "Are you sure that was a good idea, Riva?"

I shrug. "I could tell he's one of them. And he could obviously tell there was something different about us."

"If giving him that info makes it more likely this Rollick guy would talk to us soon, it sounds good to me," Zian says.

Jacob still doesn't look happy. "Stay on guard. We don't know how friendly our welcome is going to be."

It can't be more than a minute before the bartender reappears from wherever he went off to and starts pouring our drinks. He slides them across the counter to us and accepts Andreas's cash without a word.

I curl my fingers around the sweating glass, wrinkling my nose at the sour-sweet smell. I wish I had more of my custom lemonade instead.

"Now what?" Zian asks.

Andreas considers the rest of the club. "I say we stick together and wait. I don't think it'd do us any good to badger anyone else at this point."

He sips his drink with an approving expression. I simply hold on to mine for appearances, having no interest in fizzing my thoughts with alcohol.

More people drift into the club. Quite a few of them aren't actually people, from what my heightened senses tell me.

One song bleeds into the next, and the colored lights sweep over the figures, more of whom are dancing now. The beat thrums through my muscles, but I'm too on edge to immerse myself in it even if I wanted to.

We move away from the bar as more customers come over. My skin starts creeping with uneasiness.

"What if—" I start to say, and just then a woman saunters up to us out of the growing crowd.

I immediately know she's shadowkind. Even if I didn't have any special sensitivity, she'd look unearthly with her statuesque height, her sharp cheekbones and jawline, and the feral grace to her movements.

"Rollick will see you now," she says, briskly and simply, and turns as if expecting us to follow.

There isn't a whole lot else we can do. With a wary glance at each other, we trail behind the woman past the bar and through the rest of the club to a door that blends into the dark gray walls.

She unlocks the door with a press of her hand and leads us up a flight of stairs and down a short hallway to another room. When she's opened that door, she ushers us in ahead of her.

We step into a large but sparsely furnished office. A thick crimson rug covers most of the floor, leading to an old-fashioned wooden desk with a leather chair behind it. A matching liquor cabinet stands nearby, and that's it.

Well, other than the man who's getting up from the leather chair as we file in.

Like the other creatures that call themselves shadowkind that I've met so far, this man's outward appearance is totally human. Extraordinarily handsome human, like one of my soap-opera hunks stepped right out of the screen with lighting effects and makeup intact, but not monstrous in any way.

Our escort shuts the door behind us, standing with her back to it as if to block us for making an escape.

The man ambles closer. The bright glow from the light fixture gleams off his tawny hair.

He smiles, but it's a measured smile, like he isn't sure how much warmth he wants to offer us yet. He's as tall and muscular as Jacob, which doesn't mean much against my or Zian's supernatural strength—but who knows how much power *he's* hiding.

When he stops, still about five feet away from us, a waft of that power tingles over my skin. He's giving off enough don't-fuck-with-me vibes to make the hairs on the back of my neck stand on end.

"So," he says in a silky drawl, "a purple dude in Toronto told you to come looking for me."

He's quoting my words back at me. I feel it's my job to respond. "He said that you… you might be able to do something for us. That you help out shadowkind who are 'odd.'"

The man who must be Rollick arches his eyebrows. "But you're not shadowkind, are you?"

"We're hybrids," Jacob says tersely. "We have powers."

Dominic clears his throat. "We were brought up by human experimenters who I'm sure knew a lot less about living with those powers than actual shadowkind would. We just want to get a better idea how to handle that side of our nature."

Andreas nods. "That's all we were looking for. A little guidance. Not trying to make trouble or get in anyone's way."

Rollick crosses his arms over his chest. "And these

experimenters are the ones responsible for your hybrid state?"

"Yeah," Zian says, and hesitates. "I don't think— Have there been other hybrids before that you know of?"

Good question. The shadowkind guy didn't sound particularly surprised by the idea that we could exist at all.

"Not like that," Rollick replies in a bland tone that doesn't really answer anything. He studies us in silence for a long moment. "I don't run tutoring sessions."

He seems to be entertaining the idea of helping us, though. If the purple floater sent us here to be decimated, wouldn't the guy in front of us be getting on with that already?

"We just want to make sure that we're not disturbing regular people by accident," I say. "And to figure out if we can stop the people who made us from tracking us down. Things like that. Maybe you were born knowing it, but we have no idea what we're doing."

Rollick chuckles. "You obviously have a lot to learn, starting with the fact that shadowkind aren't born."

He rubs his jaw and then adds, "Well. It could certainly be interesting seeing what you've made of yourselves so far and where you could go with it. And I'd rather not have beings of any type running amok drawing attention to our existence."

"Does that mean you can give us a hand?" Zian ventures.

The unsettling man eyes us for yet another stretch of apparent contemplation. My skin starts to itch.

Then he swipes his hands together as if washing them of the dilemma. "Let's see what you can do, and I'll set you up in the hotel for a few days while I decide what I make of it."

My flare of hope is shaken by a jolt of nerves. A few days in one spot?

Andreas has clearly been struck by the same concern. "We appreciate the generosity, don't get me wrong, but I don't think it's a good idea for us to stay in any one place for very long. The people hunting us down managed to track us to Toronto in about a day."

"They might have just gotten lucky," Dominic adds. "We managed to stay in one location for about a week earlier on. But we can't know for sure."

Rollick hums to himself. "Someplace to stay while staying on the move. I might have an idea how you can accomplish that too. But it'd be dependent on you staying close enough to stop by and meet with me every day. Could you accept those terms?"

Jacob lifts his chin, his jaw set at a firm angle. "I think that depends on what your idea is."

The shadowkind man grins as if delighted by the answer. "They didn't experiment all the brains out of your heads, I see. It just so happens that I met an odd bunch several years ago who had a very useful method of transportation…"

THIRTEEN

Dominic

Zian runs his hands over the granite countertops and shakes his head, still not over his amazement. "This has got to be the nicest place I've ever stayed in, and it's a fucking *car*."

"Recreational vehicle!" Andreas calls cheerily from the driver's area up front. He's enjoying our new ride too.

I take in the RV from where I'm sitting on the convertible sofa that served as one of our beds last night. It is hard to believe that what looks like a luxury apartment is on wheels, although the faint rumble of the engine and the occasional sway as Andreas eases us through a turn give it away.

This sofa and the one across from me boast soft, dove-gray leather. The cabinets in the kitchen and overhead gleam with dark wood, and the kitchen area comes with a full-sized fridge and microwave along with a stove top and small oven.

Between the king-sized bed in the official bedroom at the back, the bunks across from the bathroom, the pull-out sofa, and the loft over the driver's seat, we even all get our own beds. The only possible comfort we could complain about missing is a bathtub, although we do have two separate bathrooms complete with glass shower stalls to make up for it—the one in the main space and the bedroom's ensuite.

And somehow the mysterious Rollick produced this amazing home-slash-vehicle for our use in a couple of hours.

I shift in my seat, my extra appendages flexing uneasily against my back. "Are we sure it was a good idea to take a gift *this* nice from a guy who openly admitted he's a demon?" Whatever exactly that word means in real-world rather than movie terms.

"I wouldn't exactly call it a 'gift,'" Jacob says from where he's poised in the seat next to Andreas's, watching the Miami suburb pass by beyond the windshield. "He made it clear that if he doesn't see us every day, he'll have it confiscated."

"Still, it's awfully generous."

Rollick didn't just hand over the extravagant vehicle but a credit card to keep it gassed and us fed as well. Which I appreciate, because it meant that we could keep cruising around the outskirts of Miami all night, taking shifts while the rest slept, but it is a lot.

"I wonder how all this works," Zian murmurs as he crouches down on the floor by the oven. I can tell from the tightening of his face that he's using his X-ray vision to study the inner mechanisms, but he hasn't completely zoned out of our conversation. "Rollick was pretty curious about us."

"Or nervous," Riva puts in as she emerges from the main bedroom, which we all agreed should be hers.

Out of all of us, she needs her privacy—and her distance from the rest of us—the most.

Her pale skin has a rosy glow from the shower she just took. She's already wound her hair back into her usual braid, and she's wearing a typical tank-and-cargos combo.

But I can't stop the brief flash of memory that sends me back to seeing her wrapped in nothing but a towel a few nights ago.

At the twitch of my dick, I yank both my thoughts and my gaze away. With the way she flinched away from me after I healed her, she couldn't have made it clearer that she doesn't want me *that* way.

And why would she? Who the hell would want to make out—or anything more—with a guy who's got two gruesome tentacles sprouting from his back?

Tentacles I admitted to her I've stolen lives with… and enjoyed it.

Jacob hums in response to Riva's suggestion. "He definitely wants to know more about what we can do with our powers. Or to make sure we aren't going to use them destroying his city."

Andreas chuckles. "If he was *that* worried, I don't think he'd have let us leave at all."

Riva's mouth twists at an uncomfortable angle. "I'm not sure he wanted to find out what might happen if he tried to stop us."

She leans against the wall next to the bathroom, her

eyes downcast. A different memory rises up: of her yesterday evening, setting her mouth in a flat line while Rollick cajoled her into demonstrating her most potent power.

He brought in a little rat-like creature from someplace, a beast the size of his hand with a strange mohawk of fur down the middle of its back and eyes that shone eerie green.

Just give it a little jolt. Shadowkind are awfully resilient. You're not likely to kill it unless you really *try, and it'll heal quickly enough.*

I suspect the only reason she forced herself to go along with the request was her hope that Rollick would know how she could keep a tighter grip on that particular talent. Finally, she fixed her gaze on the creature, her body tensing, and seemed to work up to the brief shriek she pushed out.

It wasn't much more than a squeak, but the rat-thing squealed as one of its legs dislocated from its hip.

That's not the problem, she told Rollick after, when he commented that she'd restrained herself just fine. *The problem is when I'm upset. It gets so much harder to rein the... the hunger in.*

But Rollick hadn't looked as if her clarification was a deal-breaker. He gave us all a homework assignment for today that we're off to complete now before checking in with him later on.

Now we know that our talents—and Riva's in particular—*can* work on monsters as well as regular men, though.

What would it feel like to drag the life energy out of

one of those unnerving creatures? Out of a demon like Rollick, who made the air quiver around him with all the power he contains?

I suppress a shudder and yank my attention back to the present. "We don't know much about the shadowkind. What they want. How they think. The guardians obviously have mixed up priorities, but that doesn't mean they're totally wrong to see what they call monsters as… well, monsters."

"And that's why we're going in with eyes wide open and ears pricked for any sign of trouble," Andreas says, and pauses. "We definitely should stay cautious around Rollick, generous or not. I managed to sneak a few peeks inside his memories, and… he's bashed some creatures up pretty badly at least once himself, for reasons I couldn't tell."

An uneasy shiver travels through my gut. "Then he doesn't have too many qualms about resorting to violence to get his way."

"We don't trust him," Jacob agrees. "But I'll point out that for all we know, the things in that memory deserved it."

"True." Andreas hauls on the wheel. "Here, this looks like a good spot."

We've ended up in an industrial zone on the edges of the city along the coast. Drey pulls into a vast shipping yard where a few pieces of steel machinery stand derelict.

The concrete storage building attached to this yard appears to be vacant. A grimy FOR LEASE sign hangs crookedly in one dim window.

The back of another long, low building stretches along

the far side of the shipping yard, and a line of tall metal
fencing creates a barrier to our left. A few narrower
buildings stand across the street, with little visible activity,
though I see a truck rumble toward them as Andreas
parks.

Nice and secluded. No one nearby enough to see us
flex our talents.

Andreas has brought the RV all the way over to the
unused building, as far from any potential passersby as
possible. We step out one by one into the warm fall air.

It only takes a matter of seconds for humidity to start
building beneath my trench coat, even though Andreas
picked up one about as light as they get. But I'm not
risking flashing my monstrous extras around in plain view,
no matter how isolated this spot is.

Jacob draws himself into a commanding stance. "All
right. Everyone ready for this assignment?"

I think his gaze lingers a little longer on Riva than the
rest of us. If she notices, she pretends not to.

Zian rubs the knuckles of one hand with the other.
"We're just trying to bring out a little of our power and
use it without going overboard, right?"

Andreas nods. "Yeah. Get a feel for it, seeing how
gradually you can extend it bit by bit. It makes sense. If we
get more comfortable with our abilities, they shouldn't get
quite so overwhelming even when we're under attack."

He smiles easily at all of us, but I know he's worried
about his own talents and how they affect him. I saw him
struggle to make his body completely solid again after he
blinked in and out of visibility too many times in a row
not that long ago.

How can I resent the things growing out of my back when Drey has to face the possibility of literally *disappearing*?

Zian glances toward the RV. "I guess I'd better stay totally out of view if I'm going at all wolf-man."

He's trying to sound blasé about it, but his muscles tense as he strides around the vehicle so he's sheltered between it and the vacant building.

Jacob swipes his hands against each other. "We should spread out some so we're not feeling observed and self-conscious."

I don't know how self-conscious he ever feels about *his* powers, but I can appreciate what he's saying for Zian's benefit. "Good idea."

He strides off to the left toward one of the looming machines, which maybe he's planning on manipulating with his telekinetic powers. I'm not sure if he's planning on bringing out his poison spines today too.

"I'd better pick a spot pretty far out of the way too if I'm going to be dipping in and out of visibility," Andreas says with a crooked smile, and heads to the right where there's a shadowed alcove in the side of the building.

Riva lets out a huff, her arms crossed tightly over her chest. "I guess I need to look for something alive. Do bugs feel pain?"

A little shiver passes through her body, and she catches my eye just for a second. "I don't really want to torment even them."

I offer what I hope is a reassuring smile. "I guess it's worth it in the long run if it makes sure you don't torment anyone you *really* don't want to hurt later?"

"Yeah." She bites her lip and then wanders off across the grit-strewn yard, scanning the ground.

I have a similar task ahead of me. I need to see if I can just kind-of kill something… get the high of stealing its energy without sucking it dry.

The thought makes my stomach list queasily. I don't like tapping into that side of my powers at all.

But that's exactly the problem Rollick is trying to help us tackle. If we shy away from the parts of ourselves we're afraid of, how can we learn how to master them?

I might not trust him, but I don't think he's wrong in suggesting this strategy.

Whether bugs can feel pain or not, they can definitely die. And avoiding taking enough energy to kill them will definitely require particular finesse.

I meander forward, not in the exact same direction as Riva but keeping her within view from the corner of my eye.

As much as I hate the vicious aspect of my powers, I've at least had to face it dozens of times in the past under the guardians' orders. This is all totally new to her.

She might not want me getting physically close to her, but I'll guide her through any emotional trauma that might rise up as well as I can.

Assuming I can keep a handle on my own. Memories flicker up—the nervous squeal of a pig, the death groan of a golden retriever that's etched on my soul—and I flinch inwardly.

I didn't want to. I never would have if our jailers hadn't made the consequences of refusing their orders worse than the orders themselves.

But always, in the end, some part of me couldn't get enough.

We've crossed about half of the sprawling yard before I spot a fat beetle trundling along looking lost. My gut clenches tighter, but I know it's perfect for my purposes.

I pluck it up and tuck my hand under the flap of my coat so one of my suckers can rest against the hard-shelled body.

When I'm not already trying to heal, it takes a certain amount of concentrated effort to start siphoning energy. Especially when my initial impulse is to balk at the idea.

I drag in a slow breath and focus on the soft twitching of the bug's legs against my unwanted flesh. On the faint tickle of life I can sense inside its form.

Take just the smallest sip. Only the minutest of tastes.

Let it be stunned but not killed.

Let it recover.

I hone my attention even more and then give the slightest tug with my talent.

A jolt that's barely larger than a splinter shoots through my nerves—a split-second tingle that's so temptingly exhilarating I've grasped for more before I'm even conscious of it.

I catch myself an instant later with a mental slap. It's too late.

With a sinking heart, I bring my hand back around and peer down at the beetle. It lies stiff and still in the middle of my palm.

I don't need to wait to see if it'll snap out of a trance. I already know it's dead.

That fact becomes even more obvious when I move to set it down, and its desiccated body crumbles into dust.

Guilt tangles tight through my chest. I swallow thickly, forcing myself to step forward, to look for another target to try again.

But deep inside, all I really want to do is strangle myself with my own fucking tentacles.

Maybe this is pointless. I've never *needed* to use this part of my power outside of the guardians' experiments. Who knows if I ever—

Movement from the direction Riva went in interrupts my thoughts. My head jerks around in time to spot three burly, leather-vested men marching toward her where she's standing not far from the metal wall.

Riva has seen them too—I mean, they're difficult to miss. She braces herself defensively, frowning at them as they approach.

"What are you doing here?" one of them demands. "This isn't some playground."

"I'm just taking a walk," Riva replies. "What's your problem?"

I have no idea what it might be, but apparently the men have a pretty major one, because they all launch themselves at her without another word.

Under normal circumstances, I wouldn't intervene. Not even when I see one of them flash a knife.

Riva can handle herself in a fight. If I dashed in, chances are I'd only get in the way and make it harder for her to defend herself.

Her limbs slash around her petite body like a whirlwind—an absolutely gorgeous one. But as her fist catches one of the attackers in the nose and her knee rams another in the gut, two more men who look like they came in a matching set with the first three hurtle right over the fence a short distance behind her.

One of the newcomers is gripping a knife… and the other has a pistol clasped in his meaty hand.

Alarm blares through my nerves. I'm leaping forward before I've even fully processed my panic.

She's distracted by the first bunch—she doesn't know the new attackers are coming. And no amount of feral strength can stop a bullet to the skull.

Even my powers wouldn't be able to save her if that prick shoots her in a particularly vital spot.

I threw myself toward her believing I had the chance to save her before the threat even got to that point, but I'm no sprinter. I'm still ten feet away when the jerk with the gun raises it, his fingers curling around the trigger.

The other has swung toward me, brandishing his knife. Getting in my way.

But even without that obstacle, I wouldn't make it in time.

Not with my hands and legs.

Understanding hits me in a chilly smack. It's broad daylight—there are multiple witnesses—but I have no time for doubt.

I can protect her, so I will.

I don't hesitate, despite the pang of anguish that sears through me. With one swift yank, I fling off my coat and whip my tentacles at our assailants.

Fourteen

Riva

The man stabs his knife at my shoulder, and I just barely manage to duck—blocking his friend's punch at the same time. Some distant part of my mind is protesting, *What the hell is going on?* but my fighting instinct overrides any other consideration.

These three pricks don't look like guardians—no armor, no helmets. They don't seem to have any idea what they're dealing with.

But whatever their reasons, they're trying to hurt me. And they're going to regret that decision.

I have my own blades in my cargo pants pockets just in case, but it's easier working with just my body. I knock the knife from the one guy's hand with a punch so hard the bones in his wrist crack.

He stumbles to the side with a grunt of both shock and pain. The other guy lunges at me—and does a double-take when I flash my claws at him.

I take advantage of his surprise to kick him in the gut, sending him careening through the air to sprawl several feet away.

Only then do my ears pick up the scrape of other footsteps behind me. I whirl, clocking my third attacker in the face as I pivot on my feet.

He reels backward, and I find myself staring into the barrel of a gun—just as a long, sinewy tentacle smacks into the man pointing it at me.

The gunman's arms slam sideways. The shot goes wild, clanging into the metal fence.

Dominic rushes in, his trench coat shed, both tentacles whipping around us. Another attacker, this one clutching a knife, lies slumped on the ground in his wake.

I leap in and wrench the gun from the shooter's hand. He barely seems to notice me.

His broad face has gone sallow as he stares at Dominic. At the inhuman appendages protruding from Dominic's back.

"What the fuck!" he spits out. "What kind of freak—"

A sharper fury than when it was only me they were attacking roars up inside my chest. I ram my fist into his mouth before he can finish his question.

His jaw jerks right off its hinges. With a moan, he sinks to the ground, clutching it.

Dominic stares down at him, panting. He looks almost as sickly as the man staring at him does.

He's put so much effort into hiding his strangeness. This is exactly why.

He knew what reactions he'd get.

But he let these assholes see him, let them gape at him in horror like all of them are now, to save me.

Other, more welcome footsteps thud toward us. Jacob, Andreas, and Zian race across the lot, their faces taut with confusion and anger.

"Who the hell are these fuckheads?" Jacob growls, leaning mainly toward anger as usual.

I step farther away from the five men, all fallen to the ground with their various injuries and staring at all of us. Their aggression has given way to fear.

My mouth twists into a frown. "I don't know. I haven't seen any guardians around."

Zian marches up to the guy with the broken wrist, bristling with fury. "Who sent you at us? What do you want?"

The man flinches at the bellowed questions. "None of your fucking business," he grits out, but he still looks bewildered.

"I don't think they had any idea who we are," I murmur. Or what.

"You're—you're *monsters*," mumbles the guy I kicked in the gut, scrambling to his feet. His gaze is fixed on Dominic, his face gone waxy.

Andreas snorts in derision. "I'd say the monsters are the ones going around randomly attacking people."

He grips Dominic's shoulder, and the other guy stirs out of the agonized daze he seemed to have slipped into.

"Grab your coat," Andreas says, quiet and gentle. "I'll wipe you from their memories. They'll have no idea what they saw. It'll be like it never happened."

Dominic nods shakily and hurries to where he

dropped his coat. My gaze follows him, my heart wrenching on his behalf.

It did happen. *I'm* not going to forget it.

I already knew he was willing to let the monstrous parts of himself grow to heal me. But revealing himself like this… doing that might have been even harder.

As Andreas turns toward my injured attackers, Jacob looms over the nearest one and slams the guy's back into the asphalt with a stomp of his shoe against his ribs.

"You'd better tell us what the hell you were trying to do here, or a whole lot more of you is going to end up broken. In ways you can't even imagine."

Whether because of Jacob's fierce expression, the venom in his tone, or the inhuman features he's already seen, the man lets out a whimper of surrender. "It was just a job. We got some cash and some pictures—we were supposed to get more if we offed the girl."

"Who gave you the job?"

"I don't know! It was just an envelope—left in our car a half hour ago telling us to come right away."

Andreas is studying him. "I think he's telling the truth."

"If he is, then it doesn't make a whole lot of sense," Jacob grumbles.

"It doesn't."

Andreas's eyes flare ruddy. After a minute, he shakes his head. "I'm not seeing anything that would connect these jerks to the guardians."

Jacob grimaces. "I guess you'd better wipe *all* of us from their memories then."

He turns to glower at the injured men. "You're going

to walk us over to your car, give us the pictures and the cash, and then we'll let you drive off to the hospital like none of this ever happened. Or we can kill you right now and take all your stuff anyway. It's up to you."

"We'll give you what you want," rasps one of the other guys.

I rub my arms, my nerves still clanging with uneasiness. I don't like this at all.

"After that," I say, "I think we'd better have our next chat with Rollick sooner than we'd planned."

If I had any doubts that the self-proclaimed demon took the threat of the guardians seriously, the fact that he's left behind the comforts of his hotel to meet with us elsewhere erased them. I don't know how much we can actually trust him to have *our* best interests at heart, but he seems awfully practical when it comes to his own security.

We drive into the immense underground parking garage he directed us to with our eyes peeled, but there's no sign of any danger within. After we've parked not far from the exit ramp and eased out into the cool, dim space, Rollick wavers into being near a concrete column several feet away without warning.

All of us flinch, our hands jerking up defensively.

Rollick chuckles, the corners of his eyes crinkling with well-worn smile lines. "I didn't mean to startle you. If you're going to be keeping much shadowkind company, you'd better get used to abrupt comings and goings."

Jacob studies him intently. "How do you do that? The

shadowkind we tried to talk to before—some of them just vanished, as fast as you appeared right now."

Rollick raises his eyebrows. "There's a reason we got our name. The realm we came from is made mostly of shadow, and that's our natural home. We can meld into and out of the darkness of your world whenever we want."

Zian looks down at himself as if expecting to see his own body blending into shadow. "*We* can't do that."

"That doesn't surprise me. The only other hybrid I've ever met needed a lot of practice to tap into that particular skill, from what I hear."

Curiosity jolts through me. "You know another hybrid like us?"

"Not exactly like you," Rollick says with a twinkle of amusement in his eyes. "She came by her combined nature through more natural processes, no experimentations by nosy humans."

Andreas has perked up too. "Where is she? Maybe we could talk with—"

Rollick gives a dismissive wave of his hand. "I've already attempted to reach out to her and gotten no reply. She's kind of a flighty being, in more ways than one. But also prone to taking on projects of various sorts. No telling how long she might have dropped off the grid this particular time. But I did bring a few other associates for you to meet."

He makes another motion, and three more figures solidify into sight in a semi-circle facing us.

Like Rollick, they look human as far as I can tell, but they give off an obvious vibe of supernatural energy. My muscles tense.

Is this some kind of ambush?

But Rollick goes on talking without any hint of aggression. "I thought these three might be of some use if your 'guardians' come calling again. Cinder can manipulate electricity."

The wiry-thin woman at his left snaps her tan fingers, and sparks shoot up. More dance in her pale eyes.

Rollick indicates the stockier man with a head of thick, chocolate-brown curls next to her. "Slick has a knack for tracking down objects and coaxing them into his possession."

The man tips his head toward us with a blink of his heavy-lidded eyes.

"And I insisted on coming along because you all seem so interesting!" the woman at Rollick's right pipes up.

She grins at us with no sign of self-consciousness. Her hourglass figure in its silk dress gives her a sultry look that's offset by her dimpled cheeks and the youthful glow in her smooth face.

Rollick clears his throat. "Pearl was watching from the shadows during our first meeting. But she's selling herself short. As a succubus, she can persuade most mortals to do just about anything."

"Doesn't even have to be dirty," Pearl says with a bell-like laugh, and considers the men standing around me. "Although for the bunch of you, I certainly wouldn't mind taking a—"

A snarl of warning vibrates up my throat before I'm aware of my reaction. My claws have sprung from my fingertips, and the mark that formed after Andreas and I had sex burns.

Pearl holds up her hands. "Hey, now! I don't touch where there's already a claim."

She lowers her eyelashes and peeks at me through them. "I'd mention my offer extended to *you* too, but I have a feeling it'd be the rest of them growling then."

As it is, the guys around me have stiffened at her final remark. I will my claws back into my fingertips, my face flushing with embarrassment.

"It isn't— We're not—"

But some part of me is clamoring to tear her limb from limb if she suggests so much as touching any of them again.

Rollick claps his hands together. "Well, that's the introductions. How did your first training session go?"

Jacob's attention flicks back to the demon, his eyes narrowing. "How do you *think*?"

"Well, from the tone you're taking, I'm going to guess something unexpected was involved. You'll have to tell me what that was, since I have no idea."

Rollick's tone has stayed glib, but that could be an act.

"What Jake is getting at is that we were attacked," Andreas says. "Well, mostly Riva was. A bunch of men—humans—who looked like they were part of some gang said they'd been hired to try to kill her."

Zian bares his teeth. "We sent them running."

Dominic shifts on his feet. He hasn't said anything so far, just standing a little back from the rest of us with his head drooped lower than usual.

I glance at him with a twinge of concern, but his expression gives away nothing but a mild discomfort.

What happened during the attack—revealing himself,

taking in the assholes' reactions—is obviously still weighing on him.

Rollick cocks his head. "These guardians of yours caught up with you already? That's awfully competent for mortals."

"No," I say. "That's why it's strange. The attack doesn't seem to have had any connection to the guardians at all."

Rollick pauses, and then a change comes over his body that I can't totally explain. He doesn't shift the way Zian does, his physical form altering, but somehow his presence feels *bigger*, more potent, in a way that sets all my nerves jittering.

He swivels toward Slick. "You were talking about testing them, provoking them. I *told* you to leave it be."

Any hint of good humor has left his voice. His tone is dark and cold enough to make me shiver.

Slick's eyes widen. "I wouldn't have—you know me, Rollick—"

"Yes, I do know you. And you know *me*. If you lie to me again, you won't be around to do it a third time."

The other shadowkind man draws his posture stiffly straight. "We don't know what they might be capable of beyond what they were willing to admit. We needed to see—"

Rollick's hand lashes out so quickly I barely see it. Thick black claws have protruded from his fingertips.

They slice through Slick's neck deep enough that a torrent of black smoke gushes up from his flesh.

Slick staggers and vanishes. Rollick turns back to us, his ominous energy simmering down, his claws gone. He looks perfectly calm, and so do the women on either side of him.

My body has gone even more rigid. "Did you *kill* him?"

Rollick shakes his head. "It'd take a lot more than that to kill a shadowkind. Which I could have done if I wasn't feeling mildly merciful."

He glances into the shadows behind him. "Slick knows he'll need to give a full accounting when he's done recovering from his just punishment."

My throat has constricted. This is the kind of creature we're dealing with. A demon ready to deal out a painful, even fatal punishment in an instant at being disobeyed.

The fact that he did it on our behalf doesn't set me particularly at ease.

I suspect my men feel similarly. They've all eased a little closer to me at the display.

Well, all except Jacob, who probably figures a truly "just" punishment would have been slaughtering the offender. He's stepped toward Cinder.

"Electricity," he says. "Can you use that to heat things up just like real currents—if we wanted to melt something, for example?"

The slim woman gives him a puzzled look. "What are you looking to melt? I don't do grilled cheese sandwiches."

Despite everything that's unnerving about this situation, the corner of my mouth twitches toward a smile. Then Jacob motions to me.

"Not cheese. We have—*Riva* has a necklace that's very important to her, and it broke, and none of us can fix it properly with our powers. But you might be able to work the metal so it's good as new again."

Oh. With a lurch of my heart, my hand flies to my cat-and-yarn pendant. "I—I don't know."

Jacob told me he'd find a way to see it fixed. Apparently he was so committed to the task that he's taking the first opportunity he's spotted to do so, no matter how bizarre.

Cinder considers me. "If it's your trinket, it's up to you. I could do it—it wouldn't be hard."

I hesitate and then force my hands to move to the clasp on the chain. Why shouldn't I let her if she's offering?

It's not as if she has any reason to damage the pendant.

"Very good," Rollick declares as I tentatively pass the necklace to Jacob, who hands it straight to Cinder. He turns toward Dominic. "Before we get down to larger business, I've given the matter of your tentacles some thought. Given your hybrid status, I'm not sure how this would go. But I don't think it'd be a horrible risk to attempt carving them right off you."

Dominic's body goes rigid as he stares at the demon. My pulse stutters.

He did say something about how uncomfortable they made him to Rollick during our demonstrations of our abilities yesterday. Maybe he indicated even more disgust with them than I realized.

Dom's voice comes out rough. "That's good to know, but I don't think—let's not go to that extreme an option first."

"I do have someone who's close to an expert to

consult." Rollick drops the subject as if it didn't mean much to him anyway and sweeps his gaze over all of us. "Now let's hear a full accounting of what you all accomplished with your time when you weren't fending off random miscreants. And then I'll decide what I should send you off to do next."

FIFTEEN

Riva

As Andreas steers the RV out of the parking garage, I flop onto one of the narrow sofas. The cat-and-yarn pendant slides across my chest with the movement.

I curl my fingers around it. But even though Cinder said she'd fused the metal bit I snapped fully back together, I'm too nervous to test it by clicking it apart and back together on its joint in my old fidgety habit.

Jacob watches me in his intense way that's somehow amplified in the past week. "It should be fine now. Exactly the way it was before."

I don't know how to reply to that statement. The necklace is never going to be exactly the way it was before, because I will always have broken it once, no matter how well it's fixed.

Just one small object out of the many things I've

broken when I lost my self-control, but the one that matters the most.

And I was losing control because of him. Because of the cruel words he was hurling at me.

"Do you think there's really any point to this?" I ask instead. "Talking with Rollick, doing his 'homework'?"

Zian glances around us. "He did hook us up with this nice ride. It's a lot better than driving around squished into cars and staying in dingy motels."

He does have a point there. I sigh and rub my hand over my face.

"What else would we be doing?" Andreas asks from the driver's area. "If we're going to escape the guardians or take them down—and rescue the other shadowbloods they've made—we need better control over our powers."

"I already have excellent control," Jacob mutters.

I can hear the roll of Andreas's eyes in his dry tone. "You have excellent control until you get so wrapped up in it that your brain short-circuits."

Jacob grunts, unable to argue against this point.

Zian looks down at his hands, flexing his thick fingers. "I feel like practicing with the smaller shifts helped me get a handle on it. But it's hard to tell when we're not in the middle of a battle anyway."

I glance at Dominic, who's sunk onto one of the benches by the dining table. He must have given our situation plenty of thought—that's what he does.

And I have no idea how today's experiment went for him. He hasn't said anything about it.

He still hasn't said much of anything, period. Not since he threw off his disguise to leap to my rescue.

My stomach twists.

When I was wounded and refused to say anything, he insisted on helping. Just now he rushed to my defense, regardless of the consequences.

I want him to know that I'm here for him just as much. That I believe he's on my side enough that I can be on his side too.

I push to my feet. In these small living quarters, there's no way to do this without being obvious about it, so the other guys will just have to deal with being excluded.

"Dom," I say gently. "Could I talk to you for a minute?"

His head jerks up. He blinks at me, looking a tad dazed.

Has he been considering Rollick's offer—wondering whether he should cut the monstrous part of himself right off, possible consequences be damned?

Jacob and Zian watch us too, puzzled and maybe even a little wary. I ignore them.

Something firms in Dominic's eyes. He gets up with a determined energy to his stance. "Of course."

I motion for him to follow me.

There's really nowhere we can go that's at all private—and has space for both of us to comfortably fit—except the main bedroom at the back of the RV that the guys have declared mine. As I step inside, seeing the bed right there, my pulse wobbles.

I don't want to sit on that while I'm in here with him. It reminds me too much of the things I've spent so much time longing to do with all of my guys—of the things I did with Andreas in memories that are now soured.

I glance around and hop up to perch on the ledge beneath the TV. My legs dangle against the drawers built into the wall there.

Dominic slides the door shut and stands a couple of feet away from me, looking me over. Concern darkens his eyes.

"Did you get hurt when those pricks attacked you? What do you need?"

Oh. That's why he came so easily—he thinks this is about me again.

It never even occurred to him that I'd notice *he* needs help.

I swallow thickly. "I'm fine, Dom. But you're obviously not."

His stance stiffens. "I'm totally okay. They didn't even touch me."

I hold his gaze. "Not with fists or blades. I know it couldn't have been fun hearing the way they talked about you."

Dominic's head droops. He shrugs. "It doesn't matter. It was nothing I didn't already know."

I make a rough sound. "It isn't true. There's nothing wrong with you—just because you look *different*, doesn't mean you're horrifying."

He lifts his eyes just enough to study my expression. "The tentacles bother you too, though, don't they?"

"Why would you say that?" I ask, frowning.

His lips curl into a grimace. "The other night—after I healed you…"

The memory clicks into place before he needs to

finish, and guilt squeezes my gut. "I'm sorry I pulled away. It wasn't—"

"I understand," Dominic says quickly. "With how I am—*what* I am now—I'd never expect—"

"Dom!" I break in, and wait until he meets my eyes. "It had nothing to do with how you look. It had nothing to do with you at all."

My voice wobbles. It's my turn to lower my gaze.

"Everything got so messed up after I broke you all out, it's hard to know how to come back from that. I don't know if I even *want* to with the others. And even with you… I guess I'm just scared."

A moment of silence stretches between us. Then Dominic steps forward and wraps his hand around mine.

I'm starkly aware of his thigh just inches from my knee. Of his presence right in front of me, his pensive gaze searching my face and trailing heat over my skin in its wake.

"If you really— Whatever you need, Riva. However long it takes. Even if you never decide to try again at all. I'll be right here."

I look up again, my heart skipping a beat. "I matter that much to you?"

His fingers tighten around mine. "You always did; you always will. From the first moment I was old enough to think about you as more than just a friend, I've been in love with you."

He jerks his head toward the lump beneath his coat on his left shoulder. "You know what I thought when Rollick talked about seeing if we could take these things off? No. No fucking way. Even if it could be permanent. Even though I hate them. Because they saved your life, and maybe they will again someday, and nothing could be more important than that."

More love than I knew I was still capable of feeling swells in my chest. My lips part, but saying those three words doesn't seem half as good as showing them.

"Can I see them?" I ask quietly.

Dominic's gaze stutters, startled and maybe a little disturbed. "You want…"

"To see them. Properly. To see *you*, all of you, the way you are now."

I haven't really before. The only times he's brought out his tentacles, I was either too wrecked or too distracted by a fight to really take him in.

Dom hesitates and then reaches for his trench coat. He eases it off carefully and lays it on the end of the bed.

Then he stands there with his profile to me, tensed for my appraisal.

He's taken to wearing T-shirts with a broad necklines, this one with notches cut in the back as well to offer more room for the tentacles. They protrude on either side about an inch down his back, each halfway between his neck and the peaks of his shoulders.

I lean forward and trace my fingers across the bare skin above his shirt collar. There is no clear line that separates Dominic's flesh from the new appendages.

It's as if they're not poking out of his skin but a fully integrated part of it. After the first inch or so of his normal light brown skin tone, their mottled surface takes on an orange hue, but it's a gradual transition.

Two rows of small suckers dapple the undersides, from

about half a foot down all the way to the tips. They're about twice as long as his arms now, though thin enough that he can coil them against his back.

They aren't frightening or horrifying. Like I said, they're just different.

They're a part of this boy—this man—who I loved and maybe still can.

I glide my fingertips right around the base of the closer tentacle. Dominic inhales with a hitch, and I jerk back my hand.

"I'm sorry. Does it hurt?"

A hint of red blooms in his cheeks. "No. The opposite."

A flush sweeps through me in turn, its heat pooling between my thighs. I can't resist extending my fingers again and stroking the base of the tentacle lightly.

Dominic closes his eyes. The whiff of pheromones drifting through the air gives proof to his statement.

My nerves quivering in anticipation, I slide my fingers farther along the tentacle.

Its flesh is softer than the skin of his back, almost satiny. And when I dip my thumb cautiously right into the cup of one sucker, I find that surface has the texture of velvet.

My pulse thrums through my veins. An impulse grips me, and I can't think of a single reason not to chase it.

What better way is there to show him how fully I embrace everything he's become?

I curl my fingers around the tentacle and guide it toward me. Then I dip my head down to press a kiss against one pair of suckers.

Dominic shivers, but the thickening of the desire lacing the air tells me it's not with discomfort.

"Riva," he murmurs in an unusually husky voice.

The suckers are pliant against my mouth, embracing it gently in return as if they're kissing me back. The crisp tang of Dom's scent wafts over me, and my pulse thumps even faster.

I part my lips and flick my tongue over the hollow of one sucker.

A strangled sound escapes Dominic, and then he's twisting toward me, grasping my shoulder. He buries his face in the crook of my neck, matching my kiss with the emphatic press of his lips against the sensitive skin there.

Heat sears across my chest. I wrench my head around at the same time Dom does.

Our mouths collide with a surge of heat and a longing that clamors through my veins. All I can do is emit an encouraging murmur and kiss him even harder.

Dominic loops his arm around my back and pushes closer, nudging my knees apart to give him access. While one hand holds me close, the other strokes down my side and along my thigh.

His breath wavers against my mouth. I tug him into another kiss, drinking it down.

I want him. I need him. The feral darkness winding through my blood propels me onward.

More. More. More.

Just like it demanded when I was with Andreas.

My muscles clench up despite the peal of hunger inside me.

Dominic freezes. When he starts to pull away, I grab his tee in my hands.

"No," I mumble, my mouth still just inches from his. "I—"

Words escape me. I tip my head forward, and he catches it against his shoulder, his arms coming around me again.

A tremor runs through his body. The same desire that's baying for release inside me must be reverberating through him as well.

But he holds himself still, waiting for me.

My voice spills out haltingly against his shirt. "The only other two times I've gotten close with anyone, things ended really badly. The first time with the boy I kissed dying. The second time with *me* almost dying, because of everything that happened after."

Dominic squeezes me close.

"I can't promise anything about what the guardians might have up their sleeves," he says roughly, "but I've got no secrets left. You know everything there is to know about me, Riva. Things I've never even told the other guys."

I let his words sink in. I believe them.

I'm scared. So fucking scared, more scared than I've been the entire time since that night with the train.

Am I going to let the fears own me, or am I going to take what I actually want? What every particle in my body knows I deserve?

Resolve twines with the longing in my heart. But one more thing holds me back—a concern that's not for me but for the man who's wrapped me in his embrace.

Andreas's words when he checked with me about the risks of our hookup rise in the back of my mind.

The guardians arranged it. I think they figured we needed some kind of outlet. It… didn't go so well.

I don't want to do this if it's going to stir up horrors from Dominic's past too.

"Dom," I venture. "Andreas told me that the guardians—that after I was gone, they brought a woman…"

That's all I need to say for him to know what I mean. I can feel his understanding in the tensing of his body against mine.

"It was sick. But I guess they figured that out too pretty quickly."

I nestle my head deeper into the crook of his neck, grappling with the clamoring of my desire. I didn't check with Andreas before— I didn't know it mattered. I need to be sure.

"You're not—Doing this isn't bringing up any bad memories?"

Dominic lets out a shaky sigh. "There isn't much to remember about that part. She took Andreas into another room, and then after…"

He stops, awkward around the thing Andreas didn't want to talk about either.

Something awful happened that day. But I'm not going to demand it from him if he isn't ready to talk about it.

"She never got to me," he goes on finally. "So I never had to… do anything. After that, they stuck to broadcasting porn onto the screens in our cells for a half hour a day to encourage us to get any hormones out of our system or something."

I wince. "That sounds incredibly horribly uncomfortable."

Dom manages a laugh that's only mildly strained, light enough to soothe my worries. "Better than their original plan. At least it might have given me some basic idea of what I'm doing."

He eases back just enough to meet my eyes. "Not that I'm assuming we're going to— I'd never want you to do anything you're unsure about."

I wet my lips, renewed longing flaring beneath my skin at the hunger in his gaze and the way it tracks the movement of my tongue. "Do *you* want to?"

He tips his forehead against mine. "Riva, right now I don't think there's anything I've wanted more in my entire life."

My heart hitches with exhilaration. Maybe, just maybe… we could both be okay.

Maybe it could be something as beautiful as making love is meant to be.

I tip my head and nudge myself upward, and he meets the kiss I'm offering. The hunger thrums through my veins again, melding our lips together with our kindling passion.

I grip him tighter, my fingers sliding into his soft hair. The elastic holding his short ponytail dislodges so the strands slide free across my knuckles, but he gives no sign of minding.

His mouth sears into mine. Our lips part, our tongues dancing against each other with a giddy thrill.

My hands drift down the front of Dominic's shirt to

grasp the hem. Without speaking, he raises his arms—and adjusts his tentacles—so I can peel the fabric off him.

A starker heat washes over me at the sight of his slimly toned torso laid bare in front of me. Then one of Dominic's tentacles traces along my waist, and my skin turns outright scorching.

Would other girls run screaming in terror? Let the idiots flee.

This man has two extra limbs to caress me with. To love me with.

A lump rises in my throat. I haven't said it yet.

I raise my head and gaze straight into Dominic's smoldering eyes. "I love you."

Something like awe flickers across his expression, and then his mouth is crashing into mine again.

I press against him, the heat of his body coursing into mine. The caress of my hands over his bare chest brings a groan to his lips.

More, more, more.

He yanks up my tank top, our lips breaking apart for just long enough to toss it aside. As his fingers fumble with the clasp of my bra, both of his tentacles tease over my ribs and across my belly.

I shiver with need. It isn't even close to enough.

I thought the desperate wildness that came over me with Andreas had to do with it being my first time. But it seems it was because it was my first time with *him*, and the shadows inside me crave the new connection with Dom just as much.

Or maybe it'll always be this intense with any of the guys, no matter how many times we've already been together. All I know is the haze coursing through my veins alongside my blood is straining toward Dominic.

The hunger has become a keening echoing in the back of my ears. My fingers dig into Dominic's naked back, and I have to will my claws to stay in.

Some part of me wants to split him right open and mingle our essence in that way too.

The deepest ache pulses between my legs. As Dom cups my freed breasts, swiveling his palms against my nipples, I whimper, both at the sparks of sensation and the yearning for connection not yet fulfilled.

I want to savor this moment, but my body is crying out in agony to completely unite. I arch into his caresses— and cant my hips toward the bulge behind his jeans.

Dominic groans against my mouth. He kisses me with even more force, applying the same principle to my breasts with a sharp tweak of my nipples that leaves me gasping.

Before I can even think about it, my hands have leapt to his fly.

"I want…" he mumbles. "I need… Oh, God, Riva."

I nod my head in little jerks, my fingers yanking at the button. "Yes. Please."

Neither of us has much idea what we're doing. I've only collided with someone like this once before, lost in the passion of the moment, and he's never been with anyone for real.

But the shadows rippling through us know what they want. Every movement comes to me without needing to think. Like it's meant to be.

Shove Dominic's pants down his thighs. Pump his

rigid shaft through his boxers. Inhale his moan into my lungs.

He hooks his fingers around the elastic waist of my cargo pants and yanks them down. They skip over the ledge I'm perched on and tumble off my legs.

His hand delves between my legs, somehow both satisfying some of my desperate hunger and sending my desire spiking even higher.

"You are perfect," he insists in a low voice as he wrenches my drenched panties off me. "Fucking perfect. Every part of you. Everything you can do."

I don't argue—I can't. I'm soaring too high on the heady sensations, tangled up too much in the writhing of my blood.

I grip his ass and tilt forward, and he plunges into me like he was always meant to be there.

Yes. Yes. This is what I needed most.

This is how we become complete.

We rock over the drawer unit, Dominic bucking deeper and deeper into me. His breath has gone ragged, but so has mine.

His tentacles trail up and down the sides of my body, drawing even more pleasure from my flesh. I kiss him wildly, lost in the same sense of merging I felt with Andreas.

Our essence is flowing together. Our breaths are mingling.

We move together as one being, bliss blazing through both of us in tandem.

My claws pop out. Dominic's tentacles shudder.

He sweeps them right over my breasts and grips my

hips to pull me even tighter against him. His cock sinks so deep it hits a spot inside me that makes my thoughts spin, and then fragment, and then—

Ecstasy roars through my body, overwhelming every other sensation. The shadows in my blood dance.

The words tumble out of me like a plea. "Come. Come with me. Stay with me."

Dominic lets out a raw cry and slams into me one more time. His hips jerk as he follows me into release.

He sways in and out of me a few more times before coming to a stop. His head bows over mine, his body braced against me where I'm still balanced on the ledge.

The intensity of our joining thrums through me. I should have expected this too—this electric sensation like all my feelings have risen up to the surface of my flesh.

Just like it was with Andreas.

I lift my head, seeking out one more kiss. For comfort, for confirmation, for—something.

Dominic meets me halfway. His body trembles with the expended energy of our collision, but the kiss is so sweet I want to drown in it.

When we ease apart, my gaze drops to his chest. I touch the dark dab that's formed on his skin at the top of his sternum.

"I marked you too," I mumble in my surprise.

Dominic's thumb sweeps along my collarbone. "You had one on this side already, but now you have another to match."

He pauses. "Was that—was that because we—does it do anything?"

"I don't know how it works or why it happens," I

admit. "But I—I always know where Andreas is, if I concentrate on it. It'll probably be the same with you now."

A smile crosses Dom's face, bright enough to melt any momentary insecurities about whether he'll mind being permanently branded.

"That's perfect too," he says in the softest voice I've ever heard from him. "Then I'll always be able to find you if you need me."

Unexpected tears spring up behind my eyes. I sling my arms around his shoulders and hug him to me.

Without warning, Dominic lifts me off the ledge. He spins us together and carries me onto the bed.

He lies down with me nestled against him and brushes a kiss to my forehead.

"You asked me to stay. I'm staying until you decide it's time to leave."

An ache radiates through my chest, but it's the most delightful kind of pain. Choked up, I tuck myself closer against him and let my eyes drift shut.

I have one of my guys, finally, properly. And the possessive hunger inside me will just have to accept that one might be *all* I end up taking.

Sixteen

Zian

My sharp hearing paved the way for both of our escape attempts. It warned me of the guardians' attack in Toronto.

So normally, it's one talent I totally appreciate. But right now, I wish I could carve my eardrums right out of my skull.

I brace my hands against the leather seat of the sofa, clenching my jaw with my effort to hold my claws in. I don't think shredding the upholstery in the fancy RV that isn't really ours would be a good move.

Another stuttered gasp reaches my ears. An extended rustle of fabric, like a piece of clothing pulled off.

My emotions churn inside me, burning away at my gut.

It shouldn't matter. I can't offer Riva what Dominic is obviously giving her.

I'm too fucking messed up.

I should be glad she's recovered enough from the shit we've all put her through to want *any* of us like that.

But somehow the faint sounds of their interlude are stirring up both searing jealousy… and a well of heat at the base of my groin.

I probably should not stand up anytime soon. My stupid dick that refuses to get the memo is at half-mast.

Part of me wants to duck into the bathroom and rub the growing tension right out of me, but just thinking of it makes me flush with shame.

How the hell would I ever look Riva in the eye again if I do *that*?

Instead, I train my attention on the built-in appliances across from me. With a nudge of my vision, I can see through the surfaces to the wiring beneath.

I can see the inner workings of things. Sometimes it comes with a curious itch about how those things actually work.

If I could maneuver their parts without wrecking them like I did with the computer system in the old facility we broke into. But an RV's oven shouldn't be anywhere near as delicate as computer circuitry, right?

Not that I can concentrate all that well right now regardless, no matter how I try.

A stuttered breath filters through the bedroom door, followed by a moan. And Jacob's gaze jerks up from where he's sprawled on the smaller sofa across from me.

The noise wasn't that loud, but clearly it's gotten loud enough that he picked up on it. He lowers his phone, his expression tensing.

A groan that makes even Andreas's head twitch carries

through the RV, followed by a muttered voice I can barely make out myself.

Jacob's entire body goes rigid.

A mug whips out of the RV's sink and cracks against the ceiling.

Andreas glances over his shoulder, easing on the brake at a red light. "Perfect control, huh?"

"Fuck off," Jacob snaps. He sinks back down into the leather cushions with obvious effort, putting on a picture of being relaxed without remotely looking like he actually is.

Andreas switches on the radio, and a jangly tune flows through the RV, washing away the more provocative sounds from the back bedroom.

I wince inwardly. If I'd thought to ask him to do that earlier, maybe the two of them wouldn't even have had to notice.

"It's fine," Jacob mutters, more to himself than either of us. "It makes sense. I fucking poisoned her, and Dom healed her. Of course she'd forgive him first."

His hands flex and ball against his lap, but no more objects careen through the air. Looking at him, I get the impression that if he's angry with anyone right now, it's only himself.

"Maybe we should start our sleeping shifts," I suggest awkwardly. "Rollick wanted us to meet him pretty early tomorrow."

Andreas nods. "I'm good to keep cruising around for at least a couple more hours. I'll let you know when I need to switch."

If he's particularly bothered by what he'd heard, he

isn't showing it. But then, I can't see much other than the back of his head.

And Drey has always been the best of us at putting on an easygoing attitude no matter what's going on inside him.

I clamber up into the loft over the driver's seat, where the radio will completely overwhelm any sounds from the other end of the RV, and pull the blanket over me. When I close my eyes, images of what Riva's face might have looked like as she made those sounds float by behind my eyelids.

It's a long time before I actually fall asleep.

The RV takes the turn onto the ramp into the underground parking garage with a slight lurch that has me clutching the steering wheel.

I can't say I like driving *any* vehicle, but the massive house-on-wheels is my least favorite so far. It reminds me of my own body when I'm in a shift: too bulky, too easy to accidentally smash something—or someone—into smithereens.

But I can't leave it to the other guys to do all the work.

When I can finally stop the RV in the same spot we parked yesterday and turn off the engine, my breath rushes out of me in a whoosh of relief.

I guess it'd be a little too much to ask the demon if he could supply us with a rotation of chauffeurs on top of everything else, huh?

Although, who knows? If these shadowkind creatures

can merge into any patch of darkness, we could already have been carrying around unknown passengers who've been spying on us this entire time.

The thought sends an uneasy prickle over my skin. We don't really understand what we're dealing with when it comes to these monsters.

At least, *I* definitely don't.

Is Rollick helping us because he cares at all whether we survive? Or because he sees us as a potential hazard that he wants to contain?

Would he have already slit all our throats if he was sure he could get away with it unscathed by our powers?

Those are the kinds of questions I'd expect Jacob to have thought through the answers to. And Dominic.

Who still hasn't emerged from the bedroom where he spent the whole night with Riva.

I wouldn't say I'm the most sensitive guy ever when it comes to emotions, but I can *feel* Andreas and Jacob's awareness of that fact as we gather in the main room. The jolt of tension when the bedroom door opens seems to ripple through us all.

Riva strides out first, her chin high as if daring us to comment. But it's the hint of a soft smile lingering on her lips that tugs at my heart the most.

Dominic emerges at her heels, his arrival more subdued. He looks remarkably unrumpled, his auburn waves smoothed back into their usual short ponytail.

I think that's a different shirt from yesterday. Did he slip out sometime during the night to grab his backpack?

Did they *shower* together?

My fangs itch at my gums. But it's none of my business.

Jacob shifts on his feet and opens his mouth like he's going to say something.

Before he can get any words out, Rollick's languid voice reaches us through the door. "Are you all coming out, or did you see this as just a convenient parking spot?"

Jacob's mouth flattens. He hits the control to open the door, and we tramp out into the dank air of the dim underground lot.

Rollick is waiting there, seemingly alone. I know not to trust appearances on that score, though.

"There we are," he says in a satisfied tone. "Bright and early and ready for work. Such industrious students."

Jacob glowers at him. "You *asked* us to come here at this time."

"And I'm glad you showed up. Let's get started."

Rollick's gaze slides over each of us in turn. "After giving the matter more thought after hearing your accounts of your first training session, I've decided my misguided colleague wasn't totally wrong in principle. We need to work on how you react when you're *not* prepared."

Riva sets her hands on her hips. "So you're going to send us off to some other secluded part of town to get attacked?"

Rollick waves her sardonic suggestion off. "No, we can keep things much simpler. Those of you who have talents that come out reflexively in self-defense will take a stroll around this lot right here—separately—and my few associates who you currently can't see will emerge and test your ability to restrain yourselves."

He points at me, Jacob, and Riva. "That would be you three. Go take a hike."

Jacob balks. "What about Dominic and Andreas?"

The demon narrows his eyes at Jake. "I've brought in a friend who's particularly familiar with all things tentacle-y to take a look at Dominic's situation. And I'd like to personally conduct some minor experiments to see how Andreas's talent for disappearing might be related to our association with the shadows. Any more questions?"

His voice has stayed mild, but a slight edge underlies those last three words, more a warning than a legitimate offer. A prickling sensation courses through my limbs.

Experiments. Haven't we had enough of those?

Andreas doesn't look concerned, though. I guess it makes a difference when we have a choice.

When Jacob doesn't speak, Rollick motions us away. "Shoo. In different directions."

I don't like walking away from the others any more than I did yesterday, but I force myself to amble around the RV and then drift along the concrete wall at that side of the garage.

How good an experiment is this test, anyway? We *know* Rollick's buddies aren't going to actually hurt us.

My mind darts back to the thugs who surrounded Riva outside the shipping warehouse. Okay, maybe we don't actually know that.

The thought has just passed through my mind when a bulky form even bigger than I am bursts into view right in front of me. One bulging arm swings at me as if to pummel me in the face.

I give a startled bark and fall back a step, a surge of

aggressive adrenaline rushing through my veins. Fur sprouts from my neck and shoulders, and my face juts forward into its fanged snout.

The big green-skinned dude who sort-of attacked me just drops his hand to his side and gives me a hard-edged grin. "The idea was *not* to react," he rumbles.

I make a face, which results in my wolfish lips drawing back in a snarl. With concentrated effort, I rein in my beastly side.

My jaw aches at the sharp contraction. I flex my shoulders, eyeing the figure in front of me, wondering if he'd call himself an ogre or a troll or something I've never even heard of.

"You seemed like you were going to hit me," I mutter, but I know that's a weak excuse. This guy's boss—or whatever Rollick is to him—just warned me minutes ago that I'd be tested this way.

The Grim Green Giant doesn't appear to be bothered by my excuse. He shrugs and motions me onward. "Try to do better next time."

The next shadowkind that leaps at me shouldn't scare me at all. It's the flirty woman who barely looks older than her teens that we met last time.

But she appears floating in mid-air with a swish of blond curls and her knee ramming toward my face, and my pulse jolts all over again. The next thing I know, I've wolfed out for a second time.

As she lands on the ground with a patter of her feet, I growl and contract my wolfish features. All this "test" is doing is pissing me off.

The girl—succubus?—whatever—cocks her head at

me with a coy smile. "I'm honored that you think I'd need that much beast to take me down."

I scowl at her. "I couldn't help it."

She studies me with a vaguely curious air. "You don't like it, do you? Shifting like that?"

"What's there to like about it?"

"It makes you powerful." She laughs lightly. "Just FYI, from what I've seen in my experience, trying to *avoid* something your body actually wants to do means the urge will come roaring to the surface even faster when you can't help it."

She blinks out of sight again, leaving me frowning at the spot where she was standing.

Could that really be part of the problem? I'm fighting the wolf-man so much that it's become *harder* for me to control it?

What if I assumed that I *was* going to wolf out? What if I accepted at least a partial shift as inevitable, but as a tool I want to keep in my back pocket until it's totally necessary?

As I amble on through the parking garage, I reach inward to the parts of me that activate when I transform. I feel the shape of that monstrous face lurking behind my own.

Possibility coils through my muscles and under my skin. I'm ready. If I *really* need to, I'll go full beast on any threat.

My gut twists, still not totally happy with the idea. But when the slim electric woman, Cinder, leaps from the shadows at me with a shower of sparks, my flinch isn't half as bad as before.

My fangs spring free. A few tufts of hair burst from my flesh. But my face stays almost entirely human.

I could have, but this wasn't a situation that needed it.

I glance down at my hands as my claws sink back into my fingertips. I decided I could bring out the wolf-man… so I also got to decide when I *didn't*.

Cinder gives a brisk nod, not looking particularly pleased despite the sign of approval. "That wasn't bad. If I were one of those dim humans, I'd probably have assumed I imagined the little bit of a shift you showed."

As she slips away, Rollick's voice rings out through the parking garage. "Okay, I think our would-be banshee needs a little intensive attention. The rest of you, take a break."

I turn to see Riva stalking over to join him with a shadowkind man I haven't seen before walking next to her. From her peeved expression, she didn't ask for any special training.

My protective instinct tingles under my skin. I wander closer, wanting to keep her within reach of a short sprint.

The other guys drift to join me. Dominic peers at Riva over his shoulder.

"You can let her out of your sight for a few seconds," Jacob says in an icy tone. "You're not the only one who can take care of her."

Dominic yanks his gaze back to us. Something in me bristles at the tightening of his expression, like he's going to insist that actually he is.

But it fades just as quickly, and his mouth slants at an awkward angle.

"You know," he says haltingly, "last night—it wasn't something either of us planned."

Andreas offers him a smile that looks a little sad to me. "It's overwhelming. The first time, anyway. I don't know… Something about our blood."

Dominic holds his gaze, a mix of guilt and relief playing across his features. "Yeah." His attention slides back to Jacob, and his back draws up straighter. "I'm not going to apologize. We didn't do anything *wrong*."

Jake blinks at him. Then his stance droops, just slightly but noticeable on a guy who *never* backs down.

He flicks his eyes downward. "I know," he says tightly. "It's good that she trusts at least one of us."

A chilly shiver passes through me. What would have happened if she kept being wary of *all* of us? Would she have left?

I can't have her like that, but I still want to be with her in every way I can. As much as I can without fucking it up.

I might have said something to try to reassure Dominic that I'm not pissed off with him, but right then Riva raises her voice. My attention jerks to her.

She's hugging herself and glaring at Rollick. Five other shadowkind have gathered around her, close enough that my wolf-man self niggles at my nerves.

"I told you I don't want to," she says. "So leave it alone. Just because you're helping us doesn't make us your slaves."

Rollick looks vaguely amused, which only irritates me more. "I hardly think my suggestion was anything close to *slavery*. You asked for strategies to control your inner monster. We can't find ones that will work unless—"

"No," she interrupts firmly. "Forget it. What I've already tried was bad enough. There've got to be other ways."

"Look, if you'd just—"

I don't wait to hear the rest of his appeal before I'm marching over, anger coiling through my muscles. The other guys hurry with me, tension thrumming between us, all aimed at a source where we're much more comfortable directing it.

My voice comes out in a growl. "She said no. You have to—"

A screeching sound drowns out my voice—and a grid of lights overhead breaks off the ceiling and plummets straight at our heads.

Seventeen

Riva

At a thunderous groan from above, I fling myself to the side and duck at the same time, my arms whipping up to shield my head. Which is the right move, because an instant later, shards of glass careen through the air like shrapnel.

One sliver slices across my shoulder. As I grit my teeth, the pain shoots through my chest.

A hand clamps around my elbow and yanks me farther to the side. The jolt sends a fresh pang through my shoulder, sharp enough that I can't suppress a yelp.

A voice I recognize as Jacob's swears. There's a clanging sound nearby that could be another assault or his power lashing out—I can't tell which.

The parking garage has fragmented into wavering shapes. With the nearest set of lights shattered, shadows drape our section around the RV.

I glimpse Rollick and a few of his people tensed and

staring off toward the garage entrance just before Jacob tugs me the rest of the way around the RV to relative shelter.

He's loosened his grip. As soon as he stops, he whirls around.

His gaze searches my body until he spots the cut. It's shallow, but blood is trickling down my arm.

Jacob's face goes rigid. One of the rearview mirrors snaps off its bracket like it was made of Styrofoam rather than steel.

Okay, that move was *definitely* him.

The other guys rush around to join us, their expressions panicked.

"Dom!" Jacob barks, low and terse. "Get over here. Riva's hurt."

Even after everything Dominic said to me last night, my body balks at the thought of him extending his powers. "I'm fine. It's shallow, nothing—"

But Dom is already next to me, his fingers curling around my upper arm just below the cut. The worry in his eyes and the whiff of fear he gives off stop me from protesting further.

As the warmth of his healing ability washes over my shoulder, Zian and Andreas close in tighter around us in defensive stances. They both shoot me concerned glances before peering across the dimmed parking garage.

"What the hell is going on?" Jacob mutters. "That wasn't any accident."

Zian's muscles flex. His frame grows a few inches in a partial shift with a spurt of fur along the back of his neck.

His voice comes out in a growl. "There's someone up near the entrance. A bunch of people."

A chill prickles through me. "Guardians?"

He pauses. "Yeah. It's got to be. I think I can see a few helmets."

"Fuck." Andreas glances toward the RV. "Let's get out of here. We can drive right through them if we have to."

The words are just leaving his mouth when an ominous warbling sound rises up from the RV's engine area. Like a rush of flames has just flared up inside it.

The image flickers from my memory of the fire started by one of the younger shadowbloods when the guardians ambushed us at the Airbnb.

I snatch hold of Dominic's sleeve and yank him with me. "Get away from it!"

All five of us hurtle forward, staying close to the concrete wall. The next second, the RV's hood blasts open with a burst of fire.

We're still close enough that the heat singes my skin. Zian lunges in front of me, wincing as a few bits of smoldering debris must hit him.

Our attackers must be a squad of guardians—they've managed to find us again. Did they track our presence to the garage after we left last night and lie in wait hoping we'd return?

Or have they developed some new way of finding us that takes them even less time than before?

Flames dance across the RV's inner workings. It's obviously we're not driving our house-on-wheels anywhere anytime soon.

But no footsteps come pounding across the concrete

floor. I can make out several figures mostly poised by the far end of the garage now, lurking in the shadows on either side of the entrance, but they make no move to charge.

"Why aren't they coming at us?" I murmur.

The answer comes to us in the form of a shout echoing beneath the low ceiling. "Jacob, Andreas, Riva, Zian, Dominic. It's time you came home. You don't understand what you've gotten yourself into. Those monsters will eat your souls."

I flinch at the sound of my name, but as the man goes on, understanding sinks in. They've realized we were talking with shadowkind here.

"They're afraid of completely storming the place in case the 'monsters' fight them," Dominic says under his breath, coming to the same conclusion.

Why aren't the shadowkind *already* attacking the intruders after their aggressive arrival?

I look to where Rollick is standing and find him as tensed as we are. He doesn't look particularly afraid, but his mouth is set at an uncomfortable angle like he isn't at all pleased about the new arrivals either.

The few shadowkind who've kept their physical forms around him are watching his reactions. Cinder tips her head toward him and says something I can't hear.

They're all braced for a sudden movement, twice as on edge as he appears to be.

They haven't decided what to do. The guardians raised us hoping we'd be able to destroy shadowkind—they probably have other methods of striking out at our tentative allies too.

Even if those methods aren't particularly effective, why

should the "monsters" we've turned to take the risk on our behalf? They could just vanish into the shadows and pretend this confrontation never happened.

My lips part... but I'm not totally sure I *want* to appeal of Rollick to help us get out of this standoff.

The guardians know a lot more about the shadowkind than we do. They've clashed with them who knows how many times.

They've seen enough horrors from the creatures they call monsters that they believed raising partly monstrous warriors to defend the human race was a reasonable measure.

And we've already seen horrors, haven't we? One of those shadowkind paid off a bunch of goons to try to murder me, just to test how we'd use our powers.

Rollick responded to that overstep by gouging his colleague's throat.

And just now, the demon was cajoling me into exercising my twisted powers. Insisting that I need to inflict more pain, refusing to try any tactic to simply keep that talent under wraps, no matter how much I hate it.

Was his insistence really for my benefit or for his, because some part of *him* enjoys seeing pain dealt out?

The guardian's voice rings out again. "Stop fighting and return to us, and we'll make sure you're safe. They can't touch you at the facilities. And anything they've already done that you might not even know, we'll fix it."

A creeping sensation tickles up my bare arms. I hug myself, shifting my weight from one foot to the other.

Is it possible? Could the shadowkind have inflicted powers on us that we haven't even noticed?

Of course they could have. They can slip in and out of shadows, move through the world totally invisibly. There could be thousands of them around us right now that we have no idea about.

Who knows how much else they're capable of doing without giving any sign at all?

Jacob's face has hardened even more than before. "I'm not going back to that fucking prison," he says under his breath. "*Those* monsters killed Griffin."

I swallow thickly. I don't want to go back to the facility —to one of the facilities, since it sounds like there are even more than we know about?—either.

"Can we get past them on our own?" I ask. "Without the RV? Zee, do you know how many we're dealing with?"

Zian squints through the dim light. "I think I've counted twelve inside. But we're too far away for me to look through the walls. There could be more ready to rush in if they have to."

To my surprise, it's Dominic who speaks up in favor of the shadowkind. "If we're going to ask Rollick and his crew to help us, we'd better do it soon, or they might just leave."

I glance at him, taking in his taut but always handsome face in the wavering light from the flames still licking up from the front of the RV. "You think we should trust them?"

Andreas's mouth tightens. "We don't know what kind of deal we might be making if we ask for that kind of help. What it might turn out we owe them after."

"I don't see any way we're fighting our way out through who knows how many guardians and other shadowbloods too," Dom says. "Not on our own, not when they're ready for us, right between us and the only escape route. Maybe some of us would make it… but that's not good enough for me."

My stomach knots. I shake my head. "No. We stick together."

We are blood. The words we used to say to each other as kids and teens resonate through me.

I'm not ready to say them yet, not ready to call the guys who hurt me anything like family again, but I'm also not going to sacrifice them for my own escape.

My gaze slides back to the cluster of shadowkind, just as Cinder blinks out of view, along with one of the shadowkind men whose name I didn't get. My pulse hitches.

They're already starting to leave, deciding they have no dog in this fight. Why would they want to listen to the guardians talk to them like that?

They're our blood too. We're half shadow, half human like the guardians.

How can we know which side has our best interests more at heart?

What if neither of them does?

Zian stiffens, more fur sprouting along his shoulders as he does. "A few more guardians just came in. One of them was carrying something—it looked like a gun, but I've never seen one that big."

A shiver ripples through my body. Our time is running out.

As if to add emphasis to that suspicion, the man hollers at us one more time, sounding a little impatient.

"You can't trust them. They'll use you and spit you out. Make the smart choice and end this now."

The slight edge in his voice raises my hackles. *Use us and spit us out*—isn't that exactly what the guardians have done all these years?

Why am I even considering believing a single thing they'd say?

The shadowkind might not have the exact standards of morality I'd prefer, but only one of them has actually tried to hurt us. The rest, as far as I can tell, have genuinely been trying to help, whether I've liked their advice or not.

Footsteps are starting to scrape across the concrete now.

I suck in a breath, my heart thumping, and turn to the guys. "I think we know who our real allies are, even if they're not perfect. We can't do this alone."

The guys all nod except Andreas, who hesitates. Then he tips his head too with a grimace.

The second I get his acceptance, I spin toward Rollick. He's waving off the massive green-skinned man, turning on his heel as if he's going to leave too.

Shit.

"Wait!" I burst out, darting over. "We—we can't fight them off alone. We still need your help."

Rollick halts and raises his eyebrows at me. "You want to throw in your lot with the monsters who'll steal your souls?"

I make a face at the wry note in his voice. "We're more like you than we are like them. Please. I don't know how we're going to get through this without you."

Rollick makes a gesture, and a few more shadowkind

materialize around us. A quiver runs through my veins with the sense that there are definitely several more lurking unseen.

"What exactly do you want us to do?" he asks. "Our methods aren't necessarily pretty."

My guys have come up behind me. "Give those assholes everything they deserve," Jacob says in a caustic tone.

"But not the young ones," I jump in with a skip of my pulse. "The teenagers—they're like us. They're being forced. Just—just scare them off. The guardians knew what they were getting into. I don't care what you do to them."

Rollick nods. "Fine. Let's get this done before it turns into an even bigger mess."

"Do you want—" Andreas starts.

The shadowkind near us have already leapt into the shadows. I gulp a breath—and then the chaos starts.

There's a clang and a crunch of smashed bone. Shouts that sound more panicked than irritated bounce through the garage.

By the entrance way, the figures scatter, dark shapes rearing in their midst.

A clawed hand severs a helmet-clad head right off its neck. Electricity crackles through the air, and two bodies seize up in spasms.

The smell of burnt flesh reaches our noses. My stomach churns.

"Should we… go help them?" Zian says with an uncertain expression.

Dominic shakes his head. "I think we might just get in the way."

We thought we were skilled fighters, but we've got nothing on these, well, monsters who can leap in and out of shadows and wield their powers and supernatural strength with total confidence.

There's a boom, maybe from that gun Zian saw, and a large black mark appears on one of the cement columns. The shadowkind don't even slow down.

Gurgles and pained grunts fill the air. I spot a few figures fleeing out up the entrance ramp, away from the bodies now littering the floor.

That's what we called down on the guardians. That's what we asked for.

I'm as responsible for the carnage here as I was when my scream wrenched through our attackers before.

But I can't say I regret it. Not when the vision of Griffin crumpling flashes behind my eyes.

Not when I think of all the torment they put us through over the years and the stories the guys have told me about what happened after I was dragged away.

The guardians don't see us as anything but tools. They'd kill us too if they didn't want so badly to use us.

Two final figures scramble out into the streaks of sunlight. Several shadowkind emerge into view among the slumped corpses.

"Some army," one of them mutters disdainfully.

We hustle over to join them. My gaze skims over the fallen guardians—and jars on a smaller, skinnier form.

It's the girl I spotted during the ambush in Toronto.

Her dark hair fans out around her pale face, which is

smeared with blood. Her chest has been gouged open, innards spilling across the ground and puffs of smoky essence drifting up.

Nausea rolls over me. I cringe away and jerk my attention toward Rollick. "You weren't supposed to kill the kids."

Rollick glances at the girl and shrugs. I can't read the emotion behind his dark blue eyes.

"In every battle, there'll be a few unexpected casualties. It's rarely a scenario that allows perfect precision. Would you rather that was *you* brought down by the mortals we just saved you from?"

A shiver runs through me. "No."

But I didn't exactly want this either.

Did we really make the right choice?

Rollick doesn't allow us any time to debate that question. He makes a sweeping motion toward the entrance.

"Mortals or not, they managed to find us here—and slip past my sentries, which I'll have to investigate. Clearly I underestimated this group. We need to get you out of Miami, now."

EIGHTEEN

Riva

The ocean air gusts across the pier, filling my nose with the scents of seaweed and salt. And my mouth too, because my jaw is hanging slack as I take in the big white boat ahead of us.

Big is an understatement. *Boat* might be an understatement.

The vessel docked at the end of the pier is the seafaring version of a castle. The sleek white walls stretch across three floors above the deck to the gleaming metal bars of some kind of radio tower.

Several padded lounge chairs already sit in a couple of semi-circles across the open area of the deck, beckoning us to sprawl in them. Rectangular windows decorate the sides below deck, where that massive hull could hold an entire football field, as far as I can tell.

Andreas lets out a low whistle. "And I thought the RV was fancy."

Zian's eyes look ready to pop out of his head. "You couldn't fit that on a highway."

The Miami warmth still wraps around us, but the breeze licks a chill over my skin. I rub my arms. "I don't know about this. If we don't like how things are going, it's not like we'll be able to just leave."

The vast stretch of ocean around and beyond the ship makes my nerves itch. That is way more water than belongs in any place all at once—at least, any place I'm going to be.

Jacob shrugs. "That's the point, right? There won't be an easy way for anyone to get to *us* either."

His gaze slides to me, and his mouth slants in concern. "But if you think we shouldn't take the chance…"

I grimace. I didn't ask to be the deciding factor for the group, and I probably shouldn't be when my dislike of open water is more instinctive than logical. "I don't know. It just makes me nervous."

Dominic rests his hand on the small of my back—a simple gesture, but one that sends a much more pleasant tingle through my body.

I like that he feels comfortable offering little gestures of affection. I like that I no longer panic at the thought of receiving them—from him, at least.

"It makes sense to be wary," he says. "But if things get *really* bad, there have to be life rafts and things like that. It's hard to know where we'd be safe on land with how easily the guardians keep tracking us down."

"Yeah." I let out my breath in a huff. "Where did Rollick wander off to? Are we supposed to head on board or what?"

Andreas tips his head toward the other end of the pier. "Last I saw him, he was over by the harbor office. Maybe even monsters need to do paperwork."

Zian guffaws at the wry remark. I shift my weight from one foot to the other, restlessness winding through my body, and turn.

"I'll go see what's going on with him. If there's a problem, I want to know right away."

Dominic's touch falls away with my movement, and he reaches to grasp my hand instead. "I'll come with you. It's better if none of us go off on our own."

Jacob jerks to stiffer attention. "*I'm* coming."

Zian steps forward too, hastily opening his mouth. "I can make sure—"

I hold up my hands, stopping them in their tracks. "I don't need a whole entourage. I can look after *myself* just fine, remember?"

And if the shadowkind are up to something, it'll be a lot harder for me to slink over and find that out with my self-appointed bodyguards barging along after me.

Jacob grimaces, but I don't give him a chance to argue. Tugging on Dominic's hand, I set off toward the compact beige office building beyond the line of smaller boats.

Dom must sense my mood, because he keeps quiet as we approach the building. He's always been the type to walk softly, so he's really the perfect companion.

The fact that his closeness and our deepened connection make me a little giddy is just a bonus.

Rhythmic beats thrum through the walls of the office. Apparently no one in Miami is exempt from their dance music addiction.

The bass isn't loud enough to totally drown out Rollick's voice. I catch a few barely decipherable words and hustle closer as stealthily as I can.

We stop by the corner of the office building. Rollick is standing several feet beyond it near the edge of the main harbor area, gazing out over the rippling water as he talks into the phone at his ear.

"I'm hoping it won't be too long. But this is an unpredictable situation."

He means us. We're the situation.

I cross my arms over my chest, wishing I could hear the other end of the call.

Rollick pauses while his conversation partner must speak, his head bowing. A little of his typical cool confidence has fallen from his stance, as if what the other person says could alter his plans.

I always thought the demon was the man in charge around here. Does he have his own boss that he answers to?

Then he lets out a chuckle that's almost gentle, his voice dipping as well. "You know I'd rather not be away from you any longer than I can help, Quinn. I'll be sure to make it up to you *very* thoroughly the next time we're together."

My cheeks flush. Oh. I can tell by his tone that he isn't talking to a superior but to a lover.

"I'm sure it'll be fine," he goes on. "Some of my associates panic too easily. I won't keep Torrent away too long either. And you know you can call either of us any time. If you need us, we'll be there."

The unmistakable affection in his words calms my

nerves. Rollick is capable of caring about *something*, clearly.

He isn't a sadistic beast, at least not all the way through, no matter what the guardians think of the shadowkind.

Dominic glances at me, and through unspoken agreement, we ease away from the office. We're halfway back to where the other guys are waiting when Rollick's brisk footsteps approach from behind.

"All right, all right," he says. "Everyone, on board. Let me give you a quick tour."

With less trepidation than before but still a healthy dollop of wariness, I follow him up the long, narrow boarding ramp with the others. He motions to the broad front deck with its lounge chairs first.

"Feel free to relax however you like when we're not working on those powers of yours. You have full access to the ship."

I guess there isn't much need for private spaces when he and his colleagues can slip into the shadows to talk in secret about anything they wouldn't want us to know.

Rollick leads us through a series of hallways with equally glossy floors and walls. There's a dining area that looks like an upscale restaurant, the smell of roasting meat already drifting from the kitchen beyond. A library room packed full of books and cozy armchairs.

Next we come to a lounge of cushioned seating facing a broad window that shows a view beneath the ocean water, one even I have to admit is breathtaking. And finally we peer into a huge space that could fit an entire apartment inside it that Rollick calls "the party room."

By the time we reach the section with the sleeping quarters, I'm so filled with awe I'm surprised it isn't floating me up to the ceiling like a helium balloon.

The RV was fancy, but it was still a cramped space with only the basics, as elegant as those were. This is like a full-out luxury vacation.

But the niggling voice at the back of my head reminds me that all this luxury might come at a price we haven't yet discovered.

"I'll be holding on to the main suite for myself, naturally," Rollick says. "But I don't think you'll find anything to complain about in your accommodations. And you'll all have your own rooms this time."

Each of the bedrooms he opens the doors to is as big as the entire interior of the RV. The cream-colored walls and leather finishings give off a soothing vibe.

The beds are big enough that I could sprawl at any angle and not come close to touching the edges. And they're each across from a larger TV than I've ever gotten to watch in my life.

I tread into the last room, which I decide on the spot will be mine, my feet sinking into the thick carpeting. What kind of channels can you access at sea?

No one has to know if I decide to hole up in here binging all the episodes of my soap opera that I've missed, right?

Rollick steps back with a satisfied smile. "Make yourselves comfortable. We'll gather in the dining room in an hour to discuss strategy—and eat, of course."

The prospect of enjoying whatever his private chef is whipping up has my mouth watering despite my wariness.

It wouldn't be *so* bad to enjoy the magical experience we've somehow landed in the middle of, would it?

Andreas gazes around the room with a breathless chuckle. "I've seen memories of cruise-ship vacations. Huge ocean liners with their own casinos and water slides and theaters. But none of them had cabins this nice."

"I'll take this over a casino any time," I declare, dropping my backpack on the bed to claim it.

The guys linger by the doorway. Jacob starts prowling through the room as if scanning it for threats.

I narrow my eyes at him. "You've got your own bedroom to hang out in."

He turns to me with a fierce flash of his eyes. "You're not sleeping in here alone."

I can't restrain a snort. "I'm not sleeping in here with *you*."

"I'll put a blanket down near the door. No one's getting past it without going through me."

Is he fucking kidding me?

My baleful look turns into a full-out glower. "The shadowkind can slip right around you without you even knowing they're there. And if *anyone's* going to keep me company overnight, it'll be Dominic."

My cheeks heat all over again with those last words, but the shy but brilliant smile that flickers across Dom's face makes the announcement worthwhile.

Jacob cuts his gaze toward Dominic, his jaw clenching. "No offense meant, but his skills are better for *after* a battle, not fighting one."

I plant my hands on my hips. "You're not—"

Before I can tell him off again, he raises his arms in

surrender. "You don't want me right in here, I'll stay out. I can sleep in the hall outside the door."

My mouth twists with annoyance, but I don't know how I can stop him from doing that if he's going to insist. What does he even think he's going to accomplish?

"Sounds like it's settled," Andreas says, his tone dry but mild. "Maybe we should all take a few minutes to sort out our own space, though?"

Jacob grunts but marches out. The other guys follow, but Andreas hangs back for a moment at the doorway.

When I meet his gaze, he tips his head toward me, his expression softening. "How are you doing?"

I shrug. "Other than feeling a little smothered and wondering how far in over our heads we've gotten, I'm okay."

He wets his lips. "You know if you need anything—if there's anything you'd want me to do, for whatever reason—"

The pain I've worked so hard at suppressing springs up to clench around my gut.

"We're not there yet," I say quietly. "I don't know if we're ever going to be there. And I'm not going to forget that you're around without you reminding me. Just—just leave it, okay. We've got bigger things to worry about."

Andreas nods, but his face has tightened as if he's as knotted up inside as I am. "We do. But just for the record, none of this matters half as much to me as making sure you're happy."

He leaves before I can say anything else. I swallow thickly, so tangled up inside that for a second I can't breathe.

I don't bother unpacking my bag, because even at sea, it's always possible we'll need to make a hasty exit. I flop down on the bed and allow myself to revel in the fluffiness of the duvet for several minutes, but anxious thoughts keep gnawing at the edges of my mind.

This ship is amazing, but it's never going to be home. We can't stay on the run forever.

Are Rollick and his friends really going to carve out a path to a normal life for us? Or are we going to end up almost as trapped as we were in the facility, just with different types of captors, different sorts of tests?

I wish I had a better sense of the way forward.

To try to clear my head, I run through an exercise routine and take a quick shower. But when a speaker mounted in the corner of the room activates, I can't say I'm eager for the summons.

"All passengers please report to the dining room."

I'm both ready and not. I duck out into the hall at the same time as the guys step out from their various doorways.

Dominic looks up and down the hallway. "I don't remember which way the dining room is."

Zian takes a sniff of the air and strides forward without a hint of doubt. "I'm ready to dig in."

His nose leads us well. We emerge into the dining area I saw earlier and find a few of the tables pushed together to create one long one.

Serving dishes sit down the length of it, a couple heaped with spareribs that give off spicy and tangy-sweet scents. Others hold slices of baked ham, baby potatoes glistening with butter, and two different kinds of salad, one laced with mandarin slices and another with dried cranberries.

My mouth is already watering. There's no one else around yet—at least, no one I can see—so I grab a plate at random and add a little of everything to it.

Zian goes straight to the ribs, creating a little mountain on his plate that he tops with ham. He drops into a chair and pops the first bite into his mouth with gusto.

Obviously he isn't worried about trusting the food. But then, it *would* be a pretty bizarre scheme for Rollick to arrange a massive cruise just to poison us on the first night.

As we all take seats in a semi-circle at one end of the table, Rollick saunters over seemingly out of nowhere. "Eat as much as you like," he says. "Technically the rest of us don't *need* the food. Although I wouldn't associate with anyone who can't enjoy a good spare rib." He plucks one of the dry-rub morsels off its platter and carries it to his spot at the head of the table.

As if on cue, several more shadowkind waver into being by the other seats. Pearl plunks herself down next to me with a bounce of her golden curls and snatches a mandarin slice right out of the salad.

"Fruit is the best," she says in her cheery voice, and pops it into her mouth. "Don't you think so? They taste so good, and they carry the seeds to make more fruit! And I've heard mortals say they give you nutrions or something too."

My mouth twitches, but I'm afraid she'll be offended if

I laugh. Offending a monster, even a not-very-monstrous-seeming one, feels like a bad idea.

"I think it's probably nutrients," I say. "Like vitamins and stuff."

"Oh! There are so many words. And that's just your language." She plucks up another slice. "Humans do like to make things complicated."

Okay, that's a fair assessment.

"That's what I like about you," the succubus goes on hastily as if concerned that she might have offended *me*. "It's so interesting on this side. Not that you're totally mortal. I guess we don't really know exactly how much you are one thing and the other. It's very exciting."

The other beings sitting around the table don't look all that excited. Some of them barely glance our way at all.

Others study us with apparent trepidation, as if they're as concerned about what we might do as we are about them.

What was it I heard Rollick saying on the phone—something about his associates panicking? They aren't *that* nervous about us, are they?

Why would they be?

My stomach momentarily tightens, but then I spot the dessert table over in the corner. Maybe a little sweetness will soothe my nerves.

I slip over to it, snatch up one of the smaller plates, and study the offerings. Slices of key lime pie and a cake that gives off a lemon-y scent, puffy meringues and plump cookies glinting with sugar crystals.

I scoop a piece of cake onto my plate and take one of the sugar cookies too. On my way back to my chair, I take a bite and restrain a moan at the perfect chewy, buttery dough.

Dropping back down between Pearl and Dominic, I turn to wave the cookie at Dom. "You have to try—"

As he glances up at me, my gaze slides to his plate, and I realize he's already grabbed two. Three, actually, counting the one there's only a chunk of left in his hand.

He must have gone straight to the dessert table before he even started filling up his dinner plate.

A laugh bubbles out of me, startled but genuinely happy. "I guess your sweet tooth is going to have a good time around here."

Dominic grins back. "No kidding."

As I alternate between the remains of my main dinner and my dessert, Rollick stirs at the head of the table. He folds his hands together on the tabletop and shoots a pointed look at an empty chair next to him.

A moment later, one final shadowkind being appears out of the shadows—a lean man with scruffy auburn hair, an oddly dented cheek… and two tentacles protruding from his waist, braced as if to help his balance.

Dominic brightens. "That's Torrent," he murmurs to me. "He talked with me this morning—he's going to look into reasons why my…" He waves toward his shoulders, where his tentacles are covered as usual by his trench coat. "…might act the way they do."

Why they keep growing when he uses his healing power, he means. It looks like that guy should have some idea how these things work.

Rollick clears his throat. "All right, folks. We can eat

and talk. Try not to spew crumbs at anyone else, and it's all good."

He shifts his attention to our end of the table. "Our shadowblood guests of honor. You've been through a lot today, so I'll give you a break until tomorrow. But then I think our first priority should be determining exactly how you're able to trace each other's movements. Assuming your younger counterparts are using the same methods, once we've identified them, we may be able to find ways of deflecting the connection."

"May." Not "will."

No one here is really sure what to make of us, are they? Including ourselves.

But his mention of the younger shadowbloods brings back the memory of the bloodied girl this morning. My chest constricts.

We aren't the only ones who need help. Everything my guys and I went through at the guardians' hands, they're still experiencing it every moment they remain enslaved.

"And we'll just stay on this boat until we figure that out?" Andreas asks.

"I'm hopeful it won't be too extended a process." Rollick smiles with a hint of grimness. "But you should be safe here for as long as it takes."

He casts his gaze over his shadowkind companions after those last words, with a darkening of his eyes that looks like a warning. Is he worried that another of his associates might come up with their own ideas for how to deal with us?

My skin prickles. Luxury vacation or not, I don't want

to be stuck in the middle of the ocean with this bunch any longer than absolutely necessary.

And the real answer might be something we were already hoping to accomplish for totally different reasons.

"What if there isn't any way to block the connection between shadowbloods?" I say. "Or they're using some method that we don't know about to even test?"

Rollick raises his eyebrows. "Then I suppose we'll figure that out as we proceed."

"Or we could solve the entire problem for good in one go."

His eyebrows lift higher. "What did you have in mind?"

I tap the table. "It's the other shadowbloods who are the biggest problem. The guardians only started finding us so quickly once they dragged the kids into the search. But they're prisoners just like we were. They don't deserve to be used like that. We should break them out of whatever facilities they're being kept in, and then the guardians *can't* use them anymore."

Zian nods eagerly. "Two birds with one stone. We have to help them."

Rollick pauses, and one of the other shadowkind, a tall gangly guy I hadn't noticed before, sits up straighter in his seat. The ropey muscles along his arms flex threateningly.

"We don't need more than five of the mutants running wild."

Rollick glares at him. "These are my guests you're talking about, Kudzu. They haven't caused us any trouble so far."

On the other side of the table, Cinder lets out a

derisive sound. "We've come all the way out here because of them."

"Because we chose to." The demon's voice lowers ominously. "You're welcome to find yourself new employment whenever you like."

She tenses in her chair, ducking her head apologetically. But the tension still radiating through the air makes my skin creep.

"A jail-break!" Pearl pipes up, clapping her hands together. "I think that would be fun."

Kudzu snorts. "You think everything is fun. You're a newbie and a tourist."

She winces, looking hurt enough that my hackles rise on her behalf.

I raise my chin. "This is the most direct way to deal with the problem. And if you all were helping us, I'm sure we could pull off a 'jail-break' a lot faster than experimenting with interrupting a connection we don't even understand."

"I agree," Dominic says, quiet but firm.

Jacob leans his elbows onto the table. "It's just a bunch of mortals you'd have to tackle, right? What are you all so scared of?"

From the looks most of the shadowkind shoot us then, I get the impression it's not the guardians they're scared of.

Like the big purple dude back in Toronto, for some reason most of these beings are frightened of *us*.

Maybe even Rollick is behind his suave demeanor. He waves his hand through the air as if he can dismiss all the concerns raised on both sides just like that.

"It's an option I won't take off the table," he says. "But

we don't know where these facilities even are. So why don't we start with what we have right in front of us?"

"Can you ask someone to start looking?" Andreas asks. "I wouldn't think it'd be too hard for shadowkind to figure out what locations fit—with the resources you've got, anyway."

"I'll see what I can do."

Even his noncommittal answer appears to be too much. Kudzu shoves away his plate. "You can't be serious."

Rollick studies him with a languid blink. "I believe in considering all the strategies available to us. It's worked in my favor before."

The gangly man mutters something under his breath that I can't make out. He vanishes into the shadows a moment later.

"This isn't like before," Cinder says to Rollick, her expression tense, and wisps away too.

And just like that, it looks like we've lost two supposed allies before we even got started.

NINETEEN

Riva

Whoen I flick out my claws and bring them to my arm, all four of my guys stiffen where they're standing around me.

"Riva!" Andreas protests, but I've already sliced open the skin beneath my shoulder in a shallow cut.

As a thin trickle of blood streaks down and a tiny whiff of dark smoke gusts up in the ocean breeze washing over the yacht's deck, Jacob lets out a sound like a growl. His hand jerks up as if he was going to catch my wrist but thought better of it.

"Never again," he says roughly. "You don't hurt yourself."

I look from him to Zian, who has tensed with anguish etched across his face, to Andreas's tight expression, to the horror in Dominic's eyes.

"It's no big deal." I motion to the tiny white scars that mottle my pale skin from elbow to armpit. "I did it at least once a week when they were holding me at the cage-fighting arena."

Zian's face contorts with even more distress. "Why would you—"

"So I knew you were still out there," I say with impatience I can't suppress. "That was before I knew you were all going to be asshats about seeing me again."

Standing beyond our little cluster, Rollick lets out a sudden sound that might have been a muffled snicker.

Jacob's stance has gone totally rigid. A faint creaking emanates from somewhere in the vicinity of the yacht's front cabin until Andreas gives him a punch to the arm.

Jacob shakes himself, his gaze searing into me in a way that sets all my nerves jangling—with both alarm and other emotions I'd rather not acknowledge.

"Heal her," he snaps at Dominic.

I scowl. "I can do this. I don't need—"

"You don't need to get hurt ever again," Jacob interrupts. "Not if we can help it. It's the least we can fucking do."

He turns to Rollick. "I'll handle the bleeding for the tests."

The demon shrugs. "It's up to you. I'd just like to get on with it, if you're done posturing for the woman who clearly isn't impressed by it."

A tiny smirk tugs at my lips. No, Rollick definitely isn't a completely bad guy.

Dominic has already rested his hand on my shoulder, but he searches my gaze before extending his power. Waiting for my permission rather than following Jacob's orders automatically.

I have made a lot of progress with my guys. With all of them, really, even if it's hard to know what could be enough from some of them.

"It's really fine," I tell him. "You know how quickly we heal on our own. It'll seal up in a matter of minutes."

The bleeding has already stopped. I'd have to prod it to get it going again, but I don't feel like provoking a longer argument.

Dom gives my shoulder a gentle squeeze. "If you're sure. I don't mind at all."

"*I* mind. The protecting each other doesn't just go one way, in case you've forgotten."

I reach up to squeeze his hand in return and then step away so it isn't a question anymore. We walk across the deck toward the bow while Jacob hangs back.

The test doesn't really work if we're standing right next to each other.

Rollick watches the proceedings with obvious curiosity. "The shadow part of your blood seeks out each other naturally?"

I shake my head. "It doesn't just happen. I had to concentrate on my memories of them."

Zian frowns. "How would the other shadowbloods be able to focus on us?"

"They could have watched recordings from our time in the facility," Andreas says. "There'd be years of footage."

I guess we have to assume that would be enough. Unless the guardians have found other connections we're unaware of.

Jacob pushes his rolled-up sleeve right over his elbow.

The purple spines laced with his innate poison spring from his forearm.

He mustn't be affected by his own venom, because he twists his arm and scratches open the heel of his opposite hand without hesitation.

He dug in a little deeper than I did. A thicker spurt of smoky stuff streaks up toward the stark blue of the sky.

Jacob closes his eyes, his face turning into a mask of concentration.

After just a few seconds, the stream of haze curves. It wavers through the air across the deck toward the four of us.

Rollick hums to himself. When the trickle of smoke has nearly reached us, he gestures to what seems to be thin air on the other side of the deck.

A couple of shadowkind—Cinder and a slim man I saw at dinner yesterday materialize by a plastic storage box and shove it toward us before opening the lid. The guy cringes backward, and Cinder makes a face.

"Get yourselves some shields," Rollick tells us. "Let's see if the essence can still seek you out through that."

Essence. That's what he calls the smoky stuff. He told us earlier that it's *all* shadowkind bleed, no liquid at all.

The four of us march over to the container and find gleaming serving dishes inside. When I shoot Rollick a quizzical look, he offers a wry smile.

"Shadowkind can't handle silver and iron. Those were the easiest large pieces of silver we could obtain on short notice. Hybrids don't seem to have the same issues with the metals, but maybe it'll deflect the particularly shadowy parts of you."

Silver. Something twigs in my brain—the big purple shadowkind who confronted us in Toronto accused us of using silver, didn't he? With the guns?

Were Engel's murderous guardians shooting at us with silver bullets like we're werewolves out of a horror story?

Considering both those guardians and their guns are long gone, I guess it doesn't really matter.

I heft one of the serving platters, which stretches from my chin to my waist when I hold it in front of me, and position myself across from Jacob with the plate held firm.

The other guys join me. Jacob stares at us as if he finds the whole thing ridiculous but squeezes a little more blood from the puncture wound on his hand.

The smoke wavers up—and veers straight toward us within seconds of him closing his eyes again.

Rollick gives another pensive hum. "All right. That's not doing it. I figured it was wishful thinking. If it takes concentration to establish the connection, maybe concentration can ward it off too. All of you, focus on pushing back any essence that might be flowing your way."

I can't see how this is going to help us in the long run. We can't exactly wander through life constantly thinking about pushing monster-blood smoke away from us.

But to humor him, I close my own eyes. Draw up a mental picture of the waft of smoke drifting away from me. Narrow all my attention down to that image.

When Rollick coughs meaningfully, my eyes pop open. The first thing I see is the stream of dark haze that's yet again stretched out toward us.

I exhale with a grunt. "So much for psychic shielding."

The demon trains his gaze on me. "You mentioned something about there being other ways you were in tune with each other beyond your blood. What specifically did you mean by that?"

"I think we're all a little extra aware of each other when we're nearby," Jacob puts in, pressing his other hand over his cut to stop the bleeding. "I knew something was going on the night Riva came to break us out, even though I hadn't seen her yet. But I don't think that effect is strong enough that anyone could track us from a distance using it—if it's even a general strategy and not something specific to us because we grew up together."

He's never mentioned that to me before—that he sensed my presence in some way like that. But I'm too distracted by the actual thing I meant to give much thought to his assertion.

I resist the urge to hug myself against the awkwardness the subject stirs up inside me. Instead, I hook my fingers into the neckline of my tank top.

"It's more than that. There's—when one of the guys and I have, um, hooked up, we both had a mark appear on our chest. And since then, I've been able to sense where they are through it."

I ease down the fabric just enough to show the two small black splotches that mark my collarbone on either side of my sternum. Zian's head jerks around, and Jacob stares from the other side of the deck.

Looks like Andreas and Dominic never mentioned that little side effect to their friends.

Pearl pops out of the shadows next to me so abruptly

my nerves flinch. It's only by sheer force of will that I don't jump ten feet in the air.

She waggles her finger at my chest. "You got shadow imprints from having sex? That's so cool!"

Cool is not the word I would have used. But maybe to a succubus, airing your bedroom activities in public is a lot less embarrassing.

"I… guess." I glance at Rollick. "Shadow imprints? Is that a normal thing?"

The demon ambles closer, his head tipped at a contemplative angle. "I've heard of some shadowkind who plant physical marks on beings over whom they're staking a claim, but generally those are mortals, and it's done purposefully. It sounds like you didn't mean to create them?"

I shake my head. "No, it just happened."

"Very interesting. There's so much we don't know about how hybrids might function."

He motions for me to pick up the silver platter again. "Hold it so it's totally covering the mark." Then he snaps his fingers at Andreas. "Go somewhere else on the yacht, wait five minutes, and then come back."

Cinder, who's still watching from near the railing, lets out a discontented sound.

Rollick ignores her. As Andreas lopes off, his attention stays focused on me.

"Can you follow his path without seeing him, even with the silver over the mark?"

I pause, letting my own attention center on the splotch that binds me to Andreas. A faint tickling sensation spreads through my flesh.

I try to map my sense of him onto what I remember of the ship's interior layout. "I can definitely tell what direction he's in and how far away he is. If I needed to get to him, I could find him no problem. He's stopped… I think that would be the library?"

A few more shadowkind pop into being around the edges of the deck. The gangly muscular guy who complained yesterday—Kudzu—crosses his arms over his triangular chest.

"None of this is working. They're not *like* us."

Rollick turns to him. "We've only tried a few strategies so far."

The other man grunts. "We're risking everything over—"

He cuts himself off with a jerk of his head, but the frustration in his voice digs into my bones. What's his problem with us?

Rollick looks as if he may have restrained an eye roll. As I set the platter aside, he strides toward his shadowkind companions, gesturing for them to gather with him near the front cabin.

"If you're so concerned about using our time effectively, you can use that thick head of yours to generate some other possibilities."

Kudzu lets out a huff, but he follows, along with Cinder and a couple of the others. The tentacled man— Torrent—appears out of the shadows to join their cluster.

Pearl leans closer to me, giving off a whiff of a smoky rose scent. She raises her finger as if to touch one of the marks on my chest, but I step back instinctively, releasing my shirt so the neckline springs back up to cover them with a jostle of my pendant.

The shadowkind girl claps her hand to her mouth with an abashed expression. "Sorry! I just—I've never seen something like that before."

"Me neither," I say dryly, eyeing the woman.

She's awfully nosy. Is that a succubus thing or just a Pearl thing?

Her smile springs back into place, and she waves to the slim guy who helped bring the silver platters over. "Billy, come meet them!"

The guy walks over to us tentatively, his pale eyes gone wide beneath his chaotic brown waves. As he gets close, I realize that two of those waves aren't hair at all.

He has spiraling horns protruding on either side of his head, closer to beige than brown and poking too high to be disguised by his locks.

"Billy's like me," Pearl announces, slinging her arm around his narrow shoulders. "Well, he's a faun, not any kind of cubi. But he hasn't been in the mortal world much. So many fun things to learn."

The horned guy's gaze roves over all of us, including Andreas and Jacob as they cross the deck to rejoin our group. His voice comes out breathless. "Have you ever gone in a plane before? This is my first time even on a boat. They say you can swim in the water, but I don't know…"

He tugs at a lock of his hair, glancing toward the ocean with a nervous expression. A pang reverberates through my chest.

I know what it's like to feel like a newbie in the world, even if not quite the same way as this guy.

"We haven't actually gotten to experience a whole lot so far ourselves," I say. "Most of our lives, we were locked up in one building."

Pearl tsks her tongue. "That's so unfair of them. You have all this amazing world to run around in and they shut you up in one tiny little part of it."

Is that why she's so overeager too—because she hasn't spent much time around people? Or mortals, as the shadowkind seem to call us?

That could explain the lack of manners and personal boundaries.

Dominic must be thinking along similar lines. "Where do you go when you're not here? I take it shadowkind don't start out in our world?"

Pearl laughs. "Oh, no. We come into being in the shadow realm. We can only get here through rifts. I *need* to make the trip, because I've got to feed, but I only became, like, a year ago."

Zian's brow knits. "You're only a year old?"

She motions to her curvaceous body as if putting herself on display. "We come the way we're always going to be. No growing up. We weren't there, and then we are."

"Like magic," Andreas says dryly.

Pearl claps her hands. "Yes. Just like that."

Billy ducks his head awkwardly, his face turning ruddy beneath his light brown complexion that's a lot like Dominic's. "I've been alive for longer than that. But I can't mingle with mortals when they'll notice these." He motions to his horns.

Jacob cocks his head. "Can't you just think them away like Rollick does with his claws?"

"Oh, no," Pearl says. "We can't leave our shadowkind selves behind completely. Everyone's got one thing that sticks."

She pushes up one fluttery sleeve of her dress to reveal a band of glittering gold that winds across the normal creamy skin. "It goes right across my chest to my other arm. But I can cover it up, or people think it's a strange tattoo."

"Some of us can hide our sticky features better than others," Billy says.

"Yeah." Pearl squints at all of us. "But you five don't seem to have any at all." She glances at Dominic. "Well, except for you, but you said those only grew in later. That's got to be a hybrid thing."

Footsteps rap across the polished wooden boards toward us.

"Keeping our guests entertained?" Rollick saunters over to our end of the deck with an amused expression.

Pearl grins at him. "Someone should with those grumps around."

The mention of the "grumps" brings back the knot in my stomach. I hesitate and then force out the question. "Why are some of them bothered by us? It seems like they're upset that you're helping us at all."

Rollick pauses before he answers, which makes all my nerves twinge with apprehension. He's trying to decide how to tell us something we won't want to hear.

"Our community, such as it is, has some… mixed feelings about hybrids," he says.

Zian glances down at his brawny frame. "They don't like that we're part human?"

"Not exactly." Rollick appears to weigh his words again before continuing. "None of us have much experience with beings like you. Honestly, before you showed up, I was only aware of three other hybrids in the entire length of my multi-millennia existence, and two of those were almost immediately snuffed out by our de facto rulers."

My body tenses. "They were *killed*?"

Rollick spreads his hands. "I'm sure it's difficult for you to understand from the inside. But to us, on the outside… You're the ultimate wild cards. You've already seen some of that. You have powers that can rival our own —in some cases, overwhelm most regular shadowkind— and none of the weaknesses that can keep us in check."

"We can't jump into the shadows like you," Jacob points out. "We can *die*."

I can tell from the edge in his voice that he's thinking of Griffin.

"Well, you may be able to do the former with some training. And we can die too, just with a fair bit of difficulty." Rollick offers us a crooked smile.

"So, they're… jealous of us?" I ask, still trying to wrap my head around where the resentment is coming from.

Rollick chuckles. "Maybe a little. But it's more that you're a threat. Past hybrids have proven difficult to control, as you yourselves are finding with your abilities. We don't know how destructive you might become— toward us, or toward mortals, which will draw attention to the rest of us."

Pearl nods, her voice dropping to an awed whisper. "They say the last hybrid nearly burned up the whole planet."

My jaw goes slack. "What?"

As my gaze slides to the grim figures watching at the other side of the deck, my spirits sink.

No wonder they're so hostile. No wonder we've seen signs of fear from even the powerful shadowkind.

We're an unknown quantity, and one that could screw them up and screw them over in ways they can't even prepare for.

We're lucky Rollick is sticking his neck out even this much.

My next question tumbles out, propelled by a sudden chill. "What do the others want you to do with us? Do they think you should kill *us* too?"

Rollick snorts. "Don't worry about that. *I* can see that you're not on the verge of burning up the whole world or anything so catastrophic." He gives me a meaningful look. "At least, as long as you give those powers more practice to make sure you have a grip on them."

As I squirm internally at his insinuation, he rubs his hands together. "In any case, Torrent has set off through the waters to head back to land. He'll make some inquiries along with other associates of mine to see if we can't track down these facilities your guardians are running."

Zian perks up. "We're going to go rescue the other shadowbloods?"

"We're going to see if that's a feasible course of action."

I should feel victorious. That was my idea, and Rollick is actually pursuing it.

But I can't shake the uneasy weight the conversation has placed on my shoulders.

He didn't say that the other shadowkind *don't* want us dead, only that we shouldn't worry they'll succeed in making it happen.

Is he the only thing standing between us and a total slaughter?

If the humans who made us think we're too dangerous to exist, and the shadowkind they've fought against feel the same way… where can we possibly belong?

Monsters exist, sure. And it turns out my guys and I are the only thing the monsters are scared of.

Twenty

Andreas

Rollick motions to the glasses in front of us. "All right, drink up!"

Across the small, glossy table from me, Riva studies the amber liquid. Her mouth slants at an uncertain angle.

I can't help remembering the only other time she's drunk anything alcoholic since we got out of the facility: that night at the dance club when a single cocktail went haywire with the poison Jacob had inflicted on her.

That was the night she pointed out her scars to me and told me how often she'd taken comfort in knowing we were still out there. When she asked me to dance and looked so downcast when I refused.

When she pulled me into a hug I couldn't resist, and I got to experience the full, unrestrained bliss of her embrace.

I should have known for sure then. Hell, I should have known from the start that she was telling the truth.

But instead I treated her like an enemy, schemed against her, and now here we are. Even if we didn't have a table standing between us, there'd be an invisible wall dividing us that I can't climb over.

I curl my fingers around my own glass. "It's weak stuff, right?"

Rollick chuckles. "It wouldn't be a very effective solution to have you stumbling around drunk. I just want to see if having a little interference with your normal mental state might disrupt the connection."

I raise the glass to my lips and gulp it down. The mix of sweet and sour flavors coat my tongue and send a pang through my gut.

Riva hesitates a few moments longer and then downs her own drink.

Only a faint tingle in the back of my skull suggests that I've got anything like a buzz. I could definitely handle operating on this incredibly mild level of tipsy for a while if it meant the guardians couldn't track us.

"You know the drill," Rollick says. "Riva, you leave this time. Andreas, you see if you can find her."

Riva rises from her seat and slips out of the room without a word—or a glance at me. My throat constricts.

But I can already tell that the alcohol hasn't dulled the bond between us even slightly. Her presence nibbles at my awareness from the spot on my sternum.

She's turned left down the hall. She's heading through a doorway into another room—I think that far down, it'd be the observation lounge.

I can sense her existence from under my skin, but I can't touch her. Not anymore.

"It isn't working," I say without even bothering to get up. "I can feel her just as well as ever."

Rollick rubs his chin. "I still think these marks and the connection between them could be the key. They're something that's specific to you shadowbloods."

He gets up. "Well, let's go collect her. Maybe I'll think of another tactic to try along the way."

The chef bustles out of the kitchen just then and sets a platter on the buffet table along the dining room wall. He seems to emerge every hour or two during the day with snacks, just in case anyone's hungry.

Pearl and Billy, who've been hanging on our every move through Rollick's tests, bound over to collect some of the delicate pastries on offer. I can't summon any enthusiasm in myself, but I catch myself as I turn toward the door and go back to pluck a few to set on a plate.

Riva isn't much of a dessert person, but I know she likes sour flavors, so she might appreciate this lemon tart. Or the mini-Danish topped with what looks like a blob of cranberry.

Rollick waits for me without remark.

"The observation room," I tell him as I walk to rejoin him, our little fan club hustling along behind me.

When we reach the observation room with its tall windows that offer a view both above and below the ocean surface, Riva is lounging on one of the cushioned benches. In my first glimpse of her gazing at the watery landscape, she looks almost relaxed.

Almost *happy*.

It's a crime how seldom I've gotten to see her like that in the past few weeks. A crime that she hasn't been able to *be* like that very often in those weeks.

And the way her expression tightens when she sees me walk into the room, her momentary joy falling away, is an outright atrocity. One I committed.

The gift I've brought seems pathetic now, but I walk over to her anyway. "The chef brought out some pastries. I figured these were the ones you'd like the most."

Riva takes the plate from me and sets it on the bench's armrest. She considers it for a moment.

"I'm not really hungry," she says in a slightly apologetic tone that I can't say I deserve.

I give an awkward laugh. "It's okay. I didn't want you to go without in case you were."

I haven't even gotten a flicker of a smile out of her. Nothing like the soft curving of her lips when Pearl and Billy come rushing down the aisle between the benches.

Billy presses his hands to the window and gapes at the fish flitting by. "There are so many mortal creatures even down here."

He did say he'd never been on a boat before. I guess he hadn't made it down to this room yet.

Pearl turns toward Riva with a pop of her succubus hips that I suppose a guy might find appealing if his entire heart wasn't tangled up with a different woman. "You like it in here, huh?"

Riva runs her fingers over the leather cushions. Her eyes widen as she glances around the room, awe brightening her face in a way that makes my pulse skip a beat.

"I like the whole ship. It's incredible… I feel like I've stepped into a movie or a TV show."

"Much better than underground prison cells, I'm sure," Rollick says with a grin. "Well, you can enjoy it at your leisure for a little while. I haven't come up with any brilliant new brainstorms quite yet."

Riva hesitates, and I can feel her—partly in her body language, but maybe I pick up a fragment of her emotions through our connection too—weighing her options. Deciding whether she'd rather stay here and watch the ocean life when I'm in the same room or go someplace where I'm not around.

An uncomfortable heat prickles up my neck. I open my mouth to say I'm heading back to my room, but before I can get any words out, she's already sprung to her feet.

"Speaking of TV, I haven't gotten to do any real channel surfing for most of my life, so I think I'll keep catching up on that."

She shoots another smile at the shadowkind around us, not quite aiming it at me, and slips away.

I watch her vanish through the doorway, my stomach clenching. When I tear my gaze away, Rollick is watching *me*.

"It can be rather difficult to win over a woman who sees you as a villain," he says in a mildly wry tone. "But it's not impossible. I know from personal experience."

Somehow I don't think the supernaturally handsome demon in front of me has faced quite the same challenges that I have with whatever love life he carries out, but I'll take the sympathy at face value anyway.

I exhale roughly. "It's my own fault. I just don't know how to make it up to her."

I don't know if I even can.

Rollick ambles toward the doorway. "I can't say it's a swift process or an easy one. You might have to reveal things about yourself that you're used to hiding. But if it's worth it, it's worth it."

As he heads off to who-knows-where, Pearl sashays over to me. "Maybe I can help! This boat has *everything*. There's got to be something around that would impress her."

I don't think impressing Riva is the key, but who knows? Maybe the succubus's cheerful commentary will jostle loose some brilliant brainstorm of my own.

Relationships are her specialty, after all. Well, a certain type, at least.

"All right," I say. "Let's see if I've missed anything."

We amble through the halls, making a circuit of the ship's many common rooms. Pearl natters on about Riva's eating habits—"I heard her ask if we have any extra lemons!"—and her disinterest in the library—"I don't blame her; words are a lot more boring than being someplace."

There's a spa area I hadn't stumbled on before, but I can't see Riva letting me pamper her in any way that involves putting my hands on her body.

We step into the party room where someone has lowered a mirror ball from the ceiling, and Pearl sets her hands on her hips. "Too bad she isn't much of a party girl."

The comment sets off an automatic twinge of

defiance in me. "Actually, she really likes music and dancing," I say. "But that could come with some bad memories too…"

I pause, gazing at the expansive room in front of me. An image floats up in the back of my mind of Riva's face rapt with awe like it was in the observation lounge—but years ago, tucked next of Griffin on the training-room sofa.

I feel like I've stepped into a movie or a TV show, she said today. And days ago, in the hotel room, she admitted to how much she loved that frothy soap opera Griffin would always arrange to put on for her.

The guys on that show were always screwing up and begging forgiveness. Maybe I can learn something from them.

The idea hits me in a bolt of inspiration, sizzling through my mind and knocking every other thought out of my head.

That could be perfect. It would be hard to pull off, and maybe it wouldn't do the trick, but I know her. I know—

Something inside me balks. Is that really the right direction?

If I pick something that personal, that specific to her —will she wonder if I've peeked inside her head with my talent? Invaded her privacy?

I swallow thickly, wavering between exhilaration and doubt.

Rollick said I might have to reveal things rather than hide them.

Riva knows I observe people all the time, that I remember all kinds of things about them. And doting on her in all the generic ways I can think of hasn't gotten me anywhere.

I have to try, don't I? I can't really fuck up any worse than I already have.

A little trepidation lingers, because I know it's not just her I'm going to have to win over but the other guys as well. First, though, I need to make sure my idea is possible to begin with.

"I think I've got something," I say to Pearl. "Do you have any idea where Rollick is?"

Her eyes flash with excitement. "I can find him!"

The next second, she's leapt into the shadows.

Billy, who's trailed behind us simply taking in the conversation, peers around the party room. "You're going to try to make Riva happy?"

"Yeah. I mean, it's a little more complicated than that, but… basically."

He offers me a small but genuine smile. "I don't know much about mortal parties, but I do know music. If you need any help. It comes with the whole faun thing." He motions to his horns.

An unexpected flicker of friendly warmth passes through me. I don't totally trust the shadowkind, but I'll take them over the guardians any day.

"Thanks," I say. "Let me think about this—if I can even get this idea off the ground."

Pearl hasn't returned yet, so I venture down the hall, not sure where I should head now. But I've only made it past a few doorways before the succubus blinks back into sight—with the demon right beside her.

Rollick arches his eyebrows. "Apparently there's some incredibly urgent matter you need to speak to me about."

I wince inwardly. "Sorry. It's not that urgent. But, since you're here now… Would you let me use the party room for something tomorrow night? And I'd need some supplies. I don't know how easy that'll be while we're at sea."

"I was already planning on docking tomorrow morning, just briefly, for other reasons. Give me a list, and there's very little I can't obtain. And I have no plans for any parties, so the room is up for grabs."

My heart leaps with more hope than I've felt in ages. "Great. Thank you. I'll get on with making that list."

"This is about Riva?" he asks.

I hesitate. "Is that a problem?"

The demon aims a crooked grin at me. "Not at all. I happen to think it's better for all of us if your little banshee-of-sorts found herself some more peace. See what you can do about that all you like."

He vanishes, leaving me with an uneasy knot in my gut. Why does he think it's better for *everyone*?

But then, he does seem to enjoy making vaguely ominous comments for his own amusement.

I hurry toward the residential quarters, my nerves twanging with both eagerness and uncertainty. The sound of voices from the games room draws me up short.

The other three guys are gathered around the pool table there, Jacob motioning from the cue ball to one of the others.

"You're supposed to hit it *into* that ball."

Zian frowns. "That seems like a pretty stupid way of doing things."

"Jake's right—those are the usual rules," Dominic says from where he's standing off to the side, studying the rack of cues. "But nothing says we couldn't make up our own."

They all fall silent when I stride into the room. Jacob's expression tightens.

"Training is all done for the day?" he asks.

"For now." I barrel onward before I can think better of the proposal I'm about to make—and how they might feel about it. "I need your help—I want us to do something for Riva. Something… big."

Twenty-One

Riva

I know before they even knock that Andreas and Dominic have come up to my bedroom door together. Their arrival sends two tiny pulses of awareness through the marks along my clavicle.

A strange mix of joy and apprehension tangles inside me as I reach for the door handle. I'm about to see one guy who makes my spirits lift and one who sets off painful pangs of memory.

And I'm tied to them both. Forever, probably.

I ease the door open and peer outside. A faint vibration runs through the floor under my feet—the yacht is cruising again after stopping at a harbor for a couple of hours this morning.

Both of the guys look at me with matching expressions of hopeful anticipation. Andreas is holding a large bundle wrapped in white tissue paper.

Dominic beams at me. "We've set something up for

you. Really, Drey did, but we're all helping. We thought we might as well enjoy everything we've got on the ship while we're here."

"And we haven't really taken a moment to celebrate our freedom properly," Andreas adds, more hesitantly. "It's because of you we had the chance to escape the facility when we did. I don't know that we'd ever have made it all the way without your help. We definitely wouldn't have made it out of Engel's house alive. So, you're the guest of honor."

I open my mouth and close it again, my words startled out of me. Before I can figure out what to say, Andreas holds the bundle out to me.

"I wasn't sure what you'd like best, so I picked out a few options. I hope you'll change into one of them, but it's totally up to you. Dom will bring you to the party. You can ignore the rest of us the whole time if you'd prefer that, but I hope you'll come."

I accept the bundle, finding it soft and yielding like cloth. My nerves jitter with a mix of uncertainty and curiosity. "What exactly did you set up?"

A smile touches Andreas's lips for the first time with a hint of mischief that makes my heart ache. I've missed his playful side—missed being able to take it at face value.

"You'll see," he says mysteriously, and slips away down the hall.

Dominic holds my gaze, reaching out to give my forearm a gentle squeeze. "I think you should come. And I wouldn't say that unless I was sure."

My mouth twists. "I don't think a party is going to make up for everything."

"I know. That's not how Andreas sees it." Dom pauses. "He did speak up for you before that night, you know. In the train, while you were napping. He tried to convince Jacob and the rest of us that you were on our side and we should stop treating you like an enemy. None of us totally listened. That's on us. On me. *I* could have agreed with him and argued for you too, and maybe—"

So much anguish has crept into his voice that I can't bear to let him keep going. I step closer, leaning into him, and his arm rises to encircle me automatically.

"*You* didn't lie to me or manipulate me," I murmur against his chest. "I'm not happy about how things were back then, but you never pretended to feel anything you didn't. It's different."

Dominic swallows audibly and brushes a kiss to the top of my head. "I know. I'm just saying, when you and he —when you were with him that night—I don't think he was lying at all by that point either."

I'm sure Dom wants to believe that. Andreas is his friend—the four of them had only each other for the years after Griffin died and I was gone.

But the sharp words that greeted me when I followed him after we slept together ring through my memory, still painfully vivid. *The whole reason I started getting cozy with her was so she'd open up...*

He was saying that even after. Talking about the deal he had with Jacob.

It didn't sound like it was totally over.

"Just come," Dominic says gently. "I think it'll make things a little more right. It isn't about forgiving him—he's not going to make any demands, I promise."

I let out a soft huff and straighten up. "All right. But only because *you* asked me to."

Dom's smile soothes my uneasiness. "Thank you. Now I've got to go get changed too."

As he vanishes into his own room, I carry the bundle over to the bed, more puzzled than ever. I tear open the tissue paper and paw apart the three clumps of folded fabric inside.

They're dresses. Fancy evening gowns, leagues beyond anything I've ever worn before.

I hold them up one by one, staring at them. Then I drape them against myself as I consider my reflection in the wardrobe's full-length mirror.

Sleek black silk, so glossy I can almost see my reflection in *it*, tumbles down my frame from spaghetti straps.

Dark green lace flows into a princess skirt like an explosion of forest leaves.

A mesh neckline meets a pale blue bodice with a rippling waterfall of chiffon beneath.

They're all beautiful. They're all completely separate from anything I ever imagined my life could contain.

I linger over them, running my fingertips over the smooth fabric. I still don't know what Andreas is up to, but I told Dominic I'd give it a shot.

And I can't deny that excitement shivers through me at the thought of putting on one of those gowns. Seeing myself transformed into the kind of person who *would* belong in a life like that, if only in appearance.

Finally, I settle on the pale blue dress. It's the lightest and the most flexible to move in.

And when I tug at the folds, I discover pockets hidden in the chiffon skirt. I know where my knives are going.

Just because I'm getting dressed up doesn't mean I'm throwing caution to the wind. We've been attacked when we least expected it before.

Anyway, maybe I'm going to end up wanting to stab Andreas. Might as well be prepared.

I shimmy into the dress, which falls all the way to my ankles. To my relief, the solid part of the bodice covers my cleavage, only my shoulders and collarbone revealed through the mesh.

My two shadow marks show through the transparent fabric, one on either side.

The silver chain of my cat-and-yarn pendant dangles between them. The necklace doesn't exactly fit the elegance of the dress, but I can't imagine taking it off any more than I could erase those marks.

I'm just turning toward the door when Pearl materializes out of thin air right in front of it. A yelp of surprise bursts from my lips.

Pearl cringes with embarrassment. "Sorry, sorry, I forgot, I should have started outside and knocked. I can try again and—"

"No," I interrupt. "It's okay. You're here now. What's going on?"

"I'm helping!" She flashes a smile and holds out a pair of gray ballet-style dress shoes. "You picked a good dress. It makes your eyes look more gold."

Considering she goes around wearing cocktail dresses as casual wear, her approval feels reassuring. "I'm glad you like it."

"I can do something fancy with your hair too. If you want."

My gaze veers back to the mirror. My usual braid, slightly rumpled at the moment, doesn't really fit the elegant clothes.

"Are you a hairdresser now too?" I ask with a little wryness.

Pearl laughs. "I'm good at beauty stuff. Seems to be part of the succubus skillset. I can make it pretty but not too fussy. You'd like that, right?"

I exhale slowly. "Yeah, that sounds about my speed."

Pearl really must have some kind of cosmetician magic, because in the space of a few minutes, she's unwound my hair and fixed it into a swooping coil across my head with a few waves drifting down on one side. Not how I've ever pictured it, but looking at my reflection, I could almost believe I *am* someone else.

Pearl rubs her hands together in excitement. "I'll go tell the guys you're ready."

She vanishes again without bothering with the door.

I wiggle my toes into the shoes, which have enough give to fit my feet comfortably. No heels, which is probably for the best.

The next arrival does knock. I square my shoulders and answer the door.

Dominic is waiting on the other side again, but he couldn't look more different either. He's wearing a fancy suit with a collared shirt underneath, a bulge on the back showing where it covers his tentacles. His auburn hair is smoothed back in the neatest of ponytails, and his eyes are gleaming.

He looks absolutely dashing. I think I might be drooling.

It takes me a moment to shake myself out of the initial daze and realize he's awestruck too. A hint of a flush colors his light brown skin.

"You're even more gorgeous than usual," he says.

There's so much admiration in his voice, my nerves quiver with it.

He holds out his arm, and I take his elbow, pretending to be the people we look like now. As he leads me down the hall, I glance at the other bedroom doors, but they're all closed.

Dominic rests his hand over mine. "Everyone else is already there."

I open my mouth to ask where, but right then the first strains of music reach my ears. Not the thumping of club music that surrounded us in Miami, but lilting notes that suggest a more elegant sort of dance to fit our new getup.

Dominic directs me through the doorway of what Rollick called the party room. Which I guess makes sense, because Andreas called this a party.

But it's nothing like I'd have expected.

The room has transformed. Jewel-like lights twinkle across the ceiling. Swaths of gauze in reds, purples, and pinks cover the walls.

In one corner, a mahogany table holds several champagne glasses and a selection of bottles. Another farther into the room offers trays of delicate hors d'oeuvres.

And in the middle of it all, under the shifting light

that reflects off the central mirror ball, my other three guys are waiting.

Zian stands awkwardly in his suit like he isn't quite sure how to wear it, but holy hell, does his brawny form fill it out well. Jacob looks coolly handsome as ever in his own.

And then there's Andreas. Dressed to the nines and with his normally loose coils slicked close to his head, he's outright devastating.

All three of them tense up at my first steps into the room.

Zian's eyes widen.

Jacob's expression goes totally rigid, his hands balling at his sides.

Andreas gazes at me so avidly I feel the tingle of his attention through our marks. His throat bobs as he swallows.

I can't stop myself from folding my arms across my chest, self-conscious. "I—I don't get it. You just wanted us to dress up?"

Andreas motions to the room around us. "I wanted to make it like something out of your favorite TV show. They were always going to fancy soirees and things. I thought you should get to have something like that in real life—as close as I can give you."

That's why this scene feels so familiar—it's like a moment out of the soap opera.

A nervous giggle bubbles at the base of my throat. "What do we do now?"

Andreas shrugs. "Eat. Drink. Dance. Whatever you

want. Rollick said we can have the room for the whole evening."

"Back to tests and practice tomorrow," Zian puts in with a faint grimace.

My insides have gone all wobbly. I'm off-balance but thrilled at the same time.

For just this moment, we don't have to be fugitives or monsters or anything other than people at a party. Like we don't have any problems bigger than who's been making eyes at whom.

I turn toward Dominic with a smile. "Let's dance, then."

I don't actually know how to dance with a partner to this refined music, but it turns out that's okay. Dom sets one hand on my waist and takes one of mine with the other, I rest my fingers on his shoulder, and we drift around the room under the lights, stepping in time with the melody in slow circles.

My grip on his hand tightens as one song fades into the next. "I can dance with just you the whole time, right?"

Dominic leans in to give me a quick peck on the lips. "Whatever you want."

I steal glances at the other guys as we continue our swaying path around the room. They're doing a good job of at least acting like they don't mind being here.

Jacob has poured himself a glass of one of the champagnes, though I can't tell if he's actually drinking it. Zian plucks up the meatiest appetizers from the spread.

And Andreas leans against the wall in a casual pose, watching all of us like I used to watch the TV.

Like he isn't totally part of this scene he arranged.

After the first couple of songs, Billy materializes in the corner. He raises a pan flute to his lips and adds an accompaniment to the music that lifts my feet faster.

My mouth twitches with amusement. I tug at Dominic, and he takes that as his cue to spin me in front of him.

My skirt fans out. My heart lifts.

There's plenty of magic in this moment without the work of any supernatural powers at all.

The faun gives the next few songs a spirited extra melody. Then Pearl appears and draws him over to fill out more of the dance floor.

They beam at the décor and the rest of us as if this is a gift to them too—a little piece of mortal life they're getting to try out. My own smile widens.

It's been a while since lunch. When my stomach grumbles, I ease back from Dominic and wander over to the snacks table.

Zian glances up at me. His gaze skims over my body in the dress, and a whiff of attraction rolls off him potent enough to make my cheeks blaze.

He takes a step back as if realizing his appreciation is obvious—and potentially intimidating. I come to a careful stop and pick up a morsel that looks tasty, letting him have his space.

"Are you planning on doing any dancing?" I ask him before popping it into my mouth.

Zian's jaw works. "I—I don't think that's a good idea."

My stomach tightens, even though I should have expected his answer. "It doesn't have to mean anything."

He glances at the floor and then back at me, oddly tentative. His voice comes out gruff.

"It would, though. And I don't know— I like watching you with Dom. It's good seeing you happy. You should keep dancing with him."

It's the weirdest rebuff I've ever heard. I don't think even my soap opera heroines would have known how to answer him.

So it might almost be a good thing that Jacob approaches just then, with a wary air that's offset by his usual aura of authority.

"If you're looking to mix things up," he starts, and then hesitates as if he's not sure how to finish that sentence. He sucks in a breath. "I'd be happy to dance. We wouldn't have to get too close if you still feel uncomfortable. You call all the shots."

The way he's looking at me sets every inch of my skin tingling, but I don't want to explore the feeling. I don't want to let it cloud my memories of how he treated me before even a little.

"I'd rather not," I say awkwardly. "But, um, thank you."

Jacob dips his head in acknowledgment with a flicker of regret I can't help noticing. "It's a lovely dress," he says, the compliment coming out stiffly. "But it doesn't hold a candle to the woman in it."

My pulse flutters despite my reservations.

How do I respond to that either? I'm not going to tell him he looks stunningly gorgeous as always.

Dominic saves me, tucking his arm around my waist

and tugging me back onto the dance floor. I bow my head by his chin, my voice dropping.

"I don't know how to do this. I don't know—"

"It's okay," he murmurs. "No one is expecting anything. It might be hard to believe it after everything, but we really all just want you to enjoy yourself."

Enjoyment isn't something I really got to expect from most of my life. But for another song or two, sticking close to Dominic and following the rise and fall of the melody, maybe I do manage it.

Then Dominic lifts his head and draws me into the center of the room. I realize that Pearl and Billy have disappeared.

Maybe to give us our privacy. Because as Dom eases away, Andreas walks over to meet me.

"I don't really want to dance with you either," I blurt out, and bite my tongue at my bluntness. As true as that might be, I'm also not out to hurt him.

Andreas's expression twitches with what might have been a restrained wince. But his mouth forms a crooked smile.

"That's not what I came over for. I didn't just set this up so you could have a soap-opera party. I figured I deserve a soap-opera showdown too."

TWENTY-TWO

Riva

I blink at Andreas, totally confused. A soap-opera showdown?

"What are you talking about?"

Andreas gazes steadily back at me, his dark gray eyes stealing my breath. "The characters were always confronting each other and letting out their grievances. A lot of times in places like this."

The corner of his mouth ticks a little higher. "I'm sure there are tons of things you could say to me that you've held back because... because that's who you are. But you can let them out. You can tell me just how pissed off you are with me. Yell at me. Slap me. Knee me in the balls. I deserve all of it. Lay in to me. It's the best moment I could give you to say your piece."

I know exactly the kind of moments he's talking about. I've seen them play out on the TV screen so many times.

Back then, I never dreamed that I'd be in a position where I'd have a similar tirade I could aim at one of my guys.

My gaze flits to the other three men standing around the edges of the room. They're all following our conversation but without any sign of considering intervening.

Andreas clears his throat. "They should hear this too. I'm not going to hide how badly I screwed up."

He sinks down onto his knees in front of me, so that I'm looking down at him rather than the reverse. My throat constricts.

There is so much pain and anger still churning inside me. The sense of betrayal aches like a wound that's never properly healed.

Maybe I do need this.

"You lied to me," I say in a rasp, trying out the accusation.

Andreas nods. "I did, and I shouldn't have."

He doesn't let his gaze waver from mine. Tears prickle behind my eyes.

My voice rises. "You pretended that you cared about me. You made me believe that I could trust you. And the whole time you were waiting for me to give away some awful secret for you to report back to the other guys."

My hands clench. I don't want to hit him, not even in anger.

I have none of the same qualms about shouting. It feels good hurling the complaints at him—a release without the nauseating horror I'm capable of at full rage.

The flesh-rending kind of shriek doesn't prod at me at

all. The monster inside me knows this anger isn't about dealing out hurt but holding my own up as a banner.

"You came to me and acted so sweet. You let me open up to you completely—we shared something I'd never shared with *anyone*—and the whole time—it never would have happened—I never would have let you even *kiss* me if I'd had any idea why you'd been nice to me!"

"It's the shittiest thing I've ever done to anyone," Andreas says, his voice as strained as his agonized face. "I'm not going to make any excuses. I was so fucking wrong, and I wish I could go back and pummel some sense into me."

But as the words come out, I realize that I want more. I don't want him to justify what he did, but I need some kind of explanation.

"Why?" I say, abruptly choking up. "Why would you do that to me, after everything we'd been through before, after— How could you treat me like that?"

Andreas tenses. "Riva, I don't even want to try to say it makes sense—"

"But it did," I break in. "When it was happening, you thought you were right. Make me understand."

The last sentence reverberates through the air with the firmness of a command.

A shadow crosses Andreas's face, but he keeps gazing up at me. "I—I don't know if you'll understand. But I can tell you everything along the way."

I set my hands on my hips, the smooth fabric crinkling under my fingers. Resolve steadies me. "Fine. Do that. You're always telling stories about things from the past—make this one of them."

Andreas stares at me for a moment. Then he inhales slowly.

"You already saw how it started. The video the guardians showed us, making it seem like you knew Griffin would be killed, like you'd made a deal with them."

"The one they faked."

"We didn't know that. We should have, but we were freaked out and we'd just watched Griffin *die* and you never came back... They were always reminding us how you'd turned on us, rubbing salt into the wound, and with everything else they put us through, there wasn't a whole lot of time to step back and really think."

Andreas tears his eyes away from me for a second before dragging them back. "There were times when I wondered if it could really be true. But I thought if they'd made it up somehow, then you had to be dead too. Maybe some part of me would rather think you'd betrayed us but were still living out there somewhere than that you were gone forever."

The raw note in his voice makes my eyes burn hotter. "And then I did come back. I came back to save you."

"I don't know how to explain it," Andreas says, more ragged by the second. "I'd spent four years believing you were a traitor. You seemed distant. I could tell there was something you weren't telling us, even after you started opening up. I only made the deal with Jacob because the alternative was not even trying to find out what was true —and it was something I could do. A way I could make sure the other guys were safe. I've been trying so hard for so long to keep everyone from falling apart..."

He trails off.

I resist the urge to grit my teeth. "You let me fall apart."

"I didn't mean to. I didn't— the more time I spent with you, the more I was convinced that you were telling the truth, that you'd come to break us out and you wanted to protect us. But I couldn't get the other guys to believe it. And there was still that thing you were keeping quiet about… I had no idea it was only that you'd kissed Griffin."

I remember with a queasy lurch of my gut how nervous I was when I finally admitted that to him.

But he'd already known all along from the video. That much of the recording was real.

"I did tell you," I said. "When I thought I could trust you."

"And I was so relieved it wasn't anything else. That you were exactly the woman you'd always been. I thought everything was going to be okay."

A shudder runs through my body. "You thought it was okay to fuck me."

Andreas can't suppress his wince at my harsh phrasing. His head droops.

"You were still the woman I'd always loved, and you loved me too, and when I was wrapped up in the moment, it felt like that was all that mattered. And after I came out of the daze, all that seemed to matter next was making sure the other guys knew we'd been wrong so I could fix everything else. I didn't know you'd follow me—that you'd hear…"

"Were you ever going to tell me if I hadn't?" I have to ask.

"Yes," Andreas says hoarsely. "I'd already realized I was going to have to while I was walking upstairs to talk to the guys. But it was more important to deal with them first. I guess I don't have any proof that I definitely would have in the end."

He raises his head again and meets my eyes. "No matter what I do to make up for it, I know there's no way to simply fix how I screwed things up. But I will keep trying. For the rest of our lives, if that's what it takes. I'll go to my grave trying and not regret anything but the fact that I fucked up so horribly in the first place. I've loved you my whole life so far, and I'll love you for the rest of it, even if you spend the rest of yours hating me."

The truth of those words rings through his voice—and resonates through the mark on my chest. He means it, every bit of that statement.

And I don't hate him. Even at my angriest and most hurt, I've never hated him.

I'm not sure I'm even angry at him anymore after his confession. I can follow the road he went down without all that much difficulty.

The guardians screwed all of us over. They messed with our heads and battered our spirits.

They broke us in so many ways and put together the pieces badly.

How many mistakes have I made?

All he wanted to know was the truth. So he could be sure, for the guys he'd do anything to protect.

I *can* understand that.

But even as my shoulders start to relax, a thread of

tension remains wound around my stomach. That echo of his voice wavers through my mind again.

The whole reason I started getting cozy with her was so she'd open up…

I have to know the whole truth too.

"Okay," I said quietly. "I want one more thing."

"Name it."

"I want you to show me your memory of everything that happened from when you left me in the farmhouse to when I caught you talking with Jacob."

A flicker of surprise races through Andreas's expression. Before he can speak, Jacob lets out a rough sound from where he's standing near the snack table.

My attention jerks to the other guy. "What?" A prickle of renewed irritation climbs my spine. "Are you worried it'll make *you* look even worse?"

Jacob swipes his hand across his mouth. His face hardens, but he answers evenly enough.

"I know it will. But that's my fault."

At least he can admit that much.

I tug my gaze back to Andreas. He nods. "Whenever you're ready."

Last time, when he showed me what they experienced after our first escape attempt, he suggested I sit down first. I lower myself to the floor and brace my hands on either side of me.

"Go ahead."

Drey's eyes shine crimson, and all at once I'm back in the basement.

I'm back, but not as myself. My silver-steaked hair, the

stuff that made Griffin call me Moonbeam, unfurls across a blanket beneath my new view.

It's Andreas's eyes I'm looking through this time. Andreas's arms wrapped around a much slimmer, smaller body than his own.

Andreas's body tensing in the moment before he tells me he needs to go talk to Jacob.

I think I know why he started the memory here. Because while I can't read his emotions in the memory, I can feel the way he resisted releasing his hold on me.

He didn't want to let me go. He didn't want to leave me.

But he pushes himself swiftly up the stairs with an air of determination that radiates through his body. He walks straight to the room where Jacob is sitting on the floor by the window and stops on the threshold.

"We need to talk about Riva."

The Jacob of weeks ago answers Drey with the same coolly dispassionate tone he used so often back then. "I told you on the train. We'll revisit that subject *after* we've gotten whatever we can from Engel."

As I watch from within, Andreas marches right into the room with a shake of his head. "No. All the venom— in every form—needs to stop now. It shouldn't have gone on for even this long."

Jacob's icy gaze turns into a glower. I can see why he didn't love the idea of me revisiting this conversation.

"It isn't up to you," he snaps. "You don't get to make the call."

Andreas crosses his arms in front of him. "You're not in charge here either. We're in this together—isn't that how it's supposed to go? You're not always right, Jake, and this one time you're incredibly wrong."

"I guess you can make your case once everyone's awake. In the meantime—"

Before Jacob can finish his dismissal, Zian and Dominic appear in the doorway.

Zian swipes at his bleary eyes. "We're awake. What's going on?"

Andreas turns to them with a sense of urgency winding through his limbs. "We've been wrong about Riva. I got the whole story out of her, and she hasn't lied at all. She didn't turn on us even a little bit."

I can't deny how emphatically he says the words, how strongly he clearly feels about making that statement. It's etched into the memory.

He was sure. He wanted to make things right.

Zian knits his brow and goes to sit on the edge of the bed. "But we saw—"

Andreas's tone turns terse with frustration. "I know what we saw. It's what made even *me* treat her like shit when we should have been welcoming her back. But they must have faked it—we should have realized that."

Dominic frowns from the doorway. "It looked awfully real."

Jacob's sneering voice would make me flinch if I were in my own body. "Drey just *wants* to think it was fake so he can feel better about getting cozy with the traitor."

Fresh tension tremors through Andreas's body.

"She's not a traitor," he retorts. "You think you're so smart, Jake. Do you really figure the people running the facility are skilled enough to genetically engineer us into whatever the hell we are, but they couldn't handle doctoring a minute of video footage?"

"I figure there was no reason for them to bother."

"No reason? How about giving us someone to be angry at other than the guardians—who're the ones who actually killed Griffin? How about adding that little sliver of doubt about whether we can trust even each other to try to deflect another escape attempt? The second part didn't work, but the first sure as hell did."

The part of me I'm still aware of within Andreas's mind starts to ache with the vehemence in his voice. I missed all this—I had no idea how hard he fought for me.

"You don't *know*," Jacob shoots back. "You've bought into her victim routine and now you want an excuse to make that okay."

Andreas clenches his jaw. "Do you even listen to yourself? We *did* know Riva. She was one of us, right there with us through all the shit they put us through, and she has been since she came back too. Why the fuck we ever trusted what the guardians showed us over what we'd seen our whole lives—that's the crazy part."

"I planned out every part of that escape down to the minute. We didn't let a hint of it slip. How else could they have known to be waiting for us like that?"

"Oh, so that's what this is really about. You can't admit that you might have slipped up somewhere, or that maybe you simply weren't quite as brilliant as you'd like to be."

Jacob pushes to his feet. "It's not about me at all. It's about Griffin, who's dead, because she—"

"She *loved* Griffin," Andreas interrupts. "Which you

wouldn't doubt at all if you ever bothered to listen to her instead of the angry story you've built up in your head."

Jacob's face flushes with fury. "And I suppose she told you that she loves you too, huh?"

Andreas's voice doesn't waver in its confidence for an instant. "She loves all of us. Or she did, anyway, but it seems like she could still love even you in spite of what an asshole you've been to her if you got your head on straight."

Oh, Drey. I want to cry and I want to hug him, and a million other clashing desires.

Jacob practically sputters. "What a stupid fucking fairytale. And you believe all this bullshit she's been spouting, huh?"

"Yes," Andreas says firmly, "I do. Because I've been watching her and listening to her for days, and everything adds up to it being true. In case you've forgotten, the whole reason I started 'getting cozy' with her was so she'd open up about things she wouldn't have told us otherwise. I held up my end of the deal. Now you've got to listen."

The words don't strike the same chill in me hearing them now. He was using them as a club to smack Jacob into accepting his argument, nothing more.

The last painful shards that were still digging into me melt away.

I'm not happy about what Andreas did or the choices he made when we first reunited. But he wasn't scheming against me up until the end.

He really had realized his mistake, and he was fighting tooth and claw to correct the whole group's course the best way he knew how.

In the memory, Andreas's gaze has jerked toward the doorway where that past me has appeared, sickly pale and braced defensively. Then, with a hitch of my senses, I'm falling back into my own head, faced with Drey's worried eyes here in the present.

For the first few seconds, I can only stare back at him. My innards feel so jumbled up it's a wonder I'm still breathing.

Then I reach out my hand and touch his cheek.

Andreas closes his eyes at the tentative caress. A glint of a tear seeps out from beneath one lid.

"You've got it, Tink," he murmurs. "You've got all of me."

The armor I've built up must have cracked, because the declaration sinks right into me. And I believe him.

I stroke my thumb across his cheekbone. Then I stand up on wobbly legs, not entirely sure what happens next, but knowing this is my story now.

My soap opera. My melodrama.

I might still be hurting, but I can feel more than that. I want to *be* more than that.

I tug Andreas up by the collar of his dress shirt. He peers at me, uncertain.

The lilting music is still winding around us. So I say, "Dance with me."

TWENTY-THREE

Riva

Dancing with Andreas is the strangest feeling. Like a war is being waged inside me.

The mark he gave me tickles eagerly. My nerves clamor to push closer against him.

My muscles tense in resistance, not ready to let go of the wariness I've held on to for so long.

He's tense too, holding himself a careful distance away from me, never stepping any nearer. One of his hands rests on my waist so lightly I can barely feel the pressure.

The warmth of it blooms across my skin anyway.

His fingers twine loosely with mine, leaving the way open for me to pull away if I need to. As we turn in a slow circle with the elegant tune, he gazes down at me.

No red sheen colors his eyes now. I think he's watching for the slightest sign that I've changed my mind, that he's overstayed his welcome.

The silence between us starts to weigh on me.

"I liked all of the dresses," I tell him. "It was hard to pick. This one just felt the most right for how I'm feeling at the moment."

A hint of a smile touches his lips. "I'm glad. It was hard to know—I don't think I've ever seen you in any dress. Or with your hair up like that. Was that Pearl's idea?"

I laugh awkwardly. "I just let her do whatever she wanted."

"She did a good job. You look stunning. I could hardly breathe when you first walked in." He pauses, and his voice dips. "I can hardly breathe now."

I squeeze his hand instinctively and hear him swallow. "I don't know... I don't know if I totally forgive you yet. There are pieces of me that still hurt. They might for a long time."

"That's okay," Andreas says quickly. "I wasn't pushing for anything. I just—doing this was the only thing I could think of that came close to showing you how much you mean to me."

A lump rises in my throat. "I like the party a lot too."

His lips curve into a clearer smile. "Good. That's what matters the most."

Behind the anguish and the fear that I'll pull away after all, I can see the boy he used to be in his face. The Drey who'd always have a wry remark to break through a tense moment and a story to tell to lift us out of darker thoughts.

He had four years to marinate in the lies about me. To watch his friends struggling with their new talents and their grief, unable to help them.

Would I really have held on to my faith in my guys if the guardians had told me a similar story before they'd shipped me off? If they'd claimed that Griffin and I had been caught because one of the others had turned on us?

I don't really know. I'd like to say I would have, but I wouldn't have thought I could slaughter an entire arena of strangers either.

The truth is, I want to forgive Andreas. I want to sink into the sense that we belong together, that we'll stand by each other, and leave the pain behind.

It might not be the smoothest road, but I can start that journey now. I don't have to completely forgive him for the past to trust his devotion to me in the present.

With our next rotation, I ease half a step closer. Andreas's head dips with a shaky exhalation, his breath tickling over my forehead.

My gaze drifts away from him for just a moment—and snags on Jacob still poised by the snacks table.

Poised is absolutely the word for it. Every muscle in his body looks coiled with tension, ready to spring—whether to tear me and Andreas apart or to climb the walls in frustration, it's hard to tell from his taut expression.

And in that moment, taking in the chiseled planes of his face, I remember more of the conversation when I discovered Andreas's betrayal.

With every word after I made it to their room, Jacob jabbed the knife in deeper and twisted it. He *knew* everything I only just saw in Andreas's memory—he knew how adamantly Drey had fought for me and believed in me.

And even then, he did everything possible to convince

me that the other guy was only playing at caring about me.

He's very good at it, isn't he? Got you to let your hair down and everything.

Then to Andreas, in front of me: *You can stop now. I can't see how you'll get anything more out of her than you already have.*

My feet stall in mid-turn. Andreas freezes, but the anger gripping my body now has nothing to do with him.

I spin toward Jacob. "*You* lied to me. You knew Drey was sure I hadn't done anything wrong, that he wasn't trying to mess with me anymore, but you talked like he was still using me."

How much of the pain tangled with my memories of Andreas are because of what he actually did, and how much is the wrenching sense of betrayal provoked by Jacob's jabs?

Whatever color Jacob's face contained drains from it. Somehow his stance goes even more rigid.

I half expect him to deny my accusation, but he squares his shoulders as if accepting a blow.

"I'm sorry," he says in a voice as tight as his expression. "I thought—I was pissed off—it was a shitty thing to do. You can come at me too if you want to. I deserve it a hell of a lot more than Drey did."

My fingers curl toward my palms, but from beneath the anger comes a twang of resistance.

I could yell at Jacob for the rest of the day and still not be finished letting out all my grievances. For just a little while with Andreas, I was starting to feel almost okay.

I don't want to ruin this moment that wasn't Jacob's anyway, by delving into all that pain too.

"I don't even want to *think* about you," I reply in a voice so flat and cold it could rival him at his worst, and turn back to Andreas.

Bobbing up on my toes, I sling my arms around Drey's neck and tug his mouth down to meet mine.

Am I aware that this move is guaranteed to twist the knife *I* just stabbed into Jacob? Hell yes, I am.

But the longing to get close to the man my body already claimed has been coursing through my veins for days, even if my broken heart has overridden the hunger. And the second our mouths collide, my desire is the only thing that matters.

Andreas lets out a soft, choked sound and hugs me to him tightly. Our lips meld together with a familiar electric thrill.

Every cell in me sings out with joy.

I've missed this man, I've craved him, and now he's back where he's meant to be.

The wave of emotion isn't as intense as the first time we collided. An ache to resolidify our connection completely forms between my legs, but I'm not going to hump the guy right here on the dance floor.

No matter what happened after the first time, his touch still makes me feel giddily alive in ways nothing else can.

But not no *one* else.

A nervous chill flickers through my nerves, and I draw back just far enough to seek out a different pair of watching eyes. I find Dominic where he's drifted over to the far wall.

I brace myself for anger or disappointment in his expression, but the moment I catch his gaze, he smiles. A broad, open smile, as if nothing could make him happier than seeing me reestablish my bond with his friend.

Unexpected tears flood my eyes. I clasp Andreas's fingers with one hand and hold the other out to Dominic to beckon him over.

Andreas stands with a relaxed posture as Dom comes to join us. I grip Drey's hand and tease my fingers down Dominic's lean chest.

"This is my party, right? I want to dance with both of you."

Dominic lets out a soft chuckle and sets a hand on my hip.

Andreas grins down at me, his eyes gleaming with affection. "What you want, you get, Tink."

Club music would work better for this kind of collaboration, but we can make it work.

I close my eyes and tune into the subtle rhythm beneath the melody. Sway my body from side to side with the dips and swells.

As I revolve between them, the guys follow my lead, turning with me.

Dom trails both his hands up my sides to my ribs and then down to my thighs. He leans in to press a kiss to my shoulder from behind.

Andreas shimmies a little one way and then the other, always staying in front of me. His thumb strokes over my knuckles while his other hand slips around the back of my neck.

I'm caught between the two of them, but I don't feel remotely trapped. They're the fuel to my fire, and feeding on both of them makes it burn even brighter.

I don't give a shit that the other two guys are watching. They picked their own paths away from me.

And if the shadowkind are peering at us from the shadows—let them stare if they want to.

I tip my head back against Dominic's chest and feel the faint hitch of his breath. His groin brushes my ass with a hardness that sends my hunger spiking higher.

There are some things I don't want an audience for. Things I want to share with just the two men who've marked me—and who've welcomed my mark in turn.

I caress the line of Dom's jaw and then reach to grasp the few coils that have swung free at the sides of Andreas's face. "I love the party you made for me, but I think I'd like to move on to a different kind of celebration."

Drey's voice comes out in a low rasp. "What did you have in mind?"

I draw his face closer to mine and speak so only he and Dominic can hear me. "Take me to my bedroom."

"Fuck," Dom mutters, and buries his face in the crook of my neck. The nip of his teeth against the sensitive skin there brings a gasp to my lips.

Andreas's gaze sears into mine as if he's searching for any fragment of doubt there. When he doesn't find it, he pulls me by the hand toward the doorway.

"I think the other guys will figure out the party's over."

A momentary twinge passes through me at the

thought of Zian—but he didn't even want to *dance* with me. He doesn't owe me anything, but surely I don't owe him anything either?

And Jacob can go suck rocks.

I'm barely aware of the walk back to my room. My feet might as well be gliding over the carpet, and every inch of skin is thrumming with anticipation.

With the eagerness to immerse myself in the men I've branded as my own.

We duck into my bedroom, and I slip off my shoes instinctively at the edge of the bed. Then doubt coils around me.

What am I doing? I was already out of my depth hooking up with just one guy.

Andreas hesitates with a trace of his own uncertainty, but Dominic turns me toward him and seeks out a kiss. My body melts against his.

I know him. I know how we work together, with no past pain tarnishing what we've made together.

I push at the lapels of his jacket, pulling my lips from his just long enough to demand, "Off."

Dom's smile is a little shy as he shrugs off the jacket. He's cut openings in his dress shirt from the top of his shoulders to halfway down his back so his tentacles can slip easily through.

I reach behind him to tease my fingertips over the satiny skin. Dominic hums low in his throat and claims another kiss.

As we inhale each other's breath, Andreas eases closer. He dapples kisses along the curve of my shoulders and the back of my neck.

Every graze of his lips sets off sparks through my chest.

When he tugs off his own jacket, I lift my hand to run my fingers along the collar of his shirt. He groans, leaning into my touch.

"I missed you so much," he mumbles against my hair. "Dreamed about you every night. Ranted at myself for being stupid enough to lose you after you went through so much to find us."

"I missed you too," I admit in a small voice, and he hugs me against him from behind, nuzzling the corner of my jaw.

The air turns thick with the scent of anticipation and lust. But this moment is about so much more than simple bodily cravings.

I grip Dominic's collar and gaze into his bright hazel eyes. "I love you."

Dom cups my face in a gesture that couldn't make me feel more cherished. "I don't even know how to say how much I love you."

Andreas's arms tighten around me. I let my head tip back against him. "I love you too."

He sucks in a breath and bows his head beside mine. "Then I'm the luckiest man who ever existed on this planet. I'm going to spend every second I can making sure I'm proving how much I mean it."

Dominic's fingers find the zipper beneath my armpit and ease it down. The heat of the men's bodies on either side of me ward off any chill as he peels my dress off to pool at my feet.

I still feel abruptly overly naked, but there's an easy

way to balance the scales. I grasp at the buttons on his shirt, flicking them open as quickly as I can.

When Dom takes over, tugging the shirt right off, I run my hands over his chest and tip forward to lap my tongue over one pebbled nipple. He lets out a rough sound and jerks my mouth back up to his, firm but not brutal about it.

His tentacles curl around his body to stroke over mine. The suckers press against my skin all along my torso in a multitude of kisses.

"That's hardly fair," Andreas mutters in a teasing tone. "How are my two hands supposed to compete?"

Dominic grins at him, so at ease with the reference to his strange appendages it makes my heart flutter. "You'll just have to make particularly good use of what you have. You could start by undoing her bra."

Drey hums and hooks his fingers around the band. As the pressure falls away with the drooping of the cups, I turn toward him.

Facing him again, more undressed than I ever was the one time we got intimate before, a momentary awkwardness settles over me. I don't know where to set my hands or aim my eyes.

Maybe sensing my shift in mood, Dominic's touch gentles. One tentacle wraps around my waist in a tender embrace while his hands slide around to cup my breasts as if to shield them.

Andreas gazes down at me, the rich brown of his skin even more vibrant than usual but a shadow of anguish still lurking in his eyes.

He glides his fingers along my jaw to my chin like he

did the first time he kissed me, but he simply holds them there, his face still inches from mine. His tongue flicks out to wet his lips.

"Tell me what you want from me," he says, his voice raw. "I'm honored to be invited in at all, Riva. It only goes as far as you say. You have to know how much I want you."

I do, because the same need burns inside me. We merged our souls together but never had the chance for the wonder of it to sink in before it was spoiled.

I want to do this right.

The words tumble out. "Kiss me."

Andreas doesn't need to be asked twice. He bends down to capture my lips.

The same thrill tingles through me as did on the dance floor.

My hands slip under the hem of his shirt of their own accord to fan across his taut abs and toned chest. Drey groans and fumbles with the top buttons of his shirt before yanking it over his head.

Then he's diving in for another kiss, not waiting to be asked this time. He consumes my mouth while Dominic swivels his palms in deft circles against my stiffening nipples.

A whimper climbs up my throat. The ache between my thighs expands, torturously demanding.

All I'm wearing now are my panties, and I can tell they're drenched.

The next time Andreas releases my lips, Dom twirls me back toward him. He sweeps my small frame off my feet, his tentacles helping brace me against his body, and lays me down in the middle of the massive bed.

"I've been wondering…" he murmurs, planting a trail of kisses down my sternum. "I want to try… But I don't really know what I'm doing. You'll have to show me what feels good."

I sag back into the duvet, ready to welcome whatever he has in mind. "Go ahead."

His kisses chart a path all the way to the hem of my panties. He teases his tongue across the base of my belly as he guides that scrap of fabric off me, and my nerves jump with anticipation.

Then he lowers his mouth right over my pussy.

I knew this was a thing people did, but I had no conception of how glorious it would feel. A surge of bliss races up from my core.

My head arcs back against the pillow with a moan.

Dominic doesn't hesitate. His tongue flicks over every sensitive spot down below, and his lips massage every place it isn't touching.

I can't stop myself from bucking to meet his mouth. Pulses of pleasure rock me in endless succession.

With the gasps and cries slipping from my lips, I hope he can tell he's doing fucking fantastic.

Andreas lets out a ragged breath and sinks down on the bed next to me. He nips my earlobe and nibbles my jaw, but his gaze comes back to focus on Dominic's face between my legs.

As Drey fondles one of my breasts, rolling the nipple between his thumb and forefinger, the fresh jolt of pleasure makes me buck harder. Dom raises his head just a little, his tongue swiping over my clit.

"How does she taste?" Andreas asks in a tone so hungry I shudder eagerly at the sound.

Dominic's eyes gleam. "Sweeter than a sugar cookie."

He dives back in for more.

As I writhe with their combined attentions, Dom's tentacles stroke up and down my legs. Then one delves right between my thighs.

Dominic lifts his gaze again, swirling his tongue over that most provocative place while he gauges my reaction. The tip of the tentacle glides through the slickness of my opening.

Holy fuck. I tremble with the pleasure both immediate and promised.

"Don't stop," I mumble.

He slides his lithe appendage right into me. It fills me with a slim, flexible pressure not at all like his cock but thrilling in its own way.

As the tentacle pushes deeper, shifting forward with swift pulses, I moan. Dominic smiles against my clit and sucks down hard.

At the chorus of sounds spilling from my throat, Andreas swears under his breath and drops lower to lap the peak of my breast right into his mouth. I tangle one hand in his tight coils and the other in Dom's silky auburn strands falling loose from his ponytail.

The shadowy smoke in my blood doesn't wrench at me as urgently as it did my first times with each of these men. Instead, it quivers through my veins in a heady sort of dance, urging me on with a sense of reveling.

This is where we're supposed to be. How we're meant to be.

United like one being.

All at once, the fleshy tendril inside me twists. It curls around, increasing the feeling of fullness as its end spirals into a thicker ball.

I gasp, my grip on Dominic's hair tightening. He suckles me more eagerly—and thrusts that bulging tip into me like the thickest of shafts.

I'm already so aroused the burn that comes is nothing but ecstatic. I sway with the pulsing, welcoming his tentacle even deeper.

Pleasure swells through my torso, intoxicating and exhilarating. Then Dom scrapes the tips of his teeth across my clit, and I shatter.

I come so hard I sob with the impact, clutching on to both him and Andreas. A tidal wave of delight sweeps through me.

My body clenches and then goes slack. My vision spins.

"That's how we treat our woman right," Andreas murmurs as I sag into the duvet.

The words set off a pang of resolve that resonates through me. I don't want this interlude to be only about me.

We belong to each other; it goes both ways. I wouldn't have anything else.

As Dominic straightens into a kneeling position, I convince my muscles to move, twisting me up and around. Without giving him a chance to protest, I nudge him down on the bed, the pendant I'm still wearing swinging from my neck.

"Riva?" he asks, breathless.

I yank at his suit pants so hard the button pops. "I want to taste you too."

He inhales as if to form a protest that I don't need to, but I've already freed his erection from his boxers. When I wrap my lips over the head of his shaft, any words he might have said dissolve into a groan.

"Oh, fuck," he manages to mutter as I work my mouth farther down his rigid cock. "So fucking good, Riva. Never—felt anything like—*God.*"

Hearing him unravel only heightens my enthusiasm. I have no more experience with this act than he had going down on me, but the awareness of his enjoyment floods my senses.

I stroke my fingers over the moon-and-blood-drop tattoo on his hip that matches mine.

We're bound together by blood and history, and my body knows exactly how to make his quake.

My tongue winds around his hot, straining flesh. I drink down his musky flavor.

Dominic's hips rock to meet me with obvious restraint. He touches my temple, his fingers trembling with the force of the bliss I'm conjuring in him.

Despite the force of the orgasm I've already enjoyed, a throbbing sensation forms in my sex at its emptiness. An ache for the same driving rhythm that's now focused on my mouth.

And I can have that, can't I?

I release Dom's cock for just long enough to glance

toward Andreas, who's sat back on his heels to watch us with heated envy.

"Drey. I need you—inside me."

His eyes widen. Then he's scrambling to meet me, jerking at the fly of his pants at the same time.

"Fuck, yes."

He strokes his fingers over my opening first, but I don't think I could be any wetter. I suck Dominic's cock down at the same moment as Andreas's presses into me from behind.

Pleasure spikes through every nerve. I moan around Dominic's shaft, and he shivers at the sensation.

The shadows inside me flare. If they were dancing before, it's an all-out rave raging through my veins now.

The marks on my collarbone sing out. We're joined; we're together.

We're blood, and we found our way back to each other against all the odds.

Andreas's fingers curl around my hips. He rocks into me at an increasingly urgent pace that I match with the suction of my lips.

Dominic sways with me. His eyes have gone hazy with pleasure.

His tentacles still wind around my shoulders and arms. One makes its way between us to pluck at my breasts, and I can't hold back another moan.

Dom grunts. "Can't stop—Riva, I'm going to—"

I want it all. I down him as far as I can and savor the spurt of his release at the back of my throat.

As I suck him dry, his tentacles ramp up their

attentions. My nipples tingle with the squeeze of the suckers.

Andreas bows over my back to kiss my shoulder blade. He tucks his hand around my waist and fingers my clit in time with his frantic strokes.

That's all it takes. I crackle apart again, bright and hot as a firecracker exploding.

My pussy clamps around Drey's cock, and he groans as he follows me.

Andreas loops his arm around my waist as he rocks to a stop. He presses more kisses down my spine.

Then he pauses with a shaking inhalation and tips his damp forehead against my flushed skin.

"I love you. Always."

Emotion swells at the base of my throat. I twist around, tugging him with me so I can nestle between both men on the bed.

"Never leave me again," I murmur, and I think they both know I don't mean just physically.

"Not a chance," Dominic swears. He captures my mouth in a quick but emphatic kiss, heedless of his flavor lingering on my lips.

Andreas hugs me close. "It'd take a goddamn apocalypse to tear me away from you."

But as I sink into the mellowness of the afterglow, a niggling chill seeps in.

I'm not entirely sure that an apocalypse is off the table.

TWENTY-FOUR

Riva

Rollick leans against the railing around the yacht's upper deck, the cool breeze ruffling his tawny hair. "What exactly is your objection?"

I lower my gaze to the little crab he's set in a bowl on the small table between us. It clicks its claws and scrabbles at the sides too steep for it to clamber over.

It looks more like an alien creature than a thinking, feeling being. I wouldn't be able to make out agony in the stalks of its eyes or catch a gasp of its pain.

But that doesn't mean it wouldn't feel plenty. It's still *alive*.

It has just as much a right to live that life peacefully as I do, doesn't it?

I meet the demon's gaze again. "That's not who I want to be. I don't want to use my power—I wish I didn't even have it."

Rollick lets out a short sigh. "You know you don't have

much choice. There is no operation that's going to cleave the talent—or the urge to use it—out of your body. Your options are master it or be mastered by it when you're unprepared."

I grimace. "But how is mastering it better than the alternative if it means I'm willingly torturing animals to get to that point? At least… at least when I've used it before, I had a good reason to. It was life or death."

"And you could be sparing this crustacean some pain now only to inflict much worse on some other innocent being later."

He's right. I know he's right. But—

I lift my chin. "I haven't had the urge lately, even when I've been upset. The last time I released the power, I managed to only work it on the people attacking us. Maybe… maybe I've got enough control already."

Rollick cocks his head. "You might be satisfied making that gamble, but I'd rather ensure more certainty than 'maybe.' As would my associates. If you want my help, this is a necessary condition."

I study the crab again. Nausea unfurls through my stomach.

A tremor of a deadly shriek tingles through my chest, but it wants to smack into Rollick, not the little beast in front of me. Show him what he's asking me to inflict.

But I don't. It isn't even difficult for me to resist the twinge of fury.

I hate the sadistic presence lodged inside me. Jacob and Zian can hone their brutal skills with inanimate objects that can't feel anything. Dominic can at least practice with plants.

And Andreas doesn't do anything that would physically hurt someone in the first place.

It's only me whose power *demands* agony to operate. Why did I end up like this?

But if Rollick decides we're not meeting him halfway, it won't be just me but all of my men who'll be kicked to the curb. I grit my teeth and prod at the viciousness inside me.

What kind of nerves does a crab have? What will I need to crack and sever?

The monster inside me will know. As soon as my scream ripples over its body…

I part my lips, but my throat constricts. The only sound I propel out is a choked grunt.

Frowning, I inhale deeply and try again.

The cruel shriek stays locked in my chest. The thin squeak I force out does nothing at all.

"I'm trying," I say, bracing myself for Rollick's anger.

He only studies me in his usual implacable way that always makes me feel like he's seeing way more than I'd prefer.

"But you don't want to try, and you don't have the proper motivation. You're working against your purpose."

With another sigh, he straightens up. "As much as I'd like to get on with this, I don't think enraging you is a great way to begin a regimen of self-control. I have some things to take care of on land this afternoon. See if you can't meditate on the issue and come to accept the act as necessary so you'll get out of your own way."

He doesn't say what'll happen if I *can't* manage to get

out of my way, but his prior comment about necessary conditions is warning enough.

I swallow thickly and follow him down the steps to the main deck. The harbor of a city I can't recognize from the skyline is coming into view up ahead across the dark water, glossy high rises interspersed with older-looking structures in pale pastels.

"Where are we?" I ask. "And how long are we going to be here?"

"Havana. And how long depends on how quickly I can conclude my business. But I'd imagine you're decently safe with a good chunk of ocean as well as national borders between you and our foes."

Havana, Cuba. I've never left the United States before other than our brief foray into Canada.

But his reply relaxes me. I'm not sure how the guardians could figure out we've come here even if the younger shadowbloods are tracking us from back in the US.

They'd need to get in their own boats to narrow down our location across the ocean. Rollick's people would see them coming from miles away.

I think I'm starting to warm up to sea travel.

"Stay on the yacht," Rollick tells me as we reach the lower deck. "You should all do some meditating on deflecting your fellow shadowbloods too. You've got all those shadows in you—they ought to be able to work with you a little if you can focus them enough."

I nod. "We can do that. I'll get the guys together."

I'll even work with Jacob if it means we come up with better protection against the guardians.

But after the yacht docks, I linger for a few minutes by the railing, watching the activity in the harbor and the cars cruising by on the streets beyond. Whiffs of brine and gasoline reach my nose.

A strange pang forms in my chest, like I'm homesick for a place I've never been before.

Even though I have no marked connection to him, I recognize the solid footsteps that tread across the deck toward me as Zian's. He comes to a stop by the railing a couple of feet away from me and hesitates.

"Everything okay, Shrimp?"

He says the old, teasing nickname like he's testing it out. The sound of it in his gruff voice brings a sudden shock of heat to the back of my eyes.

"You mean, other than the fact that we're being hunted across the continent by slave-drivers who want to use us as weapons?" I say, matching the vibe he's offering.

Zian lets out a huff. "Yeah, I guess it's a silly question. You just looked kind of… sad. In a different way from usual." He glances down awkwardly and moves as if to walk away. "I didn't mean to—"

"No, it's fine." I turn my attention back to the city. "I was just thinking that maybe we could get away from the guardians if we just settled down in some distant country. They can't be all over the world, right?"

"It would be pretty crazy if they were. Drey says all the memories he saw from them, it seemed like they weren't talking with people far away."

"Yeah." I swipe my hand across my mouth. "But then I realized that they'd find us eventually anyway. Given enough time, they could probably track us down anywhere on the planet. Maybe we'd buy ourselves a week or a month, but would that really be worth it if we'd just have to pick up and run again?"

Zian stands in silence for a moment, contemplating the question. "No. Not really."

"And there's the other shadowbloods too. I don't want to just abandon those kids."

Not to the same horrors we went through. Not if we can spare them some of that torment.

Zian's muscles bulge as if he's already imagining an assault on a facility. "We won't. We'll get them out. You managed to get us four free, so with all five of us together, we've got to be able to pull off a whole lot of prison breaks."

In spite of the uncertainty lingering between us, the determination in his words makes me smile. "Let's hope so."

Maybe because of that momentary sense of understanding, I find myself glancing over at him. "Zee… Is something bothering you—about me?"

His gaze jerks from the scene ahead of us to me, startled. "What?"

My fingers tighten around the railing. "You obviously don't have to want to dance with me or whatever. But sometimes it seems like you're still upset with me or concerned about what I might do, or *something*. You apologized for distrusting me—it seemed like you weren't scared about my power—but if you still have doubts about anything that happened—"

Zian shakes his head so forcefully I stop speaking.

"No. No, Riva, I—" He extends his hand toward me and then catches it before it's quite reached me.

We both gaze down at that truncated gesture for a moment before he lifts his head again, his mouth tight.

"It's not you," he says. "I swear it's not you. You have been so… incredible. Fuck, I'm grateful you're even talking to me after… after everything."

"Then…?"

He swallows audibly. "It's me. I don't know what *I* might do—I don't trust myself."

That doesn't make any sense. If he doesn't hold any animosity toward me, then why would he need to worry about doing something that could hurt me?

I drag in a breath, struggling for the words to ask him, and just then the other three guys come hustling out onto the deck.

As Zian and I spin toward them, several shadowkind, including Cinder and Kudzu, emerge as if ushering our friends out. None of the guys look happy, Jacob scowling darkly enough that it's a wonder the sun hasn't blinked out.

My pulse stutters. I push toward them, Zian stalking over at my side. "What's going on?"

Kudzu turns to us with his ropey arms folded over his chest. "It's time for you to go."

I blink at him. "What?"

"The five of you mutants. Get the fuck off our ship. Stay the hell away from Miami."

"But—Rollick said to—"

Cinder slashes her hand through the air with a crackle of electricity. "Rollick's got millennia under his belt.

Staying alive even longer either doesn't mean that much to him or he's too curious to do the right thing. So we're deciding now. We're done with you."

She's serious. They all are.

My gaze travels over the faces of Rollick's colleagues, and every single one of them stares back at me with hardened eyes and determined expressions.

They waited until he was out of reach, and now they're staging a mutiny… against us.

"This is ridiculous," Jacob snaps. "It's not your call to make."

"I'm the one in charge while Rollick is away," Cinder says. "So yes, it is."

She snaps her fingers, and sparks shoot into the air.

As if summoned by the display, Pearl and Billy burst into being on the deck next to us. Pearl's normally coiffed locks swing in frantic disarray.

"What are you doing?" she demands, facing the other shadowkind. "You can't just—"

"As if you newbies get any say," Kudzu sneers at them.

Billy squares his narrow shoulders and steps toward him. The faun is a full head shorter than the smallest of our antagonists, but he doesn't let that stop him from glaring at them on our behalf.

"I might not have spent much time mortal-side, but I know that Rollick wouldn't like this. If you have a problem with what he thinks is right, why don't you—"

Kudzu slams a fist into the smaller man's face, hard enough to send Billy's slender form flying across the deck. Billy crashes to the floor with a groan and smoky essence pouring from beneath the hand clamped across his nose.

"Hey!" Zian growls.

He steps between Billy and the other shadowkind while Pearl dashes to her friend. Cinder sends up another threatening spurt of sparks, and a chilling rush of air sears over us from one of the other beings.

My heart thumps so loud it reverberates through my entire body. In a detached sort of way, it occurs to me that us leaving isn't want these shadowkind really want.

They want us dead. They want to know for sure we'll never cause any problems for them.

But they're still wary of us. They're not totally sure what we'll do if they attack us the way Kudzu just lashed out at Billy.

They're settling for running us off to preserve themselves. If we make it a fight, I don't know how long they'll stick to caution.

I don't know if any of us would survive that fight, outnumbered and against monsters who have a hell of a lot more experience wielding their powers than we do.

Dominic has rushed over to join Pearl and Billy, his tentacles shifting beneath his trench coat. "Is he okay?"

"He'll heal," Pearl murmurs. "But it'll hurt."

Billy's gaze seeks out mine from across the deck. I can see anguish in his eyes that isn't just because of his broken nose.

"I'm sorry," he mumbles. "I—" He shoves himself to his feet, glowering at the other shadowkind again. "We're not letting you do this."

My gut wrenches. The shadowkind who'd befriended us are willing to fight too, and their companions clearly aren't afraid to pull out all the stops to shut *them* down.

"No!" I call out before anyone can throw any more punches—or sparks, or whatever. "We'll go. Just let us grab our bags, and then we'll leave."

The guys' heads jerk toward me. I aim a determined look at all of them, willing them to follow my lead.

Jacob's eyes flash, but his shoulders come down through what looks like sheer force of will.

"What she said," he bites out, turning back to the shadowkind.

"Fine," Kudzu snarls. "You have five minutes to get your things and get the fuck out of here. But we'll be taking your phones first."

So we can't get in touch with Rollick. My stomach balls tighter.

He holds out his hand, and I can't see any option but to pull the device out of my pocket and toss it at him.

The guys follow suit, their expressions grim.

"All right, get on with it," Cinder says. "And that five minutes is one each. We're not giving you a chance to conspire together."

She motions to Zian, the closest to her. He glances at me as if for guidance.

At my sharp nod, he takes off into the ship.

Apparently he's worried about the shadowkind changing their mind partway through, because he hurries back onto the deck carrying not one but five backpacks—all of ours. He tosses them to each of us, shooting the shadowkind a challenging glower.

"We're going to tell Rollick what you did," Pearl declares, her face flushed with anger.

Cinder narrows her eyes at the shorter woman. "The

two of you will keep your stupid mouths shut, or we'll smash you right out of existence. Maybe you've forgotten, but you can die in this realm."

"It's all right," I say quickly. "We're going."

I catch the guys' gazes and set off toward the boarding ramp. With obvious trepidation, they follow me one by one.

My heart feels heavier with each step over the frothing waters toward the pier. What if *this* gamble is the wrong one?

But the price of forcing the issue feels way too large for me to want to place my bets there.

I grip the straps of my backpack as we tramp through the harbor. At the city-side end, we merge into a bustle of other bodies, but apprehension keeps prickling through my nerves.

Most of the faces around us are tan or darker, framed by hair in shades of brown and black. Dominic and Andreas blend in just fine, and Zian might not draw attention from anyone who doesn't look closely at the shape of his features, but Jacob's pale coloring stands out starkly in the crowd.

And me—my moonbeam braid must shine like a beacon of abnormality.

My fingers itch to pull one of my hoodies from my pack, but sweat is beading on my skin even in just my tank top. I'll be a liability if I get heatstroke too.

We might draw a few odd looks, but the locals will simply assume we're tourists, right? They must be pretty used to those.

Voices flow around us, but the ones I make out are all

speaking Spanish, which I know maybe three words of. I weave through the crowded streets beyond the harbor and finally find a narrow side-street to duck into that's little more than an alley between two tall stone buildings.

It's dim and quiet, which is what mattered the most to me.

The moment we've all gathered in the side-street, Jacob turns to me. "What are we doing?"

The question is brusque enough that my hackles rise. "Making sure we don't get murdered by bigger monsters than us."

His mouth twitches with a wince. "I wasn't criticizing. I just wondered what your plan is now."

Oh. I'm still not used to this new accommodating attitude he's taken toward me, and the memories stirred up last night have brought the early days of our reunion back into uncomfortable clarity.

I exhale roughly and peer at the busier street beyond us where men and women are ambling by, caught up in animated conversation. "That shouldn't be only up to me. But I figured we'd get our bearings and stake out the harbor someplace where we'll spot Rollick when he gets back."

Andreas's downcast expression brightens a little. "We can intercept him and tell him exactly what happened."

"Right." I might not want to put us or Pearl and Billy in the other shadowkinds' crosshairs, but the demon can look after himself.

Dominic's expression has stayed pensive. "We might not see him at all. He could go to the ship through the shadows."

"We should at least be able to tell when they're preparing to disembark," I point out. "They'll have to bring in the ramp. If that happens, we can rush over and make a fuss."

Jacob nods slowly. "Sounds like our best bet. We just have to pick a good vantage point so we can watch the yacht without those pricks noticing we're hanging around."

Zian cracks his knuckles, his lips drawing back from his teeth. "I wanted to pummel them into the deck. We might have been able to take them."

A queasy chill wraps around my gut. "We don't know that. And they'd have *wanted* the excuse to kill us. You heard what Rollick told us about how the shadowkind see hybrids."

A gloomy silence descends over us all.

Dominic adjusts his pack against the bulges on his shoulders. "Maybe we shouldn't go back right away. It wouldn't make sense for Rollick to dock for a five-minute errand. We can give the other shadowkind a little time to believe that we've left for good and go back to whatever they're usually doing all day."

Zian frowns. "What do we do until then?"

Andreas glances toward the street. "I've heard good things about Cuban street food. Who's up for dinner?"

"Will they take American cash?" Jacob asks doubtfully.

A flicker of a smile crosses Andreas's face. "Dom and I got Spanish lessons in the facility. I guess they were counting on sending us places like this to do battle with shadowkind while blending in with the locals. I don't have a ton of practice, but I'm sure I can manage to get some money converted. We'd just need to find a bank."

I ease toward the wider street and peer down it at the signs on the buildings. Even my limited grasp of the language doesn't prevent me from guessing what *Banco* must mean.

"I think there's one by the corner," I say, pulling back.

Dominic glances at the rest of us. "Maybe you three had better stay here where you won't be too noticeable. Drey and I can handle dinner."

My body tenses at the thought of watching them walk away, but I'll always know exactly where they are. And Dom has a point.

"Be fast," I say.

Dominic steps over to me and raises his hand to the side of my head to tug me close. He kisses my forehead and then manages a reassuring smile that soothes my anxious spirits just a little.

"I wouldn't stay away from you for long, Sugar," he murmurs. "We'll be right back."

The new nickname sparks a welcome warmth in my chest, followed by a flicker of heat across my cheeks when I realize where it's come from.

Sweeter than a sugar cookie.

Dom shoots me another smile that's somehow both shy and sly and steps away from me with obvious reluctance.

"I'll look after her," Jacob says in his commanding way.

I don't bother to hold back my snort.

As Dominic and Andreas slip out into the busier

street, I lean against the smooth stone wall behind me. The faint pulse of my marks traces their journey away from us.

Jacob shifts his weight on his feet. "Riva."

He waits until I look at him. It's the first time he's spoken directly to me since I told him off in the party room last night.

My jaw tightens automatically. "What?"

He holds my gaze unwaveringly. "I know you hate how I treated you before. I hate that guy too. If I could kill him, wipe him right out of existence, so you never had to think about him again, I would. But if I did that, then I wouldn't be here to stand between you and the assholes who are still around. That's why I'm here. It isn't enough, but I'm giving it everything I can."

My throat closes up. I yank my eyes away, my hand rising to grip my pendant.

"You *are* that guy," I say. "Realizing you were an asshole doesn't turn you into a whole new person."

Jacob scowls. "No. I guess it doesn't. But if I can find a way to turn myself into one, I will."

He says the words so vehemently that I can't help believing him.

The trouble is, I don't think that way exists.

Zian clears his throat, cutting through some of the building tension. "The guys didn't even ask what we wanted for dinner. I hope they get something good."

A laugh tumbles out of me despite the ache around my heart. "I'm sure they know what you like by now."

As we wait, restless anxiety ripples through my limbs. The ache in my chest expands to encompass more than just my feelings about Jacob.

Is it my fault the shadowkind are afraid of us? I'm the one with the most brutal talent.

I'm the one who's refused to attempt the steps Rollick's asked me to take toward controlling it.

Why wouldn't they see me as a threat?

When we get back on board, when Rollick can sort this out, I'll do the practice he's asking for. I'll deal out a little pain to make sure I don't slip up when it really matters.

It's the least I can do when the shadowkind are risking so much just having us around.

The uneasiness tangled inside me doesn't loosen until Dominic and Andreas appear at the mouth of the side-street several minutes later, carrying several items wrapped in foil paper.

Andreas starts handing his cargo around, the heat of the contents seeping through the paper into my hands. "I caught a few happy memories from people who've stopped by this food stall a gazillion times, so I think it was the best of the bunch around here. If you—"

With a sharp hissing sound, a streak of silver sears through the air and plunges into his shoulder.

TWENTY-FIVE

Riva

Andreas stumbles, a splotch of red blooming on his shirt sleeve. Even as the foil-wrapped food falls from my hands and I leap to him, more bolts hiss through the air.

Another strikes him across his temple, digging a gouge through his dark skin. Then there's a clattering sound like a shower of hail.

I fling my arms around Andreas to pull him closer to both the nearest wall and the ground. Dominic is already racing over to us, his face tensed.

As I press my hand to the wound on Drey's shoulder, as little as I can do for him with *my* touch, my head jerks around to seek out the source of the shots.

Jacob is crouched on the ground between the rest of us and the depths of the alley, his hands raised defensively. Several more gleaming bullets whip toward us and crash into the forcefield of telekinetic power he's pushing them back with.

Those aren't tranquilizer darts. Someone's trying to *kill* us.

A clammy sensation squeezes around my gut.

"I can't see who's attacking us," Zian says in a rough voice, his head swiveling as he scans the narrow street. "It looks like they're shooting from someplace above. There!"

There's a flicker of movement by a window. An arm jerking out, flinging something down toward us.

Alarm blares through my nerves. "Get out of here! Onto the street—where there's more people."

We hurtle out of the alley like one being, desperate for the shelter the crowded throughway can provide. Whoever's attacking us, they won't risk shooting innocent bystanders, right?

A *boom* reverberates from behind us, jolting the ground beneath my feet. I sling Andreas's arm over my shoulders, holding him awkwardly with my lesser height even though my muscles are up to the challenge.

He curls his fingers into my shirt but runs alongside me, only swaying a little. But the sight of the blood streaking down the side of his face makes my stomach churn.

Dominic dashes next to us, gripping Drey's hand. "I need something—" he gasps out. "The wounds are too deep—I have to get the energy from somewhere."

Oh, hell, I didn't even think of that.

The people on the sidewalk jerk away as we plunge into their midst, murmurs and exclamations rising up in our wake. I don't need to understand the language to recognize that they're disturbed.

Who wouldn't be?

I spot a sapling growing from a pot on the far side of the street. That's got to be enough, right?

I jab my hand toward it, and Dominic veers in that direction. Zian and Jacob thump along behind us.

"We've got to get farther away," Jacob rasps out. "Whoever they are, we don't want them following—"

He doesn't even have time to finish his warning. Hollers ring out, bouncing off the bright pastel storefronts.

Dominic lunges forward and smacks his free hand against the tree. I let Andreas slump against the pot and spin around.

A squad of figures in military-style uniforms are barging into the street from the same direction we came from, a few of them right out of our side-street. Whatever they're shouting to the pedestrians clogging the wider throughway, the crowd is parting.

People are hurrying off in either direction. Cars grind to a halt, some of them backing up to navigate nearby cross-streets.

The soldiers raise their guns and point them straight at us.

"Shit," Jacob hisses through his teeth. He catches my arm and pushes Andreas forward, herding us toward another street just a few buildings down.

Then his hand lashes out behind him. Two of the figures running toward us topple like action figures kicked by a toddler.

The other soldiers are barking orders at each other. They dodge their fallen companions and start shooting again.

More of the bullets ping against Jacob's hurled power, but one whizzes right past my ear. I swallow a yelp and throw myself faster toward the corner, yanking Andreas with me.

The wound on his arm has to be killing him, but that's better than him being *literally* killed.

As we dart around the bend, I fling a quick glance over my shoulder at the uniformed combatants pursuing us.

They all look like locals. I don't see a single metal helmet either.

They aren't guardians. So who the hell are they, and why the fuck are they trying to kill us?

"What's going on?" I manage to say as we barrel past the bystanders on the less crowded street we've turned onto. "We haven't even done anything!"

Dominic drags in a breath, his forehead already shining with sweat—probably because he's managed to seal Andreas's injuries enough to slow though not stop the bleeding.

"They're saying something to each other about monsters. About the ones they were warned about."

The clammy sensation from before turns into blades of ice lancing through my gut. "They were tipped off."

Like the gangsters who came at me back in Miami— except a dozen times deadlier.

At least one of the shadowkind in Rollick's crew took a page out of his disgraced colleague's book.

Ursula Engel did tell us there were other organizations

dedicated to ridding the world of shadowkind. One of our supposed allies must have found a local group and pointed them straight at us.

They found a way to arrange our deaths without having to risk their own hides even slightly.

Jacob lets out a string of curses through his gritted teeth. My own fury, sharpened by a sting of betrayal, surges up through my chest.

We never did a thing to the shadowkind. All we asked for was whatever help they'd freely give.

We turned to them instead of turning *on* them like our creator wanted, and they repaid us by trying to destroy us just like she did.

My power reverberates through me with the prickling of a scream at the base of my throat. But everywhere I look, I can't help seeing the startled civilians darting away from us as more yells echo from down the street.

Whether this group of monster hunters are actually part of the military or they've stolen uniforms to make it look like they are, they've found a winning strategy for clearing their way. My talent isn't as easy to aim as a gun, though.

Even as it claws at my lungs, begging me to pay our attackers back for the pain they've already caused the man beside me, I gird myself. I'm not going to tear through all these unknowing people on a rampage.

I don't even know if doing it would save us. Who can tell where more of these assholes might be coming from?

All at once, I'm wishing I had tormented a few crabs and the other creatures Rollick would have set in front of me. Maybe then I could have chosen who I ripped into.

We shove toward the opposite sidewalk where there are still enough confused bystanders around to offer us some cover and hurtle onward into a broad courtyard that opens up in front of us.

But our attackers have obviously been warned that we wouldn't go down easily. Another half a dozen of them come charging into view from the far end of the courtyard.

I whirl around, but the figures behind us are marching into view, closing in.

The two groups are trapping us between them. How much longer will Jacob be able to hold off even one set of bullets?

Andreas touches his still-bleeding forehead. "If I could mess with their minds—I can't concentrate."

"It's not your fault," I say urgently.

Zian waves his arm, his voice low and urgent. "Guys! Over here!"

We dash forward to an alley he's spotted at one of the unguarded corners of the square. The thunder of more gunshots blares behind us.

A body slams into me from behind. We spin, my claws springing out, and then I see it's only Jacob, wrenching me to the side.

Wrenching me to the side… while blood bubbles from the bullet he just took to his ribs.

He took it for me. Shielded me with his body when his power couldn't offer enough protection.

"Jake," I mumble, still scrambling forward.

His pale blue eyes dart wildly from side to side. "Just go. *Go.*"

"Dom!" I call out instinctively as we throw ourselves into the dingy alley.

But our healer is already a few steps ahead, still helping Andreas along—and he's got nothing in this gritty laneway to draw energy from except himself.

If Dominic falters, then we might all be dead.

Jacob hustles along behind me, but his breaths sound labored, his steps uneven. Steadier footsteps and another barrage of shouts carry from the road beyond.

The lane swerves, giving us a momentary reprieve. We push ourselves faster, swing around another bend—

And find ourselves staring at a six-foot-tall wooden fence that blocks the entire passage ahead.

Zian lets out a snarl and hurtles toward it like a battering ram. He hits the fence shoulder-first.

The boards crack but hold in place.

As he backs up to try again, the rest of us hurry over around him. Jacob lists to the side, clamping his hand against the bullet wound on his torso.

And at the same moment, the first of our pursuers springs around the bend.

Bullets boom out. Jacob grunts and casts out his power, but not quite fast enough.

Even as I leap toward the wall, a metal bolt catches me in the back. It sears into my chest with a blazing pain.

My lips part. A croak tumbles out of them.

I can't get my breath. My lung is collapsing.

"Riva!" Jacob cries out, and sputters a sound that's as much groan as growl.

Then something else groans, with a grating earthen

quality. The sound resonates all around us, behind us, stretching through the alley.

Zian rams his shoulder into the fence again, and three of the boards shatter completely. I stagger toward him and trip over a stone.

I spin to catch my fall against the stone building beside me—and gape as the far end of that building comes crumbling down over the man who shot me like a landslide.

It's Jacob. He's lifted his blood-drenched hand alongside the other, the muscles flexing through his arms as he hauls the entire three-story structures on either side of the alley off their foundations.

Chunks of stone roar down into the narrow lane. In a matter of seconds, the alley is blocked off as high as the second-floor windows still standing on the opposite side.

I get a glimpse of the wreckage, and then Zian's arm is whipping around me. He scoops me up against his brawny frame and hauls Jacob off the ground too.

"I've got them!" he shouts to Dominic, and heaves us through the remains of the fence.

Zian is supernaturally strong, but even I wouldn't have thought he could carry both me and Jacob at a sprint. Either I didn't give him enough credit, or I should be incredibly grateful for the effects of adrenaline.

I can't focus well enough to really think about it. The pain of my failing lung radiates through my body and my mind, and the next span of time fades into nothing but ragged gasps for breath and the caustic throbbing.

I'm vaguely aware of a cool breeze lapping over my face. My ass hits the ground, and a tendril it takes me a moment to recognize as one of Dominic's tentacles wraps around my torso.

"Bring him over here!" he shouts out.

Warmth washes through my chest. The pain jabs deeper—and then starts to melt away.

My wheezing smooths out. Air flows into both lungs with a renewed pang of pain, but also the relief of oxygen.

I open my eyes. We're sprawled under a short stretch of trees.

The one right over me is starting to sag, its leaves shriveling.

There's a creaking sound, and a crash. I jolt upright to see a car rocking where it's tipped on its side.

"Jake!" Zian snaps, grasping the other guy's shoulder.

Jacob has sat up too, his face so wan you'd think all the blood from it had drained into the splotch soaking his shirt. No fresh blood streams from his side now, but his face is frozen in a mask of tension, his eyes both dazed and fiercely frantic.

"They shot her!" he rasps out. "They fucking shot her."

Another car flips off its tires.

Andreas swears and waves his hand in front of Jacob's face. "We got away. We're all okay now. But we won't stay that way if you make it obvious where we've ended up."

"Fucking—asshole—pricks—I'll kill—every one—of them."

The words grate out in anguished hitches. A telephone pole snaps off its base like a twig.

I've seen Jacob like this before—not this bad, but the same basic state. After the guardians ambushed us on the university campus.

Ignoring the splinters of pain lingering in my lungs, I shove myself toward him. I can take the same tactic that brought him back to reality then.

Straddling his sprawled legs, I smack my palms against the sides of his face and yank it toward me. "We're out. You stopped them. It's done."

Jacob's pupils jitter in his eyes. His hands snatch at the air.

"Riva—they shot her—the fucking bastards—they tried to *kill* her—"

This time, one of the trees crashes over. My gut twists into a ball.

It's me he's so agonized about. Me he's still fighting for in whatever battle he's gotten trapped in inside his mind.

I shake him. "I'm right here. Dom healed me. I'm okay."

His twitching eyes don't see me. His body shudders in my grasp.

Dominic at least partly healed Jacob's physical wound like he did mine, but I have no idea how much other kinds of damage our escape has taken out on him.

I had no idea he even *could* tear down an entire building—let alone two of them—with his talent. And that was after he'd already deflected dozens of bullets.

"Jake!" I yell, as loud as I dare, and slap his cheek with a prick of claws. "I'm here. Listen to me."

The blow has no discernable effect. Jacob lets out another anguished groan, and something thuds and shatters down the street.

"Riva!" he calls out like I'm not there at all.

The shadows inside me tug me toward him, and I'm so worried that I let them.

I lean in with one last-ditch effort of convincing him I'm with him and slam my mouth into his.

Jacob's breath stutters against my lips. His hands fly up, fingers curling around my neck, tangling in my hair.

But not to choke me or torment me like he might have weeks ago. He holds me in a desperate embrace as another shudder passes through him.

His mouth drops from mine as his head bows.

"Riva," he murmurs in what's little more than a breath.

My insides feel as if they've been entirely rearranged all over again. "I—I'm okay. I'm here."

I push myself farther back so I can see his face. Jacob stares at me, still dazed but back with us.

I will down the flush burning my cheeks and scramble right off him. "We need to get out of here before they catch up with us. Can you walk?"

His mouth opens and closes. Instead of answering with words, he sways to his feet.

My own chest is aching, but I hold myself as steady as I can and glance around at the others. "Where do we go?"

A tremor runs through Dominic's body where he's leaning against the tree he sucked most of the life out of. He's burned out most of his energy too.

His gaze slides along the landscape beyond the trees. Following it, I realize we've come down to the coast again, though not the same stretch as the harbor where the yacht was.

In the near distance, a range of smaller boats bob in

the water along narrower docks, stretching as far as I can see.

"We could find a boat no one's using," Dominic says hoarsely. "One we can figure out how to start if we need to. It'd be easier getting away on the water."

Zian hesitates. "Should we see if we can find Rollick?"

Andreas's mouth twists. "We don't know for sure that he *wasn't* in on that attack. And even if he wasn't, we're obviously not safe anywhere near his ship until he's dealt with the others."

I might have protested if I didn't feel so weak myself. We're in no condition to fight with several shadowkind along with any other unwitting human accomplices they rope into their campaign against us.

"We rest and then we regroup," I say.

Dominic's gaze slides to the wreckage around us. "We should definitely put some distance between us and this spot."

Jacob winces and trudges forward on wobbly feet. Zian falls back to steady him with a hand against his back.

Dom and Andreas fall in on either side of me. I reach to grasp Dominic's hand, as concerned about his well-being as he clearly is about mine.

We walk until I think I'm going to collapse. Zian picks out one of the larger private boats nearby and peers through the walls to confirm it's empty.

After we scramble on board, Jacob extends a little jolt of pressure to start the ignition. Andreas steers the craft away from its harbor, in search of a hiding spot where it won't be noticed in the descending darkness of evening.

The rest of us tramp down into the cabin area. There's

only one level, but it has two cramped bedrooms and a set of freestanding bunks behind the stairs.

I don't bother to ask, just flop right down on the double bed in the first of the bedrooms. Before I can relax, Jacob sinks down next to me.

"I'm not leaving you alone," he says in a raw voice. "I'm not letting them get one more chance to come at you."

I could point out that I don't have to be alone even if he isn't in the room. Or that he can stand between me and any attackers just fine from anywhere else on the boat.

But I don't have the energy to fight with him. Not after all the fighting we've already done.

Not after seeing how desperate he was to defend me even after he'd already saved me.

"Fine," I mutter, and squirm under the blankets so there are at least two layers of fabric as a barrier between me and his side of the bed.

Then I close my eyes and sink into oblivion.

Twenty-Six

Jacob

I wake up with a pounding ache in my head and a flutter of unfamiliar emotion in my chest. My pulse hitches in the second it takes me to orient myself.

I'm sprawled on a bed that's rocking gently with the water that buoys this boat up. And Riva is lying next to me in the darkness, her fiercely sweet scent wrapped all around me.

My heart keeps thumping at its heightened rate. I lift myself gingerly into a sitting position and peer at her in the dim light that seeps through the bedroom's small, curtained window.

Her petite body swathed in the covers I'm poised on top of, huddled with her back to me right at the far edge of the mattress.

As far as she could get from me without falling off the bed.

The ache in my head has retreated, but a new one winds around the base of my throat. I only vaguely remember insisting that I would stay in here with her.

Did she let me because she understood or because she was too worn out to argue about it?

I close my eyes. *You are such a fucking prick, Jake.*

The thrum of my blood through my veins pushes me toward her. Clamors at me to hug her close and prove to her how much she means to me.

But hugging her wouldn't accomplish that. She'd flinch away the second I touched her.

The only time she's willingly embraced me was when she felt she had to or I'd screw us all over.

My hands ball at my sides, my fingernails digging into my skin with pinpricks of pain.

My memories of the attack and our escape are hazy and disjointed, as much blaring anger and horror as any concrete imagery. But I remember the press of her lips against mine, the shock of elation and longing cutting through the savage emotions that were gripping me.

Elation and longing immediately tainted by my realization of how wildly my powers had been flailing around.

I saved us and then I practically called our attackers right back down on us. Nice work.

The thought sends a different sort of thrum through my body. The assholes who tried to gun us down are still out there.

They shot Riva. They almost killed her.

They *wanted* to.

My teeth set on edge, a surge of rage welling up inside me—the one emotion in me that's comfortingly familiar.

I can't change what's already happened. I can't undo all the shit I put this woman through.

I can't make different decisions years ago. I can't bring Griffin back to life.

But I sure as hell can make sure that anyone who's tried to hurt Riva never gets a second chance.

This kind of rage, the slow-burning kind like a forge smoldering inside my soul, wafts a cuttingly frigid sort of fire. My thoughts harden with cold efficiency.

Every movement, every consideration narrows down to the goal in front of me. Every thud of my pulse propels me forward.

I slide off the bed, pick my pack off the floor where I dropped it, and stalk out of the bedroom without a sound.

As I tug the door shut behind me with a soft click, a form stirs on one of the bunks beneath the cabin stairs. Andreas gets up and squints through the dimness at me.

Yes, that's perfect. He's the one I need.

"Zian's standing watch," he whispers, tipping his head toward the deck above. "He just took over from me."

"Where's Dom?"

Drey motions to the other bedroom. "Out like a light. I think he needs all the sleep he can get after patching the rest of us up."

I nod. "Can you stay awake a little longer?"

My friend studies me with a trace of hesitation that makes my gut twist. Though we've been there for each other through so much, his pause brings back all the ways I let *him* down too.

But all he says is, "What did you have in mind?"

I motion in the direction I think is toward land. "Those fake soldiers are out there. Probably still looking for us after I bashed up their city. I think we should find them first."

"And then?"

A tight smile grips my mouth. "And then we make sure they never get anywhere near Riva again."

Andreas swipes his hand back over his coiled hair. He doesn't give me an immediate agreement, but the clench of his jaw tells me he's on board.

"We shouldn't leave her by her—"

"Not all of us," I say. "Just you and me. Zian can smack down anyone who comes at him, and Dom'll be here if the worse comes to worst."

Drey's gaze slides over me again. "Are you sure *you're* up to another fight?"

I adjust my weight, flexing my muscles to test them. A faint throbbing lingers inside my skull from how far I strained my powers this afternoon, and a twinge runs through my side where the bullet hit me.

It's all distant compared to the vengeful chill warbling from that forge inside me.

"I've got most of my strength back. And what we're going to do shouldn't take too much of my power."

One corner of Andreas's mouth curls upward, and then I know I have him for sure.

"I distract them, and you knock 'em down?"

A matching smirk crosses my face. "That's the plan."

He turns toward the stairs. "First we have to find them."

"I don't think that'll be a problem."

I pause to yank my sparse belongings out of my pack and stuff in a clear plastic trash bag the boat's owner left crumpled in a corner. Then I climb the stairs after Andreas.

Zian glances over at me from where he's staked out in front of the cabin, but I can tell from the acceptance in his face that Drey has already told him the gist of what we're up to. He dips his head to me.

We leap out onto the rickety dock we tied the small yacht to and scramble up the rocky shoreline to this much more derelict section of the city. Down a dingy street, I spot a car that's rusty and dented enough for me to be sure it has no alarm system.

"We go back to the scene of our 'crime,'" I murmur to Andreas, heading toward the car. "At least some of them will be searching for us around there."

And this late at night, the windows on the city's buildings are nearly all dark, the streets around us empty. It shouldn't be difficult to spot a squad of supposed soldiers marching around on patrol.

I pop the locks on the doors with a tug of my talent and twist the ignition the same way. As Drey drops into the split leather of the passenger seat, the engine rumbles to life.

I have a general sense of where we are relative to the part of the city we fled through earlier—approximately southwest. Easing on the gas, I pull away from the curb.

In the first few minutes, nothing crosses our path except a mangy dog that trots faster at the sight of us. The digital clock on the dash says it's three thirty in the morning.

"We won't want to get too close in the car," Andreas says. "It'll draw attention when the streets are so quiet."

"This is just to get us closer fast enough that it's still dark."

We lapse back into silence. Drey runs his fingers over the mottled armrest.

A flicker of an image passes through my mind: his hand sliding over Riva's dress as they danced together.

My own hands tighten around the steering wheel. For a second, my anger flares hot enough to cut through the chill that's keeping me focused.

But the only one who deserves that anger is me.

"I'm sorry," I say abruptly.

Andreas's head snaps around. "What?"

"You tried to tell me I was fucking up. More than once. And I didn't listen to you. And then, with Riva—I purposefully made what you did sound so much worse…"

Acid gnaws at my stomach as if I've poisoned myself. The part I hate most is that I don't even know how much I really believed I was defending my friends in that moment and how much it was jealousy I was tamping down so hard I couldn't even recognize it.

Andreas says nothing for long enough to leave me queasy. Then he swipes his hand over his face.

"We all messed up. We *are* all messed up. I know that I can't even imagine how hard it's been for you the past four years, without Griffin, believing she sold him and the rest of us out… And I know that I haven't been able to do much to make it any easier."

A splash of shame chases my guilt. "It wasn't your job to make *my* life easier. I never expected—"

"Of course you didn't. I'm just saying I'm not holding any grudges. Were there a few moments in there when I wanted to punch you in the face? Sure. But I don't think that would have fixed things any faster."

His tone has turned lightly wry. He watches me as if to evaluate my reaction.

I swallow thickly. "Maybe not, but I bet it'd have been awfully satisfying. If you get the urge again, feel free to actually punch me."

I tried to match his tone, but Drey has spent enough time in other people's heads that he can be almost as perceptive as my twin was. He must be able to tell I'm serious.

"You already beat yourself up plenty without me adding to it, Jake."

I don't know what to say to that. Then the beam of a flashlight flickers across the street several blocks in the distance, and my foot jams on the brake.

"We'd better stop here."

It's easier, focusing on the mission I intend to carry out. Sinking down into the welcome simmering of icy fury, letting the searing chill carry me out of the car and stealing down the street.

Andreas keeps pace. We dodge the pools of light beneath the sporadic streetlamps, sticking to the thickest of shadows.

From some club or bar in the area, energetic bass is still pounding, distant to our ears. A laugh spills out of a high hotel window that's open to the night breeze. A single car putters by.

Otherwise the night is still and silent. I wouldn't be surprised if the supposed soldiers managed to clear most of the locals out, if any had wanted to still be up.

After seeing what I did to those buildings, maybe it wouldn't have been too hard.

When I spot the gleam of the flashlight again, we're only a couple of blocks away. The figure holding it is beyond our view.

We creep closer with even more care. My ears pick up the scrape of footsteps moving away from us down the cross-street.

Andreas stops me with a hand on my shoulder. "Let me take a look," he says under his breath.

He vanishes from view, as neat a trick as the way the shadowkind can merge into the shadows. I wait in a darkened doorway, grappling with my impatience, as he must venture after our potential targets in his invisible state.

A minute later, he reappears next to me.

"It's them. Some of them. I counted seven, spread out along the street, but one guy talked into a radio, so they're in contact with others. They're patrolling, looking into all the buildings."

Satisfaction sweeps through me. "Good. Then we'll just have to give them some bait."

They think we're in hiding, on the run from them. That we're too scared to face them head on.

The truth is, we just needed a chance to turn the tables and get the upper hand.

I backtrack, seeking out an ideal site for our ambush. After prowling up and down a few streets, I come across a parking lot behind a bar that's closed for the night.

The backs of the surrounding buildings close off the rectangular space, the only entrance and exit a short lane onto the street. The bar itself has a rear second-story patio with a thick stone wall undulating along its border.

Now we just need to lure the bastards here.

I motion to the patio above us. "Get up there and wait for me. I'll bring them around. We want to gather as many of them as possible before I start taking them out. Once they're in, if they look like they're aiming to leave, flood their heads with enough memories to keep them confused."

Andreas nods and reaches for a window ledge to help him scale the lower part of the building.

The training the guardians put us through wasn't a total waste. I hope someday they find out we put it to use cutting down monster-hunters rather than monsters.

I slip out of the parking lot and glance up and down the nearest street. There's no sign of our targets, but I know they aren't far from here.

I train my attention on a statue fixed to the roof of a building on the corner. With a shove of my power, it cracks off its ledge and plummets to the ground.

The cracking thud of the stone form hitting the pavement echoes through the night. I pull back into the mouth of the lane and watch.

It's less than a minute before footsteps pound close enough for me to hear. Several uniformed figures charge into view down the street.

They gather around the fallen statue, glancing from it to the roof with tensed poses and guns in hand. One of them has something that looks like a glittering net slung over his shoulder, whatever the hell that's for.

Definitely not normal soldiers. I have a sneaking suspicion that those shiny bullets they fired at us—and into us—were made out of silver, not lead.

The hunters fan out again to search the street. One of them speaks into his walkie talkie.

Good. Bring more of them this way.

With a nudge of my ability, I send an empty pop can rattling across the sidewalk just a few feet from where I'm standing.

The nearest figures jerk around. I let out a curse I muffle badly and take off down the lane, deliberately letting my shoes smack the asphalt harder than they need to.

Hushed hollers pass between the hunters. They rush after me, the sound of their pursuit mingled with more crackling of radio static as they call for backup.

That's right. Let's get everyone together now.

Every murderous prick who nearly slaughtered the woman I would die for.

I sprint into the parking lot and throw myself toward the patio using the same route Andreas took. He bobs up from behind the surrounding wall to give me a hand up.

We duck down again behind the jutting chunks of stone just as the first men race into the parking lot in pursuit.

I have to keep them engaged while the others pour in

after them. Searching rather than shouting warnings to flee.

Peeking over one of the lower sections of wall, I set a window rattling. As soon as the soldiers rush in that direction, I flick a shingle off a roof on the opposite side.

More hunters are storming into the parking lot. Some of them are whirling with obvious wariness in their stance.

We can't afford to wait long enough for them to get suspicious. It's time to end them now.

Like shooting fish in a barrel.

The rage inside me flares through my chest. I lean forward, gripping the edge of the wall, just as the first man steps toward the lane and then stumbles as Andreas's power floods his mind with memories that aren't his.

Before my target has had a chance to let out more than the start of a yelp, I whip him against the corner of the nearest building, head first. His skull bursts open like a smashed jack-o-lantern.

More shouts of alarm rise up, faltering as confusion spreads through their ranks. I grin with my teeth bared and topple them one after the other.

Neck snapped. Back cracked.

Shove that one into his own knife, straight through the heart. Slam this one's face into the pavement until it's a bloody pulp.

My body hums with the energy whipping out of it. Not a single emotion stirs inside me except the burn of resolve.

Die. Die. Die.

No pausing, no resting. Blazing from each to the next the second I've struck them down.

Every last one of the pricks, until Riva can walk safe through these streets again.

But as the skulls shatter and the heads slump, the stabbing sense lances through me that none of this will *ever* be enough.

TWENTY-SEVEN

Riva

The boat rocks, and I jerk awake with a jolt of alarm. My body springs into a defensive crouch, tossing off the covers before I'm even fully aware of where I am.

No shouts or crashes carry from beyond the small bedroom's door. The thin gray light of pre-dawn drifts through the small window, making the plain furniture look outright dingy.

The boat settles, whether from a wave or one of my guys moving around. I sink back down onto my ass and retract my claws.

I've taken one calmer breath when the door swings open and Jacob marches into the room.

He smiles at me immediately, but the friendly expression doesn't quite reach his eyes. His pale irises have darkened like churning storm clouds.

Dark splotches dapple the fabric of his light blue shirt

as well—streaking across the sleeves where they're rolled to his elbows, splattering his chest. When he steps to the foot of the bed where the light is a little sharper, the spots glint with a ruddy crimson sheen.

My stomach lurches all over again. "What happened?"

Jacob's smile stretches wide enough to bare all his teeth. He reaches around to yank a bulging plastic bag from his backpack.

"I happened."

He upends the bag, and a deluge of bloody objects tumbles onto the far corner. A meaty smell floods the air.

I stare and abruptly recognize the details—the jutting fingers, the stumps of wrists, a glint of a thick silver ring.

They're all hands.

Hands severed from their bodies and dumped on the end of my bed.

My claws spring back out automatically, my ears tufting with their catlike peaks. My gaze jerks to the door that's clicked closed behind him in anticipation of some even larger threat.

Jacob tosses the bag aside with a plastic warble that brings my attention back to him. "There's nothing to worry about. They're never going to squeeze a trigger at you again. I made sure of it."

His voice is even but fervid. The gleam in his eyes looks almost feverish now.

I stare at him. "You— Those are from—"

"Every last one of them," he says with a slight rasp. "Drey and I tracked them down, and I slaughtered them like they tried to do to us. To you."

He glances down at his trophies. "I'd have brought

their heads, but they wouldn't all have fit in the bag. Their hands are what they tried to hurt you with most anyway."

"I…" I don't know what to say.

I should be horrified, right? There's a heap of chopped-off hands lying on my bed.

Some part of me *is* horrified, with a thread of nausea creeping through my gut. But at the same time, a strange lightness is rushing up inside me.

We're safe. Safe from the hunters who tried to murder us.

Because Jacob went out and took care of them before I even had the chance to worry about them again.

He's watching me so intently my skin flares under his gaze. But whatever reaction he was searching for, he must not get it, because something in his expression falters.

The sight sends a twang of regret through me, knowing the lengths he's just gone to on my behalf, but I don't know what he wants. I don't know if I can give it.

"They aren't the only ones who hurt you," he says, his voice gone raw, and jerks a knife out of his pocket. The blood smeared across its heavy blade suggests it's the one that sawed through all those wrists.

Then he brings the knife to his own arm, right below the roll of his sleeve.

Something in my brain stalls. I can't fully process what I'm seeing until he angles the blade to dig it in.

A cry breaks from my throat. I throw myself forward and grab his wrists just as blood starts to spring from his skin.

My hands look tiny against his bulging muscles, but

the supernatural might in me gives me the strength to wrench his knife hand away from his forearm.

More blood is flowing from the cut he managed to make before I sprang in. Another pained sound hitches out of me, and I press my palm against it.

"We need Dom."

I suck in a breath to call for our healer, but Jacob shakes his head.

"No. I hurt you. I *poisoned* you with this fucking arm. I don't deserve to keep it."

He means it. Every word propels from his lips with the same fierce resolve I used to hear when he accused me of murdering Griffin.

He barrels onward. "I can't change what happened, but I can show you it's over. I can pay the price. I—"

"Not like this," I break in. "Never like this, Jacob."

I squeeze his arm harder. Only a little blood is streaking out from beneath my hand now—I don't think he'd managed to cut very deep yet—but my heart still aches to see it.

Jacob stares down at me like he can't quite believe I'm refusing him. When the tears burning behind my eyes brim over, he flinches.

With a shudder of his fingers, the knife thumps to the floor. His legs give.

He slumps to the floor, his head tipping forward to lean against the edge of the bed by my knees. But he doesn't pull his arm away from me.

"I hurt you so badly," he mumbles. "I can't take it back. I can't make it better. I don't know how to do this right."

My throat closes up. I keep clutching on to his forearm, but I have no idea what to say.

The boy in front of me seems so lost and alone, but he's already pushed me so far away that I don't know if I could ever reach him.

But I don't want to lose him. Whatever we still have, however much all our history before the past few weeks matters, that one fact resonates through me beyond a shadow of a doubt.

"I don't know either," I say, my voice coming out rough. "But you have to be here, in one piece, to do it."

He inhales with a hiss through his teeth. "What if I'm never going to be in one piece the way I was again?"

I frown. "What do you mean?"

Jacob is silent for a stretch before he speaks again. "I wasn't lying when I said I died that day, even if it wasn't you who killed me. When I saw Griffin fall on that screen, when I knew he was gone… It was my fucking fault. I should have taken lead. I shouldn't have let him—"

He cuts himself off with a strangled sound.

My other hand drifts over as if of its own accord to rest on the rumpled strands of his hair. My tentative touch seems to give him the resolve to go on.

"Everything was wrong, and there wasn't anything I could do. I just wanted to be gone too. There wasn't any point. The only thing… The only thing I felt other than empty was rage at the pricks who shot him down. If I hadn't known I might still get to pay them back, I would have slit my own fucking throat four years ago."

Fresh tears prickle in my eyes. "What about the other guys? You still had them."

Jacob manages a shrug in his slouched position. "I look out for them. I'm not letting them fall if I can help it. Because that's what we do for each other. I don't—there's nothing *in* me—I couldn't manage to be a brother properly so I sure as hell can't handle being a friend."

He lifts his head to gaze up at me. "Until I watched you racing toward that train, and I—I cared, so fucking much, and I was terrified and ashamed and I wanted so many things that I haven't even thought about in years. But I'm not fixed. It's like I just broke more. The emptiness is all filled in with total fucking chaos. I can't even keep my goddamned powers from going haywire."

I feel as if I can see the broken pieces of him behind his distraught eyes. I didn't know that moment made such a difference to him.

But I still have to ask, with a quiver of nerves that rises up despite everything he's said, "So you're not at all angry with *me* anymore? I didn't—I didn't know what would happen that night, but I got distracted; I distracted Griffin. If I hadn't kissed him…"

Jacob is already shaking his head. He meets my gaze again.

"The guardians figured out what we were up to somehow. I don't see how it'd have happened any differently no matter what you did out there. At least he got that little bit of happiness before they murdered him."

I can't sense any trace of rancor in his words. I think he means that too.

But I can't help prodding a little farther. "You believed it was my fault for a long time."

"I—" He exhales harshly. "Maybe it was like Andreas

said. Maybe it was easier hating a you that was alive somewhere than believing you were dead and having to mourn you too. I hated and hated until it was all I could do. I didn't know how to turn it off until I hurt you *that* badly that it jolted me out—"

Jacob cuts himself off with a growl that seems directed entirely at himself. He pushes himself onto his feet but stays crouched enough that we're on the same level, and lifts his hand to touch my cheek.

"I'm glad you got to have that moment with Griffin before everything went to hell. I know—I know *you* would rather they'd taken me out than him—I know he was always—"

"Jake," I interrupt with a burst of emotion that cuts off the rest of my words for a moment. My heart feels like it's breaking now.

I rest my free hand over his against my face and repeat the words I know Andreas already told him. But Jacob wasn't in a place where he could hear them then, was he?

Maybe he can now.

"I loved all of you," I say quietly. "Nobody more than anybody else. You were all different but not more or less. I loved *you*. The way you'd spot answers to problems so quickly. The way you could cut through any worries or confusion we got caught up in."

Jacob lets out a sputter of a laugh, but I keep going.

"You could always get us focused and on track, right there with you. It was the best feeling when we'd make it through a training exercise together, and you'd smile at all of us like we'd already defeated the guardians… If I started feeling out of sorts, I could always hang out with you, and you'd have some new challenge we could tackle together…"

His head droops, his hand falling though he's caught my fingers in his. "I don't even know where the track is anymore. I'm the one all out of sorts."

The corner of my mouth ticks upward with a bittersweet smile. "I can't think of anyone else who'd set out on a crusade to kill all the monster-hunters in town before they could find us again."

His gaze jerks back up with a flare of the passionate determination I loved so much too. "Anyone who comes at you has just signed their death sentence. Maybe I can't promise much, Wildcat, but I can guarantee you that."

After this morning's bloody present, there's no way I can doubt his declaration.

"Just don't think you're ever handling them on your own," I retort.

Jacob's mouth twists, but he doesn't argue.

A breeze drifts past the thin curtain. Its cool taint reminds me of the sticky dampness beneath my other hand where it's still pressed to Jacob's forearm.

"Let me bandage your cut? If you're going to insist that Dominic doesn't take care of it right away."

Jacob's expression pulls into an outright grimace. "It'll heal fast enough on its own. He shouldn't have to extend himself any more than he already has." He lays his arm down on the blanket. "Go ahead. Thank you."

He replaces my hand with his as I reach for my backpack to find the first aid gear I stashed there for my own past injury. I can't help thinking that his concern for Dominic sounds a lot like being a damn good friend.

He's cared all along, even if his grief overwhelmed his awareness of it.

I brush an antiseptic wipe over the cut before wrapping a wad of gauze in place with a longer strip of the stuff. As Jacob flexes his arm to check the tightness, I lean back on the bed and wipe my blood-streaked fingers on the sheet.

We really owe a major apology to whoever we stole this boat from. Maybe leaving a nice wad of cash as a thank you will balance the scales?

I'm struggling to decide what to say next when a series of thumps emanate from above, forceful enough to set the boat bobbing in the water.

My pulse stuttering all over again, I jump to my feet.

Zian's voice bellows down from the deck. "Guys! It's those asshole shadowkind."

TWENTY-EIGHT

Riva

Jacob and I don't speak, only dash for the door. One of my hands fumbles in my cargo pants' pockets for a knife; the other flicks its claws free.

I don't know how much good either of those weapons will do me against the monsters and their powers, but I'm not going in unarmed.

Jacob must have the same thought, because the purple spines that hold his poison spring from his forearms. He takes the stairs two at a time, every movement honing to brutal intensity.

I can see in each stride the vulnerability he showed me falling away, his icy confidence snapping back into place as he prepares for battle.

This is what his anger did for him. It gave him armor to face all the shit the guardians threw at him when he had nothing else to hold him together.

I still cringe at the memories of how he aimed his rage at me, but I'm not sure I can say I wish he'd never had it.

Andreas was already hurtling up to the deck ahead of us. At the rasp of footsteps behind, I glance over my shoulder to see Dominic following us.

His tan face has taken on a sickly tone, but he manages to shoot a tight smile at me.

We burst out into the warm morning air on the deck, right on each other's heels. On this small yacht, there's barely room for us to fan out in a semi-circle without bumping into the railing.

Zian stands with muscles bulging threateningly in the middle of the deck, facing the dock. His face is still mostly human, but his wolf-man fangs jut from his mouth, claws twice as thick as mine arcing from his fingertips.

In the crisp early sunlight, five figures watch us from the dock, a few steps away from the bow of our boat.

Cinder has her slim arms folded over her chest, the fingers of one hand drumming the opposite elbow. Kudzu matches Zian's aggressive pose with his ropier muscles flexing.

I don't know the names of the other three, but they stood with Cinder and Kudzu when they kicked us off the ship.

It's almost definitely one of those five who pointed the hunters at us.

There's no sign of anyone potentially friendly to us. How did this bunch track us down?

Why did they track us down? Did they realize their human dupes didn't perform adequately and decided it was time to finish the job?

As that last question passes through my mind, a tremor of caustic energy wakes up at the base of my chest.

These beings wanted us dead. They cast us out, treated us like *we* were the monsters.

My mind feels jumbled from the wrenching conversation with Jacob, but one clear, quivering thread of resolve winds through my body.

I am not letting these fiends hurt any of us again.

In the split-second of that decision, a sixth figure materializes farther up the dock, just across from our yacht's hull. Rollick studies us with a typical air of nonchalance, but there's a fiery smolder in his eyes that I don't like the look of.

"See," Kudzu says in a brusque tone. "I told you they'd all be here where I saw the one guy."

Rollick lets out a dismissive sound. "That's hardly an impressive revelation. I'd have been more surprised if they'd split up."

Cinder hisses through her teeth with an electric sizzle. "They've made a mess of their stolen boat too. Blood and body parts all over the place. They're *beasts*."

I wince inwardly at the reference to Jacob's gift.

His jaw only hardens. "I took care of the real beasts. The ones you sent after us."

One of the other shadowkind scoffs. "You can't blame us if you're such a hazard the local hunters caught on the moment you stepped on shore."

A choked guffaw tumbles out of me. I know we aren't that noticeable.

"We've roamed all across North America before now and never been attacked by anyone other than guardians… oh, and the thugs one of your crew paid off to kill us."

The tremor spreads through my limbs beneath my skin. I want to tear through every one of them—but I don't know if I can.

I don't know how bad the backlash might be if I try and fail. I could make things even worse.

And there's still a chance—Rollick has stood up for us through everything, hasn't he?

The demon is eyeing us with the same edge of skepticism I sensed at first glance. "You did make an awful mess of this city. Pulling down entire buildings, leaving mutilated bodies strewn around parking lots."

Andreas raises his chin, and I remember that Jacob said Drey came with him on his mission tonight. "We did what we had to do to protect ourselves. It'd have been a lot less messy if your people hadn't set us up to be attacked."

"And if they hadn't kicked us off the ship in the first place," Zian growls.

A fierce crackle runs through Cinder's voice. "We were protecting *our* own. You're like rabid dogs—and we all know what humans do with those. Is it so awful for us to take the same tactic?"

Her sneering words fling me back to Ursula Engel's living room, to hearing the woman who created us call us abominations she couldn't wait to see slaughtered. My claws shoot from my knife hand, pricking into my palm.

"We didn't ask to be this way," I snap.

She narrows her eyes at me. "You're not trying very hard to rein yourselves in. You've been arguing with Rollick every step of the way."

"Well, forgive me for not wanting to go around torturing random creatures for my own training." My claws dig right into the flesh of my hand, the pang of pain grounding me just a little against the internal claws scrabbling to break free from my lungs.

The shadowkind woman in front of me isn't an innocent creature. She's made it amply clear that she's my enemy.

But lashing out at her is exactly what they all expect, isn't it? It'd be an excuse to justify slaughtering us all if I can't carry through.

And then where will we be? Stuck here in a country we're not familiar with, where only two of us even speak the language, with resources that'll quickly dwindle and possibly more hunters already on the alert?

"We all make sacrifices," Kudzu mutters. "It's obvious you'd rather hold on to your delicate sensibilities than do what's necessary to keep anyone else safe."

I can't hold back a snort. *My* delicate sensibilities?

Maybe when I was two years old, if then.

Jacob has turned his full attention on Rollick. I can tell from the tension in his stance that he's braced to whip out his telekinetic talent the second it's needed.

"What about you?" he demands. "They tossed us out against your orders, and that's just fine with you?"

Rollick's voice turns slightly brittle. "No, it's not. And they'll face consequences for their actions. But that doesn't mean I can't reevaluate my own decisions in light of new information."

"You're really blaming us for fighting back when those hunters nearly killed us?" I burst out. The quiver of a shriek climbs partway up my throat, nipping at my vocal cords.

"Your methods appear rather overblown compared to the actual threat. I have mentioned at least once or twice how important it is that we keep our abilities under wraps around the regular mortal population."

Cinder nods sharply. "Exactly so that more of those pricks don't decide to take up arms against us."

Dominic speaks up, his voice as even as always but propelled with more force than usual. "We wouldn't have needed to fight at all if *you* hadn't tipped them off. It wasn't because of us. None of us had done more than walk up the street and buy some dinner."

Kudzu grunts. "It makes a lot more sense that you fucked up than that we went running to ally with humans."

"Except one of you already did before," I remind them, my temper flaring hotter. "It wouldn't even be the first time this week."

Rollick swivels on his heel to contemplate his companions. "It is true that there's a precedent for sending murderous mortals after this bunch. If you deliberately provoked them, then—"

"Oh, for fuck's sake," Cinder breaks in, her words warbling with frustration. "Let's just end this. *She's* the biggest problem."

Her slender forefinger jabs at me, and in the same instant, the four shadowkind standing with her spring into action.

Kudzu and one of the beings hurl themselves right over the railing onto the deck of the yacht. Another flings his hand forward, and blazing light sears across my eyes.

I throw myself down on the floor to dodge any other attacks, braced to strike out or roll away. Dark spots stay hazed across my vision.

Jacob lets out a yell, and one of the figures on the deck goes flying all the way across the dock to crash into the rocky shoreline. But Kudzu charges at Jake and heaves him over the side to plummet into the water.

Blinking hard to try to clear my eyes, I lunge at the gangly shadowkind man—but Zian shoves in front of me with a roar. He slashes at Kudzu and reels backward with a bone-cracking punch to his wolfish snout.

Andreas blinks in and out of view, jabbing a knife at Kudzu. But another of the shadowkind has leapt onto the deck and kicks him in the ribs with a spike that juts from the back of her heel.

Kudzu rams Zian over the railing after Jacob. And Cinder steps to the edge of the deck with a current of electricity hissing between her hands.

I leap to the railing, my stomach flipping over. She's going to electrocute them—burn them to oblivion right there in the water.

Because they rushed in to help *me*. They're going to die because they wanted to defend me from the only real villains around here.

The furious anguish of that realization tears up through my chest. The scream explodes from my mouth at full throttle.

I don't even have to think to deflect its effects from my men now. The vicious thing inside me recognizes them from the thrum of our blood, the torture already entwining us through our shared history.

Inflicting more of that torment isn't what it wants. It wants the monsters who tried to tear us down to suffer, every possible drop of agony wrung out of them.

My scream reverberates across the yacht and the deck, slamming into all six of the shadowkind who confronted us. I can taste them yanking and flailing against its grip like bugs on flypaper—and my hunger doesn't know how long I can hold them.

I might not have much time to drink down all the pain this part of me is craving.

My fury narrows down onto Cinder first, my nerves buzzing at the electricity still sizzling in her hands. My intent rips through her from feet to forehead.

Hit her as hard as I can. Batter her, break her.

The shriek still ringing from my throat twists her ankles and shatters her kneecaps. It digs through her innards like a jagged blade.

Split open her ribs. Dislocate both her shoulders. Then blast her menacing skull right in two.

Send her crumpling into the smoky mishmash she's actually made of.

Just as my attention jerks away from her crumpling, mutilated form to latch on to a new target, a slim form bursts out of the shadows at the foot of the dock, racing toward us.

"Leave her alone! You're making her—"

The focus of my scream veers to the newcomer, pummeling him with a hitch of breath and a shock of alarm through my senses.

More, there's more of them than I thought—I have to crush them all before—

"Riva, don't!" a voice I vaguely recognize cries out. "It's Billy! He wanted to help; he was trying to—"

Billy. The name sinks in through the shriek that's echoing through my mind.

The delicate frame that's cracking so easily under the pressure of my voice, the horns poking from the jumbled waves of hair—

Horror hits me like a wave of icy water. I wrench myself backward and trip onto my ass—but the impact of my body against the deck breaks the momentum of my scream.

My voice cuts off with a stutter. And I stare with pulse thrumming and throat aching at the two smoking bodies sprawled across the dock.

The one I meant to destroy—and the one that tried to be my friend.

The cry that tumbles out of me next has no pain in it but my own.

No. Oh, no.

What the fuck have I done?

TWENTY-NINE

Dominic

R iva slumps onto the deck, her face drained of all color. The features that had gone rigid as she let out her scream slacken; the white sheen fades from her eyes beneath her plummeting eyelids.

There's chaos all around us—yells of horror and anger, shadowkind looming on the deck in front of me, plumes of dark smoke gushing through the air—but my entire world narrows down to the woman I love. A splinter of her anguish spears through me from the mark on my sternum.

Before I've even processed that I'm moving, I've dashed to her side.

A shudder ripples through her body, and then she keeps shivering despite the warm air, like she's freezing. When I touch her arm, her skin feels clammy.

I yank off my trench coat without a second thought and crouch down next to her to wrap it around her trembling shoulders. The ocean breeze licks over my exposed tentacles, but right now I don't give a shit.

The rest of the world barges into my awareness, as much as I'd like to keep tuning it out.

"You see?" Kudzu is hollering, stomping toward us with his sinewy muscles flexing across his tall frame. "*She's the fucking monster. We have to destroy her before she—*"

My tentacles have already lashed out to defend Riva as well as I can. Andreas steps in too, his face taut but determined, and from the splashing and sputtering that carries from below the boat, I'd imagine Zian and Jacob are doing their best to fight their way back to us.

The second shadowkind being that leapt onto the boat has stepped back to the railing, his eyes bulging with fear. But the other springs forward, joined by the one of their group that'd stayed on the dock before, scrambling after Kudzu with seething hisses and murder in their eyes.

Oh, fuck.

Then Riva raises her head. She doesn't seem to see the monsters bearing down on us—she focuses on the railing as if she can see through the hull to the dock beyond.

"Billy—is he—" Her gaze yanks to me. "Can you heal him, Dom? I tried to stop before it went too far…"

Three raging supernatural fiends are storming toward us intent on ending her life, and she cares more about the life she almost took. She'd send me to protect him rather than have me stay here defending her.

I don't feel like I have a lot of choice, though. I snatch up the knife she dropped and shove between her and Kudzu a second before the massive guy barrels down on her.

"Don't touch her!" I snap, tentacles whipping around me, knife hilt clenched in my hand.

He could probably pummel me into the deck without breaking a sweat, but he'll have to if he wants to get to Riva. He's not setting one fucking finger on her while I can still stand in the way.

The shadowkind man snarls with a hint of a smirk, as if he's *glad* he gets to bash through me first—

And then a voice so deep and dark it sounds like it's echoing up from the depths of hell reverberates through the air.

"Get away from the girl."

The rush of supernatural power that comes with that order washes over me in a prickling wave that sets all the hairs on my body on end.

Kudzu jerks around, his body clenching up like he's been punched.

A monster stands on the dock, glaring at the shadowkind on the ship with eyes like smoldering coals and razor-pointed teeth glinting in his grimace. The inhuman figure has to be well over seven feet tall, muscle-bound beneath his ruddy skin, two long black horns curving upward from the sides of his head.

My mind jars against the image, my thoughts scattering.

Then Kudzu says, in a cringing tone, "But, Rollick—"

"Get. The fuck. Away from her," the monster says in a firm but almost sardonic tone that does remind me of the demon's voice, even if this version is way more booming.

Is that… is that what our benefactor *really* looks like?

I guess he's called a demon for a reason.

There's no missing the brutal energy that radiates off him, even more potent than in his human form. The shadowkind on the deck fall back, one of the smaller beings wincing as if Rollick's demonic presence outright hurts her.

And just like that, it becomes very clear why he's the boss. Even if his associates sometimes turn a little mutinous.

"Billy," Riva says again, louder—a wrenching plea.

"He's alive," Pearl's voice calls up from the dock, unusually squeaky with strain. "He's— It's not good."

The demon that is Rollick meets my eyes and jerks his head toward the dock as if to say, *Well, get on with it.*

I don't want to leave Riva, but knowing that someone is helping Billy in ways she can't obviously means more to her than keeping me here. Rollick's influence seems to be holding his comrades at bay.

My stomach knotting, I dash to the side of the boat.

As I straighten up with my approach, the crumpled bodies on the dock come into view. They're even more unsettling than I expected from my glimpses while Riva's scream cut through our attackers.

I can barely make out the heap of matter that was once Cinder through the streams of smoke gushing off her corpse. It looks as if her flesh is disintegrating into the smoke essence.

There's a knob of something there that might be a knee. A long, lean chunk that's probably her torso, though contorted beyond recognition.

I drag my gaze away to the other, smaller form huddled closer to the shore.

Billy is at least still identifiable as the slender, horned faun. His head appears to be intact, though it's tucked toward his chest with a twisted grimace.

But the rest of him…

The gleam of a rib juts from one side, right through his torn shirt. Both of his legs sprawl bent at unnatural angles.

Wafts of essence trail off his wounds. Pearl is crouched over him, tears shimmering on her rosy cheeks, her pale hands flitting over him as if wanting to piece him back together but not knowing how.

No, that's not good at all.

I shove open the gate and push down the ladder so I can rush down to the dock. The rickety surface bobs under my sudden weight.

Jacob and Zian are just pulling themselves onto the boards farther down, adding to the unsteadiness. Jake swipes his hand back over his drenched hair and stares at the boat as if he's about to launch himself back onto it, his eyes blazing like ice-blue flames.

"If those fuckers touch Riva—"

"They know better," Rollick says in that echoing demonic voice that sends another shiver under my skin.

I dash over to Billy and sink down across from Pearl. My tentacles swing forward, one of them tucking around his waist, and the other trailing through the air.

"I need—I need an energy source," I rasp out.

Rollick snaps his fingers. "Kelp, get the kid some fish. *Now.*"

An eerie warbling sound carries up from below, with a tremor of the dock. Then a gleaming fish as long as my forearm flips out of the water onto the boards next to me.

I don't question it, just smack my other tentacle around its scaled body. The suckers clench on, and life races into me in a tingling torrent.

I compel the energy through my body and out the other tentacle, pouring every shred of the life I'm absorbing into the broken man in front of me.

Billy's shadowkind body doesn't feel the same as the people I've healed. Instead of catching hold of solid bones and organs, the healing power I'm sending into him seems to pool through his entire form. Like it's condensing inside him, making every particle of him stronger and more solid.

Whatever it's doing, my efforts appear to be working at least a little.

The rib vanishes into Billy's body. His legs morph back into a more normal configuration.

The plumes of essence taper off, but thinner ribbons of smoke keep winding upward.

Another fish flops onto the dock, and my tentacle flicks to that one, nudging the desiccated corpse of the first into the water. I yank more life energy through me, but I can't tell if my renewed efforts are actually fixing anything in the muddy sense I have of Billy's internal state.

My voice comes out in a croak. "I don't know what else to do. I don't know if I can do anything else."

Pearl smooths her hand over Billy's tan forehead. To my relief, I spot the halting but visible rise and fall of his chest with a breath.

"I think—I think he needs to be back home to totally heal," the succubus says, and glances at Rollick.

The demon nods. "There's a rift just down the coast. Take him as quickly as you can. You'll be able to find me later."

Pearl gathers her friend up in her arms and murmurs something by his ear. A second later, they both waver out of sight into the shadows along the dock.

My chest feels hollowed out. I look up, my thoughts shooting back to Riva, and find her standing near the railing, watching.

She still looks sickly, and in my first glimpse, another shiver ripples through her frame. But she pulls my trench coat tighter around her and draws her back up straighter as if ready to face judgment.

Seeing her in my clothes sends a strange wobble through my gut that's not at all unpleasant. Somehow I manage to reach the ladder before Jacob or Zian do, hurtling up the rungs so I can sling my arm around her.

Riva leans into me, taking comfort in my embrace. Just like that, I'm complete.

I don't care that my mutations are out for everyone to see. I don't care if I look like a monster to anyone looking on.

I am what I am, and I am hers. If she can love me like this, then I'm damn well going to figure out how to at least like what I've become.

"Are you really going to just let them off after what she did to Cinder and the wimp?" Kudzu demands, scowling down at Rollick but, I notice, not daring to step right up to the railing.

Rollick's attention shifts to the gangly shadowkind with a mild glower. Before my eyes, his body contracts.

The ruddy skin pales to a peachier tone. His frame shrinks to a more realistic six-foot-and-a-few.

The horns vanish, and an elegant suit reforms over the planes of now more subdued muscle.

But the aura of power doesn't diminish. It's as if he twisted a dial up to max, and the force of it keeps humming through the air like the peal of a warning bell.

The demon crosses his arms over his chest. "I never said anything about 'letting them off.' There are gradations between turning a blind eye and slaughtering people."

"She *should* be slaughtered—she tore Cinder apart! They all—"

I can't keep my own anger bottled up any longer. I step away from Riva to face him with my hand still on her shoulder.

"You were going to massacre us! Why the hell should we just roll over and die because it'll make you feel better?"

Kudzu bares his teeth at me, but his attention snaps back to Rollick at the clearing of the demon's throat.

"I will decide what's to be done with them on my own time. But frankly, Cinder got what she asked for."

Kudzu's face hardens. He glances at his companions, some silent communication passing between them.

"Fine," he spits out. "Have fun with your psychotic playthings. We aren't sticking around to help."

He leaps into the shadows, there and then gone, and the other four blink out of view within the next thump of my heart. Then it's just the five of us on the deck, clustered around Riva, staring down at the demon who might have saved us... or might be planning a more complicated doom.

Rollick brushes his hands together as if washing them of bad business and meets our gazes steadily.

"You'd better come with me back to the ship. I have some news about your 'facilities,' but it wouldn't be wise to stick around here any longer what with all the commotion we've already caused."

The harbor area we picked is secluded from the rest of the city by a strip of brush, but the faint grumble of early morning traffic reaches my ears. Has some part of this conversation been seen or overheard?

All the same, I balk. "What news?"

Rollick shoots me a baleful look. "Nothing earth-shattering, but enough to potentially point you in the right direction. Are you coming or not?"

At his question, the others all glance... at me. Even Jacob.

As if the fact that I questioned Rollick, the fact that I told off Kudzu however ineffectively, means my opinion carries the most weight.

"Are you going to hurt her?" I ask. I don't know if he'd tell the truth, but I want to at least evaluate his answer.

Rollick's unperturbed expression doesn't shift. "I have no interest in doing so. As long as she doesn't try to shriek the bones out of my body, I think we'll be fine."

"I won't be doing any shrieking if you don't come at us," Riva says in a raw but firm voice. "So there shouldn't be any problems then."

He did stop the others from continuing their attack. I

don't know what changed his mind, or whether it hasn't changed at all and he's wanted more time to evaluate us all along, but accepting his offer feels like a safer bet than taking our chances on our own here in Havana.

"Fine," I say.

"But if any more of your idiot 'associates' try to—" Jacob snarls.

Rollick cuts him off with a flick of his hand. "I believe the trash just took itself out, as some of you mortals like to say." He steps toward our boat. "Come on, then. Since you can't travel by shadow, it'll be easiest if we make use of this convenient craft you've already commandeered."

Andreas moves toward the cabin. "I'll drive."

The rest of us unmoor the boat, always making sure there's someone between Riva and Rollick. Not taking any chances about his good graces just yet.

As Andreas starts the engine and sets us cruising out into the low waves, Riva sinks down on one of the benches. She turns toward the demon.

"Will Billy be all right? He'll heal once he's back... home?"

Rollick is already lounging on the bench across from her. "I can't say how long it'll take, but he'll recover. We *can't* die in the shadow realm. We rarely die even in this one unless we're hit with the right tools—or very thoroughly eviscerated, as you demonstrated with another of my colleagues."

Riva's mouth tightens. She gazes out over the water for a few minutes, the rising sun glancing off her silver and slate-gray hair.

Then her fingers twitch toward the trench coat. She slides it off and offers it to me.

"I'm sorry. I should have given this back earlier."

I drop down next to her and grasp her hand. "It's all right. I'm actually… kind of enjoying not being sweltered."

A soft smile crosses her lips, but it looks fragile, like it could easily be shattered. There's still so much pain shining in her gold-flecked eyes that the sight makes my heart ache.

When we approach the large harbor where the massive yacht is docked, Rollick steps into the cabin to direct Andreas. We pull up beside the vessel to scramble onto the pier and then the larger ship.

Rollick jerks his thumb toward our previous ride, looking at someone I can't see who must be lurking in the shadows. "Take care of the boat and head back to Miami for further instructions."

As he sets a few other members of the crew who waver into sight about casting off immediately, one more figure emerges from the patches of darkness along the deck. Torrent leans back against the cabin wall, taking some of the weight off his supporting tentacles that are much thicker than my own.

My heart leaps. If he's back, then Rollick must have been telling the truth at least about the search for the facilities.

I head over to the shadowkind man with my hand still wrapped around Riva's, the other guys following. Rollick strolls over too, although I assume he's already heard whatever Torrent has to report.

"You found the facilities?" Zian asks with a hopeful expression.

Torrent's mouth slants crookedly. "I've identified three spots I think are likely locations of the type of facility you described. I can't tell you for sure whether any or all of them are actually holding other experimental subjects like you."

"Then we'll have to check them out," Andreas says without hesitation.

"We can make decisions about that when we're back in the right country and I have a better idea what we're working with," Rollick says. "For now, why don't you take a moment to breathe and then you can come back to the discussion—and the others we need to have—fresh?"

Riva's free hand tightens around the strap of her backpack. She doesn't say anything about a potential rescue mission, no eagerness showing on her face.

She tips her head toward me, letting her forehead graze my jaw. "I'm going to my room. I think I need a little time alone."

I press a quick kiss to her temple. "Are you sure?"

"Yeah. Don't worry about me."

She squeezes my hand and then lets it go. As she heads into the ship's interior, the ache that formed before clenches hard around my chest.

But the wound inside her now is one I have no idea how to heal.

THIRTY

Riva

The light knock on my door makes my lungs constrict where I'm lying on the bed on top of the covers.

Andreas's softly cajoling voice filters through. "Hey, Tink. I brought you a plate from dinner, whenever you're ready to eat."

"Thank you," I say without stirring.

I know he's hoping I'll come to the door or invite him in, that he'll have a chance to talk to me face to face. But the weight bearing down on my chest holds me in place until I sense him stepping away and heading back down the hall.

When I'm sure he's out of view, I push myself up and trudge over. A large part of me doesn't want to do anything except sink into oblivion, but the rest of me knows that's not really an option.

I need food to keep my strength up. I can't just fall apart.

As much as I feel like I already have.

The scents wafting off the plate Andreas prepared provoke a pang in my stomach, but when I sit cross-legged on the bed with the dish on my lap, I find I can only force down a few bites of the creamy pasta and braised asparagus. After that, my throat closes up.

Grimacing at myself, I set the plate on the bedside table for picking at later and flop down on my back again.

The daylight is dimming beyond the small window. I wonder how far we are from land—where exactly we're headed to.

I haven't talked to Rollick about his plans yet. Every time I think about facing him or any of the other shadowkind, I cringe down to my bones.

Our demon benefactor hasn't pressed the issue, so I've avoided it for now. Maybe if I lie here a little longer, I'll know what I want to say.

I'll know how to sort out the mess inside me into something worth hearing.

I'm not sure how much later it is when another set of footsteps approaches my door. I can tell they don't belong to Andreas or Dominic.

My body tenses, bracing for a summons or impatient questions. What actually happens is the lock clicks over and Jacob barges right into the room.

I jerk upward on the covers with a lurch of my pulse. "What are you doing?"

He kicks the door shut behind him but then simply stands in front of it with his arms crossed over his chest, like he sees no problem with invading my privacy but draws the line at infringing on my personal space.

"You've been hiding away in here all day," he says, with an emotion I can't identify smoldering in his icy eyes. "At this point, it's obvious whatever you're doing on your own isn't helping."

I scowl at him automatically, partly because I can't say he's wrong. "And you figure that *you* can help me?"

His gaze seems to pierce right into me the way his poison spines once did. "I think I'm the only one here who knows what it's like to have to live with the fact that you chose of your own free will to hurt someone who didn't deserve it."

His words sock me right in the gut. I flinch, my head drooping.

My voice comes out raspy. "I stopped as soon as I realized who it was."

"I know. And you realized your mistake a hell of a lot faster than I did. So you can at least give yourself credit for that."

I draw my knees up to my chest and hug them. "I proved the shadowkind who wanted us dead right. I showed that I *can't* really control myself—I'll hurt people I wouldn't even want to. I almost *killed* him."

"I almost killed you," Jacob says quietly. "Maybe not quite as directly, but we both know I'm the one who pushed you to the edge. You might not have forgiven me, but you don't seem to think I deserve to be scrubbed off the face of the planet for it either."

Pain and regret resonate through his words. I swallow thickly before looking up at him.

He's got a fresh bandage wrapped where he tried to cut his forearm off this morning. The one I used would have gotten soaked when our shadowkind attackers tossed him in the ocean.

He sounds calmer than he did when he broke down in front of me, but the anguish he expressed clearly hasn't gone anywhere.

I can understand that urge in a way I didn't totally before. If I could cut into my chest and dig out the parts of me that hold my shrieking power, I'm not sure I wouldn't try.

I grapple for a way to respond to his statement. "We had all those years together before. Billy barely knows me except for what I did today. Anyway, him forgiving me isn't the point."

"You forgiving you is," Jacob agrees. "Do you think you were somehow worse than I was? That you deserve worse than I do?"

I close my eyes. Somehow it hurts even trying to answer that question.

"I don't know. I argued with Rollick about practicing more to make sure I had a better handle on my power. I took that gamble, and Billy paid for it."

Jacob's feet whisper across the carpet. The bed dips as he tentatively sinks down on the edge, still a couple of feet away from me.

"You were scared. You were scared, and you got backed into a corner, and you *mostly* managed to only lash out at the people who were actually a threat."

"I'm not sure mostly is ever good enough."

"Maybe not. But I was there too, Riva. He jumped out

of the shadows and bolted up the dock so fast—*I couldn't even tell whose side he was on in that first second, and I wasn't caught up in my powers."*

I peek at him through narrowed eyes. "So, what, you're saying it's okay that I bashed him up?"

Jacob's mouth twists as he holds my gaze. "I'm saying it was an honest mistake. If you'd erred in the other direction and he *had* been joining the attack, we could all be dead."

I can't help snorting at the idea of Billy the faun, the sweetest of all the shadowkind we've met, racing in to slaughter us all, but there isn't much humor in the sound.

"I don't like it," I say after a moment of silence. "The way I feel when I'm sending out that power. Or maybe it's that I like it too much. What if using it even more makes it *harder* for me to back away?"

That's the question that's been simmering inside me all day. The fear that's made me balk rather than march straight to Rollick and say we should get on with my training.

What if I end up hurting even more people than I already have?

Jacob considers for a moment before speaking. "I think you'll be able to tell if that's happening, and then we can figure out other strategies to deal with that problem. You don't like how things are now either. Even when you don't know how to fix something, the only thing you can do is keep trying whatever seems most likely, over and over, until hopefully you get there. Right?"

I think from the shadow that's come over his face that he isn't talking just about me now.

I incline my head. "I guess that makes sense. I just— this isn't anything like how I wanted to be. *Who* I wanted to be."

"The guardians took away a whole lot of our choices. But I'm trying to make the most of the choices I do have. I know you, Riva, just like you know me. You aren't going to let yourself become an actual monster. If you could take on the whole fucking facility to get us out of there, you can handle this."

The confidence in his voice brings an unexpected burn to the back of my eyes. "I wish I knew that for sure so I didn't have to be so scared."

Jacob's expression softens. He leans toward me, his hand reaching out—and then falling to the duvet still several inches from where I'm sitting.

His hesitation hangs in the air between us like a tangible thing. He's afraid too—afraid I wouldn't have accepted even a brief touch of comfort from him.

But he was right to come in and insist on talking to me. It is better not being alone, even when my company is him.

Maybe especially because. He's also right that he understands the guilt that's suffocating me in a way I don't think any of the other guys could, not exactly.

As far as I know, they've never hurt anyone that badly except in self-defense or forced by the guardians.

Sitting with Jacob, talking with him, has opened a crack in the weight that was pressing down on me. And seeping through that crack is not just a hint of relief but a tingle of longing.

He brought me back the severed hands of our enemies.

He would have cut off his own arm in retribution if I'd let him.

I hate what he did to me… but I have no doubts any more that he hates his past cruelty just as much. That he is trying, in every way this damaged man knows how, to save me from any further pain.

To give me something better.

I lift my gaze from Jacob's fallen hand to his uncertain face. It takes another moment before I can push the words from my throat—but they feel right when I do.

"If you want to make up for how brutal you were before, why don't you show me how gentle you can be now?"

Jacob's eyes flicker with a momentary widening. Then he eases across the bed and ever so carefully tucks his hand around mine.

He skims his thumb over the back of my hand, feather light. Just his increased closeness and that simple touch wakes up a sharper quiver of need through the shadows in my blood.

I don't have to act on the sudden awakening. I can take the comfort he wants to offer without it having to turn into anything else.

A faint whiff of pheromones suggests that Jacob is grappling with the same desires, but he restrains himself, sticking to my request for gentleness. His thumb skims back and forth over my skin in several slow strokes.

He turns my hand over against his palm and glides the fingers of his other hand over my wrist. A fresh burst of tingles shoots over my skin.

My skin heats, but I sit still and silent, watching him.

He traces the bones of my forearm up to my elbow and back again with the same care. His lips slant into a bittersweet smile.

"You've always looked so delicate. Quite the trick when you're the strongest one out of all of us."

The corner of my mouth quirks upward. "I think Zian might object to that assessment."

Jacob lets out a soft huff. "I'm counting powers *and* physical strength. Zian can't tear someone apart without even touching them."

Somehow he makes my ability sound admirable rather than horrifying. I suddenly remember the way he talked about the massacre in Ursula Engel's house after we'd first escaped.

He said it was "fucking amazing." Called me a superhero.

I was too scarred and incapable of trusting him then for the knowledge to sink in, but he really did mean it, didn't he?

He doesn't think my power is something wrong with me. He thinks I'm amazing, mistakes and all.

Why else would he be here right now, trying so hard to make me believe the same thing?

Jacob twines my fingers with his and raises his other hand to slide his fingertips across my shoulders.

"Even before," he goes on, "I always thought Griffin's nickname for you was silly. *Moonbeam.* Like you something fleeting, fragile. You were a wildcat all the way through, fierce and unshakable."

My smile tightens. "I don't know about the unshakable part."

Jacob circles his thumb against the crook of my neck in a soothing massage that makes me want to purr. "Look at all the shit everyone's thrown at you, including me, and you're still standing. I say that counts."

I reply with a noncommittal sound, resisting the urge to press into his touch.

Jacob traces his fingers down my spine and up again, with just enough pressure to be soothing. There isn't a trace of his usual rigidity in the caress.

His voice lowers again. "I did understand it better after a while, though. There was this one day at the facility—a few years before we tried to escape; we must have been around thirteen—when we were doing some training thing outside, and the sunlight caught on you just as you turned around and smiled at the rest of us. And I'd swear you fucking glowed."

"Like a moonbeam?" I joke, with a bit of a wobble.

"More than that. And not only your hair. *All* of you just shone."

His hand pauses against the middle of my back, resting there. "You're a hell of a lot more than a moonbeam, Riva. You're our whole goddamned sun. Wherever you go, you bring that warmth with you. You tether us so we don't spiral out into the abyss. How many times have you pulled each of us back from the edge just in the past few weeks?"

The burn comes back to my eyes, hotter than before. "We all had each other's backs."

"But without you there during those four years, the rest of us got lost."

"Without me and Griffin," I feel the need to say.

Jacob starts rubbing my back with his slow, careful rhythm again. "I don't know that it really would have been better if he'd still been there without you."

He falls silent for a stretch, and I don't know what to say.

The brush of his fingers is siphoning off my ability to speak. More heat kindles under my skin with every stroke, but the ache winding around my heart holds the sting of loss.

My losses. His. All of ours.

Jacob drags in a breath. "That moment in the field was when I realized how much I wanted you. But I also knew I wasn't going to act on that feeling. Griffin loved you too, so much—he might have been the one who could read people's feelings, but he was my *twin*, so I sure as hell could read him—and I could see how you were with him… I never would have thought there was even a chance you'd fall for more than one of us."

My throat constricts. "Jake—"

He shakes his head. "It's okay. That's what I'm trying to say. It was okay then, and it's okay now. You don't ever have to want me the way you want Dominic and Andreas. I never expected to have it anyway. I just hope, so much, that we can get to the point that you believe I'll be standing with you through whatever comes at us. Having that would be enough. I'd be happy—hell, I'd be fucking ecstatic with that."

The emotion swelling in my chest bursts through the crack that'd opened, and I don't know how to do anything but turn toward him and tug his mouth to mine.

Jacob's chest hitches beneath my hand, and then he's

kissing me back. There's so much tenderness and heat mingled in the press of his lips that I could melt with it.

Nothing about him is icy now. He cups one hand against my cheek and rests the other on my waist.

The shadowy essence inside me flares, clamoring for more.

My fingers slide into the smooth strands of his hair to grasp them and yank him closer. A groan reverberates from Jacob's lungs.

We fall into each other farther, our kisses deepening, our tongues dancing. Every nerve in my body shivers with anticipation.

When my hand creeps up under the hem of Jacob's shirt to trace the ridges of muscle across his abdomen, he groans again and slides his arm farther around my torso. Then he tips us over, pulling me with him so I'm bowed over his body, straddling him.

His voice comes out in murmurs between the collisions of our mouths. "I'm yours. Whatever you want with me, you can have it. This is your show, Wildcat."

His palm grazes my breast, and a whimper tumbles out of me. I know this feeling, this rush of overwhelming hunger that can only be sated one way, and for a moment, I'm lost in it.

Then I turn my head to give Jacob access to my neck. As his lips sear against my skin, my gaze falls across his forearm raised toward me.

This close, I can't miss the faint pock marks where his toxic spines can emerge.

Something flips over in my gut. The remembered sting

and the rippling pain flash from the depths of my mind—
and break loose a deluge of other memories.

The frigid blue of his eyes when he hurled his
accusations at me. The cutting edge to his voice when he
chose the best remarks to flay me open from the
inside out.

All the thorns he jabbed in my side, over and over,
hoping to tear me down.

I gasp for air, and a sob comes out instead. A different
sort of crack splits me down the middle with a flood of
tears.

Jacob jerks back from the kiss as I sag over him. His
hands hitch against my body as if he doesn't know what to
do with them.

I can't stop the tears from streaming out. They're
streaking down my cheeks and pattering across Jake's shirt,
and more seem to breach the walls I've held so firm inside
me with every choked breath.

All the anguish and confusion I bottled up, all the pain
I tried to bear unflinchingly—it never left. It's been
stewing inside me all these weeks, and now it's boiling over.

"Riva," Jacob says raggedly, framing my damp face
with tentative hands. "Riva, I'm sorry. I'm so fucking
sorry."

I tip my head right against his shoulder, and his arms
finally come around me, catching me against him in their
solid embrace.

This is Jacob too. This is the Jake I knew, even if parts
of him have hardened and turned embittered over the last
four years.

He said the boy he used to be died, but he's here. He fought his way up through the rage and misery that consumed him so he could be with me.

But maybe I'm still not capable of forgiving him for how much of that rage and misery he inflicted on me before he pulled free from it, not completely.

With a slight rock of his body, he pushes us so we're sitting upright on the bed. "It will never happen again. I swear it. I'd rather cut off my own *head* than hurt you."

Even through my sobs, I believe him.

I'm smearing tears and snot all over his shirt. "Sorry," I mumble as I struggle to rein all that emotion in again.

Jacob only squeezes me tighter. "*You* have nothing to apologize to me for. Not ever." His lips brush my temple. "You're so strong, Riva, but you don't always have to be. I can be your armor when you need it. I know I can do that much."

He *feels* like a suit of armor braced around me, shielding me from the world while I grapple with my tears. Maybe it doesn't make sense that he could protect me when he's the one who set me on this crying jag in the first place, but most of my uneasiness at the explosion of vulnerability fades away.

The embarrassment lingers. When I finally swipe the last tears from my eyes and inhale without a stutter, I keep my head tucked against his shoulder, not wanting to meet his gaze just yet.

"I love you," Jacob says, his voice rough. "You are my sun, my fucking soul. I'm going to keep showing you how true that is for as long as it takes."

I know I'm not ready to say those three words back to him, even if I could have four years ago.

I know I'm not ready to form the connection that would fuse his essence with mine, even if I teetered on the verge just now.

But that doesn't mean I can't recognize that he's been knitting my heart back together from the moment he stepped into my room.

Here with him, with his words and his embrace, I've found some kind of peace.

"Stay?" I whisper against his chest.

Jacob hugs me with a shuddery exhalation that sounds like relief. "As long as you'll let me, Wildcat."

THIRTY-ONE

Riva

I wake up with Jacob's sharply cool scent filling my lungs and a needy ache pulsing between my thighs.

At some point during the night, without really thinking about it, I kicked off my cargo pants, which make for poor sleepwear with all their lumpy pockets. Unwise move.

Now my bare knee is hooked over Jacob's leg beneath the duvet he pulled over us. At least *he's* still wearing his slacks, thank all that is holy.

The rest of my body decided to press up against his while we slept, my hand resting on his chest. My head lies against his shoulder, cushioned by the arm he's still got tucked around me.

I feel the rise and fall of his breath beneath my hand and try to convince myself to pull away. But it isn't just the shadows in my blood shouting at me to twine myself with him even further.

I've recognized how gorgeous he is even when he was acting like a total jackass. My hormones have gone haywire every time he's been close to me, regardless of how the rest of me felt about it.

And now he isn't being a jackass. He shook me out of my self-berating funk yesterday like I'm not sure anyone else could have.

He held me through the whole night like the armor he promised me he'd be.

The thought of giving him my whole heart is still a little terrifying. But fuck, I don't know how I'm going to concentrate while I'm around him when my defenses against my attraction have crumbled so much.

Is it possible I could satisfy some part of that itch without giving in to the most vulnerable bits?

Is it selfish of me to even want that?

Jacob's breath speeds up a little, and the waft of pheromones that laces the air tells me he's awake… and not exactly unaffected by our current position either.

His hand rises to stroke carefully over my hair. I can feel the tight control he's maintaining over the simple movement, over his entire body where it touches mine.

"Okay, Wildcat?" he murmurs.

"Yeah," I say, but even with that one word, my voice comes out a bit ragged.

Jacob twists a little so he can peer down at my face, managing not to dislodge my hand or my knee. I'm not sure if that's for the best or a precursor to my impending doom.

"What?" His tone firms with a protective edge that only fans the flames nibbling away at my own control.

I swallow hard, my cheeks flushing. Am I really going to say this?

I should peel myself off him *now* and jump in the coldest of cold showers.

But somehow I'm still not moving.

Jacob lifts his other hand to brush his thumb over my cheek. He's definitely taking my instructions to prove himself with gentleness to heart.

When I lift my gaze, the worry shimmering in his eyes nearly cracks me apart. "If something's wrong—"

It suddenly feels ten times more selfish *not* to tell him what's actually on my mind.

Which doesn't make it any easier to spit the truth out. I lower my gaze back to the muscled planes of his chest that show through his button-up shirt and fumble with the words.

"No, I just— I think I want— It doesn't seem right to ask—"

Jacob waits out my babbling patiently, his fingers stilling against my face. When I halt completely, he studies me.

"Ask for what, Riva? You can ask me for *anything*. Hell knows I fucking owe you."

My mouth opens and closes again. My flush spreads down my cheeks. "I—Do you think we could—"

I squeeze my eyes shut and force my thoughts into something vaguely resembling coherency. "Could we… enjoy ourselves a little, without it being anything permanent?"

Jacob goes even more rigid, but a fresh whiff of desire tickles my nose at the same moment.

"Without leaving a mark, you mean," he says, his voice lowering in a way that sends my temperature spiking. "Nothing binding us. Just to get off."

"Yeah," I mumble, and then feel I need to make one thing clear. I meet his gaze again even though my face is flaming. "For now."

I'm not making any promises, but I don't want him to think I expect it to be never. That nothing he's done has meant anything.

A small smile that brings a flutter into my chest crosses Jacob's lips. "I told you last night that I'm yours, didn't I? Whatever you want with me, I'm right here. Take as much as you need."

A tight, hungry sound works from my throat, and then I'm rolling right onto him, straddling him like I did last night.

I splay my hands against his sculpted chest and wet my lips. Leaning over for a kiss feels too risky.

If I'm not going to lose myself in the moment and end up careening past boundaries I'd rather not, I need to keep a little distance.

Jacob trails tentative fingers down my neck, but his eyes have gone stormy with his own desire. "What can I do for you, Wildcat?"

The ache between my legs seems to be pulsing all through my body now. "I—touch me. Make me feel *good*."

A groan he can't quite suppress seeps from his lips.

He drops his hand further to trace the side of my breast through my tank top. I press into the contact, shifting my hips at the same time—and my pussy, covered only by the thin panties, grazes the rock-hard bulge behind the fly of his slacks.

Both of our breaths hitch in unison. As the pleasure of the friction spirals from my core, Jacob cups my breast completely.

He rolls his finger over my nipple and then squeezes it. I whimper at the heady sparks the gesture sets off.

My hips rock. I can't stop myself from grinding against him, seeking more of that delicious friction that's quickening both our pulses.

"Fuck," Jacob mutters shakily. He massages my breast with more forceful strokes that bring a whimper to my lips.

He bucks up to meet me, his erection locking against me even more firmly through our clothes, and my fingers dig into his shirt. I'm afraid to do anything else, to ask for anything else, or I might lose my grip on the reins.

Maybe I should stop this. Maybe it was a stupid idea.

But I'm not sure I know how to stop.

Jacob must see the inner conflict playing out on my face. He hesitates for just a second, and then both his hands slide to my thighs.

"I know what you need. Come here."

Before I can ask what he means, he hefts me up without the slightest sign of effort. My muscles might be supernaturally powered, but I'm still tiny compared to him.

In one smooth movement, he lifts me so I'm kneeling over his face instead of his groin. My hands grasp onto the top of the headboard instinctively.

Then Jacob tugs my panties to the side and swipes his tongue over my throbbing cunt.

The starker rush of pleasure shocks a cry from my lungs. As if that's the confirmation he was waiting for, he pushes up to plant his entire mouth against my folds.

His tongue flicks over my clit and down across my opening. He moves his lips against every sensitive part of me, sending quivers of delight racing through every nerve.

Oh, God. I clutch on to the headboard and sway with his attentions, my body outright quaking with the sensations he's conjuring through it.

It felt incredible when Dominic kissed me there, but something about this position makes the act even more potent. I can set the pace; I can adjust the angle when he moves from what's just the right spot.

Jacob follows my lead without complaint or any sign that I'm smothering him. His hands work up and down my thigh muscles as he devours me from below with every part of his mouth, even the softest graze of his teeth.

He plunges his tongue right inside me and then laps all the way to my clit, and I shudder against him with a moan. My hips can't stop bucking, urging him on.

"That's right," he murmurs with a torturous vibration against my pussy. "Ride me for all you're worth."

He dives back in like I'm the best meal he's ever eaten. The pleasure swells until it's resonating through my whole body.

One of my hands falls to grip the rumpled strands of his pale hair. The other grips the headboard as if for dear life.

He sucks down on my clit, and the rising wave breaks.

It crashes over me, washing away every sensation but the surge of blissful release, whiting out my vision. I sputter another cry, lost in the haze.

Jacob keeps moving his mouth against me until my body starts to sag. Then I ease off him, sated but also a little awkward at how up close and personal we just got.

He's buried his face in the most private part of me, and he hasn't even taken off one piece of clothing.

Of course, that was by my choice more than his.

The shadows twist through my veins, yanking at me, but my baser desires are satisfied enough that I can ignore them as I sink into the mattress.

Jacob licks his lips, the gesture so unexpectedly erotic after what he just did that I practically come all over again. He grins at me, looking nothing but satisfied himself.

I've forgotten how absolutely breathtaking he can be when he's actually happy. I don't know if I've gotten a chance to see it since our escape.

He can't be that happy, can he? His erection is still straining against his slacks.

But he sits up before I can think about offering to repay the favor, his grin unwavering.

"That is exactly how you should always look, Wildcat."

I hesitate. "Do you want—"

He shakes his head before I can finish. "I'm good. That was about you. And it's *really* good to be able to give you something that lights you up for a change."

A different sort of embarrassment heats my cheeks. "I feel like I used you."

He fixes with me a look both heated and determined. "Riva, it's a fucking privilege to be used by you. If that's what you need, I will eat you out every day of the year and take the blue balls as a badge of honor."

Okay, now my cheeks might scald right off. "Um…"

Before I can decide how to respond, reality crashes back into the room with a jaunty rapping on my door.

The heat of our interlude drains out of me. My body tenses, knowing it's Rollick before the demon even speaks.

His voice calls through the door, as lively as his knock. "Rise and shine, little banshee. Breakfast is being served, and then I think it's time we talked. The porcupine can come too."

His summons wipes away the last wisps of the afterglow even as Jacob grunts in mild objection at the sardonic description of him. My heart sinks.

We're on Rollick's ship. We're alive and well because of his mercy.

And after seeing his full demonic form, I'm really not inclined to test his patience or his generosity.

I caught up even *him*, with his millennia of built-up power, in my scream for at least the short while it lasted before I wrenched myself out. That fact is both incredible and unnerving.

I don't think he's going to forget any time soon that I can be a threat to him. One he might want to squash if I start looking like I'm more trouble than I'm worth.

"I'll be there," I reply, sucking in a breath, and gird myself to face the comeuppance I got to put off yesterday.

THIRTY-TWO

Riva

I'm not really in any state to immediately head to breakfast, regardless of the gurgle of my stomach reminding me that I barely ate anything all yesterday.

I dig through my backpack for a change of clothes and then look up at Jacob. "I'm going to take a quick shower. Er, alone."

The corner of Jacob's mouth ticks upward with a hint of amusement even as his eyes smolder.

"I think I'd better grab one of those myself, with the water set to ice-cold."

He gets off the bed and then reaches to give my shoulder a quick squeeze before he leaves.

"You are all right, aren't you?"

After everything that passed between us last night, that question could refer to a whole lot of things. Maybe all of them.

I pause in the stream of sunlight pouring through the window and really take stock of my internal state.

A whole lot of me still feels tender when prodded. The lump of guilt in my gut hasn't completely dissolved, and I can't say my emotions about the guy I just got awfully close with are free of snarls either.

But beneath the jumbled, painful bits, or maybe around them, my sense of myself holds steady. I was shaken yesterday, but I seem to have found my footing again.

"I will be," I say, and Jacob nods as if that's the best answer he could have expected.

"I'll see you in the dining room, then."

I can't let him just leave like that. He reaches for the door, and his name tumbles from my lips.

"Jake."

He glances back at me, his forehead starting to furrow.

I find I can manage at least half a smile. "Thank you."

For talking me down last night. For shielding me through the night.

For helping me work out other tensions just now…

Jacob's stance relaxes, as much as the guy ever relaxes. "I should be the one thanking you."

He strides out of the room with the athletic poise I can't help admiring now that I'm letting myself feel more than angry at him.

In the ensuite bathroom, I scrub myself all over hastily, taking just a moment to enjoy massaging the fancy shampoo that was part of the bath set Andreas got for me into my hair. The citrus tang wakes up my senses even more.

To face the conversations ahead, I need to be alert and honest and bold. But I have my men with me, in more ways than one.

We're going to get through this too.

I twist my hair into its usual braid even though it's still damp after the toweling and slip out into the hall. Dominic emerges from his room at the exact same moment—which is probably not a coincidence, since he must have known I was on my way out.

It gives me a little thrill I can't totally explain to see him standing assured with his tentacles out in the open. To stop them from dangling at his feet, they fall to his waist and then loop back around to hook over their bases, swaying a little as he steps to meet me.

He'll have to cover up again when we venture out into normal society. But he isn't ashamed for me or any of the shadowkind here to see them anymore.

Even with all the worries still weighing on me, I can't resist pulling him into a hug. Dom hums happily as he hugs me back and presses a kiss to the corner of my jaw.

"You look like you're feeling better, Sugar," he murmurs by my ear.

The new nickname sends a giddier thrill right down the middle of me.

I tip my head against his chest. "I just… needed some time to come to grips with things. Jacob helped."

Another blush tingles in my cheeks, but if Dominic can guess what some of that "help" entailed, I don't think he minds. He strokes his hand over my hair before we ease apart to head to the dining room.

"I'm glad you and him are sorting things out. He was

awful, and of course you've been angry, but I know that's not who he really is."

My smile turns crooked. "Maybe we're all still figuring out who we really are now."

Dom pauses for a moment in his contemplative way. "That sounds about right."

The smells of buttery eggs and fried sausages tickle into my nose and set my stomach growling again. My mouth is watering before I even step through the dining room doorway—and then it dries up as I halt in my tracks with a stutter of my pulse.

Pearl has come back. She's perched on the edge of one of the tables, talking with the hulking green-skinned shadowkind who's occasionally emerged as part of Rollick's crew.

As my legs lock, she tosses her glossy blond waves over her shoulder and glances around. When her bright eyes meet mine, the succubus's friendly expression twitches.

I expect her smile to stiffen into a frown, but instead she hops off the table and ambles over to me, if with a little less energy than her typical pace.

"Have you eaten yet? The croissants are extra good today."

My mouth opens and closes and opens again. "I—No. I was just going to get breakfast now."

"Well, come on then. Rollick's stalking around looking like he's building so many plans in his head he'll fall over if he doesn't get the chance to let them out soon."

I follow her tentatively over to the buffet spread. Dominic veers over to the other guys, who've all gathered around one table.

Zian nods to me, and Andreas shoots me a warm grin, but they seem to recognize that they shouldn't interrupt.

I didn't think I was going to see Pearl again. I didn't think she'd want to see me.

I haven't prepared for this conversation, but it's one I know I need to have at least as much as whatever's coming with our host.

Food ends up on my plate somewhat by random rather than any conscious selection process, because my mind is too busy spinning around what I'm going to say to focus on my options. Pearl grabs herself another croissant and plops into a chair at an otherwise empty table.

I'm not totally sure she wants me to follow, but a day hiding from my screw-ups is long enough.

I carry my plate over and sit down across from her. "I didn't realize you'd come back."

She shrugs in her artfully careless way and takes a bite of her croissant. "I like working with Rollick. And you all have been very interesting."

Interesting isn't the word I'd have thought she'd use. I hesitate, poking my fork into a sausage. "Is Billy healing okay?"

"Oh, yeah, as soon as we got into the shadow realm, everything started binding itself together just fine. It's a pretty dreary place, but it's easier to relax when you're surrounded by the same stuff you're made of."

The reassurance only eases a little of the tension inside me. I force myself to dig into my breakfast, thinking she might bring up any grievances she has, but Pearl chews merrily away, apparently content in my silence.

"I don't know if he's going to want to see me again," I

say finally, "so the next time you visit him, if you could tell him how sorry I am. I never meant—I wouldn't have done it if I'd been totally in control."

Pearl snorts. "I didn't think you would have."

I peer at her, still struggling to gauge her reaction. "Aren't *you* upset at me? He's your friend, and I— It could have been you."

The succubus hesitates, turning the last bit of croissant between her fingers. She glances at me.

"You think I don't know how powers can get a grip on you when you haven't had much practice using them?"

I stare at her. "I—I have no idea." I'd kind of gotten the impression that shadowkind came into being simply knowing what they could do and how to wield those talents effectively.

Pearl's gaze slides away from me again. "In one of my early feeds, I had my hand down the guy's pants before I realized that he was terrified under the lust I'd stirred up. He didn't want it at all. We cubi can get glimpses inside people's heads, you know. To make sure they're a good target. The more they're into it, the better it is. But I was *really* hungry, and he was curious at first, and I… just kind of tuned out the bad signs until I'd practically…"

Her mouth tightens, and my chest constricts in sympathy. I can imagine how that kind of realization feels all too vividly.

Pearl shakes herself and manages to brighten as she yanks her gaze back to me. "So I'd be an awful hypocrite if I got mad at you for not having perfect control over your scream-y power."

Even so, I feel the need to make one thing clear. "I'm

going to do some training with Rollick, like he's been pushing for. I want to get as much control as I can."

"I'm sure he'll be *very* happy about that. He does like to get his way."

Pearl pops the last piece of croissant into her mouth and lets out a pleased hum. Watching her, it's hard to reconcile the bubbly young woman she looks like so often with the pained regret she expressed just moments ago.

After she swallows, she wags a finger at me. "It's everyone, really. I don't know why, because I've never talked to another cubi who has this—although I guess I haven't met a whole lot of them yet—but after I hook up with a mortal to feed, they always start spilling some deep dark secret they feel awful about. Maybe they can tell I'm not going to blab to anyone they know, so it's a safe way to unload."

I grimace. "That sounds… unpleasant."

"Yeah, it kind of kills the mood. I haven't figured out how to stop it happening. But hearing all those confessions has made it very clear that everybody's done bad things. I figure what matters is whether they care enough to try to do better afterward."

She sounds so genuine that more of the guilt congealed inside me disintegrates. I still want to apologize directly to Billy if he's willing to give me the chance, but maybe I don't have to feel like a total monster.

Or at least not more of one than the actual monsters.

As if summoned by that thought, Rollick saunters into the dining room and sweeps his gaze over all of us with an imperious air. "Are you semi-mortals fueled up yet? We've got decisions to make."

I gulp down the rest of my breakfast at lightning speed and dart over to join my guys. Rollick stays standing, leaning his hands against the back of an empty chair as he considers us.

"I'm sorry about the mess in Havana," I say right off the bat, even though technically the messy parts were mostly Jacob's fault. But he was acting to protect me. "And, um, pissing off most of your crew."

Rollick makes a dismissive sound. "Over the centuries, I've come to terms with the fact that most of my kind are very narrow-minded."

Dominic is studying him, his eyes wary. "When the bunch of you first showed up, you sounded like *you* weren't sure we were more than a liability."

Zian's brawn tenses at the reminder, but Rollick simply chuckles.

"It *was* a mess. I can't say I appreciated needing to clean it up. But it became obvious in the confrontation that my people were at least as much to blame for that as you were."

I can't hold back my incredulous question. "The confrontation… where I killed one of them and nearly did the same to another?"

The demon cocks his head. "You enforced your authority when the people you cared about were threatened and reined yourself in before you went too far overboard. What more proof could I need that you *can* control yourself, if imperfectly? I can work with that. And I think you understand the necessity of said work now too."

I swallow thickly. "I do."

"Why do you want to work with us?" Jacob asks brusquely. "Why don't you figure it'd be easier to destroy us like the others wanted to?"

Well, that's one way to put it all on the table.

Rollick offers a slanted smile. "I have hundreds if not thousands of years more experience than most of my associates can draw on. And some very specific experiences that have suggested that the merging of human and shadowkind can save the world more often than ending it. It seems that the mortal side acts as a decent moderator for those talents… Possibly being so much closer to possible death makes you more inclined to prevent it on the whole."

"You said you'd only met one other hybrid before," Andreas says.

"Yes, well…" The demon's voice softens slightly. "The mortal I happen to love once wielded a power that was more threatening and horrifying to shadowkind than anything the bunch of you have, and she proved it could be used to boost us up rather than bind us. So I have learned not to make assumptions."

He rocks back on his heels, scanning us with renewed analytical curiosity. "And in general, I don't believe in destroying potential resources. I'd very much like to see what you shadowbloods can do given the freedom to make your abilities your own—and that includes your younger counterparts, if we can locate them."

I'm not sure how I feel about being considered a "resource," but his last words capture my attention. "We're going to break them out? You're going to help us do it?"

"I think that course of action is the most likely to

diminish your 'guardians' ability to track you, since none of our experiments have borne any fruit so far." Rollick glances toward the dining room windows. "My people in the cities along the southern coast have noticed some activity that suggests they're aware that you've been at sea and are attempting to be prepared for your return."

My stomach knots. "So we'll have to go through them to get to the younger shadowbloods?"

"If what you've said is true, I'd imagine most of their experimental subjects are still back in their facilities. We could start there. The more allies we have on our side, the greater our options."

Zian perks up. "Torrent said he'd found a few facilities —or he thought he had."

Rollick nods. "It would simply be a matter of determining which if any of those your counterparts are being held at and getting them out."

Nothing in that statement sounded particularly simple, but my pulse kicks up a notch in anticipation.

"How are we going to figure out the first part?" Dominic asks. "Are your people going to sneak inside and scope things out?"

Rollick's expression darkens a little. "Unfortunately, that's impossible. Your guardians are obviously familiar with shadowkind ways—and weaknesses. One of the factors that helped Torrent identify the likely locations was the presence of a lot more silver and iron than most of us can easily tolerate. Going straight in would likely be a suicide mission."

My spirits deflate. I guess the shadowkind could watch

from afar, but who knows how long it'd taken them to confirm what's going on in those places?

Whatever shadowbloods might be in the facilities, they'll be locked away down in the depths like we were most of the time. Who knows how securely the guardians are holding them now?

At the new building where I found the guys after our first escape attempt, there wasn't even a training field for a small break from captivity…

The answer hits me so squarely I could smack myself for not thinking of it right away.

"*We* can find them," I say. "It's in our blood. We've lived the same lives as them. Maybe we don't know their names or what most of them look like, but I think—if we focus on the parts we do have, the things we all would have gone through—I think our essence will lead us to them."

Those experiences are imbedded deeper in us than anything you could see in a video recording. We *know* the other kids the guardians have held captive, better than anyone else could.

The guys all sit up a little straighter, their eyes flashing at my words. I can tell the idea feels as right to them as it does to me.

Rollick rubs his jaw. "We don't know for sure that your blood play will work with impressions that vague."

I raise my chin. "It's worth a try. It'd be a hell of a lot faster than hoping your spies will spot something from outside the buildings." I hesitate. "But we'd have to make sure the guardians don't track *us* down while we're following the trail."

A small smile crosses Rollick's lips. "That much I can help with."

He leans forward with his hands braced against the top of the chair. "I'm willing to help you with this because it serves my purposes too. But most of the risk won't be mine. As I've already mentioned, we won't be able to go into the buildings with you."

Andreas frowns. "You have some abilities you can use at a distance, don't you?"

"To a small degree. Even with those… The helmets and vests these mortals wear will protect them from most influence we could exert from afar."

So that was what the guardians' strange uniforms had been about. They must have hoped the metals would give them some small bit of protection against our powers too.

But it hadn't worked. We hybrids really are that much more powerful than the full shadowkind.

No wonder Engel was afraid of us. No wonder the shadowkind are too.

I inhale slowly to steady myself. "What does that mean for us, then?"

Rollick's smile has turned grim. "My people would do what we can on the outside—to draw the mortals out and dispose of any who step beyond the stronger protections. We can be prepared to carry the young ones you rescue to safety as soon as they're out. But it'd be up to the five of you to handle everything inside the building, on your own."

A solemn silence descends over the table as we let that declaration sink in.

Just the five of us, unaffected by the guardians'

protective measures but with powers we're still struggling to control, no ability to dart away into the shadows if the fight turns against us, no shadow realm we can turn to in order to repair our injuries.

The demon's voice softens. "Do you really want to do this? We can hold off your pursuers from this ship for a long time. If you'd rather, I have no problem with simply continuing to cruise around while continuing our experiments. We may still find another way to cut off their ability to track you."

The thought of sticking to the security of the yacht, of enjoying gourmet food and curling up in my cozy bedroom at night, wraps around me like a warm blanket. It's so tempting.

But the next image that floats through my mind is of my cell in the facility.

The cramped space with its narrow, hard bed.

The plates of bland food delivered through a slot.

The barrage of orders, day in and day out.

All the hurt and destruction we carried out on the guardian's whim.

All the pain they dealt out to us if we resisted.

The younger shadowbloods are living like that right now. If Engel's notes were correct, their powers are weaker than ours.

They have no hope of escape unless we come for them. How could I sit on my ass in luxury while they're being tormented?

And Rollick can't be sure that we really will stay safe on this ship anyway. For now, the guardians are simply preparing for battle along the coast—but they've taken us by surprise before.

None of us—me and my men, our shadowkind allies, or the younger shadowbloods in captivity—will really be safe and free until the guardians can't reach us any longer.

Glancing around the table, I see the same resolve forming in my men's eyes. I feel it humming through my marks from Andreas and Dominic.

I broke in to rescue them all on my own. With the help of Rollick and other shadowkind, with the five of us working together, we have to be able to take on whatever the facility holds.

Or we'll die trying.

I turn back to Rollick with a knot of apprehension forming in my gut but not a single trace of doubt.

"We need to get them out of there. Whatever it takes. As soon as we can find them."

THIRTY-THREE

Zian

I should probably stop being surprised by how fancy every vehicle Rollick owns is. I mean, do private jets that *aren't* fancy even exist?

The leather seats are wide enough that I don't feel at all squished even when the middle arm is in place, and padded enough that I can sink right into the cushioning. The bathroom is nearly as big and shiny as the one attached to my bedroom on the yacht.

It's too bad I can't enjoy the fanciness more. My pulse is thrumming through my veins at a heightened pace, and it speeds up even more when Rollick swivels his seat into the aisle so he can face all five of us.

"It'll be difficult to come up with a definitive plan before we know what location we're dealing with," he says. "But I've made my calls, and I have people on standby with the supplies to create some excellent disruptions."

Riva straightens up in her seat. "And to get the shadowbloods we break out to someplace safe."

The demon inclines his head. "Of course. I'm not sure how close we'll be able to bring any vehicles while avoiding detection, but we'll carry the young ones on our backs if we need to."

He pauses with a slight grimace. "Unfortunately I won't have as much backup for this mission as I'd prefer… Kudzu and his friends have spread the word through the community. Quite a few of my typical associates balked at getting involved, and I prefer to work with willing help."

"We wouldn't really be able to count on them if you were forcing them into it anyway," Andreas says from where he's sitting in front of me.

"There's that too. But qualms don't apply to my material resources, so we're still well covered there." Rollick's dark eyes glint with amusement.

I haven't been able to tell how much this "mission" is important to him and how much he sees it as a game to pass the time. But I guess it doesn't really matter as long as we pull it off.

He clasps his hands in his lap, squaring his shoulders as if bracing himself. I understand why when he makes his next announcement.

"Also in the interests of avoiding detection… you need to be prepared that if we identify a facility where your counterparts are being held, you won't be able to charge straight at it. That'll give them time to realize you're coming."

I knit my brow. "Won't they have more time if we take longer getting there?"

Rollick's gaze settles on me. "The problem isn't really the time. It's how obvious you make it where you're going. If we don't want them picking up on your route… the five of you will need to split up to make the journey."

A jolt of horror shoots through my body. We haven't been more than a few hundred yards apart from each other in weeks.

The whole point is that we're in this together.

Dominic tenses in his spot behind Riva. "You want us to go off on our own?"

Rollick shakes his head. "Not entirely. I think it should be enough to break off into two groups and then take an indirect route to reach the facility. I have two helicopters already standing by at the airfield we're headed to. We only need to confuse the tracking efforts enough to obscure your intended destination."

Jacob leaps out of his seat, his eyes flashing. "I'm staying with—"

He cuts himself off as he swings around and his gaze sweeps over all four of us. His stance goes rigid, but he dips his head. "No. Never mind. Riva should have Dom and Drey with her. They've proven themselves."

My throat constricts with a pang, both at his clearly pained acceptance—and the knowledge that I'm excluded from that proven circle too.

Before any of the rest of us can jump in, Riva clears her throat. "I don't like the idea of us splitting up at all. But it does make sense. And if we have to, I think either Dominic or Andreas should be in the other group. That way, no matter what happens, we'll be able to find each other."

Her hand brushes over her collarbone where she showed us the marks that've formed on her skin.

The two guys who share those marks tighten their expressions, but neither argues.

The demon is watching our discussion with apparent interest. In the momentary silence, he speaks up.

"That sounds like solid strategy. I'd also suggest that your two physical powerhouses should split up between the groups, so that both have physical might if you need it."

That means me and Riva. There's no chance of me staying by her side, even if I deserved the spot.

But he's right. "That's fine," I mutter reluctantly.

Andreas pushes to his feet like Jacob has so he can more easily look at all of us. "I'll go with Zian, then. The two of us should make a good team if we run into any trouble before we meet up again."

He hesitates and catches Riva's gaze. "As much as I'd like to be right there with you the whole way, I'd rather know you've got Dom nearby in case you're injured."

Riva aims a baleful look at him. "I don't want any of *you* dealing with injuries on your own either."

"I can't be with both groups, as much as *I* would like that," Dominic says in his usual quiet way. "I think we'll all feel better if I'm with you."

I can't help nodding.

Riva lets out a huff. "So I'm outvoted, is what you're saying?"

Jacob has noticeably brightened since it turned out he was getting to stick with Riva after all. "Four to one. No complaining."

She wrinkles her nose at him, but there's more fondness in her gaze than I've seen her direct at him in weeks.

He's reconnected with her too, if not as fully as Drey and Dom have. All at once, my skin itches with the sense that I've found myself separate from our group in a totally different way.

I tried to talk to her the other day on the ship, but I don't know if she really understood what I was getting at. I don't know how to convey half of the things I'm feeling.

And one very big part of it I'd rather not even think about.

I want her to know I'll be here for her as much as I can be, though. That she means just as much to me as she does to the other guys.

How much more time do we have before she's going to be walking away from me, and I might not even get the chance?

As I grapple with my doubts, Rollick chuckles. "It sounds like it's settled, then."

With the discussion over, Riva squirms over toward the window where the sunlight is beaming in. We've all taken a double row for ourselves, sliding the armrest in the middle out of sight so it's like one long seat instead of two.

My chest clenches up as if my ribs are closing in on my lungs. I close my eyes, picturing the move I want to make.

Reassuring myself that I can do this, just this, and it won't be anything like the moments I'm avoiding.

Bit by bit, I gather my self-control. Then I push myself out of my seat and cross the aisle with two careful steps.

"Can I sit with you for the rest of the trip?"

Riva's head snaps around. She blinks at me, obviously startled—and then a small smile crosses her lips.

"Of course. I'd like that."

It feels like a much greater feat than it probably should to lower myself into the seat next to her. Even with my broad frame taking up plenty of space, she's so tiny in comparison that I don't need to worry I'm crowding her as long as I keep to my side.

Riva peers up at me with a little mischief dancing in her bright brown eyes. "Got lonely all by yourself?"

Despite her teasing, I can see the uncertainty in her expression. That's exactly why I needed to do this.

I fumble with my words. "I—I wanted to be close to you for a while, before we have to split up. So you remember that I've got your back too. Even if I'm not right there with you."

The amusement fades from Riva's gaze, softened into something more bittersweet. "I know that, Zee."

"Well, I thought—I thought it'd be good to really show it."

My face has heated to the point that I think it might burn right off my skull, but Riva doesn't laugh at me. She just keeps looking at me with that soft shimmer in her eyes that makes my heart beat twice as fast.

From the tilt of her body, I think she might have reached over and held my hand or something if the situation were different. If I hadn't flinched away every time she's touched me in the past.

I've come this far. I can manage a little more, right?

Slow and calm, totally controlled. Only one precise movement, nothing a friend couldn't offer another friend.

I lift my arm and ever so carefully extend it in offering to wrap around her shoulders. Riva's eyes widen, and then she scoots a little closer to accept the gesture.

I rest my arm across her back, my hand settling loosely to cup the peak of her shoulder. Riva exhales, and her muscles relax against mine.

"Are you sure this is okay?" she asks in a voice as careful as my embrace.

My nerves are jumping around like they've been zapped with a live wire, half panicked, half begging for more. But when I hold still in this position, I can tune them out enough to say, "Yeah. It should always be. We're blood, right?"

"Always," Riva murmurs happily, and leans in to nestle her head against my chest.

I don't have words for the joy that clangs through every inch of my body at her acceptance. I just wish it didn't come with an equal portion of fear.

I have her with me now. What's going to happen in the fight ahead of us?

For the rest of the flight, I barely dare to move. I know that no unwanted flares of emotion will spark inside me as long as I stay just like this.

As we begin the descent, Riva straightens up so she can buckle her seatbelt. The loss of contact wrenches at me.

But once she's secured the belt, she holds out her hand. Not touching mine, just giving me the option.

I hesitate, gathering my resolve, and curl my fingers around hers.

The plane touches down with a bump and a light jostling. My stomach sinks with the knowledge that the hardest part of this mission is still ahead and approaching faster by the second.

We tramp out of the private jet into a field of close-cropped grass surrounded by nothing but trees. There are no buildings in sight, but the two helicopters Rollick mentioned are waiting at the far end of the field.

The demon turns to us. "All right, let's get on with your essence trick. Who's doing the honors?"

"I will," Jacob says without missing a beat.

Riva shakes her head. "I think we all should. We all went through something a little different. If we're all focusing together... we can go by wherever the most essence flows. That should give us the clearest picture."

Her suggestion makes sense to me. I will my wolfish claws from my fingertips.

Riva gives Jake one last pointed glance. "We shouldn't need very *much* from each of us."

He offers a crooked grin in response. "I won't cut too deep this time, Wildcat."

Jacob extends his spines. Andreas and Dominic retrieve the knives they've armed themselves with from their pockets.

Without speaking, we slice thin scratches across our forearms at the same time.

A streak of blood seeps across my skin—and a puff of dark smoke wavers up into the fresh, foresty air. I watch it for a moment and then close my eyes.

Remember the halls and the training rooms. The little bedroom where the guardians shut me away every night.

The blades they sliced into me.

The prod they jolted me with.

All the things, inanimate and living, they made me smash with tests of my strength and will.

Are there other shadowbloods like me trapped in their facilities now? Being tormented in the same ways?

I want to find them. I want to reach out to them so we can pull them out of that nightmare.

So we can all live free together.

Rollick lets out a soft chuckle. "Well, I'd say that's fairly definitive."

My eyes snap open. My breath stops at the sight of the smoke trails streaming out in front of us.

All five wafts of essence have converged into one larger current. A few little trickles veer off in a variety of directions, but by far the most floats away from us to my right, toward the sun that's dipping toward the western horizon.

"One of the locations we had our eye on is a couple hundred miles in exactly that direction," the demon says with the slightest hint of awe. "The other two are nowhere near it. I suppose we know where we're going now."

As we lower our arms, he swipes his hands together in a brisk gesture. "Which means you'd better get going. I've left tablets and phones in the helicopters along with the rest of the equipment we discussed—I'll be sending your pilots flight plans and you all the details I have so far on that specific possible facility. You can look them over on the way there and discuss how you want to proceed. And please keep me in the loop."

"Where are you going to be?" I ask.

He motions to the jet. "I'll take a more direct route, as close as I can get, and make sure our ground support is in place."

Andreas has moved to join me. Riva turns toward the two of us, a flicker of worry crossing her face.

She darts to Drey, and he catches her in his arms. I avert my gaze as they collide with a kiss so potent my skin prickles with my awareness of it.

"We'll see you soon, Tink," he promises, a little hoarsely.

As Riva eases back from him, her gaze slides to me. My body balks, but the images from the facility are still floating in the back of my mind.

What if I never get another chance to do anything at all?

I step forward and tentatively wrap my arms around her. Riva hugs me back with all the strength that's wound through her slim form.

My pulse hiccups, but I find the determination to lower my head and press a kiss to her hair.

My stomach twists itself into a dozen knots. I can feel the other guys watching me, wary and concerned.

On my behalf, or hers?

None of that really matters, though. Not when she releases me and I see the brilliant smile that's lighting up her face, just for me.

"Stay safe, Shrimp," I tell her, as if I'm not worried at all.

Our two groups veer apart as we hustle over to the choppers. I clamber on board, ignoring the nervous tension coiling around my gut as well as I can.

Our pilot materializes out of the shadows into the cockpit. "Your equipment's in the bag there," she says, and starts the motor whirring.

Andreas yanks the door shut and drops into the seat next to me. He glances over, his gray eyes a little darker than usual.

"You've got to tell her, you know."

He doesn't need to spell out what he's talking about. My body goes rigid.

I push through it, reaching for the duffel bag on the floor. "Did you tell her how it was for *you*?"

Drey sinks into the seat with the lurch of the chopper taking off. "Yeah. She didn't blame me for it. She knows none of that shit was our choice."

My hands ball, my claws prickling at my fingertips again.

What he told her isn't half as bad as my own story. It's not even in the same ballpark.

"You could figure something out with her if she knew what you're dealing with," Andreas adds in a gentler tone.

My voice comes out gruff. "We'll see. We've got bigger things to worry about right now."

We're about to break back into one of the facilities. The last place on Earth I'd ever have wanted to go.

And I've got to make sure every one of my friends and the woman I love make it back out again with me.

Thirty-Four

Riva

I pull the black cap tight over my hair and tuck the end of my braid under the springy fabric. Then I slip my cat-and-yarn pendant under my shirt collar, both for safe-keeping and to keep it out of view.

We might not be able to merge right into the shadows, but the stealth gear Rollick got for us cloaks us in darkness from head to toe.

As I hop out of the helicopter after Dominic, Jacob right at my heels, the thick fabric of the mock turtleneck and athletic pants presses against my flexing muscles. The Kevlar in it should protect us from knife slashes and the jab of a tranquilizer dart.

If the guardians decide they'd rather kill us than recapture us, the thin but dense padding across the torso and throat should help protect us from regular bullets. There isn't much that could properly shield our heads, though.

We're working with a balance of security and flexibility so we can dodge the attacks we can't absorb.

Pistols of our own rest against our hips in the dual holsters that hang from our belts. We're prepared in every possible way in case our supernatural abilities aren't enough to get us through the trials ahead.

The military-grade gear should add to my confidence. But as we hustle through the stretch of forest between our landing site and the facility, draped in the shadows of the early night, my pulse wobbles with uncertainty.

No matter how much reconnaissance Rollick's people were able to gather, they've only observed the outside of this place. We have no idea what's waiting for us *inside*, other than it'll probably look uncomfortably like the prisons we've already escaped.

I can't help feeling like a kid playing dress-up, pretending at being the superhero Jacob once claimed I am when I don't actually have any clue how to fight a war.

Go in, take down any guardians who get in our way, get the other shadowbloods out. That's our mission, boiled down to its simplest essence.

Whatever complications arise along the way… we'll just have to deal with them as they come.

A familiar figure wavers out of the gloom up ahead. Rollick tips his head to us silently and makes a few brisk gestures.

After our urgent phone conversations hashing out the initial plan, I follow his meaning well enough.

His people have disabled the few guardians who were patrolling outside the facility's protections. They're waiting to escort the younger shadowbloods to the camouflaged vans parked on the nearest road.

The facility itself is just up ahead.

We nod in acknowledgment, and Rollick vanishes again. My stomach twists tighter.

The shadowkind have a few more tricks up their sleeves, but once we cross the protective barrier that wards them away, we're on our own.

Then again, that's how we started. And for all Rollick's wealth and influence, it's always come down to the five of us when the shit has hit the fan.

If we can't pull off this mission, if we can't even protect the kids who are going through the same things we did, then what was the point of claiming our freedom to begin with?

As the trees start to thin, a glimmering trail catches my eyes through the underbrush up ahead. One of Rollick's allies—one of the few who wasn't too terrified of us to join in the operation—laid down a line of phosphorescence to show us where the boundary of anti-shadowkind protections lies.

They can't cross over that line—at all or without being significantly weakened. Our job is to get the younger shadowbloods past the barrier so the shadowkind can escort them the rest of the way to safety.

All of us know how to slink silently across terrain like this. I don't hear or see our companions approach, but the tingle of my mark tells me Andreas is getting closer.

Jacob, Dominic, and I pause at the edge of the clearing that holds this facility. I glance in the direction where I can sense Andreas is just arriving, twenty feet away.

We can't risk any sound passing between us. I have to assume he wouldn't be here if he and Zian weren't ready.

Then I turn my attention on the structure ahead of us.

From the photographs and descriptions Rollick's people passed on, I had some idea what to expect. Still, seeing the place for real, turned ominous by the darkness, makes my gut drop to my feet.

Here, the guardians took a different tactic from what we're used to. There's no electrified fence, no secure concrete bunker hiding the labyrinth of levels underneath.

They were counting mainly on disguise this time. The nearest proper road is miles away, so no one's likely to stumble on it. All their supplies must be coming on foot or by helicopter to the small clearing at the base of the cliff we're facing.

The cliff that holds the gaping black maw of a cave.

The guardians built this facility into the intimidating natural features of the landscape. The cave opening looms at least ten feet high and nearly the same across, surrounded by mossy crags of stone.

It's pitch black beyond the small strip of moonlight that touches the very edge of the yawning entrance. We have no idea what we're dealing with even before we've gone inside the building itself.

Andreas and Zian steal over to join us. Relief washes through my chest at having our group all together again.

Without speaking, we move farther around the clearing, over to the side. We're going to help clear the way into the facility, but the shadowkind are going to kick off our invasion.

Our allies must be watching. The second we've gotten

into place, a resonant *boom* reverberates through the woods, shaking the ground beneath our feet.

As I grab hold of a tree trunk to steady myself, the sound of another blast rattles my eardrums.

Firelight dances through the trees beyond the other side of the clearing. We pull back a little deeper into the forest to ensure its glow doesn't reveal us.

Then we simply watch.

Three guardians in the familiar metal helmets and vests dash from the mouth of the cave. Guns glint in their hands.

One raises a walkie talkie with the other to report to colleagues inside. They march to the edge of the clearing, peering at the flames, but don't venture farther into the forest.

They're being more cautious than when I broke the guys out. Maybe the surviving guardians from that escape told stories about how I diverted them.

This bunch *shouldn't* have any idea that we were heading their way or that we'd even want to invade their workplace. But with every passing moment, the chances increase that the guardians who've been tracking us will figure out where we've converged and spread the word.

Every instant could make a difference.

Thankfully, it doesn't take long for more guardians to come loping out of the cave. A dozen of them set off through the trees to investigate the fire, but five hang back by the cave entrance, scanning the entire clearing.

Yes, they've definitely gotten smarter. But I don't think they've gotten stronger.

We can take five no problem.

I flick my claws from my fingertips.

We don't want to use the guns yet if we can help it. It's better if the guardians who've ventured farther away from the facility don't realize there's trouble back here.

The main force of guardians vanishes into the darkness of the woods. And we launch ourselves forward.

Before we've even reached them, Jacob has already flung two of the figures against the cliffside, denting their helmets and cracking their skulls against the jutting crags. Zian snarls and pummels one into the ground with a heave of his fist.

I throw myself at the figure nearest to me and plunge my claws right into his throat.

The final guard lets out a bark of warning that's cut off with a gurgle. Andreas has blinked out of invisibility behind him, jabbing a knife into his heart.

More shouts echo from the depths of the cave. The hairs on the back of my neck stand on end, but I glance around at the guys and see a resolve in their eyes that solidifies my own determination.

We aren't the monsters here. We're freeing tormented children from the real beasts.

I *can* be a hero, in every way that counts.

And we're working like a team again—a real one with all the trust and understanding that should go with that word. With only a look and imperceptible nods, we spread out to either side of the cave and dash in close to the walls.

The guardians come charging forward down the middle of the space. One has a light fixed to her helmet, the beam bobbing through the darkness.

We spring.

Bodies smash against the walls as Jacob lashes out with his powers.

I sever another throat.

Dominic's tentacles whip from his back to slap around a neck and crush a windpipe.

A guardian next to me stumbles, and Andreas is on him with his knife before I need to whirl around.

"The door!" Zian calls out, his voice low but urgent.

The lit helmet has spun toward the far end of the cave —where we can see a solid wall with a steel door on the verge of slamming shut.

Jacob jerks his hand forward, and the door jolts to a halt just a crack from locking. The muscles in Jake's arm bulge with the strain.

Zian heaves himself forward, and I dart after him just as fast. He catches the edge first, but his thicker fingers can't push inside the crack to yank it farther open.

There's no handle on this side.

I dive in and squeeze my own fingers into the tiny gap. With an ache I feel all the way through my shoulders, I haul at it.

The door shifts toward me, just enough for Zee to get a proper grip too. He yanks it wide—

And another squad of guardians barrels into us.

Electricity crackles with a prod that smacks my arm. My limb spasms, but I hold on to enough control to kick my attacker aside with a force that must crack several ribs.

Jacob hurls himself at the man who jolted me with a growl that could match Zian's wolf. He crushes the guardian's skull against the rocky floor with his bare hands.

Darts whiz toward us, and I fling myself around so my

face and head are protected. With another jab of my heel, I snap someone's jaw.

Zian roars. There's a gristly tearing sound and a thump that's probably an arm or maybe a head torn right off.

These people want to destroy us. They've always wanted to destroy us, even if only our free will and our spirits.

They managed to slaughter Griffin, but we won't let them take another one of us.

An arm swings upward with a flash of an unexpected blade. I throw myself between the fallen guardian and Jacob just in time to deflect the slash so it only glances off his cheek.

My claws rake across the woman's throat, and she slumps with a gush of blood. When I glance up, Jacob swipes the thin scarlet streak from his cheek and offers me a smile that reaches all the way up to warm his cool eyes.

Yes, we're a team now—all of us.

The five of us push into the space beyond the steel entrance. Dim light illuminates a short hallway with a door on either side and an elevator at the end.

A helmet glints in the crack where the door on the left is pushed ajar.

Before the guardian there can pull the trigger on his weapon, Jacob's power batters him into the tiled floor. Zian crushes the man's head under his heel as we storm past.

We burst into what's obviously the control room, screens mounted all across three of the walls over a long console of controls.

The guy seated in front of the console whips up a gun,

but it flies from his hand to smack against the wall. Jacob and Zian loom over the guardian while the rest of us hang a few steps back, Andreas keeping watch by the door.

"Where are you holding your experimental subjects?" Jake demands. "The ones with powers, like us?"

The man's panicked eyes leap to the screens and back to us. I scan the footage projected from various security cameras around the building.

There's a vast training area that looks more like a cavern than a room. Hallways full of more doors.

No one stirs in any of the images. Have we really eliminated the entire staff of this facility already?

If that's true, then all that stands between us and getting the kids out is this prick.

But we might need him. We don't know what codes or keys it might take to open the cells our fellow shadowbloods are locked inside.

"I—I—" the guardian stutters, and then squares his shoulders, his mouth clamping tight.

Jacob raises his hand, his fingers curling toward his palm, and I have a sudden vision of what he means to do. How he could strangle the life out of this man as easily as clenching a fist.

But we don't need to. The guy is unarmed, defenseless —and I'd like to leave one person here knowing that we're so much more than monsters.

"Wait," I say, quiet but firm.

Jake grimaces but eases to the side as I prowl forward.

What I can see of the guardian's face around the plates of his helmet pales. He swallows audibly, but he still doesn't speak.

I pin him with my stare, every muscle braced for action. "I don't want to—"

I cut myself off, realizing what I was going to say isn't true. And maybe the truth will mean more, even if it's not as pretty.

"No," I correct myself. "I *do* want to hurt you. A whole lot of me would like to make you feel just a fraction of what you and the people you work with put us through."

I flex my claws for emphasis. A shriek tremors in my chest, eager to feed off the pain I've denied it so far in this battle.

The man remains silent, but his jaw ticks with a restrained flinch.

I take another step closer to where I could scrape my claws across his face if I decided to.

"I want you to know that. I want you to know that I'm holding myself back from what I'd like to do right now, because no matter what you people put in me or did to me, I'm not a monster. I can believe there are people out there who'd care if you died, who don't deserve that pain. I can have compassion even for *you*."

"I'm not going to help you," the guardian rasps out.

I shrug, staying tensed. "That's up to you. We've broken out of places like this twice before. We can manage it again without you. We know to leave your eyes and your hands and your face intact in case we need those to unlock the system. The rest of you…"

Leaning in, I hook one claw under his helmet and flip it right off his head. His fear saturates the air, so pungent I wouldn't be surprised if the others can smell it now too.

"I'm giving you the option," I say. "If you want to survive another day to see those people who care about you, who maybe you care about too, you can show us how to find and open the cells. Or we can kill you and then figure it out anyway. The only thing that changes is whether you live. That's your choice."

Jacob inhales roughly behind me but doesn't argue with the bargain I'm attempting to strike.

I don't know if it's going to work. The man's posture has gone even more rigid in his chair.

But then Andreas speaks up from the doorway, even but with a hint of his cajoling tone.

"Chloe would miss you an awful lot, don't you think? And what would she tell Ava? Is this job really worth losing *them*—leaving them alone?"

The man can't suppress his wince this time at the names Drey has pulled from his memories. His face turns an even more sickly shade.

"Do whatever you're going to do to me," he spits out. "But don't—don't touch them. They had nothing to do with this."

He spins his chair toward the console. My teeth grit at the thought that he's only acting because he thinks we were threatening his family—but he's doing something.

I really shouldn't look a gift horse in the mouth, should I? I'm getting what I wanted even if not exactly the way I wanted it.

And he'll know that I meant my promise when he walks out of this building alive.

His hands dart over the controls. He points to one of

the screens—a blue-print style rendering of a hall lined with small rooms on either side.

Uncomfortably familiar.

"That's where they are. Three floors down, past the training complex."

"And unlocking the doors?" Dominic asks.

The man wavers for a second and then leans toward a glass pane on the console. A flash of light washes over his face. He jabs a few buttons, and the symbols marking each of the cells blink from red to green.

"There. It's done. Now don't—"

Zian brings his fist down on the man's head with a *thwack* that makes me cringe. But even as he tumbles off his chair, I can see the angle and the impact were only enough to knock him unconscious.

"Tie him," Andreas urges.

I'm already springing over. My claws slice off a few strips of the man's shirt.

I tug one piece of fabric through his mouth as a gag while Jacob and Dominic hurry to secure his wrists and ankles. Then I scan the screens again.

"No more guardians. Everyone else must be outside."

Dead or still dealing with our shadowkind allies.

Jacob smiles grimly. "Let's get those kids out, then."

My heart thudding with a mix of adrenaline and joy, I dart with the others to the opposite door. A stairwell awaits on the other side.

The guardians know better than to put all their faith in an elevator and the electricity that runs it. I'd rather not count on it either.

We hurtle down the stairs as fast as our feet can carry

us, Zian's head swerving from side to side as he listens for sounds of pursuit.

On the third floor, we shove out into another hall that leads into the cavernous room I saw on the surveillance. Our footsteps echo eerily through the vast, darkened space.

But there's light up ahead. The gleam of florescent bulbs shines through the window on the door at the far end.

I push myself faster. We have to get the younger shadowbloods out of their rooms and all the way back up to the surface.

We have no idea when reinforcements might be arriving.

The hall beyond the window lies empty. Zian shoulders the door open.

We spill into the hallway, our gazes whipping over the dozens of closed doors we unlocked upstairs.

And half of those doors fling open as a horde of hidden guardians charge out to meet us.

THIRTY-FIVE

Riva

A yelp of warning breaks from my throat, as if the guys won't have seen the threat in the same instant I did. I propel myself backward—

And bang against a set of steel bars that've just dropped from the ceiling to cut off our access to the doorway.

They've locked us in. Was this a trap?

We all duck low instinctively to make ourselves smaller targets. Tranquilizer darts whiz through the air only to be smacked to the side by a wallop of Jacob's telekinesis.

I have only a second to register that the guardians are wearing something odd under their usual helmets before one of them tosses a hissing cannister our way. A plume of blue smoke gushes up into the air around us.

Gas masks—that's what they're wearing. They think they can knock us out this way instead.

Zian sputters and aims a brutal kick at the cannister,

sending it spinning past our attackers. The smoke wafts away from us with another push of the invisible force Jacob can conjure, but a hint of dizziness prickles through my mind.

Several of the guardians let out startled shouts, shaking their heads as if trying to clear them. When I glance at Andreas, his eyes have flared red.

He's confusing them with projected memories. But there are so many of them, more tramping out of a door at the other end of the hall.

Dominic yanks out his pistol and fires at our adversaries, but the power Jacob is hurling out to deflect their assault carries bullets from our side too. Dom flinches as the projectile ricochets off the wall.

Shit. We can't shoot at them without opening ourselves up to their own ammunition.

More darts fly. My ears catch the click of another cannister.

If we don't figure out something fast, we're going to suffocate in here.

The thought sends a jolt of panic through my nerves. I sway on my feet, claws out to slash at anyone who dares to come close, knowing it won't be enough.

The vibration in my chest reverberates through my lungs with a swelling scream.

I could end them all—but they know that, they're tossing everything they can our way to stop me first. If I'm doing this, I have to cut them down *now*.

But they're not the only ones with us in this hallway.

Nervous eyes peek from one of the doors that hasn't been thrown fully open. As my power resonates through my bones, I can feel them—the ones like us, the ones with shadows in their blood, shut away in this place for so long.

I can't save us by killing them too. And my scream…

It prickles up my throat, and I clamp down on it. My body balks like it did before when Rollick tried to get me to practice my powers.

But with my next gulp of air, laced with the desperation of all my men around me, my mind latches on to a different memory.

Last night, under Rollick's supervision. Letting out a sliver of a shriek and lancing it through one creature and another.

There are too many guardians. I can't hit them one at a time.

But I shielded my guys before. I *know* them—and I know the kids huddled behind those doors too, in all the ways that matter most, enough that my blood could lead me here.

I won't strike at them. Not the ones like me.

I'm not a killer. I'm a *protector*.

Images flash beyond my eyes of all the moments I've shared with my men over the past week. Not just battles and bloodshed, but tenderness too.

Showing Dominic I adore him even with his strange new features.

Stepping back into Andreas's arms with forgiveness.

Stopping Jacob before he sliced himself open on my behalf and bandaging his wound.

Cuddling up to Zian on the plane just hours ago, proving that whatever he's able to offer me is enough.

I can heal in my own ways. I can defend and champion.

And I will do that now.

I part my lips and let my power out.

The shriek bursts from my throat and blasts down the now-crowded hallway. I aim it past the bodies that pulse blood and shadow together and stab it into every figure before me that's only human.

Human and totally monstrous.

My hunger surges up to saturate my nerves. I wrench through one body and another, devouring their pain, letting the satisfaction of it drown out any tremors of guilt.

All my focus, all my self-control stays on keeping my vicious talent on target.

I'm distantly aware of my men moving around me, not frozen in shock like the first time I let my fury loose.

Zian braces himself in front of me, guarding me from any physical attack, smacking away a dart that careens my way. Jacob heaves one cannister and another back toward their source, his power warbling down the hall as he compels the noxious gas away.

At the back of the crowd, the new figures who barge into the hall stumble into their colleagues in the grips of memories that aren't theirs. In the muddle Andreas is casting over them to distract them for the few instants before my scream catches hold of them too.

And Dominic crouches next to me, one tentacle wound around my bare hand, another clasping the neck of an injured guardian who collapsed on the floor after he attempted to charge us. My healer is flooding me with more and more energy even as I drink down the giddying waves of pain I'm dealing out as well.

We're in this together, and we'll leave together. More of us than came.

Strength thrums through my muscles. The shriek belts on and on as bones snap and tendons tear and—

And then there's no one left. No one who deserves my rage.

My legs wobble with the sudden rush back into normal awareness, but it's all eager adrenaline, not a hint of weakness. When Dominic touches my side to steady me, I've already caught my balance with a flare of urgency.

"We've got to get the kids out. There could be more guardians coming."

There's no way the staff here didn't manage to contact their colleagues elsewhere, right? But we don't know if anyone was close enough to help all that quickly.

It's better not to take the chance.

We hurry down the hall, yanking open the doors that the guardians weren't hiding behind. I find a skinny, dark-complexioned girl who can't be more than twelve and a stout, redheaded boy who looks maybe fifteen.

"Come on," I say, beckoning to them. "We're getting you out of here. No more tests. You'll be free."

As they stir to their feet, apprehension and hope flashing across their faces in tandem, Zian gives a shout of triumph and fishes a controller from one of the mangled guardian's pockets. He hits the button, and the barred gate rises.

Andreas ushers two other kids out through the

doorway. "Let's take only a couple each," he shouts over his shoulder. "We need to be able to protect them."

I nod. "And hurry!"

Dominic directs two more kids toward the training area. As I encourage my shell-shocked charges to follow them, motioning toward the door to try to avert their gazes from the bodies on the blood-stained floor, Zian wrenches open the last of the cells and frowns.

"That's all of them down here. Only six?"

I pause in the doorway and glance at the boy, who looks slightly less terrified than the younger girl. "Was it just the six of you in this facility?"

"I—I'm not sure," he says. "We didn't always train with the same people. They came and went."

Well, six is better than none. Six is a start.

Maybe the guardians didn't manage to make all that many more shadowbloods with Engel's adjusted methods after all.

Jacob kicks the last of the still-smoking cannisters into one of the empty cells and yanks the door shut to seal the noxious smoke away. He turns to Zian.

"Go with them! Make sure they get to Rollick okay. I feel like there's something else important down here— come back as soon as you've dropped the kids off and we'll see what else they've been hiding."

I don't love leaving him on his own, but getting the kids to safety matters more. "Don't go too far," I order him.

Andreas and Dominic have already crossed half the cavernous room. I hurry my charges along as quickly as I can, not wanting to slow down the others' escape by calling for them to wait.

They vanish into the stairwell, and we dash after them moments later. The kids finally come out of their stunned state enough to pick up to a run.

I wonder if they've been drugged like the guys say they were after our first escape attempt, their senses dulled.

We'll see them free of that internal prison too.

We scramble out into the short upper hall. Muffled grunts carry from the control room where the man we tied up must have regained consciousness, but I ignore him.

Zian pulls ahead before we race outside and wedges a stone in the door to hold it open. As we approach the mouth of the cave, we both scan our surroundings quickly.

I catch a few shouts off in the distance, and the flames are still crackling as part of Rollick's distraction. But there are no guardians I can see or smell nearby.

A spark of victory lights in my chest. We did it—we saved them.

There's no one left here who can hurt any of us.

Andreas and then Dominic lope past us back toward the facility, their kids already safely passed on. I wave my two charges on toward the gleaming phosphorescent line.

"We have friends here who are going to make sure we all get out of this place without the guardians catching us again. Stick with them, and the rest of us will join you soon."

Pearl and a shadowkind man wave to us from just beyond the boundary, the succubus bouncing eagerly on her feet. I shoot Pearl a quick smile and give the kids a gentle nudge toward them.

"These are the last of them."

Pearl returns my smile brightly. "Are you coming back with us, then?"

My sense of Andreas and Dominic through my marks tugs at me. I think of Jacob still searching below, and shake my head.

"We're going to give the building one last check and then we'll be right with you."

As the shadowkind figures hustle the kids onward through the woods, I wheel around with Zian by my side and dash back into the cave.

That's it. All six of this facility's prisoners are in protective hands now.

But maybe we can hurt the whole organization of guardians even more if we just look a little harder. Find out whether they're holding other young shadowbloods elsewhere.

We could be only just beginning this war.

The upper hall of the hidden facility is empty—I can feel that Andreas and Dominic have headed downstairs. They weren't there to hear that we'd already gotten all of the kids who were being held here, but we need to get back to Jacob anyway.

I dart into the stairwell, and Zian stalls in his tracks behind me with a confused grunt. "What…?"

I start to glance back at him, but Jacob's voice carries up from below. "Riva—hurry! We've got to deal with this fast."

I have no idea what he's found, but my heart lurches

with a sudden jolt of panic so sharp it practically shoves me toward him.

"Come on, Zee!" I holler, and take off down the steps.

Jacob has pulled off his black cap. His blond hair gleams in the florescent lights as I dash after him around the twists in the staircase, a couple of levels above him.

He marches past the third-floor landing to the fourth basement level and pushes aside the door there. I run after him, propelled by the still-growing wave of anxiety.

What have the guardians been doing down here?

I barge into the fourth-floor hallway just in time to see Jacob disappearing past a door partway down. His voice carries back to me. "This way! Quick!"

I spring after him and burst past the door. My momentum hurls me forward a few steps before I slow, realizing I've come into a narrow, empty room that appears to have no other exits.

Transparent panes shoot from the walls on either side of me. They smack into place, hemming me in.

With a stutter of my pulse, I slam my fist into one to smash it.

It's definitely not any normal kind of glass. My supernaturally powered blow doesn't open the slightest crack.

My gaze jerks to Jacob, who's standing beyond one of the panes, expecting him to be launching himself at it from his own side. But he's just standing there, watching me.

In the space of a thump of my heart, I notice a few things.

There's no cut marking his cheek where I deflected the jab of the guardian's knife.

His slicked-back hair curls a little longer around his ears than seems quite right.

His clothes, though all black, don't totally match mine. The collar only reaches the base of his throat instead of covering his neck.

And his eyes. The pale blue eyes that've seared into me with anger and lit up with joy look utterly empty in a way I've never seen before, not even at his worst.

The bottom of my stomach drops out.

That's not Jake.

The man who isn't Jacob pushes his mouth into what looks more like an imitation of a smile than the real thing.

"It's been a long time, Moonbeam."

About the Author

Eva Chase lives in Canada with her family. She loves stories both swoony and supernatural, and strong women and the men who appreciate them. Along with the Shadowblood Souls series, she is the author of the Heart of a Monster series, the Gang of Ghouls series, the Bound to the Fae series, the Flirting with Monsters series, the Cursed Studies trilogy, the Royals of Villain Academy series, the Moriarty's Men series, the Looking Glass Curse trilogy, the Their Dark Valkyrie series, the Witch's Consorts series, the Dragon Shifter's Mates series, the Demons of Fame series, and the Legends Reborn trilogy.

Connect with Eva online:
www.evachase.com
eva@evachase.com

Printed in Great Britain
by Amazon